Little River
The Other Side of Paradise

by
James L'Etoile

Astra Press

ISBN: 978-0-615-88389-2 (trade paper)
ISBN: 978-0-578-47904-0 (ebook)

Book Design: Evernight Designs, Elle J. Rossi
Interior art: original painting by Larina L'Etoile

Second Edition

Titles by James L'Etoile

AT WHAT COST
BURY THE PAST

You may choose to look the other way but you can never say again that you did not know.
— William Wilberforce

Original Little River cover art by Larina L'Etoile

Chapter 1

Island Time in Montego Bay means there's no rush for anything. On the surface, the notion of being on time holds little value. Scratch below that placid, carefree exterior and you'll find a desperate underbelly that feeds on fear. The thing about fear is that it festers and thrives when time matters.

For two passengers on the morning flight from Los Angeles, time worked against them. They were the only ones who seemed to care about the delay, fifteen minutes behind schedule. The plane lumbered to the gate. When the cabin door opened, the passengers rushed down the jetway, a single herd migrating toward the required customs checkpoint. Bodies pushed and jockeyed for position, eager to celebrate a honeymoon, anniversary, a family vacation, or cheat on their spouse with the office secretary.

One of the hurried passengers, a tall man, separated himself from the crowd. He looked more haggard than the others and rubbed a hand through his short hair. It started to grey at the temples a few years ago, and in spite of the calendar putting Grant at forty-two, he didn't feel middle-aged. Stepping out of the crowd, he unhitched his shoulder bag and parked a black carry on at his feet. Grant stretched his shoulder muscles from the long flight and paused in the departure lounge at the gate area long enough scan the waiting passengers for a particular face.

All he saw were blissful, sunburned souls who sat in the terminal, waiting for their departing flights. The joyful faces on the resort posters promised fun in the sun and other hedonistic pleasures if you patronized their establishments. Grant's hands trembled when the face he hoped for failed to greet him. His drooped shoulders, low hung face and pinched expression starkly contrasted the vivid tourist murals that adorned the terminal's walls. A ragged deep breath betrayed his fear and exhaustion.

Grant didn't travel well under normal circumstances, and the long, cramped flight from Los Angeles left him bone tired and on edge.

A few moments later, a small-framed blonde woman, dressed in simple jeans and a red tee shirt walked up and stood next to him. She wore scant makeup, only enough to accent her warm brown eyes. She carried a bulky overnight bag slung over a toned arm, but the heaviest burden was one not measured on any scale. She carried a dark foreboding that tugged at her soul.

"Anything?" Andrea Carson asked.

Grant Turner shook his head. He'd scanned the terminal departures twice–nothing. "We need to get down the corridor and clear customs." Grant visited Jamaica a couple of times, once with his wife and once with his daughter. Unlike those trips, this stay was no vacation.

Andrea looked across the lobby; her shoulder-length honeyed hair fell across one side of her face. Athletically trim with a simple beauty, Andrea looked younger than her age. In fact, many of her friends said that she and her daughter could pass for sisters. Her daughter hated the comparison. It bothered the sixteen-year-old so much that she once cut her hair shorter and died it red. That was five years ago. Much had changed since that simpler time, and Andrea would trade anything to turn back the clock.

Without another word, she picked up her bag and joined the tide of arriving passengers toward customs and baggage claim. Her hair bounced with each quick, determined stride. A pair of porters moved from the path of the woman on a mission.

Grant watched as she weaved through the crowd, a slender, determined blonde missile honing in on her target. He shouldered his bag, followed in Andrea's wake and caught up with her as she joined a line that snaked through a large, open room with two rows of customs stations along the rear wall. The cavernous space held the passengers from their plane, joined by over a hundred others from a flight that had arrived minutes before. Placards posted in the brightly lit and newly remodeled customs area promised efficient processing—if all passengers had their passports and other documents ready.

Progress was slow for the first flights each day; all the customs personnel on Island Time hadn't arrived. Four of the dozen stations held crisply uniformed customs inspectors. The tourists didn't seem to mind. Some of them cuddled and cooed at each other, while others took the delay in stride and looked at brochures, or resort posters, starting their vacations early. Grant and Andrea looked edgy and out of place among the party crowd.

All the non-Jamaican citizens held their customs declaration forms, filled out and ready to hand over to the customs officer, along with their passports. The heat in the room was bearable, but the rising humidity of the day would make the fragrance of a hundred or so travelers less inviting.

"Is the guy you talked to going to meet us here?" Andrea asked. Looking up at Grant, she noticed grey and black stubble on his chin. "Thank you for doing this, for coming with me," she said.

Grant noticed a slight glisten of tears. "I couldn't do this alone either. I'm glad we're doing this together. The guy wants to meet somewhere quiet and private. He said the airport isn't the place. He gave me an address of a place near Negril and said to meet him in the bar."

"He's in a bar at this hour of the morning? No wonder we haven't heard anything. How can you trust this man?" Andrea's jaw tightened with frustration.

As Grant and Andrea approached the customs station, the officer in the booth waived them forward. Passports and forms changed hands, as a young Jamaican woman examined and stamped each of them. Each name from the passport went into a computer terminal.

The young customs officer wore a white, long-sleeved shirt under a navy-blue blazer, designed for an impeccable first impression for the tourists. Her name tag identified her as Tami, from Jacmel, Haiti. She asked the same series of questions that she had asked a thousand tourists before. "Where will you be staying while here in Jamaica?" She didn't even bother to look up from her computer keyboard.

Grant read from a rental agreement, "We're renting a bungalow in Negril, off of Norman Manley Boulevard…"

The customs officer apparently needed no further information about the location, so she asked, "What's the purpose of your trip? Business or pleasure?"

Grant paused.

The customs officer lifted her face from the computer screen and repeated, this time a bit louder, "Business or pleasure?"

The words came hard; they clung to his throat, bitter and harsh. If you say the words, they become true. Unable to hold them back any longer, Grant softly uttered, "Our daughters have disappeared. We came to Jamaica to get them back."

Chapter 2

The words spilled out faster than expected. A father's fear and failings laid out for the world to judge. There was no magical explanation—he failed to protect his daughter. It wasn't a bad dream. His daughter vanished without a trace. With Andrea's daughter disappearing at the same time, Grant had no answers and an amplified sense of fear hit exposed raw nerves.

The young customs officer paused and looked again at the passports on her desk. The expression on her face changed. The woman's eyes carried a mix of confusion, but also something darker. She picked up the phone at her podium, dialed a number and waited. She whispered, "Monsieur Baptiste?" A few heavily accented words followed in a rapid urgent tone, similar to French, but different, somewhat clipped and abrupt. She promptly ended the call and snatched up the passports.

"Come with me, please," the customs officer said. Curious glances guessed the authorities had singled them out for drug smuggling or some other notorious crime. There were cutting glares from passengers in the lines behind them. A few snickered at the unlucky forty-something couple getting nabbed on the way *into* Jamaica. Grant and Andrea followed the customs officer through a set of pale-green doors and into a windowed space that looked out into the processing area.

A dark-skinned man in a police uniform sat behind a small desk piled high with documents, newspapers and magazines. Cigarette smoke wafted up from an ashtray stashed in the midst of the flammable clutter on his desktop. A nameplate sat half-toppled in the mess identified him as Constable Hickson. Hickson ground out a cigarette butt in the ashtray and left it smoldering among a dozen other remnants. He waived his hand through the smoke and moved the ashtray to a shelf behind him, the ashes spilling onto a disarray of an expandable baton, handcuffs, and a canister of pepper spray. Constable Hickson hung a bulky automatic rifle and a ballistic vest on a hook behind his desk. A thin layer of dust on the rifle and vest bore evidence that they hadn't been touched for weeks.

"These people believe their daughters are missing." The customs officer handed the passports to Hickson, avoiding eye contact with the American couple. She quickly walked back to the lines of waiting tourists.

The constable opened one of the passports, gave it a brief glance, and casually tossed both documents in the middle of the sea of paperwork without looking at Grant or Andrea. He lit up another cigarette, took a long pull and held it between his thumb and forefinger, in a European fashion. "From my experience, young people often decide they want to stay longer than planned and forget to tell their families."

"I know my daughter, and I'm certain she would call if she were able to," Andrea said.

"Young women sometimes fall in love and they fear telling their parents. I suggest you go back home and wait for them," Hickson said as he stretched, took another drag from his cigarette, and placed his feet on the desk, knocking off a pile of customs forms, reports and wanted-persons notices. The documents fanned out onto the floor. Among them were missing persons reports filed in Montego Bay.

Andrea held back the urge to dive across the desk and choke the arrogance out of the man. "We're not interested in what you think. We simply want to find our girls," she said.

Andrea's face reddened. Grant placed a hand on her shoulder in an attempt to remind her; an escort out of the country would end their search before it started. Andrea did not shrug it off, she glared at the officer instead.

"Are you going to help us?" Grant asked.

"No, I'm not gonna help you, and you won't get any official help from the Ministry of Justice on your crusade." He picked up the passports and tossed them against Grant's chest, "Welcome to Jamaica. Enjoy your vacation."

Grant and Andrea hefted their bags, and another stiff-backed officer escorted them to an unmarked door that dumped them into the main baggage claim carousels. The airport funneled the passenger traffic past the baggage claim area, through a multicolored mall festooned with resort welcome centers, duty-free shops, and transportation services. Grant made for the car rental counter while Andrea sagged on a bench in the center of the bustling space.

Anxious and stunned from sheer exhaustion, feelings of guilt, fear and inadequacy fueled a fire in Andrea's mind as if she had an espresso intravenous drip. She replayed every conversation with her daughter over the last six months and condemned herself for pushing Holly into the island vacation.

Worried about how introverted and isolated Holly had become, Andrea encouraged her daughter to take the trip. The withdrawal from social situations had begun ten years earlier. After Holly's father walked out, abandoning the eleven-year-old and her mother, Holly, blamed herself for the family's disintegration. She begged her father to come back, promising that she would be a better daughter. She never got the chance to prove herself worthy to the father who abandoned her.

In the years that followed, Holly grew sullen, lonely and untrusting of any social situation that required emotional attachment. Andrea, armed with a mother's intuition, pushed her daughter into social events, clubs and after-school activities through junior high and high school. It wasn't until her second semester at college that Holly started to come out of her shell. She met Grant's daughter, Jena, in one of her classes, and the two hit it off quickly, developing a close friendship. Andrea encouraged the newfound independence, but she never dreamed it would lead to her daughter's disappearance. She shouldn't have pushed so hard. The guilt tasted bitter. Even with hundreds of people around, she'd never felt so alone.

Andrea paid no attention to the celebratory mood of the resort employees who plied their guests with Red Stripe beer and rum-based frozen concoctions. She glanced up at Grant, and for a brief flash, wanted to blame him for allowing Jena and Holly to take the trip together. Then she recognized, from the dark circles under his eyes, drooped shoulders and exhausted appearance, that he also hurt from Jena's disappearance. It wasn't his fault. He loved his daughter and, like Andrea, had dropped everything in their lives to come to this place together and find their girls.

Boisterous reggae music spilled out from the duty-free and souvenir shops. Tucked behind a rum-tasting bodega, a long, modern counter housed the rental car agencies that serviced the island. The rental car counters were sleek and efficient. The only thing that set them apart from any other airport was an assortment of posters behind the counter that featured island tourist spots. Grant checked his reservation documents, located the company and walked up to the open counter. He gave the attendant his name, handed over a credit card, and quickly signed the rental car agreement.

The short, grey-bearded Jamaican man behind the counter handed the keys to Grant. "Is this your first trip to Jamaica, Mon?" The man's voice was slow, relaxed and lilting, reflecting his joy at meeting new people from far-away places.

"I was here a few years ago. I want to see more of the island this time. Do you have a good roadmap?" Grant asked.

The man laughed, "Welcome home—nothing changes on the island." He pulled open a drawer and fished out a detailed roadmap and a handful of tourist brochures. "Your car is outside to the left. The red one in space five. Please enjoy our beautiful island."

Andrea saw Grant finish at the rental counter. She furtively wiped her eyes and joined him. When a group of college-age revelers passed her, she felt a twinge of panic. Holly and Jena would have been exactly like the carefree travelers, without a concern in the world. She silently ached for her daughter.

Grant joined Andrea and pointed to a door that opened into the rental car lot. Grant opened the door, and she walked through. The early morning heat and humidity clamped down on them. Within seconds, their clothes stuck to their skin.

A red compact car sat, as expected, in slot five of the small rental lot. Grant opened the trunk and placed their bags inside. Slamming the trunk lid, Grant raised his head and looked toward the traffic on the main terminal access road. The hair on the back of his neck pricked on end. Was someone waiting for them beyond the line of cars, vans and busses? He couldn't see anyone, but he was certain someone was there. He felt the presence.

Andrea picked up on Grant's uneasiness. She touched him on the elbow. "What is it?" She gazed off beyond the road and into the lush vegetation.

"I don't know—maybe nothing. I'm worn out and edgy," He, rubbed his jet-weary eyes with the palms of his hands. "I'm tired, I guess. I could be seeing things that aren't there."

Grant spread the island roadmap over the trunk and found their current location at the Sangster International Airport, on the northernmost point of Montego Bay. "The last place we know the girls were, for certain, was their hotel in Negril. Where do you want to start?"

Before she could respond, an unsteady engine whine came from the hillside beyond the main access road, the same spot that had drawn Grant's attention moments earlier. A battered Toyota Land Cruiser, crudely hand-painted in the green and black colors of the Jamaican flag, burst from the brush line, took a sharp left up the road, and accelerated out of view.

Andrea watched the vehicle race out of sight. "That was strange. Did you catch the dreadlocks on the guy in the front passenger seat? They must have been two feet long."

The sudden appearance of the off-road vehicle, coupled with the sensation that someone watching them, put Grant even more on edge. The main access road was less than fifty feet from their car, so he saw the man with the dreads clearly enough, but it was the man behind the wheel that caught his attention. It was a man he would later have difficulty describing. A big man, with an olive complexion, and short dreadlocked braids. The man was not dark skinned, like the local Jamaican people, nor did he appear to be a pale European; his features were something in between. He turned and looked directly at Grant for a moment before he sped away. Something in the man's cold, steel-blue eyes grabbed at Grant's soul. A tingly charge shot up Grant's spine.

Chapter 3

Grant and Andrea watched the Land Cruiser disappear over the crest of a small hill to the West. They climbed into the rental car's cramped front seats. Grant backed out from the parking slot, paused at the mouth of the airport road, then took a left at a sign for Little River and Ocho Rios, followed by a quick right turn to Negril.

"We know the girls were in Negril. That's where their group stayed. Let's head that way and find our bungalow so we have a point to work from and a place for the girls to find us," Andrea suggested.

"That sounds like a good plan," Grant said.

As Grant pulled into the traffic on the highway to Negril, he noticed the green and black Land Cruiser, driven by the blue-eyed man, a few cars ahead of him. When the gap between them lessened, the Land Cruiser sped away, darting in and out of city traffic, leaving Grant and Andrea stuck in the thick Montego Bay traffic.

"Let's find a grocery store. Why don't we stop and grab a few things," Andrea said.

Grant piloted the small car through the snarled morning vehicle traffic of Montego Bay, where solid lines on the asphalt meant very little. Cars shot through intersections, passed on the right shoulders and cut each other off in a high-stakes game of chicken. At this hour, foot traffic outnumbered the cars, people off to the markets for daily fresh produce, or laborers pretending to look for work.

The locals eyed the two Americans with the resignation that the foreigners represented tourist dollars. The faces held delayed judgment, wondering if these two were here to exploit the island people, or boost the local economy. Often, the two intertwined.

Andrea pointed, "There's a market up ahead on the right."

Grant nodded and turned into the parking lot. Andrea agreed to stay with the car while Grant went in and attacked a grocery list she had made up on the fly.

Andrea pulled open her bag and locked eyes with a photograph of her daughter, Holly. The image of the girl, in happier times, copied onto several hundred posters, which begged for any information about Holly's whereabouts. Andrea stared out the car window, and the thought of Holly and Jena passing this very spot on their way to Negril caused a tremor in her hand. The car felt even smaller, and Andrea grew unsettled as the sea of unfamiliar faces passed outside. Someone had to know what happened to the girls, yet no one offered a shred of help.

She stroked the curve of her daughter's face with the tip of a finger and wondered what Holly was doing at this moment. She fumed over the callous manner and lack of any sense of urgency from the customs officer at the airport. The same attitude over long-distance phone lines demanded that she come here, to Jamaica, to find her daughter. No one else seemed to care, except Grant. He seemed quiet in his thoughts, but Andrea knew he had to be crumbling inside, as was she.

Everyone, other than of the two of them, had given up trying to find the girls. The tour company that had booked the college summer tour disclaimed responsibility for the girls' absence when the remainder of the group returned to Los Angeles. Over long-distance connections, not one person at the hotel recalled anything that would help locate the missing girls. Other participants in the group's trip were unable to give any useful information. So Andrea found herself in Jamaica, in a scrubby section of central Montego Bay, clinging to a single thread—a report from a taxi driver who may have seen the girls the night before they disappeared.

From the parking lot, Andrea could see panhandlers, street-corner hustlers and open-air drug transactions taking place with no effort to conceal their actions. There seemed to be little police presence in the squalid streets away from the main tourist areas. After a moment, she saw Grant heading out from the market, loaded with translucent plastic bags, a selection of fruits, coffee, bottled water and paper-wrapped deli meats all visible from across the parking lot.

Grant stuffed the bags on the floor in the back seat and slid inside the car. The windows were down, but the humid heat inside was uncomfortable. The air conditioning pumped tepid air from the vents on the dash and slowly cooled the interior.

"I'm sorry; I should have left the air on while I went in. I wasn't thinking," Grant said. He noticed the open satchel in Andrea's lap, the daughter's photo peeking through the opening.

Grant looked at Holly's likeness and put his hand on hers. "We'll find them."

"We *will* find them." She nodded, put the bag down, and put on her sunglasses to shield her eyes from the bright Caribbean sun. Were she to admit it, the glasses shielded her from Grant as well. She had to pretend to be as strong as he was. She could not fall apart now; she needed to stay strong for Holly.

Grant returned to Highway A-1, the main route through the commercial district of Montego Bay, parallel to the coastline. He merged into traffic and headed west toward Negril. Traffic moved briskly through construction zones where workers repaired erosion and filled potholes caused by the last hurricane. Vehicles swept inches from road crew workers without pause. The route hugged the coastline's breathtaking views of a vivid blue ocean—all within a few feet of the edge of the road.

After a half-hour of driving, Grant and Andrea pulled into Lucea, a small coastal town whose entire populace seemed to be out on the streets and sidewalks. The main street narrowed, and the modest cinderblock buildings that lined the street blocked the intense sunlight. The shaded roadway gathered knots of locals who cooled themselves on the sidewalks and curbs. Other drivers, it seemed, took comfort in the shade, with traffic nearly at a standstill, barely creeping through the village.

The roadside market stretched the entire length of the main street. Street vendors in makeshift booths on the curb, locals haggled over the price of bananas, ackee, callaloo, pineapples, and an assortment of fish.

At the far end of Lucea, a collection of townspeople, with full shopping bags, waited in the open bus transit yard. The bus schedule was a fluid thing, a driver might give up his seat in the shade when enough people asked for a bus to a certain destination. Only then would he amble off to one of the empty busses and load up.

Grant swung the car to the right and continued on A-1 out of town. Within twenty minutes, they hit Negril, one of the island's premier tourist destinations. Pristine-white sand stretched for miles along the roadway.

"The last time I was here, Jena and I walked out there forever. That seems like a lifetime ago." He cleared his throat, "I bet our girls spent hours on that beach…"

"I can see why, it's gorgeous," Andrea said as she scanned the faces of those who sunned and strolled.

They continued down the highway, where brightly colored resort banners flashed past. Most specialized in singles or couples and promised all sorts of pleasures of the flesh.

A gravel road, marked with a small sign with the words "Negril Retreat" etched in the weathered wood, pointed out the entrance to their rental. Grant swung the car up the steep, sweeping left-hand turn for a bumpy half-mile ride. When they reached the top of the hill, he parked in front of the bungalow, and looked out on an expansive ocean vista. The bungalow sat high above the vegetation near the highway, and the effect was startling. Transparent blue ocean waves gently caressed bright-white sand beaches, while the warm breeze pushed in from offshore.

Andrea approached the front door of the bungalow and found it unlocked. A note addressed to the two of them lay on a small shelf in the front entryway. She pulled it from beneath a carved wooden paperweight and read it to Grant: "Welcome to Negril. Keys are on the kitchen counter." She lowered the note, "That's awfully trusting, leaving the place open."

"I told them I wasn't sure what time we'd make it in," Grant said.

Grant grabbed the bags from the trunk. Andrea gathered up the plastic grocery bags from the back seat and they carried their provisions inside. The entry foyer transitioned to a large, covered, open-air living room with a view out to the beach below. Large overstuffed furniture in heavy cane frames added to the stunning scenery.

Grant put the bags down and wandered out onto the patio, which extended beyond the room to an infinity pool and wet bar off to one side. Opening up the wet bar, he found it fully stocked with Appleton Rum, of light, dark and coconut varieties, and a number of bottles of cold Red Stripe beer.

The kitchen was to the left of the entry and bedrooms were on either side of the living room. Andrea put the grocery bags on a marble island and asked, "Which room do you want?"

Grant replied, "I don't care, you choose."

The bedrooms flanked the open living area, and both promised a view to the ocean. Andrea, opting for the bedroom to the right, picked up her bags and carried them off to the room. The well-furnished suite included heavy mahogany pieces and featured large French doors that opened onto the patio. She pulled the doors open toward her and felt the ocean breeze against her face. Andrea noticed that Grant had stepped onto the patio from his room on the opposite side.

Andrea gathered her hair up in a ponytail with a hair tie, ventured out onto the patio and joined Grant, who stared out at the view. "Under any other circumstances, this would be a beautiful place for a vacation getaway," she said.

Grant nodded. "Jena and I stayed here the last time. The place is familiar to her. I hope she'd think to come here." He turned and faced Andrea, "They are out there. If they had any ability to contact us, they would have. So we need to go to them."

"I want to get into town and start asking around, but other than the taxi driver who claims he saw them, I don't know where to start," Andrea said.

"Let's start with the taxi driver, Paulo. He's the last one we know who says he saw the girls. When I spoke with him, he said they were in his cab. We'll talk to him, and that might take us to the next lead."

Somber, but sure, Andrea left the ocean view and grabbed her blue backpack. "I'm ready."

They climbed back into the compact red car and Grant drove down the rough road to the main highway. At the bottom, they turned left toward downtown Negril, past a score of high-end resorts, with names like Couples and Hedonism, offering the tourist every indulgence imaginable.

Grant turned right on Norman Manley Boulevard and followed the road along the coastline. "There's Rick's Café," he said, pointing off to the right. "The name of the bar where we're supposed to meet Paulo is called 'Johnny's.' It's a bit farther down the road."

Grant drove slowly down the Boulevard, looking for the place Paulo mentioned over the phone. The buildings thinned out, and he thought he must have missed it. He was about to turn around when Andrea pointed at a small wood and cane shack tucked back from the road. A ratty looking sign, attached to the structure by a thin wire, gently rocked in the breeze. The crudely painted letters, washed thin by seasons of rain, were barely legible: "Johnny's."

They parked in the red dirt lot next to the only other car there, a faded-blue Toyota mini-van, which boasted large patches of rust along the front fender wells. As they stepped from their car, they noticed the humidity was much heavier down by the water. It was stick-to-you steamy.

The couple didn't notice the battered green and black Land Cruiser that had followed them and parked across the street from the bar. The blue-eyed driver remained in the vehicle while the dreadlocked passenger trotted across the road and approached the side of the bar, unseen by the occupants.

Grant and Andrea walked into the establishment. Reggae music played from an old boom box stereo system behind the counter, and there were a number of makeshift tables made from doors with reclaimed planking arranged around the space. A counter, salvaged from an apartment kitchen, served as the bar in the center of the rectangular room. A gaunt older Jamaican man stood behind the bar, wiping glasses with a tattered towel. The only other person sat at a table in the far back corner.

Grant walked over, "Paulo?"

"That's me, Mon," The heavy-set Jamaican replied. "You must be de father of da girls, yes?" Paulo asked in a thick Jamaican accent.

"Yeah, we're their parents," Grant confirmed, while pulling out pictures of the girls from his shirt pocket. He slid them across to Paulo. "You remember them?"

"Oh yeah, I 'member these two ladies," Paulo said, holding the photographs of Holly and Jena up to his face. "You have something for me?"

Grant slid an envelope across the table.

Paulo opened the envelope and flipped through a number of fifty-dollar bills with his thick thumb.

Andrea stepped closer to the table, "When was the last time you saw them?"

Paulo's face furrowed in thought. "They call for a taxi after midnight to take dem from one of the clubs to their hotel, it was the Grand Lido. I can't 'member where I pick dem up."

Grant slid another fifty-dollar bill across the table, "Think hard. Where did you pick them up?"

Paulo's thick calloused hand swiftly grabbed the money from the table, "I think I 'member now. I pick 'em up at de Ocean Palace."

"How did they seem to you?" Andrea asked, "Were they okay when you dropped them off?"

"I think they was fine, but they did seem worried about sometin' and want to get back to the hotel."

"Did they say what it was they were worried about?" Grant said.

"No, only that it had to do with going to the police," Paulo said.

Andrea became alarmed, "What about the police?"

"That's all I knows. That's all I want to knows. You can't trust all the police here. Some of dem protect powerful bad men."

"Who do they protect?" Grant said as a shadow at the door caught his attention. The old man at the bar saw it also, who calmly put down his bar towel, and ambled out the rear of the building.

The long dreadlocked man appeared through the shadows of the door and raised the black stubby barrel of an automatic rifle. He looked at the trio at the table. "You talk too much, Paulo," he said.

The weapon jerked in the man's hands, and three loud bursts echoed in the small bar. Paulo slumped back in his chair, three crimson spots blossoming on his chest. With a malevolent glare on his face, the gunman walked up to the table and turned the barrel of his weapon at Grant and Andrea. When he spoke, the sound came from deep in this throat, "Go home now. There is nothing here for you."

Andrea started to protest, but the gun barrel was now aimed at her head. Grant grabbed her arm, pulled her toward him, and covered her with his body. Grant waited for the sound of gunfire.

The gunman didn't fire. "This is your only warning. Leave here."

The dreadlocked gunman backed out of the bar, jogged to the Land Cruiser across the street and got into the passenger side. He clipped his weapon into a bracket in the door, turned to his blue-eyed companion and said, "They should be no problem now."

The driver grabbed the gunman by the collar of his sweat stained polo shirt and spat, "For your sake you had better be right. Your carelessness brought them here."

He released his grip on the gunman and put the Land Cruiser in gear. His blue eyes burned in the rear view mirror as he pulled away. He saw the troublesome American couple run to their car and leave, heading back toward Negril.

"Back in Haiti," he said, "no one would dare speak of my business. Maybe now, people here learn the same thing."

Chapter 4

Grant pinned the gas pedal to the floorboard, sending the little sedan into a fishtail in the red-dirt parking lot. The tires spun as they lost their grip on the edge of the asphalt, and the rental car shot away from the scene. Grant and Andrea put as much distance between the ramshackle bar and them as possible. Hillside buildings on the outskirts of Negril flew by in a blur. A speeding ticket was Grant's last concern.

"Why did he do that?" Grant said as he slipped the car around a sharp bend. "Paulo was our chance to get a handle on the girls. Why did that thug have to kill him? Paulo didn't deserve that. He was only trying to help us."

"The guy with the dreads knows where Holly and Jena are. Why didn't you let me ask him?" Andrea asked, anger flared in her voice.

"Did you forget what he did to Paulo?" Grant said, his eyes flicking up to the rear view. "We could have been next. Then where would Holly and Jena be?"

Andrea slumped back into the seat, seething that they let an opportunity slip through their fingers. "What now?"

"I don't know. We need to think this through for a moment. It might not be safe to go back to the bungalow," Grant said.

He slowed the rental down as they closed on the central area of Negril. Convinced that nobody followed them from the bar, Grant turned into the Times Square shopping center off Norman Manley Boulevard. The rear parking lot was three-quarters full, and he pulled the car in the middle of the lot, hoping the red sedan would blend in with the rest. The shops were busy plying the morning tourist crowds with high-end jewelry and island fashions. In this place, Grant and Andrea looked like everyone else. They could buy some time, lost in a sea of foreign faces.

They walked into a crowded, open courtyard with a small café tucked to one side. Grant snagged one of the empty tables, sheltered from the sun beneath a bright-yellow umbrella. Out of the sun, but more importantly, they were partially hidden from view. They both ordered coffee from a ten-year-old girl who served as the café's waitress.

The young girl returned in minutes, balancing two steaming cups of rich, bold Jamaican Blue Mountain coffee on a polished silver tray. With a delicate touch, the young girl placed each cup and saucer on the table. Her face brightened as she backed away, proud that she had not spilled a single drop. The girl's mother, watching from behind the coffee counter, nodded in approval.

Andrea emptied a packet of raw sugar into the coffee and absently stirred the cup with a spoon. She licked the spoon and set it on the side of the saucer. As she lifted the cup, her hand trembled, threatening to spill the coffee. She closed her eyes and the image of the Jamaican man killed in front of her made her shake, as if a cold winter's wind crept up her neck. She looked up and said, "Before Paulo died, he mentioned that the police can't be trusted. That they protected somebody."

"The bad people. Like the police were on the criminals' payrolls," Grant said.

"He died before he said who the police were protecting. Whoever that was could be the person responsible for taking the girls. Paulo knew where the girls were taken, and the creep killed him to keep us from finding out. They have to be alive, or they wouldn't have killed Paulo."

It was the first time that either of them mentioned out loud the possibility of death.

Grant took a sip of the hot brew, hoping the rich, dark flavor would somehow make all the answers appear. "Let's start with what we know. The girls went from the club to the hotel, and they were worried about the police. Paulo told us the police can't be trusted, and that guy with the dreadlocks made sure he didn't say anything more to us."

"He said, 'You can't trust all the police,' which means maybe there are some we can trust," Andrea said, while looking into her coffee cup. "Maybe we should go to the police. We just witnessed a murder."

"But, who can we trust? If we talk to the wrong cop, we get deported, or worse. If that happens, it's game over for the girls and us. It seems like a risky idea. What about checking out the girls' hotel? Someone there has to know something they wouldn't tell us over the phone."

"The resort manager and their attorney were very clear that none of the staff had any knowledge of their 'departure,' as he called it. Remember the last call we made? The attorney threatened to sue us if we made public accusations that Holly and Jena were taken from the premises," Andrea said.

"If Paulo was telling the truth, that's the last place they were seen."

"He was killed to keep that from us. Maybe the resort management doesn't know anything about the girls, but the staff might be willing to talk. We have to be a bit sly about it and not let the management know what we're doing," Andrea said.

Grant threw a few dollars down for the coffee and a generous tip. He stood and saw a strange look on Andrea's face.

"What?"

"You have blood on your shirt. Are you hurt?" she asked.

Grant looked down and saw several large drops of blood. Paulo's blood. It had spattered up the front of his shirt. He remembered how close he was to Paulo when the man died. An inch or two in another direction and he'd be on the dirty bar floor along with Paulo.

"I'm fine, but I need to get out of these clothes. I'm surprised no one noticed," he said. A slight rattle caught in his throat.

She gave a quick smile. "You tried to protect me back there. With the gunman…" She looked away as if visualizing the scene unfolding again. "Thank you, Grant." She took a breath and stood up, "You go back to the car. I'm going to duck into one of these shops and find you some-thing."

"Let me come with you."

"Trust me," Andrea said as she walked into the complex and disap-peared into one of the shopping warrens.

Grant hadn't really known Andrea before they came together on this trip. Their lives never intersected. They lived in the same general area of the San Fernando Valley, but if not for Holly and Jena's ill-fated trip, Grant and Andrea may have gone the rest of their lives without meeting. Grant admired Andrea's passion and feverish commitment to their daughters' recovery, something he shared equally.

He hadn't noticed Andrea as a woman—an attractive woman—until now. A burst of embarrassment hit when he realized that he harbored such thoughts. Grant hadn't felt that way since his wife died, five years earlier. He assumed that people got one chance at love, and he had had his. The drunk driver that killed his wife took away everything meaning-ful in Grant's life, save for one thing—his daughter. Jena had comforted him as much, perhaps more, than he was able to help Jena through the loss of her mother. He depended on her more than he cared to admit.

He could not bear to think what would happen if he failed to find Jena.

As he plopped into the car, anxiety took over. What if he failed? He didn't think he could live with himself if the worst happened.

Grant was lost in the midst of a fear-fueled daydream when Andrea opened the passenger door. She plopped on the seat next to him, clutch-ing a clear plastic bag.

She looked at him. His expression couldn't conceal pain and sorrow. She reached over and grabbed his shoulder. "Hey, snap out of it."

He shuddered, shook his head and tried to get rid of the remnants of the dream. "What if we can't find them? I don't know what my life would be without her, or even if it is worth living."

"We are going to find them. But first—you need to change." She handed him a fresh button-up linen shirt from the plastic bag. "Put this on and stuff the bloody one in the bag."

Grant pulled his blood-stained polo over his head and took the new shirt from Andrea. "Thanks for not picking out a tie-dye tourist tee shirt." He wriggled into the new shirt and caught a slight blush on her cheek as she watched him dress.

"That looks better," said Andrea. She tied the loose ends of the bag, the blood stained shirt secured inside. She hopped out of the car, tossed the bag in an overflowing garbage bin near the rear of one of the stores, and hurried back to the car.

"How did you know to do that? You have some experience running from the law?"

"I've watched my share of true crime shows."

As Grant started the engine, the air conditioner mercifully blew semi-refrigerated air at them. Tension filled the cramped small car as they headed to the last place where anyone had disclosed seeing the girls. The man who had told them was dead. People didn't want them poking around here, that much was clear. Legal threats, the risk of deportation, Paulo's murder, and the dreadlocked man's vile warnings couldn't keep them from the search. They had to know what happened to Holly and Jena, no matter the personal cost. The mystery of their disappearance centered on the Grand Lido resort; any slender thread that unraveled the path to the truth was precious. Everything depended on it.

Chapter 5

Impressive and opulent described the Grand Lido Hotel, perched on an outcropping of rock that overlooked Bloody Beach Bay. The open-air lobby and registration bustled with frantic activity after a busload of tourists and their stacks of luggage hit the lobby. Lines formed in front of the huge polished wooden registration desk, where each guest received a welcome cocktail and personal attention. Porters grouped bags in small manageable lots; trays of ice water passed through the waiting guests. The unhurried and slow pace of the registration process offered a chance for guests to peruse the tour and excursion desks, strategically placed in the lobby. It was another reminder that nothing moved quickly in this country; everything found its own opportunity. For Grant and Andrea, the milling crowds provided an opportunity, a diversion that allowed them to enter the property unnoticed.

In the thick of the lobby, Grant and Andrea surveyed the crowds, discounted the throngs of travelers, but paid particular attention to the staff. The people who worked in the Grand Lido were their best chance for new information on the girls.

Andrea tugged on the sleeve of Grant's shirt. "I think we need to split up. I'll head down-stairs to the main bar and talk to the bartenders," she said.

"That's probably a good idea. Hotel management wouldn't give us anything over the phone. You hit up the bar staff and I'll talk to some of the porters over there," Grant said, pointing to a group of men in white uniforms near the concierge desk.

Andrea took copies of the posters, with photos of the girls, from her purse and handed a few to Grant. She walked down the stairs to the bar, blending in with the other tourists in the sprawling resort. She passed an enormous, deep-blue pool that overlooked the bay and a stretch of white sand beach.

Grant lost sight of her after she meandered past the sunbathers lined up along the edges of pool. He turned and approached the group of porters. As he grew near, they quieted down and stood a little straighter, with the hope that the American was a big tipper.

"What can we do for you, sir?" said the one closest to him, flashing a brilliant smile.

"I need your help, gentlemen. Do any of you remember seeing these two girls last week?" Grant gave each one a copy of the poster with the girl's photographs.

On the lower level, Andrea took a seat at the long, darkly lacquered wooden bar. It featured over a hundred liquor bottles displayed on shelves, with blenders and huge tubs of ice for the day's libations. The bar and a dozen tables sat under a gazebo with a grey tile roof. It looked nothing like the bar where she had witnessed Paulo's murder, but the smell of alcohol and cigarette smoke brought back a flash of the blood, gunpowder and violence. A chill spread across her back. Three men in crisp white shirts worked blenders filled with frozen concoctions with names like Dirty Banana, Hummingbird and Jamaica Sunrise. The loud purr from the blenders was constant, the tourists enjoying their cocktails in the early afternoon sun.

One of the bar attendants approached Andrea, his name tag identifying him as Tommy. "What can I get for the pretty lady?" he said as he wiped down the lacquered bar surface.

She looked him in the eye and slid one of the posters of the missing girls across the bar. "Do you remember these girls?"

Tommy took the poster in his dark, calloused hands and concentrated on the girls' photos. Andrea thought she detected recognition in his face. Her heart skipped a beat.

Tommy looked at Andrea, then turned and hollered, "Marcus, come over here a second."

Marcus walked over from the other end of the bar, a smile on his face, and looked at the paper Tommy handed him. His smile melted immediately. "What happened? This says they went missing," Marcus said.

Andrea nodded. "They did. They were due to come home last Friday, four days ago."

Marcus looked stunned, "I saw them last week, I think Wednesday or Thursday night. They came in and asked me to make them the usual, a Green Grass."

"Did you notice anything strange going on with them? Did they seem like they were in trouble?" Andrea said.

"They were fun. I mean, they always had a good time. They had guys coming up to them all the time. Only a couple spent any time with them. They seemed like they were here for fun, not hooking up with someone. Know what I mean?" Tommy paused. "I thought it was weird that they didn't come out here on their last night," he added.

"I remember a guy asking about them that night," Marcus volunteered. "He wanted to know their names."

The comment piqued Andrea's interest, "What do you remember about him? What did he want?"

Marcus scratched his closely shaven head. "He asked if they were here alone, if they were American, and if they were buying drugs."

Andrea jerked. "Drugs?"

Tommy stepped close to the bar, lowered his head and whispered, "The government tries to keep it out of the travel brochures, but ganja is a major cash crop here on the island. Go walk down the beach and you'll see the activity."

"Did the girls buy weed?" Andrea asked.

Marcus shrugged his shoulders. "I don't know. They could have, but I didn't see nothing."

"What about the guy that was asking about them?" Andrea said.

"The guy comes in here sometimes. He's not from here, mid-thirties, about six feet and looks like he can take care of himself." Marcus recalled. "But the thing I remember most are his steel-blue eyes. They were just cold, you know."

Andrea wrote her cell phone number on the poster and requested, "If you think of anything, or if you see this guy again, please call me." She passed each of the men a twenty-dollar bill and thanked them for their time.

She walked back through the pool area and noticed a few pale tourists were on their way to a wicked sunburn. Some of them certainly showed more skin than they did at home. She looked up ahead and saw Grant at the top of the stairs. Andrea motioned for him to join her.

Grant trotted down the wide staircase and met Andrea by the pool, where she found a table under a huge umbrella. He pulled out one of the metal chairs for her and they both sat down. He took a breath and collected his thoughts. "It seems our girls were very popular. The porters said they recognized them, and one helped them in with their bags." Grant adjusted his sunglasses up on his head. "The girls had a good time; relaxed out on the beach, danced, drank, but weren't problems."

"When did they last see them?" Andrea asked.

"That's the strange part. Two of the porters recalled seeing the girls Thursday night on the way to their room." Grant sat forward: "They said Holly and Jena looked upset, nervous, and acted—different."

"Different, how?"

Before Grant could respond, they were interrupted by a young woman dressed in shorts and a resort uniform green shirt. Her name tag read Toni.

"What can I bring you two?" she asked. Before either of them had the chance to reply, Toni said, "Hey that's Holly and her friend," pointing to the posters in front of Andrea.

Andrea looked up at Toni. "Holly's my daughter, and she's missing."

Grant asked, "When did you last see them?"

"I think it was the middle of the last week, over at the bar. Maybe Wednesday," she said, motioning toward the long covered bar. "I work there in the evenings." She had confirmed the descriptions from the others about how fun loving the girls seemed and that nothing indicated they were in any sort of trouble.

Andrea took one of the posters and jotted her phone number. She handed it along with another twenty-dollar bill to Toni and said, "Please call me if you remember anything. Even the slightest detail could be important.

"I will. I really liked those two. Let me get you a couple cold Red Stripes, OK?"

Grant nodded, and Toni walked off towards the bar.

Andrea looked at Grant, "The guys at the bar recognized the girls and said they seemed like they were having fun." Andrea leaned in. "They did mention a man hanging around the bar asking about the girls."

"Did they get a look at him?"

"Mid-thirties, about six feet tall, with blue eyes. They told me he wasn't from around here."

Grant leaned back in the chair, the driver of the Land Cruiser reflecting in his minds' eye. "So what does a guy like that need with a couple of twenty-year-old girls?"

Andrea added, "They said the guy asked if the girls scored any pot."

He shook his head. "I don't think they were into anything like that, but I could be just plain naive."

Toni returned with two bottles of Red Stripe beer and left Andrea the change from her twenty dollars. The young girl left silently after she took one more look at the posters on the table.

Grant took a long pull from the cold bottle. He wasn't much of a beer drinker, or a mid-day drinker, for that matter, but right now, most things in his life seemed upside down. He put the bottle down and stared at the condensation on the label.

"Something got the girls worried their last night here," Grant explained.

"And the man who was asking about them has to figure in the middle of it," Andrea added. She had not touched her beer but absently peeled the paper label from the bottle.

Grant quickly downed his beer, and the cold liquid sat like a frozen orb in his stomach. In spite of the constant off-shore breeze, he felt confined, almost claustrophobic. Jena was out there, somewhere—and here he sat. He needed to move forward, he needed to press on. Unable to contain the anxious energy any longer, he stood. "I have an idea. Let's take a walk."

They left the change on the table for Toni and walked past the bar and through a manicured archway that framed a stairway to the white sand beach. In the open sand, away from any shelter, the heat chased all but the most determined off the beach. Rows of lounge chairs lined the stretch of sand and most of them were empty.

Grant pulled off his shoes and socks and let the warm water lap up against his ankles. He looked far down the beachfront and scanned the sandy outcropping all around the bay. Each resort roped off their little section of sand from the others with different colors of heavy-braided nylon rope. In several locations, signs advised that locals were to stay away. That seemed odd to Grant. It had been their beach before the resorts came.

"See that roped off section," Grant gestured down the shoreline. "The Grand Lido has a security person to keep an eye on things. Let's talk to him."

Andrea followed suit, removing her shoes, rolling up her pant legs and walking in the gentle surf. It was easier to walk at the water's edge, and much cooler on their feet than burrowing through the hot white sand.

Walking down the beach, they found the dress code here was rather lax. Several women chose to go topless, and middle-aged men wore thin Speedos. It seemed odd that people who shouldn't show so much skin were the first to do so. One of life's great contradictions.

As they arrived within ten feet of the rope, a man in white shorts and green resort shirt stepped from a shabby little shack. The thatched hut was big enough for him to sit at a chair but little else. He walked toward Grant and Andrea, cutting off their path down the beach.

"Are you guests of the resort?" he asked in a thick, lilting Jamaican accent.

Grant shook his head, "No, but can we talk to you?"

"This area is for guests of the resort only. You need to leave," the dark skinned man said bluntly. He seemed like he lived for the moments he could order non-conforming tourists around.

"We just want to talk to you," Grant added, with a bit of vinegar in his voice.

The Jamaican walked closer, looking ready to toss Grant from the stretch of sand that he protected.

Sensing a clash of testosterone, Andrea smoothly walked over, stepped between the two riled men, and placed her hand on the Jamaican's chest. She looked up at him and softly muttered, "Can you help us find our daughters?"

The effect on the security guard was dramatic. Now deflated, he looked down into Andrea's face and his expression softened. The reaction surprised Grant, and he recognized it was time to step back and let Andrea continue.

Andrea handed the security guard one of the posters, and he looked at it intently. After a moment, he handed it back.

"I think I saw them last week."

"Holly and Jena. When did you see them?" she asked.

"They were talking to a man I have chased off many times."

"Do you know who he was?" Andrea asked.

"I don't know his name, but he is involved in all kinds of stuff—drugs, prostitution, and guns. He's a Haitian man, always up to no good."

Andrea's anxiety now elevated, she pushed on. "Did you hear what they were talking about?"

The security guard thought for a moment. "No, I didn't hear what it was, but it looked like an argument of some sort. The man grabbed one of the girls by the arm, and I told him to leave." The guard put his hand up, "Wait here."

He trotted back to the shack, and after a few seconds came back to Andrea. "The man pulled this off one of the girls when he grabbed her arm." In his large calloused hand he held a small gold chain, with a gold tag inscribed with the name, Jena."

Grant's knees buckled at the sight of the bracelet he had given his daughter for a high school graduation present.

Andrea took the chain and gave it to Grant, who clutched his hand around the thin gold trinket. The touch of something that Jena wore caused a ripple somewhere in his soul. This is what it felt like when your world started to crumble.

Grant opened his eyes and looked at the security guard. "Where can we find the Haitian?"

"I hear he lives in Lucy Town, but you be careful poking around out there. You get out in Cockpit Country and you get lost, no one will ever find you," the security man said, referring to the dense, isolated forest where runaway slaves had hidden themselves over a century ago. "There be places up in there where even the police don't go."

Grant and Andrea worked their way back to their car, walking silently past the pools and through the hectic lobby. A few glances from the porters reflected their concern, but most turned away and avoided eye contact with the troubled couple.

"I guess Lucy Town is our next stop. You know where that is?" Andrea asked, breaking the silence.

"Lucea is about thirty minutes down A-1. We went through it on the way here," Grant said.

"We can't just go into the middle of town and start asking around about this Haitian guy. If he's as connected as the security guard says, he will have people waiting for us." Andrea cautioned.

"That's true." Grant paused, "It's not a main tourist destination, so we are going to stick out like a sore thumb. And he knows who we are. So we are at a huge disadvantage."

"Let's grab some lunch on the way and think out our next steps," Andrea said.

Grant nodded, "That's a good idea. I didn't know I was hungry until you said something. But we can't spend a lot of time—we need to—" Grant choked up.

"I know," Andrea said, placing her hand on Grant's arm. "We are on the trail, but we need to figure out the best way to follow it. We are closer now than before. From Paulo, to the Grand Lido, to Lucea. We are making progress."

A few minutes down the road, Grant pointed. "How about there?" The place was a small roadside shack with a sign that read "Mama's, The best Jerk Chicken and Fresh Fish in Jamaica."

Andrea nodded, "Sure. Mama says it's the best," she said, pointing at the flimsy sign.

Grant pulled the car into the dirt parking area alongside a few other cars. They got out and walked under a tattered blue plastic canopy serving as the dining area's shelter, where an older woman greeted them. "Sit anywhere you like."

Grant pointed to a table at the far end of the dining area, away from other patrons, so they could talk. Grant held Andrea's chair for her, and then seated himself. The table was an old door, complete with the hole for the door knob. Stained paper menus on the table proclaimed, again, that Mama's Jerk Chicken was the best on the island. The smell of all-spice and jack bonnet pepper in the air backed up the claim.

The same older local woman who had greeted them came to the table to take their order. She smiled, "Now what can I be getting for you?"

Looking up from their menus, both ordered the Jerk Chicken, with a cold Red Stripe. Their lunches came in short order, and they both picked away at the spicy chicken dish.

"This guy in Lucea has got to be the key to what happened to our girls," Andrea said after a sip from her cold beer.

Grant nodded and waited until he finished chewing, "What worries me is what the Haitian is into. And what he wants from Jena and Holly."

"How are we going to find him? We're going to stand out as one of the few non-Jamaican faces in town," Andrea said, fear in her voice.

"Don't forget, he's not local either. Maybe we approach it directly. We go into town and say we're looking for our business associate," Grant responded.

Andrea shook her head, "I don't know. That sounds pretty risky. We don't know anything about him. Not even his name."

"Wherever our girls are, he knows something." Grant paused and looked out at the lush island countryside which his daughter Jena had passed through only days ago. It seemed like a lifetime since he'd seen her.

They did not delay after their meal. Grant left money on the table to cover their bill, as well as a generous tip for Mama. They quickly got in the car and continued east on the main highway.

In a well of deep shadows alongside the diner, the blue-eyed Haitian and his dreadlocked partner sat in the Land Cruiser, intently watching the American couple. The Land Cruiser waited until the Americans were a hundred yards ahead, then pulled out onto the road, following the red sedan. The two predators followed their prey at a cautious distance toward Lucy Town.

"These two didn't take your warning to heart. Perhaps they need another lesson," the Haitian said to his comrade.

Chapter 6

The dreadlocked gunman rode in the passenger seat, the squat black automatic rifle nestled in his lap reloaded following his assault at the bar a few hours earlier. He pulled the round black handle backwards and chambered a round. Ahead in the roadway, the red sedan cruised steadily onward, three other vehicles in the eastbound lane separated them from the Americans.

"Get me next to their car and we can be rid of them," the gunman said.

"Let's follow them, for now," the Haitian driver said, his blue eyes hidden behind dark, reflective sunglasses.

The gunman grew more agitated. "We can get them now! We have them!"

"I said not now! You will have your chance, but not until I say so! You got that?" The Haitian's anger allowed his French-accented speech to surface. Years in the squalid public schools in Port-Au-Prince had instilled the patois of the Haitian language deep in his subconscious. He hated the French intonation, which to Jon-Pierre's ear sounded guttural and unrefined. He had spent his adult life repressing his upbringing, only to have it rear up and hint at his past. He spoke slowly, "Do you understand me?"

The subdued gunman lowered his head, scolded and submissive, "Yes Jon-Pierre. I understand."

The Land Cruiser continued down the coastline toward Lucea in the wake of the red car. The tail proved easier than Jon-Pierre had planned, because the highway traffic filled in the space between them and their target. The Land Cruiser never came within fifty yards of the Americans and he kept at least one car in between them at all times. As they approached Lucea, Jon-Pierre pulled the Land Cruiser onto a dirt road that circled the main part of town.

The red sedan arrived in the center of Lucea where the pace of traffic slowed as people walked across the street, seemingly unconcerned about oncoming cars. Grant pulled behind a local bus packed to capacity with people and packages. The windows of the bus were down, and passengers stuck heads, hands and arms out into the cooler air.

Grant turned the car into a small parking lot out front of a boxy, whitewashed concrete block building with blue painted trim. A rusted rectangular sign labeled the building as the Lucea Police Constabulary.

Andrea looked confused. "Paulo said that we can't trust the police. We shouldn't be here." She grabbed Grant by the arm in protest.

"He said we couldn't trust *all* the police. Remember, you caught that," Grant said. "We have to trust someone, somewhere, even if it is only rattling some cages."

"Grant, I don't like this. We could hurt the girls if this guy is connected with the police." She tightened her grip on his arm.

"I know you don't like this. I don't either, but how else are we going to find this guy unless we make enough noise to get him out in the open."

Andrea sat silently in the car. She hoped Grant was right, but was unconvinced this was a smart next move.

Grant looked over, gently took her hand off his arm, and held it in his. "Andrea, we have to do this. We have to flush him out. Please trust me."

Andrea looked up, tears in her eyes, "I'm scared."

"I am too. But I don't know any other way to get to him."

Andrea nodded, opened the car door and stepped back out into the oppressive humidity, which intensified her wariness. She bit on her lip and followed Grant to the main entrance of the police station, ready to bolt at the sign of any threat. Her instincts shouted for her to turn away, *now*!

Across the crowded street, Jon-Pierre stood under a fruit seller's canopy at the farmers market. He held a ripe, red-fleshed papaya to his nose and pretended to smell the fruit while he watched. The Americans entered the police station and closed the door behind them. He waited until they disappeared, tossed the papaya back onto a produce cart and moved in between the passing cars until he made it across the street into the police station parking lot.

Jon-Pierre went directly to the red sedan. He smiled. The car windows were down, out of respect for the stifling afternoon heat. Jon-Pierre looked around, made sure no one saw him, and tossed a small package into the driver's seat. The Haitian turned and blended in with the people in the streets.

The police station lobby was empty except for three sweat-stained vinyl chairs. Apparently, no one in this busy town had crimes to report. On the far wall, a small counter hung beneath a sliding glass window. The paint peeled in several places, and the window carried spiderweb cracks and scars from angry fists and elbows. Grant pressed the button mounted on the wall beside the window.

An electric buzzer rang out, loud enough to wake someone from a deep sleep. The uniformed officer came into view and that's exactly what it looked like. The man's uniform shirt was untucked and unbuttoned and he rubbed the slumber from his face as he approached.

The officer stepped to the window. "You get pick-pocketed? You tourists are never careful with your money, flashing it all around. What do you think is going to happen?"

He pulled a piece of paper and a pencil from a drawer in front of him. "Let me guess, the description you are going to give me is, 'a tall thin black man'. That's three-quarters of the island's population. What do you really think we are going to do?"

Grant responded to the officer. "We did have something taken." He passed one of the posters with the girls' photographs through the window.

The officer took a quick look at the photos and put the poster aside. "Young women run away from Mommy and Daddy all the time while they are on vacation. They be back before your plane leave to go home. No worries." The accent became more marked.

"They aren't runaways! They were supposed to be home a week ago," Andrea explained. Her voice filled the small, enclosed lobby.

The officer started to close the window on them and Grant shot his hand out to stop it. "Please, have you seen them?" Grant asked.

The officer pulled his sweat-soaked undershirt away from his body for a moment. "I don't remember seeing them," he said, pointing at the poster. "We don't get that many tourists here. They go on to Negril, or back the other way to Mo Bay or Ocho Rios."

"We are also looking for a man." Grant decided it was time to ask. "He is sort of olive skinned, shorter braided hair, about six feet tall, with blue eyes. He's with another man, much darker, long dreadlocks. I think they live here in the area, and we need to talk to them." Grant described the green and black Land Cruiser that had burst through the brush line near the airport.

Andrea went stiff when Grant asked about the man. It was such a risk. Paulo's warning that you couldn't trust the police echoed in her mind. A single misstep could put their daughters in the crosshairs. She held her breath.

The officer pushed the poster back to Grant, and the expression on his sweat-drenched face grew hard. "You need to leave. Forget about that man; he bring evil and death to the island."

Grant pressed, "Who is he and where can we find him?" Grant stepped even closer to the window and pleaded, "He has something to do with our girls. Please help us; we have to talk to him."

The officer shook his head. A fog of sadness passed over him. "If this man has something to do with your daughters' disappearing, then it's too late," the officer said.

"What's his name?" Andrea said softly.

The question bothered the officer. He swallowed hard, bit his lip, then leaned in close to the window. In a low conspiratorial tone, he said, "Jon-Pierre—his name is Jon-Pierre Baptiste. He a very bad man. He run the big mob in Haiti and come here after the earthquake. He think there's more money here than there be in stealing medical supplies from the Red Cross in Haiti."

"What is Baptiste into here in Jamaica, and why don't the police do anything about him?" Andrea said.

"Jon-Pierre be into a lot of things. He trade drugs for guns, make people pay for protection, but mostly…"

"Yes?" Andrea prodded.

"Trafficking. Human trafficking. He take women and boys and sell them," the officer said.

"Why aren't you stopping him?' Grant asked.

"Jon-Pierre runs most of the North Coast where many Haitian immigrants live together in camps, or small towns. They fear him. Jon-Pierre was Tonton Macoutes. People think the Macoutes went away after Papa Doc Duvalier's reign of terror ended in Haiti. They never stopped. Now with the Haiti in disarray, they are more powerful than ever."

"Where can we find Baptiste, Sergeant Collins?" Grant asked, using the name on his uniform.

The officer looked around nervously. "He lives up on the hills east of town. He has a number of places all over the North end of the island.

I cannot tell you more. If he finds out that I've told you this much, he will kill me and my family."

Andrea nudged Grant and tilted her head toward the door. Grant thanked the officer and moved with Andrea toward the exit.

"You know what Tonton Macoutes means in Creole? It means the bogeyman. Forget where you heard any of that and forget you ever came here," the officer said while he tore up the poster.

They walked to the car in the blinding sunlight, and as Grant opened the driver's door, he spotted the small package on the driver's seat. He picked up the brown paper package, came to attention and immediately looked around for someone, anyone who seemed out of place. He scanned the faces all around him, but nothing appeared unusual on the bustling street.

Andrea walked around the car, stood next to Grant and asked, "What's that?"

"I don't know, but I don't like the feeling," Grant said.

He held the small package in his hands and slowly pulled on the stained brown paper until it revealed a five-inch white cardboard box. He sat the box on the roof of the car and slowly pulled the top open. His heart stopped at what he saw. A clump of blonde hair wrapped in thin, blood-soaked tissue paper in the bottom of the small container. Along with it, a necklace tangled in the strands of hair.

He fell backwards and caught himself on the car doorframe. "What have they done?"

Andrea pulled the necklace from the box. It was broken at the clasp where it had ripped from someone's neck. She recognized the delicate piece of jewelry as Holly's.

Grant picked up the grotesque box and noticed another object under the bloody hair. Another gift, tightly wrapped in newspaper and secured by rough twine, awaited. He pulled the oddly bound package out of the box, carefully untied the twine and unrolled the stained newsprint.

Andrea screamed at the top of her lungs. Grant cradled a severed finger in the paper. Under the finger, a message scrawled on the crimson-stained section of the morning newspaper read, "Tonight, Savanna La Mar, at the intersection of B-8 and A-1, at 8:00."

Again, Grant looked around to see if anyone had watched them unwrap the present. Dozens of townspeople looked in their direction with only mild interest after Andrea's scream. The locals took a hysterical tourist in stride. Grant saw nothing out of place, but the hair on his neck pricked out on end. He knew the watchers were there.

Andrea shook uncontrollably, and Grant grabbed her tight in his arms. He put his mouth to her ear and whispered, "We are going to find them, I promise." He felt the soft warmth of her cheek and held her close.

She looked up at him and whispered, "What if we are too late?"

"We're not too late. I can't accept that. We have come this far, and we can't give up. That's what Jon-Pierre wants us to do. He's trying to scare us away, and I'll admit he's doing a damn good job."

He walked Andrea to the passenger door and placed her in the car. He got in the driver's seat with the box and headed back toward Negril.

Holding a pair of binoculars and a smile of satisfaction on his face, Jon-Pierre looked on from a second-story window across from the police station. "Let's get prepared for tonight," he said to his gunman. A crooked smile grew on Jon-Pierre's face.

"I'm ready. I don't understand why we can't kill them now," said the grim-faced, dreadlocked man.

"Patience, my friend. You'll have your chance. We are going to make them work first, and perhaps make a little money in the process." He put the binoculars away and said, "Not to mention have some fun, at their expense."

Chapter 7

The short drive back to the Negril bungalow seemed to take forever. The matted clump of hair, Holly's necklace and the severed finger screamed in silent horror from their hiding place in the white cardboard box. Neither Grant nor Andrea wanted to picture how these macabre bits and pieces came to them. The only certainty was that Jon-Pierre Baptiste was a monster, and this particular monster took pleasure in tormenting them. His years in the Tonton Macoutes had left him well practiced.

Grant and Andrea barely spoke a word during the drive from Lucea. Uncertainty and fear filled the air between them. When the rental car pulled into the space in front of the rented bungalow, a pallor of sadness descended over the couple. They had hoped that by now they would have their girls back with them, or at the very least, confirmation of where they had gone. Instead, they had nothing. Worse than nothing, they had a mutilated body part with an implied threat of more to come if they failed to meet at a place and time of Jon-Pierre's choice.

A red light blinked a greeting as they entered the bungalow. The light flicked on and off from the counter where an answering machine sat tucked behind a piece of stoneware.

"Nobody has this number. It can't be the girls. Jena didn't have the number, and I couldn't tell you what it is. It's probably the rental company asking if the place is okay," Grant volunteered.

He hit the play button and the machine replayed a message. As Grant suspected, the rental manager called to ensure that the bungalow was to his liking.

After Andrea heard that the message from the rental company, she said, "I'm going to take a quick shower to clear my head and wash off some of the grime."

Grant heard the shower start to run. He walked over to the kitchen and grabbed a bottle of water from the refrigerator. Taking a cold swig, he leaned back on the counter and noticed the phone machine light blinking. *Must have forgotten to erase the message.*

He returned to the machine and pressed the play button once more, so he could delete the message from the rental company. His finger readied above the delete key as the message started, but it was a different voice.

The machine beeped and the second message started. "This is Lieutenant Washington, from the Ministry of Justice. Please call me regarding the location of your daughters. I need to discuss this with you. It is most urgent." The Lieutenant gave a phone number in Montego Bay and requested a return call as soon as possible.

Grant felt promise for the first time since they arrived in Jamaica.

"Andrea!" he said. The water in the shower continued.

In his excitement, Grant dialed the number twice incorrectly. On the third attempt, he connected with the Ministry of Justice.

"Lieutenant Washington, please," Grant said.

"The Lieutenant is not available at the moment. Would you care to leave a message?" the person on the other end of the line said.

"My name is Grant Turner. Lieutenant Washington left a message regarding my daughter Jena and her friend Holly Carson. I need to speak with him, it's very important…"

"The Lieutenant is expecting your call. Please stay by the phone, and he will call you back."

Andrea came out from the bedroom, dressed in fresh khaki shorts, bare feet and a blue tank top. She looked fresh, but worn from the events of the day. Andrea cocked her head and dried her hair in a thick towel. She looked to Grant and saw that he was excited.

"What?" she asked.

"We got a message from a Lieutenant from the Ministry of Justice. They have information on the girls. I called, and we are supposed to wait for a call back."

Andrea's face brightened, and the worry started to fade as she ran to Grant. She hugged him and dropped her towel in the process. She squeezed him tight, "I knew we would find them, I can't wait to give them both great big hugs," she said.

Grant hugged her back and felt the same sense of relief and comfort settle within him. Even when the phone rang again, he held Andrea's embrace, taking in her warmth.

Grant snatched up the phone, "Hello?"

The voice on the other end said, "This is Lieutenant Washington. Have I reached Grant Turner and Andrea Carson?"

"Yes, we're here. Let me put you on speaker so we can both hear," Grant said, and tapped a button on the phone console, activating the speaker function.

"I understand, from our officers at the Montego Bay Airport that you are looking for your daughters. Is that right?"

"Yes, that's correct," Grant said. The excitement grew, and he squeezed Andrea's hand, hoping they would soon be with their girls.

Lieutenant Washington paused. "From the pictures and descriptions you provided, we may have found one of them."

Grant and Andrea looked at each other. What was happening? The girls would not have separated on purpose. Andrea asked, "One girl? Which one?"

The Lieutenant curiously added, "I don't know."

Andrea's excitement was close to bursting. "What do you mean you don't know. Just ask her."

The silence on the other end of the line was unsettling. Finally, the Lieutenant's heavy voice responded, "We can't ask her, because we found her dead. The remains somewhat match the description of your girls. We need you to identify the body."

Chapter 8

Elation tumbled into a darkened chasm of complete despair. Their worst fears had come true; they had failed as parents. The single inviolate rule of parenthood is to keep your children safe. It doesn't matter how old they are, two or twenty, your kids aren't supposed to end up like this. They had failed, and words eluded them. Neither Grant nor Andrea responded to the lieutenant. Andrea's knees buckled as she stumbled back onto into the sofa. Grant stared at the phone, shocked and horrified.

"Hello, did you hear me? We need you to come in and identify the body," Lieutenant Washington said over the speaker.

Grant's voice croaked, "It can't be."

"We have a young white girl here, and she matches the description you provided. Unfortunately, I must request that you come to the morgue in Montego Bay and make an identification of the remains. I'm very sorry," Washington added. He gave Grant the address and directions to the facility before he disconnected.

Grant hung up the phone, went to the sofa and collapsed next to Andrea. One of them had lost a daughter, and it was too painful to comprehend which one of the girls had been lost.

Andrea scooted close, leaned her head on his shoulder, and said, "I can't believe it. They were good girls. This can't be happening—not to them."

Grant felt her shudder as he held her. "What could have happened? Jena and Holly wouldn't separate, so what happened to them? If the police found one, where is the other?"

"I don't know what I'll do without my Jena. She's everything to me," Grant said as tears formed and slowly trickled down his cheek.

Andrea looked up at Grant, slowly reached up, stroked his stubbled face and gently kissed him on the cheek.

Grant cupped her hand on his cheek and pulled her close.

She looked up at him. "You're not alone, Grant."

They embraced, without another word spoken. Both knew the horror that awaited them in Montego Bay, and neither wanted to leave the temporary comfort they found with each other. It was Andrea who broke away first. Grant saw that she held Holly's necklace, cupped in her hand.

"I don't want to believe she's gone," she said.

"How did the lieutenant know where to find us?"

"This is harder than I thought. I can't do this." Andrea began to shudder.

"I know. I know it's hard, but we have to go and identify—"

"One of our girls." Andrea cut him off, her fear bubbling over.

"We need to get the girls home," he said.

"What kind of home will it be without them?"

"It won't be the same, ever." He shifted on the sofa, took one of Andrea's hands and looked into her eyes. We have to do this. We need to go and take her home."

Andrea clinched her eyes against the tears and nodded. She leaned into Grant one more time, drawing from his strength. A moment passed, and neither of them spoke. Drawn by the inevitable, they rose from the sofa and headed for the car.

The hour's drive to the morgue in Montego Bay passed with excruciating torment, borne with tension that grew mile by mile. After they arrived, Andrea and Grant sat for a moment together in the car outside. Neither was prepared for the terror waiting for them inside the morgue.

"Do you want me to do this?" Grant said.

"No," she said, shaking her head with determination, "I have to do this, Grant. I have to know."

Both exited the car, and Andrea grasped Grant's hand tightly before they entered the front door. Air conditioning strained to keep up with the heat inside, but it couldn't overcome the stench of decay and formaldehyde. Andrea gagged at the horrible smell. The odor alone told her that nothing good ever happened in this place.

Andrea trembled and Grant placed his arm around the small of her back in an attempt to settle and support her. She leaned her head on his shoulder and melted into Grant's side.

A woman in white medical scrubs sat behind a desk in the reception area. She seemed oblivious to the horrendous odor of death. She looked up but said nothing to greet them.

"We're here to see Lieutenant Washington," Grant said.

The woman nodded and gave a consoling glance. She picked up the phone, dialed a number and said, "Tell Lieutenant Washington the people he was waiting for are here."

She listened for a response and then hung up. "The lieutenant will be out in a few minutes. Would either of you care for some coffee, or water?"

The thought of drinking anything in this place made Grant's stomach turn. Mama's Jerk Chicken wasn't a good idea after all. "No, thank you," he said.

Less than a minute later, a tall, dark man, in a crisp, tan linen suit, stepped through the door into the lobby. He walked over to Grant and Andrea and introduced himself. "I'm Lieutenant Washington," he said, extending his hand.

Grant shook the lieutenant's hand. The police officer's eyes studied the two Americans.

"Mr. Turner, Miss Carson, I regret we must do this, but please follow me to the viewing area." He backtracked across the lobby and held the door open for Grant and Andrea.

Their staccato footfalls echoed in the hallway, which only served to heighten their apprehension. The walls were a pale blue, marked with chipped paint where gurneys had bounced off the walls. The impression was that sadness dwelled here. Neither Grant nor Andrea would say it aloud, but both held the same selfish wish: *Please, not my daughter.*

A single door beckoned at the far end of the hallway. Grant thought it looked like the kind of place a convicted murderer would walk his last steps before execution. The poorly maintained overhead lighting flickered, making the facility appear somewhat otherworldly. Washington stopped at the door.

"The girl is in here. I need you to tell me if she is yours. We must be very certain about the identification," Washington said.

Grant nodded and took a step toward the door when the Lieutenant put his arm out, "You need to prepare yourself. The body is badly decomposed and—damaged."

Grant made no response, but tightened his grip on Andrea as they walked through the door. In the center of the room was a gurney, with a plastic sheet covering the remains. The only light in the room, a bright spotlight, illuminated the gurney and gave the covered body a spectral appearance.

They walked up to the gurney, held each other tight and braced for what promised to be the worst possible ending to one young life. The Lieutenant slowly pulled down the plastic sheet revealing a young face.

Or, where the face would have been. The features were unrecognizable and misshapen. Patches of flesh, torn and peeled, white bone visible beneath. The girl's face was broken, and a limp jaw hung to one side.

Andrea went limp. She turned away from the body and tucked her face into Grant's chest, muffling a sad groan. Grant froze and couldn't look away from the grotesque display. There were answers here. He had to find them. Although the girl was battered and not recognizable, Grant knew this wasn't his Jena. He noticed a patch of hair pulled from the front of the woman's head. His mind flashed to the clump of hair and flesh in the package they had received in Lucea.

"Let me see her hands," Grant said.

The lieutenant looked at Grant, folded the sheet and exposed the right hand with a missing index finger.

"Care to tell me how you knew about her finger, Mr. Turner?" Washington asked.

Grant noticed a small tattoo on the right shoulder. He gently nudged Andrea, "Does Holly have a tattoo of a butterfly?"

Andrea closed her eyes tight; she couldn't look at the dead woman. "No, she doesn't. No tattoos that I'm aware of anyway."

She felt Grant's embrace loosen. She turned, slowly bent closer and examined the girl on the gurney. She had to remind herself to breathe.

"This is not my Holly. She didn't have a tattoo. Holly's hair is a little darker. My daughter is only about five foot five, and this woman seems—taller," she said. Her face betrayed relief mixed with a rush of guilt.

Grant also felt a reprieve that the body wasn't his daughter. However, the dead girl was somebody's little girl. "This isn't Jena either. My daughter has a small tattoo on her arm—and there is nothing here."

Lieutenant Washington looked down at the remains. "Water can drastically change what a body looks like. Are you absolutely sure this girl is not one of your daughters?"

Both Grant and Andrea nodded. With another small measure of guilty relief, Grant said, "Yes, we're sure."

"I accept that she is not yours. However, you need to tell me how you knew to look for the missing finger." Washington said. He threw back the sheet, covering the girl's body.

After a brief moment of uncomfortable silence, Grant finally spoke. "Lieutenant, we have been looking for our girls and talking to anyone who may have seen them. In the process, we stopped and talked to the police in Lucea." Grant recalled Paulo's warning—You *can't trust all the police,* and he wasn't about to trust this police officer with the whole story.

At the mention of the police in Lucea, the lieutenant's face hardened, but he continued to listen to the American's story.

Heeding Paulo's words, Grant kept some of the facts to himself. "While we were in the police station, someone wrapped up a finger and lock of hair in a box and placed it in our car," Grant said.

"Where is this box now?" Washington asked.

"It's in the car." Grant said. Had he implicated Andrea and himself in this young woman's death?

"Why don't you go retrieve it while I talk with Miss Carson, here," the Lieutenant said.

Andrea stiffened at the thought of being alone with the lieutenant and the body of the poor dead girl, but she gathered a bit of resolve from the fact that her daughter was still out there. "Grant, go ahead. I'll be fine."

Grant nodded and walked quickly toward the door. He looked and saw Andrea in the glow of the harsh spotlight. She looked vulnerable and hurt, but within her, he saw a rekindled ember of strength. He needed her and that sliver of strength more than he cared to admit.

As soon as Grant disappeared from view, the lieutenant turned to Andrea. "How did you end up in Lucea?"

Andrea didn't know who to trust and feared giving this man any information that might end up hurting the girls. She paused, looked the lieutenant directly in his dark brown eyes, and said, "We went to the police station in Lucea to give them a poster with the girls' pictures. We hoped they could give us some information."

Washington looked down at Andrea with a stone-faced glare: "Young lady, Lucy Town is not in any tourist brochure. Tell me why you were in that place. You are hiding something. Perhaps you are connected to what happened to this young lady." The Lieutenant undraped the dead girl's body.

Andrea, unable to look at him any longer, turned away. She faced the doors and wanted to bolt through them to Grant. Her heart raced when she heard his footsteps approach from beyond the doorway.

Grant walked in to the room, the box in hand. The pained look on Andrea's face caused him to stop in mid stride. The discomfort she held in her eyes made him boil. He looked over at Washington and back to Andrea. "What's going on?"

Washington leaned on the gurney, looking somewhat smug, and said, "We were talking about what brought you to Lucea. I don't think it was the farmer's market."

"We went there to see if the police had any information on the girls' disappearance," Grant answered.

The Lieutenant sighed deeply. "No one goes to Lucea unless they have a reason. What was your reason? The only thing I know is that you claim to have a finger belonging to this young lady," he said while patting the girl's bluish leg.

Grant walked to where the Lieutenant stood and passed him the box. "We want to find our daughters." He took a second to calm himself, then added, "We found this in our car after we came out of the police station."

Andrea joined alongside Grant. "Please, believe us. Help us," she said.

"Dear lady, I do believe you that you are trying to find them. What I don't believe is why you went to Lucea. What are you not telling me?"

Grant looked at Andrea and ever so slightly shook his head. He knew if Jon-Pierre Baptiste found out they had gone to the police, their girls would end up like this, on a steel gurney.

"We are going to hit all the police stations between Negril and Montego Bay," Grant explained. "Lucea was one of the places on our list."

Washington looked at Grant suspiciously. The lieutenant hefted the small box in his hand and said, "Let's see what you have in here, eh?"

Washington put the box down on a nearby counter and gently pulled back the top. He peered into the box, looking intently for a clue. "What else was in here?"

Grant had removed the blood soaked note and placed it in the glove compartment of the rental car. "That's it, the finger and lock of hair. The finger was wrapped in paper, but I threw that away because it was bloody."

Washington looked in the box again and said, "This is a message from someone. So where is the message?"

Grant remained silent for a few seconds. He looked over at the girl's body and asked, "How did she end up here?"

"Most likely she got herself sold into the sex trade. Human Trafficking. The people who run that activity treat young women as disposable things. They dumped her body in the Little River when they were finished with her. The body was found in the water by tourists on a rafting trip."

Washington stepped closer to the body and pointed out a number of indentations on her limbs. "See those marks on her legs? Those are crocodile bites. This woman was dead when she hit the water. Otherwise the animals would have taken the girl and hidden her under the water. They prefer live prey."

"Do you think our daughters are involved? Were they taken by the same men?" Andrea asked. Her faced paled with the thought that the same monsters had Jena and Holly.

The lieutenant looked at Andrea directly. "Yes. The fact you were sent her finger tells me we are dealing with the same people."

"What kind of person does this? Surely people can't go missing without someone noticing," Grant said.

Washington took a seat in a dented metal folding chair by the counter. He stretched out his long legs in front of him, looking weary. "The people who did this are from off the island. Don't get me wrong, there are Jamaicans who get involved in prostitution and smuggling people in and out of the country, but they are small potatoes compared to this. The ones who grabbed this girl are vicious and target young women on vacation at the island resorts. Their victims come from Europe, Latin America, and the U.S., all far from home, and alone."

"How many women are we talking about?" Grant said.

"We have no idea. Unless someone is concerned about them, like you, we never know. These stories don't have happy endings. The few we find are dead, their used bodied stashed away in the Little River. The rest? Taken out of the country or buried somewhere in the hills. Jamaica has the world's fourth highest murder rate, behind only South Africa, Colombia, and Namibia. It has gotten worse since the quake in Haiti."

"The State Department and the Jamaican government know about this—why don't they warn travelers?" Grant said.

"The tourist trade is a big deal here. American businesses profit from it too. The travel industry knows we need them as much as they need Jamaica. So everyone turns a blind eye to the problem. The criminals who run these trafficking networks manage to stay a step ahead of the authorities. The Ministry of Justice has Operation Kingfish, and we in the Jamaican Constabulary Force put together a Trafficking in Persons Unit. We rescued about a dozen women last year, but I don't have the resources to eliminate the problem. So we continue to have women like her dying." The Inspector put his hand on the stainless steel table.

Andrea fumed at the matter-of-fact revelations from the lieutenant. "You do nothing while young women die!"

"We can only do so much, and the corruption of local law enforcement officers only serves to further shield the ones behind these gangs."

"So then we are on our own, searching for our girls. Tell me I'm wrong," Grant pleaded.

"I can't help you unless you can tell me what message you received from the people who sent you this." Washington held up the box.

"We don't know who placed the box in the car," Grant said.

Andrea boiled over. "We are wasting time arguing. We need to get on with looking for Holly and Jena." She headed for the door, uncertain if Washington might try to stop her.

Grant watched Andrea storm through the door, turned to the lieutenant and said, "I'm going to find them with or without your help." Grant turned to follow Andrea as she burst out through the door.

Washington made no move to stop him, but as Grant hit the door the lieutenant called out, "Careful, or you and your girls will end up in Little River."

Chapter 9

Andrea pushed her way through a knot of uniformed morgue attendants who gathered outside the building before their shift, cutting through the cloud of cigarette smoke that hung nearby. She stormed to the red rental car, flung open the door, got in, and slammed it shut.

Grant followed a few paces behind and when he opened his door, she vented her disgust at Lieutenant Washington's cavalier attitude. She balled her fists as she spoke. "How dare they! It might hurt the tourist trade? I can't bear to think how many girls are gone, exploited or killed, and they don't care. Washington and the rest of them stand around and do nothing, absolutely nothing."

Grant listened, careful to avoid the steam from the volcano next to him. He waited for a pause, then said, "Paulo said it and the lieutenant confirmed it. Corruption and payoffs to police and local officials help keep these men in business."

"We are no closer to finding the girls than we were in Los Angeles, because people like Washington don't care about anything but their own pockets," Andrea fumed.

"I know we both hoped we'd find the girls by now. We are inching our way to them. Bit by bit, we get closer. Paulo, the taxi ride and the hotel, remember? Then we finally have the name of the blue-eyed monster who took them from us—Jon-Pierre Baptiste. The cop in Lucea confirmed that much for us."

"That creep wants to meet us tonight. How can we trust him after Washington told us about organized criminal drug, gun and sex trade business? It could be a plan to delay us," Andrea said.

"It could be a move to throw us off track, but it is a meeting we can't afford to blow off. Any chance at getting to the girls, or talking to the men who have them, is a chance we have to take. Washington mentioned a place called Little River. Hand me the map in the glove compartment, would you?"

Andrea popped open the glove compartment and recoiled at the sight of the blood-stained scrap of newspaper that carried Jon-Pierre's invitation to tonight's get-together. From beneath the grisly remnant, Andrea pulled the island road map with a thumb and forefinger, careful not to touch the bloody newsprint. Then she slammed the glove box closed.

"I thought you gave Washington everything when you handed him the box," Andrea said.

Grant took the map, unfolded it on the console between them, and said, "I couldn't risk the police showing up at the meeting tonight and ending our chance at the girls. It didn't matter if they were good cops or bad cops. They can't be there when we meet Baptiste."

With a fingertip, Grant traced the main highway east from Montego Bay. "Here it is. Little River is about twenty kilometers from Montego." Looking at Andrea, he continued, "You any good at metric? How far is that?"

"Twelve-point-four miles."

"How do you know that?"

"I used to run a few 10K races. Ten kilometers is six-point-two miles."

"You still jog?" Grant asked, picturing her determined stride, passing other runners.

"Not jog, run," she said.

"Is there a difference?"

"If you're a runner there is. Joggers plod around aimlessly. Runners go from point A to point B with a purpose." She brushed her hair back while she looked at the map.

"Good to know. Little River is twelve miles up the coast."

"Twelve-point-four," Andrea said.

"Whatever. Let's take a drive out there and see what stands out. If there are houses and buildings around, maybe someone saw something."

Andrea folded the map so the section with Little River faced outward. She clutched the map in her lap and said, "Grant, I can't get over why no one seems to care about the women who disappeared."

"I think they care. I think Lieutenant Washington cares. I get the feeling the problem is so big, so overwhelming, and he doesn't get much help. Like back home, the special interests want to keep a lid on the problems so the money keeps flowing."

"And young women like that one, in there, die," Andrea said.

Grant started the car, pulled from the morgue lot and headed east toward Little River. On the left side, the coastline came into view, deep blue waves crashing over dark rocks that jutted out from the shore. Strands of pristine-white sand beaches dotted the coast near the road. Green thickets of trees and brush crowded the road on the opposite side, except where clearings revealed golf courses, commercial buildings, or local markets. As the miles ticked past from Montego Bay, the developed areas made way into smaller local gathering places, taverns, and half-built concrete block homes. The local economy at the far edge of St. James Parish seemed forgotten by the tourist trade, as evidenced by the resort vans that sped past this stretch in favor of Ocho Rios, farther east.

Twelve-point-four miles later, a green and white sign on the center of a highway bridge announced their arrival at Little River. A mile before the river crossing, a resort hotel was under construction along the coastline. A few ramshackle buildings dotted the countryside, but any collection of local townsfolk lived up the hillside, which offered cooling trade winds and incredible views of the ocean.

Grant slowed and pulled the rental car off the road into a wide dirt shoulder before the roadway crossed the river. They both got out of the car and walked to the edge of a fence made of tall, thin wooden stakes, spaced three to four feet apart and connected with strands of wire.

"I'm not sure what I'm looking for," Grant said.

"The lieutenant said that the girl was found in the water. I can't even see the water from here." Andrea touched the fence and it wobbled under her touch. "This wouldn't keep much from going through, but I don't see any signs of anyone passing this way. The fence isn't cut or bent, and the grass isn't trampled."

"If you were going to drop a body off in the water, how would you do it?" Grant said.

"I'd go to the water," Andrea said.

Andrea walked out to the edge of the roadway and stepped up on the yellow curbing that warned motorists of the crossing. She went to the center of the bridge, leaned over the waist-high metal guardrail, and saw the river below her. "Washington lied."

Grant joined her on the center of the bridge. Below them, a narrow, murky tributary flowed out toward the sea. Upstream, the channel widened slightly before it disappeared into a thick grove of mangrove trees.

"There is no way that tourists found the girl's body. Who would raft in this stream?" she said.

"Then why would he say that?"

"He didn't want us to know who found her. He's keeping that from us," she said.

"Like we kept the meeting with Baptiste from him," Grant rubbed at the tension that grew at the back of his neck.

Andrea looked across the traffic lanes and saw thick fields of grassy marshland. Then she pointed at a spot on the riverbank below. "On the other side of the bridge, look over there. You see where the fence ends?"

"It looks like a path that cuts back up the hillside along the river," Grant said.

Andrea stood on her tiptoes. "You could back a car almost halfway down to the water's edge, hidden from traffic, while you did whatever."

"Like toss a body in the water. Look at that dark pool of still water. What do you think?' Grant said.

"I think we need to check it out."

They reentered the car, drove over the bridge and eased up onto the yellow curb at the head of the path. The matted grass and tire tracks showed that theirs was not the first vehicle to pull off in this spot. The two of them got out and started down the trail, Andrea in the lead.

The path was wider and went much deeper into the thick grove that they had first thought. After nearly one-quarter mile, they found tire tracks in the damp clay that appeared recent. When they reached a spot near the water's edge, the brush line and a mangrove thicket completely shielded them from the road above.

This tree-covered river basin was dark in the afternoon, with foliage blocking the direct sunlight, but the heavy humidity collected there like a bowl of muggy water near the river. Grant pointed to a mark in the dirt along the brackish water.

"This has to be the spot. These look like drag marks; but we don't know if it was the girl being dropped in, or the police pulling her out," Grant said.

A reflection from an object near the water captured Andrea's attention. She bent over and picked up a button, torn from a woman's garment. "This is the spot," she said.

Andrea turned and imagined the girl floating in the brackish waters. Mosquitoes buzzed feverishly around her, and a ripple in the water gave evidence of life below the surface. An eye peered from beneath, watchful and patient.

"Crocodile," Andrea said, swatting insects from around her. This would be an awful place to die."

"Holly and Jena aren't dead," Grant said as he stared at the murky water. "They aren't dead," he repeated mantra-like, to convince himself.

The watchful eye disappeared below the surface. Maybe later, someone would drop another fleshy package for him.

Grant glanced at his watch. "It's getting late. We should get ready for the meeting this evening. It's across the island from where we are now, and it's only a few hours till eight. Let's get going."

They backed away from the riverbank and the repressive humidity of the mangrove trees. They had seen a place where women died, or were tossed away like garbage. That knowledge that was hard to shake off. It clung to them like a shroud, telling them that the clock was ticking down for Holly and Jena.

Chapter 10

Hope. With each minute that passed, anticipation ratcheted a notch tighter. The meeting with Jon-Pierre promised reunification with the girls. Everything depended on trust in a man who, from all accounts, was a violent monster, capable of unimaginable terror. The young woman in the morgue served as an example of how far Jon-Pierre would go. Grant and Andrea found themselves balanced on a razor's edge, a murderous Haitian crime lord on one side and shady government cover ups on the other. One misstep and they might never see Holly or Jena again.

Andrea held the map on her lap, the cross-island route visible. The route south on Highway B-8 wound through thick trees and vast sugar-cane fields so dense they could see only a few feet in from the road. The highway inclined steadily as the landscape transitioned into a heavily forested plateau. Small shacks, assembled from leftover building mate-rials, dotted the side of the road. There were no glass windows in the structures, though each had a set of wooden shutters, which protected the occupants during heavy storms.

"This is a part of Jamaica they don't include in the tourist brochures," Andrea said.

"It doesn't look so bad," Grant said, as he pointed to the humble dwellings, then continued, "Look at them. They aren't much, but it's ob-vious that they are cared for and are extraordinarily clean. The people out here don't have much, but they take pride in what they do have."

Farther along the isolated road, women in their finest dresses and white gloves, and children in bright clothing, walked to church services, a glaring contrast from the homes in which they lived. Their faces re-flected contentment and peace—something to be learned from being happy with what you have. The adage resonated with new meaning for Grant and Andrea.

Approximately two hours into the drive, a plywood shack came into view. The building had no sign, but the small cluster of cars and smoke that vented through the thatched roof attested that it had a hot, wood-fired grill working.

"Hungry?" Grant asked.

"I guess so. It's hard to tell if I need to eat, or if it's my nerves."

Grant turned the red sedan into the trampled grass that served as a parking area. A group of eight Jamaican men walked from under the awning and headed their direction. They yelled their thanks for a meal to unseen people in the shack.

"Blessed be the Princess. Much love to you," one of the men said.

As the group passed Grant and Andrea, one of the men nodded a greeting and said, "Respect." Another glanced at Andrea and tipped his faded, ratty baseball cap, and said, "Hello, Love."

Six of them loaded into the back of a small Toyota pickup truck and sat on the side rails of the bed. The remaining two entered the cab, and the truck left, all hands holding onto their precarious perches.

Grant and Andrea entered the establishment under the large tin awning. The place looked temporary. A small generator sputtering behind the shed provided power for a small refrigerator, and the flooring was just trampled grass and packed red clay. The tables were rough-hewn timbers balanced on used car tires and tree stumps. No one looked up from the bar to greet the American couple, not the bar keeper, nor any of the six patrons who huddled over their plates of local fare.

Grant led Andrea to a table near the back of the shack, and a small dark woman walked over, put a hand on her hip, and said, "We don't have no menu. What we have is Escovitch Fish, Cho-Cho, and Red Pea Soup. What do you want?"

Both ordered the Escovitch, which came to their table in minutes. The fresh fish was pan fried, with a mixture of diced onions, hot country peppers, lime juice, allspice, salt and pepper. A traditional pea and rice side dish came with the spicy fish. Grant and Andrea, hungrier that they had thought, devoured the delicious meal, cooling their palates with cold bottles of soda.

"Do you think Holly and Jena will be there tonight," Andrea mused. A spark of hope danced in her brown eyes as she spoke.

"I don't know. The message didn't say they would be there. I'd like to believe that, but I know that Baptiste wants to hold the upper hand. If I were him, I wouldn't bring them."

"Then what do you think we *are* going to find tonight?" Andrea asked across the table.

"Whatever it is, it is another step closer to the girls," Grant said.

"What about Lieutenant Washington? Do you think he's on the level?" Andrea said.

"Maybe he is—but, I don't think we can take a chance. We don't know who's been bought off."

"Why aren't the communities combing the hillsides for the missing people? There's no public outcry," Andrea said.

"Who would they complain to? The police? Paulo told us that they don't trust the police. That probably extends to all the official authorities. Washington said there was nothing he could do about the violence."

"But I don't see him doing anything at all. He's complaining—but what is he doing? Nothing," Andrea said.

Andrea took the last bite of her fish and sat back on the rough-hewn wooden chair. Her mind started to race. "We should get some supplies for tonight."

"Like what?"

"Flashlights and stuff. I don't know. What do you need for a nighttime hostage rescue," she said, a bit more sharply than she intended. The frustration made them both a bit frayed around the edges.

"Yeah, I guess that's a good idea." Grant took the last swallow from the cane-sugar-laced soda.

They pushed back from the table and Grant left a few bills, more than enough to cover the tab. Once in the car, they continued south to Savannah La Mar. When B-8 ended at A-1 on the coast, Grant turned into Savannah La Mar, just past the intersection where Jon-Pierre Baptiste's note said to meet.

Grant took a curve onto Great Georges Street, into an area of businesses and homes. Several buildings showed damage to their roofs as well as to their thin vertical sides, and the Savannah La Mar Baptist Church lay in a collapsed heap.

A small store near the church remained open, in spite of damage to its tin roof. An old man tended to the store, arranging items on shelves. When Grant and Andrea entered, the old man smiled and walked to the cash register, expecting a sale.

"Good day," the old man greeted them.

"Hello," Andrea answered. "What happened to the church and your store?"

"Ah. A great windstorm. No one hurt 'cause God keeps them all at home because of the rain," the man said.

Grant went down an aisle and collected flashlights, heavy hemp twine, a small folding knife, bottled water and duct tape. Not knowing what else to grab, he felt a little like a movie character preparing to manufacture a dune buggy out of a Styrofoam cup. He paid for the items, pocketed the knife, and placed the twine and tape in the trunk. The flashlights and water bottles went into the interior pockets of the front doors.

"We have about an hour and a half before we are supposed to be there. You want to head out and wait?" Grant said as he got back into the car.

"Maybe if we show up early, they will too," she said.

Grant drove back down the highway to the intersection of A-1 and B-9, exactly as Jon-Pierre directed. The intersection was a bare, wide spot where vehicles parked. It had the feel of a carpool lot back in Los Angeles, where commuters dropped off their cars for the trip into the city. There were ten cars parked there, by his count. Grant eased into the lot and nosed the rental car in the middle of the lot of empty cars.

"Now we wait," Grant said, putting the car into park, and turned off the ignition.

They rolled down the small car's windows, immediately grateful for the slight ocean breeze that washed over them as they waited.

Time ticked by slowly as they watched the roads and parking area around them. Slowing vehicles or strolling locals kept their attention until darkness followed the sunset. Two ancient streetlights hung from heavy strands of electrical wire, illuminating the parking lot. Periodically, people came, retrieved their cars from the lot, and drove off. It was eight o'clock and Grant and Andrea had no sign of Jon-Pierre.

"What are they waiting for?" Andrea said.

"I don't know. Maybe they don't see us. I'm going to get out and walk around." Grant pushed open his car door, leaving it open so the dome light spilled out onto the parking surface. He walked to the edge of the road, stood on the side of the lot for a minute, then walked back to the car. "We'll see if that did anything."

Another two painful hours passed, and by and now their little red sedan was the only car in the lot. It was well after ten.

Grant fidgeted in his seat. "I don't get it. They tell us to come here two hours ago, and then nothing."

"I don't understand it either. Did they change their mind and they aren't going to talk to us about Holly and Jena?"

"Or they never intended to meet us. Maybe they just wanted us out of the way," he said.

Grant noticed a road sign to his left. He had seen it when they pulled in but paid little attention to it till now. Squinting to get a better look, he saw that the sign served as a makeshift community bulletin board. At least twenty pieces of paper and cardboard were fastened to the post, fluttering in the breeze.

"I'll be damned!" Grant shouted.

Andrea watched him throw the door open and run to the road sign. She joined him, "What is it?"

"Look. This is how the locals leave messages for each other," he said.

Grant pointed out job bulletins, messages from wives looking for their adulterous husbands, and assorted items for sale. He was almost to the bottom of the post when he saw it.

At the very bottom, a freshly typed half sheet of paper grabbed their attention. In bold letters, it read, *"Mrs. Carson and Mr. Turner. The two packages are ready for pickup. The cost is $50,000 apiece. The packages are undamaged, at this point. Funds must be available for deposit tomorrow by a time I will set. Will contact you for pickup. This is a one-time offer."*

Chapter 11

"I didn't think to watch the signpost. Jon-Pierre could have been right here, and we let him get away!" Andrea said.

"Or he told one of the locals to stick this on the post. It doesn't matter who delivered it, we got the message."

Andrea pointed at the note in desperation. "Jon-Pierre doesn't consider the girls as human. They're only objects to him. Objects that he wants to sell for profit and he knows how desperate we are."

"The important thing is that we know Holly and Jena are alive," he said.

"But, can we—can we believe anything this monster says? What if he's toying with us and has no intention to give them back. Or—"

Grant cut her off before she said what he didn't have the strength to imagine. What if? He diverted from the dark web of uncertainty and fear in the recesses of his mind. "We have a chance to get them back. That's more than we had this morning, and now we know exactly what we have to overcome."

"But, that poor girl they dumped in Little River... I'm afraid that no matter what we do, something really bad could happen to Holly and Jena," Andrea offered.

"Fifty grand by tomorrow. I don't know how I can make that happen," Grant said as he folded the message and shoved it in his back pocket.

"I have it—but not by tomorrow."

"We have to come up with something to tell Jon-Pierre when he contacts us," Grant said.

"What are we going to do, ask for more time? From the 'one-time offer' in his message, I don't think he will let us have more time to come up with the money."

"What can we do?" For the first time, Grant sounded a bit hopeless.

They stood alone in the wide spot of the intersection. Night had long since blanketed the isolated crossroads. Even the shadows melted into the blackness that surrounded them.

Andrea shuddered. "Why don't we get out of here. This place is beginning to creep me out."

Dark countryside passed by on the hour-long drive back to Negril. It was near midnight, and the only visible activity was close to town. A group of men carried grills fashioned from fifty-five gallon drums, and bundles of wood to the beach for tomorrow's daylong Independence Day celebration. Freedom and independence for Jena and Holly would have to wait another night.

Physical and mental exhaustion caught up with Grant and Andrea. The numbing drive back to the bungalow threatened to melt away any sense of hope. Might all return to normal with the sunrise and a new day? It was the only way to keep hope alive—and the girls. They talked about their daughters, and life in the hectic Los Angeles metropolis where they almost, but never had met one another. They focused on the past—not the future. The future was too bleak.

"How did Jena manage after her mom died?" Andrea asked.

"Jena was fifteen when it happened. A car crash caused by a drunk driver isn't like losing someone to cancer. You can't plan for the loss. It just hits you. She went to work like any other morning and never came home."

"Well, I think you did a terrific job with Jena. She really is quite something. You have to be proud of her, she has done so many great things, like the full academic scholarship she got to CSU-LA."

"Yeh, I'm proud of my Jena. She's grown so much. But now that she's on her own, it kind of makes me feel—I don't know, unneeded," Grant said.

"I know what you mean. I used to help Holly with her clothes, and her homework, and everything else a mom does. She does it all on her own now."

Grant paused. "How's Holly dealing with the divorce."

"It's been a few years since my husband left. Ex-husband." Andrea corrected herself. "Holly refuses to talk to her dad. She can't understand why he would leave his family for someone else. I can't say that I blame her for that one."

"It sounds like she needs you."

"They both need us now. More than ever," Andrea said as the approached the bungalow.

A sadness set in as the car pulled up to their resting place with only the two of them. It was well after midnight. They entered the front door, and as Andrea turned on the lights, a faint yellow glow spilled onto the patio. The gentle sea breeze pushed the sound of crashing waves up from the beach and intertwined with the sound of trickling water cascading down the patio fountain. Grant stepped out onto the patio, listening quietly to the water, hoping it would wash away the fatigue and anxiety.

Andrea joined him, she took in the nightscape and didn't seem to find comfort and solace. She softly tapped him on the shoulder. When he turned, she placed her hand on his cheek, lifted herself up on her toes and kissed him softly. "Goodnight."

Grant, taken off guard by her kiss, looked at her and stammered, "Goodnight to you, too."

Andrea, surprised by his startled response, seemed to take a measure of comfort in the warmth she felt in their short embrace. She turned and walked off to her bedroom suite, glancing back at him over her shoulder.

Grant watched as she entered her bedroom. He felt the blood rush to his face and then he quickly disappeared into his bedroom suite. Drained from the search and comforted by Andrea's presence, Grant barely finished stripping off his clothes before he fell into bed.

Sleep was elusive for both of them, fitful and full of night terrors—one or both girls found dead and dismembered, displayed like the girl in the morgue. After one such vivid nightmare, Grant awoke in a cold sweat. He swore he heard Jena calling for him.

Grant got out of bed clad in his boxer shorts and walked out to the kitchen in search of decaffeinated coffee or tea. He padded around on the balls of his feet and made sure to close the drawers silently, so as not to awaken Andrea. He knew she was every bit as exhausted as he felt, but he was awestruck at her determination and inner strength. She hadn't a clue to how resilient she was—the way she just kept pushing forward and refusing to take no for an answer. Grant had seen other examples of her feminine-fired willpower during the last twenty-something hours. He rummaged around until he found a box of sorrel tea and, following the directions on the container, put a spoonful in a large white coffee mug. Grant used the instant hot water dispenser on the kitchen sink.

As he turned he nearly dropped the hot mug when he saw Andrea standing in the kitchen behind him in a longish tee shirt. Her hair was slightly mussed, and the light from the patio reflected off her bare skin. The effect took his breath away.

"I--um--I hope--I woke--I mean, I hope I didn't wake you. I was trying to be quiet," Grant apologized, standing there in his tree-frog-print boxer shorts.

Andrea ran a hand through her hair. "I couldn't sleep, and I heard you out here. I didn't want to be alone." She looked away, uncomfortable with her need for another person's company.

"I couldn't sleep either. Care to join me? I'm not much of a tea drinker, but it's not bad. It says it's non-caffeinated, made from hibiscus, ginger, allspice and lawn clippings, I think. I was going to drink it out on the patio next to the fountain..." Grant trailed off and reached for another mug in the cabinet.

"No, no thank you--but I'll sit with you."

An overstuffed patio sofa faced the fountain, beyond which lay a stunning view of the night ocean. Grant sat down, leaned his head back, and rested the warm tea mug in his lap. Andrea sat down next to Grant and pulled her feet up under her, hesitantly leaning closer. For a moment, the sound of water from the fountain and waves washing up on the shore was all that filled the silence.

Grant took a sip of tea and closed his eyes. "I couldn't sleep. I kept dreaming we didn't get the girls back."

"Me too. I couldn't get that poor dead girl's face out of my mind."

He looked into her soft eyes and pulled her close. "Andrea, I promise you, we will find a way to get them back with us."

She relaxed into him. "What is Jon-Pierre going to do when we can't come up with the cash?"

"He can't find out. We have to get the girls before he has a chance to get the money."

Andrea sat up and looked at him. "How are we going to do that?

"We need to stall on the money for as long as we can, then demand that we see them. At least then we have a shot to grab the girls," Grant said.

"There is no way Jon-Pierre will let us take them, Grant."

"Trust me. Since he sent that gunman to warn us, we've followed his demands and directions. We have got to turn that around and get him to budge, when we say so."

"How are we going to do that?" Andrea said.

"The officer in Lucea and Lieutenant Washington both said Baptiste is into drugs, guns--"

"And selling women," Andrea finished.

"So he is motivated by greed, plain and simple. We use that against him."

"How do we do that?" she said.

"Extort the extortionist."

Grant started to talk out how to accomplish what sounded so easy to say. He fell silent while his mind worked out and discarded various scenarios. Get Jon-Pierre to deliver the girls, get proof of life and get him to believe we have the money. How do you extort a criminal when you don't have any leverage? Finally, exhaustion took hold, and they both fell asleep on the sofa in each other's arms.

Andrea awoke from her restless sleep. The sun crept over the hill behind the patio, and warm rays of color bathed the area in yellow highlights. She stayed in place for a little while, still half-asleep, enjoying the comfort of Grant's arms. She leaned in closer, and thought how in another time and place this could feel so right. As she lingered a few more moments, suddenly a flood of thoughts about Holly filled her mind. She snapped back into where she was and what she and Grant faced today.

She gently got up and stood back from the sofa where Grant slept soundly. He looked sexy, relaxed there in his boxers and tee, she had to admit. She shook her head, cleared the cobwebs from slumber and tiptoed off to the shower in her suite.

Minutes later, the sun touched Grant's face. Stretching, he noticed Andrea gone. A jolt of anxious tension shot up his spine before he heard the shower running.

He stood, stretched and felt the kinks from his cramped sleep on the sofa. His sore muscles served him notice that he wasn't getting any younger. He walked to his bathroom, turned the shower on to nearly scalding, and let the steam envelope his body.

Following his long shower, Grant dressed and thought he heard reggae music coming from the kitchen. He walked out of his room to find Andrea making a breakfast of pancakes, fruit and strong smelling coffee.

"Wow. This looks great. I didn't know you were so multi-talented," Grant said.

Andrea cocked her head in his direction and gave him an eye roll any teenage girl would envy. She turned the music down and worked on a reluctant pancake with a spatula. "Good timing. Come and sit."

They ate the fresh mangoes, papaya and berries along with the hot pancakes. The strong coffee shot a heavy dose of invigorating caffeine into their systems. Neither wanted to talk about what they faced today, it felt good to enjoy breakfast like a normal couple. But they weren't a normal couple. The very thing that had brought them together and now bound them was dark and sinister. Their two girls depended on them—depended on them for their lives. Grant and Andrea kept that burden unspoken, between them, brewing below the surface. The artificial bliss shattered, the instant the phone rang.

Grant jumped to the phone and looked at Andrea. He hit the speaker button, picked it up, and answered, "Hello."

The accented voice on the other end said, "You got my message last night, yes?"

"Yes, we got it, Jon-Pierre," Grant said.

"Good, you know who I am. Then you also know that I am not one to be toyed with. If you fail to please me in any way, then your little darlings will be disposed of like the girl you saw in the morgue yesterday. Do we have an understanding?"

"Yes, I get it. Let me talk to the girls," Grant said.

"You are in no position to ask for anything. You can talk to them soon enough. Do you have my money?"

"You have to give us more time to get the money together," Grant said.

"That is very disappointing—more so for the girls. Apparently, they thought you cared more for them. I am going to have to show them that you don't care," Jon-Pierre said.

"Don't hurt them! We are pulling the money together. We need more time. Please, we need to see the girls. We need proof of life!" Grant said.

"You dare demand anything from me?" The Haitian man's voice boomed over the speaker.

"Unless we have proof they are alive, why should we pay you any-thing?" Grant said.

"Mr. Turner, you have just killed one of the girls. You pick which one will die," Jon-Pierre said.

Andrea stood frozen as she listened to the evil on the other end of the phone. Tears welled up and streamed down her cheeks. She silently mouthed, "No. God no."

Grant was at a loss for words with this psychopath. He couldn't let his daughter die, but he couldn't condemn Holly either.

Jon-Pierre's voice returned with an icy calmness. He said, "I take it that you cannot decide. Let me do it for you." A gunshot rang out, and the phone line went dead.

Chapter 12

The gunshot reverberated in the room long after the call ended. A reminder that life was fragile and easily lost.

"What happened?" Andrea said as she crumpled into a chair.

"I don't know, but that sadistic bastard couldn't ask us to make a choice like that."

"What do we do now?" she said.

"He will call back. He wants his money and wouldn't do anything to jeopardize his play," Grant said, with more confidence that he felt.

The phone rang, and Grant picked it up before the first ring finished. "Yes," Grant said.

"So you know I'm serious, yes?" Jon-Pierre said.

"Yes, we know you're serious. When can we see our girls?" Grant's hand tightened on the receiver as he spoke.

"They are *my* girls now, and you're assuming that I have not already killed one."

"If you had, you wouldn't be asking us for the money," Grant said. For the first time, he felt a shift. The balance of power moved a notch in their direction.

"Yes…well there is that."

"Where can we see the girls?"

"You are persistent. I will give you that. Be at the Negril Beach by ten this morning. Wade out into the water; there is a buoy line from each of the resorts. Swim out to it and wait." The line went dead again.

Jon-Pierre Baptiste closed his cell phone, tossed it onto the table and smiled. He looked out on the warm beach from his hillside home perched high above Lucea. He enjoyed the game with Turner and Carson, because it was his game and his rules and that meant it would not end well for the two desperate Americans. Tormenting them was a diversion from business, but one that offered the opportunity for profit. Jon-Pierre compared it to a game of roulette—a winner and a loser. Since he owned and rigged the table, the house usually won.

The Haitian rose from his breakfast table on the patio and walked back into the house. He headed down a long hallway and took a key ring from his pocket. With a silver key, Jon-Pierre unlocked a thick padlock on a steel-plated door.

He pushed the door open, spilling light from the hallway into the windowless space. No other light or illumination filtered from the outside into that dark room, only the light that came from him. Jon-Pierre looked inside the space where both girls remained tightly bound, their wrists wrapped with heavy strands of duct tape, and sections of the silver colored tape covered their mouths. Holly and Jena looked terrified, their eyes beyond tears. They shrank from Jon-Pierre.

"Time for you to get pretty, my little ones. We are going to see how much your parents care about you. If they do not care enough, someone else will," Jon-Pierre threatened.

Chapter 13

The venom-laden conversation left Andrea lightheaded. She buckled, putting her head to her knees to stop the room from spinning. She and Grant were bargaining with a murderer, and they held a losing hand. The cold, malevolent voice belonged to a man who wouldn't blink before killing Holly and Jena, once he knew there was no money. She curled up, held her head in her hands, worried that she would never see her daughter again.

Grant knelt in front of her and took her hand. He lifted her chin until her eyes met his. "We will get them back. I promise."

With tears flowing, she said, "I'm scared, Grant."

"So am I. I'm terrified. But we got him to agree to show us the girls. That's a huge step. We're getting closer. He'll try to use our fear against us, and we can't show him any weakness. I know it will be hard, but this is our chance."

"I don't know if I can do it."

"We can. Holly needs you to be strong. I need you to help me be strong for Jena."

Grant stood and helped Andrea to her feet, forcing himself to move so that he didn't crumble. If he showed how fragile he really felt, he'd let Andrea and the girls down.

"We have about an hour to get to the beach. He's smart getting us in the water. It makes it harder to follow him. He'll know we're alone and didn't bring the police with us," Grant said.

"He has the police in his pocket," Andrea reminded.

"Some of them."

"When we see Holly and Jena, do you think we'll be able to grab them and run?" Andrea asked.

"It depends on how convincing we are. To Jon-Pierre, this is business—cold, hard math. He lets us see the girls and he gets his money. If he gets careless, if he underestimates us, we may have a chance to snatch them back."

"Well, let's get ready for a day at the beach," Andrea said.

She took a step towards her bedroom suite, then returned to Grant and hugged him. "Thank you for being here, Grant. I don't think I could do this alone."

"You aren't alone. We are together in this, and that is something that Jon-Pierre isn't counting on. You are a strong woman and he has no idea what he's up against."

She pulled away and headed to her room. Grant went to his and changed into shorts and a t-shirt.

He returned to the main living area, gathered up his cell phone and keys, and put them in a plastic bag he'd found in the kitchen, to protect them from seawater and sand. Grant heard Andrea behind him, turned, and dropped his bag of cell phone and keys on the tile floor. She wore a pair of khaki shorts over a one-piece, deep-blue swimsuit that clung to her every curve. Grant felt his face blush.

Noticing his red face, she merely smiled. "Thanks. That's the nicest thing anyone never said to me."

Grant turned away, trying to hide further embarrassment. "We should get going."

They got in the car, hurried down the highway to the resort area, hoping to find the beach before they were made out as interlopers among the resort guests. They couldn't afford to get tossed off the beach by an over-zealous security guard when they were this close. Grant picked one of the resorts at random, parked across the street and headed for the grand lobby. It was near the Times Square tourist Mecca, so the streets bustled with pedestrians and vehicles in every direction.

Andrea made it past the lobby, then stopped and held onto Grant's arm while she pulled off her shorts. In the tight bathing suit, she looked like most of the other resort guests at the pools and swim-up bar. She held her shorts in one hand, looked to Grant and said, "Follow me and act like we belong here."

They walked past the sun deck and pools to the edge of a green belt a few yards inland from the white-sand beach. A resort staff member prepared to check them for resort wristbands, but Andrea's figure distracted him. He watched her walk all the way to the waterline.

"I can't believe how warm this water is," Grant commented while walking out into the calm blue water.

Andrea waded out until the water was waist high, then swam out from the beach. She pointed in the distance. "There is the buoy line, about 50 yards out."

Both started toward the buoy, accompanied by dozens of small fish that followed them through the clear water. It took a few minutes to reach the floating buoy line. They hung from it against the slight pull of the tide and waited.

"Now what?" Andrea said.

They both looked back at the shore and at the others that hung at the water's edge. The people on the shore paid no attention to them.

"Where will Jon-Pierre have them? On the beach? From this distance, we couldn't even tell if it were Holly and Jena," Andrea said.

"I don't know. Would he risk bringing the girls out in the open like this? I mean he's made sure we can't rush to grab them while we're stuck in the water. We'll need to get closer and claim that we need to make certain they are Holly and Jena," he said.

From the West, a small, brightly colored wooden fishing boat putted along the buoy line. The Jamaican boat pilot asked resort guests who swam nearby, "Hey Mon, you want some ganja?"

No takers, so he angled the boat further up the line to make a sale. Increased resort security and competition from resort staff chased many of the local entrepreneurs to the water.

The boatman wore a tie-dye shirt and hair stuffed into a bright-green knit cap. He motored up to Grant and Andrea. "You two want some really good ganja, Mon?" The man wiped his sweaty face with the back of his arm.

Grant wanted the man to move on so they could focus on spotting the girls. "No. We don't want anything," Grant said.

The boatman smiled, revealing a few missing teeth, "Everyone want something."

In that instant, Grant recognized him as the gunman who had murdered Paulo yesterday. With the dreads tucked under the knit cap, the man had managed to catch them unprepared.

The Jamaican glanced around to make sure they were alone, then showed a pistol in his waistband. "I can shoot you both and nobody could get here in time to save you," he said.

A surge of panic raced through Grant. He and Andrea were vulnerable out in the deeper water away from shore. Jon-Pierre had planned it that way.

"I know you want what I got," the boatman said. He reached to the floor of the boat and pulled Holly up into view by the back of her collar. As Holly saw her mother, a muffled scream came from her taped mouth.

"Holly, I'm here, baby!" She reached for the boat, but the boatman placed his pistol against Andrea's forehead. "Don't come any closer, or Holly won't have a mommy."

Andrea grunted angrily, the pistol held tight against her head. She paddled backwards. The gun's barrel left an ugly red mark on her forehead.

"Baby, please listen, we are going to get you back," Andrea said.

The boatman threw Holly back on the floor of the boat and pulled Jena, similarly bound and gagged, into view. She tried to yell beneath the tape when she saw her father. She had a bruise on the side of her head.

Grant clung onto the buoy line, the sheer weight of what he saw threatening to pull him under. "Jena, I'm coming for you, sweetie."

The boatman put the girl on the floor of the wooden boat and held his gun on the couple in the water. "Boss says you get to see them. So now you see them." He put the motor in the water and pulled on the starter cord.

"Wait! If you hurt those girls, I will hunt you down!" Grant threatened.

The dreadlocked boatman laughed. "It is we who do the hunting." He pointed at Andrea, made an exaggerated hand signal to someone on the beach, and sped away from the Americans.

Grant looked at Andrea when the boatman pointed and noticed a red dot bouncing on her forehead. A laser sight. *Where?* Grant looked back to the shore and caught the red flicker from a second floor room in a resort off to the East.

Grant yelled, "Dive now," and he motioned for her to follow him.

They were under the water for perhaps a second or two when a bullet ripped through the water inches away from Andrea. A second shot creased her left side and sliced open her flesh. Grant grabbed her and headed for the surface. He didn't know if another shot awaited them, but he had to get Andrea up.

They burst through the surface and gulped air into their lungs. Andrea grimaced in pain and grabbed her side. Grant held her tight against him and checked her wound. The bullet tore a slice through the swimsuit and cut a shallow wound through her side, under her ribs.

"Can you swim back to shore?" Grant said.

"Yes," and she pushed away.

Grant spotted a trickle of blood that washed down Andrea's hip. He needed to get her out of the water fast. Jon-Pierre had planned this ambush well. He left them exposed for another shot while they were out in the open away from shore. Sunbathing resort-goers heard no gunshot. Grant expected to see Jon-Pierre on a balcony, rifle in hand. He shielded his eyes as he swam with Andrea and searched the beachfront properties. Jon-Pierre had disappeared.

"I don't see him. He could have finished us, but he didn't," Grant said.

"Is he playing with us?"

"I think that's part of it. He distracted us while his man rode away with the girls."

"Ouch, dammit all," Andrea said as she reached out with her left arm.

"Here, let me help you," Grant offered.

"I can do it myself, leave me alone," she protested as she pushed away and stroked toward another group of swimmers close to shore.

Grant paced behind her. Her movement was steady and strong. Andrea's anger diminished the pain.

They reached a point where they stood in the low surf, then walked onto the beach with slow heavy strides.

A sunburned tourist sat up from her recliner, lifted a hand to shade her eyes and looked at Andrea. "God, what did you do to your side? It looks awful."

Andrea looked at the blood that darkened her torn suit, and replied, "You gotta be careful of the coral out there." Andrea held her side and walked past the woman and toward the lobby.

"Head to the car. I'll meet you there in a minute." Grant pulled his keys out of his plastic bag and handed them to Andrea. "I'm going to find the resort's on-call doctor."

Andrea grabbed his wrist. "No. I'm fine. Besides, a doctor will ask too many questions."

"I need to take care of you..."

Grant's excitement caused a few people in the lobby to look in their direction. Grant noticed some leaning into one another sharing whispered conversation. "You need someone to take a look at that," he said in a lower voice.

"Not here," Andrea said, aware of the unwanted attention they drew from the lobby crowd.

"I'll meet you at the car," Grant said.

Andrea crossed the lobby and headed out while Grant ducked into the resort's gift shop. He pulled a tube of antibiotic ointment, gauze bandages and a roll of tape from the shelf. The thin Jamaican behind the counter eyed Grant's purchases suspiciously, but never questioned why Grant needed the medical supplies. The proprietor removed a small flask from the counter behind him and put it with the items Grant selected. The bottle contained clear overproof rum from an island distillery.

"This will take the sting out of jellyfish. Keep mosquitoes away and clean scraped knees. If that don't work, then drink it," the Jamaican man said.

Grant paid for his first aid items, including the 159 proof rum, and trotted back to Andrea and the car.

He handed the bag of supplies to Andrea, who held it in her lap. "Let's find a clinic," he said.

"No. Take me back to the bungalow. The bleeding has almost stopped. I'm fine."

"You're not fine."

"Grant. No. Take me to the bungalow. I feel safe there with you."

Grant piloted the sedan across the island roads and looked for signs of Jon-Pierre along the short drive. He slid the car to a quick stop at the bungalow and ran to the passenger door. He supported Andrea a few steps, but she shook him off and headed to the front door on her own.

Once inside, Grant pointed at the sofa. "Sit down and let me take a look."

"I will. Give me a minute to get out of this bathing suit," she said in a tone that sounded more angry than hurt.

Andrea returned, dressed in shorts and a short crop top that revealed an angry red slash that cut across her left side.

She stretched out on the sofa, and Grant knelt alongside. He prepared a warm washcloth from his bedroom suite and gingerly cleaned the dried blood from her skin. The bullet had not penetrated, but the track left a laceration that grazed the surface of her smooth skin.

"Any pain from your ribs?" he inquired as he felt around them.

"No. Feels more like a burn than anything."

Grant cleaned the slice and considered the Jamaican shopkeeper's advice about the overproof rum. He figured that anything that degreased engines and repelled insects would melt Andrea's soft skin. He placed a generous dollop of the antibiotic gel into the wound and taped a gauze pad in place.

"How are you doing?" he said.

"It stings. I'm mad and I want to get my hands on that son of a bitch."

"That's a good sign, I guess," Grant replied.

She sat up and held her side. It had to hurt more than she let on. Andrea touched his worried face, and said, "Thank you. You patched me up and you forced Jon-Pierre to show the girls. That meant a lot to me. It gave me hope again. I was starting to doubt..." She looked up into his strong face.

She paused for a moment, as if she were going to say something more. She rose, her eyes locked on his, her lips parted to speak, but nothing came out. She subtlety shook her head and walked into her bedroom.

Grant stood, antibiotic ointment in one hand, washcloth in the other, and watched Andrea. For one of the few times in his life, he was without words. The way she looked over her shoulder as she disappeared in her suite made his breath catch. He wondered if, when this was over and they had the girls back, would they be able to have some kind of relationship? The thought both excited and terrified him.

He walked to his room and changed out of his damp clothes. As he was finishing up, the phone rang. He grabbed the receiver, expecting Jon-Pierre's next demand.

"Yes?" he said

"Hello, Mr. Turner, this is Lieutenant Washington."

"Good morning, Lieutenant, what can I do for you?"

"It is a good morning. Good time for a morning swim, perhaps?"

Grant paused, "I don't understand."

"Mr. Turner, you think someone can get shot while recreating near one of the resorts, and I would not hear about it? It is a rather small island, after all."

"What is it you want from us, Lieutenant?" Grant asked.

Andrea came from her room, dressed in fresh, white shorts and a blue tee shirt that covered the bandage. She looked at Grant and mouthed, "Who is it?"

Grant caught her concern and hit the speaker phone button, "Lieutenant, I don't know what you expect from us."

Hearing the Lieutenant's voice, she sat on the sofa, half relieved, and half frustrated. She'd been expecting Jon-Pierre. Washington's lack of interest in Holly and Jena's disappearance had left a sour taste.

"I'm concerned for both of you and your daughters, Mr. Turner. It seems since you arrived on the island, a trail of violence follows you. A man shot in a local bar, a dismembered girl, and this morning, a fishing boat owner killed for his boat. Now it seems that someone is intent on shooting you."

Andrea's eyes grew big, and she whispered, "How could he know all this? He has to be involved with Jon-Pierre."

Grant nodded in agreement.

"Perhaps all of this violence would stop if I were to take you both into protective custody?"

Grant grew weary of the lieutenant's bluster. "Washington, you know full well, if we are taken into protective custody, we will have no chance to get our girls back."

"What are we to do, then?" The lieutenant paused on the other end of the phone. "Since you seem determined to do what you think you need to do, let me offer you some advice. The people you are dealing with care nothing about human life and suffering. They see it as sport. You need to prepare yourself. Go and see a man named Joseph down by the Negril River. He has a bait stand where he sells various things for the local fishermen."

"You want us to go fishing?" Grant asked.

"In a manner of speaking," the lieutenant added and hung up.

"What do you make of that?" Grant asked Andrea.

She shook her head. "I don't like it. He seems like he's in Jon-Pierre's pocket."

"I get that feeling too. I'm not sure who we can trust. The thing with this guy Joseph down at the river is plain weird. Why send us to him? I don't get it," he said.

"You think we ought to check it out, don't you?" Andrea asked, placing her hand on his shoulder.

"I don't think we have a choice. Is this another setup like we went through in the water?"

At that moment, Andrea's cell phone rang. "Hello?" she asked.

"Well it's nice to know you are resilient, Mrs. Carson." It was Jon-Pierre's icy voice on the other end of the line.

Andrea motioned to Grant, waving him in closer so he could listen. Grant put his head up to the cell phone in time to hear, "Now that we had our little show and tell, it is time for you to come up with the money, yes?"

Andrea trembled, "We need more time to get the money. You've asked for a lot of money and we can't just walk up to an ATM machine and pull out a hundred grand."

"Well, if your precious little Holly is not worth it, I truly understand." A metallic snapping sound echoed in the background, followed by muffled screams and cries. "I can put a bullet in her head right now." Jon-Pierre said.

"No. Wait, please wait!" Andrea said.

"Do you love your daughter, Mrs. Carson?"

"Yes, yes I do!".

"How much do you love her? I have other buyers who love her too. They think she would be a great addition and bring them much pleasure."

"I love her more than anything. What do you want?" Andrea wept.

"Now, let us get down to business. I require fifty-thousand per girl. It's your choice if you wish to purchase both, or only one."

"We want them both," she said.

"I understand. Now *you* need to understand. Have a pen handy? To save you all the trouble of gathering up all the cash, you are to wire transfer the money from your banks to an account in the First National Bank of Grand Cayman. Use this account number: 264-930-000."

Andrea snapped up a pen and scribbled down the account number. "I have it."

The voice responded, "Good, you have twenty-four hours to complete the wire transfer. If you fail, I will move on to my secondary buyer. They will take the parcels out of the country immediately after the purchase. You will never see them again."

"Please don't. We will try to do as you ask."

"There is no try. You do it or you don't do it. I really don't care; I get paid either way," Jon-Pierre said with a tone that carried indifference.

"We'll do it! We'll do it!" Andrea said.

"Oh, I almost forgot. If the funds are not wire transferred and verified in time, the secondary buyer asked to sample the merchandise. He tends to be a bit on the rough side."

Grant grabbed the phone from Andrea and yelled, "You sick bastard. I'm gonna kill you with my bare hands."

"You have twenty-four hours." The phone went dead.

Chapter 14

A long abandoned sugar cane processing plant deep in the remote reaches of Cockpit Country bore witness to the ravages of heat, stifling humidity and a down economy. Buildings that once housed a thriving family business were more rot and rust than substance. Rainforest encircled the compound and sent out thick, dark vines in all directions, threatening to erase any sign that man had once occupied the land.

A pale yellow glow peeked between the slats of metal siding attached to the dilapidated main building. Above a small table, a single light bulb burned, offering enough light for Jon-Pierre Baptiste to attend to his business. Jon-Pierre put the satellite phone down and tapped a command on his notebook computer. He smiled at the message on the computer screen.

The Haitian was pleased with his phone call to the Americans. Kidnap and ransom were routine psychological tactics he had used during his years with the Tonton Macoutes in Port-Au-Prince. The neighboring Haitians had enough evidence of the machete-wielding thugs to take their threats to heart. Some of the time, the kidnapped family members returned home, generally intact.

The Americans would never see their girls again—what a sorrowful tale. Jon-Pierre never believed in fairytale-happy endings. The computer screen on the table in front of him confirmed the outcome for the Americans. The details scrolled down the screen; Jon-Pierre sold the girls to a buyer from Syria. The two girls would be gone before the American's wire transfer was complete. Jon-Pierre was pleased with his business acumen, ensuring two payments for the girls, one from the Syrian and one from Turner and Carson.

He closed the notebook computer, disconnected it from his satellite phone and walked to a rustic wooden bin. The container, which originally held raw sugar cane for processing, held two terrified girls. Jon-Pierre held no-ill feelings for these two; in fact, he held no feelings about them at all. They weren't human; they were a commodity that he could sell as he desired.

He looked in the bin and verified that both girls remained bound with duct tape and gagged to suppress their screams. Oh, how they tried to scream and beg. Such wailing made Jon-Pierre's head pound. The tape over their mouths wasn't to prevent detection; it was to muffle their annoying, plaintive squeals. Satisfied that both of his charges were intact and silent, Jon-Pierre left them, returned to his perch at the table, and dialed a number on his phone.

Jon-Pierre's dreadlocked companion answered. "Yes?"

"As soon as the Americans complete the wire transfer, kill them," Jon-Pierre said.

"I'm looking forward to it," the gunman said.

"Wait for my call. Once I confirm that we don't need them any longer, take them out. Until then, keep them in sight."

"I understand," the gunman hung up.

The Dreadlocked gunman sat in the shadows of thick foliage twenty feet from the American's rented bungalow. He wanted to charge into the bungalow and kill them now. He was quickly losing patience with Jon-Pierre and could barely contain the impulse to kill the two meddling Americans. He decided he would kill the man first and then take his time with the woman before he strangled her. That would be the most satisfying. Until then, he watched the bungalow, the pressure building within him like a steam pipe.

Chapter 15

The creep with the blue eyes kept a close watch over them. They pretended they were asleep, and didn't move when he came to look at them. Holly and Jena were on their sides in the bottom of a dirty wooden container. The splintered side of the box was only four feet high, but it could have been fifty feet tall, because their legs were immobile in layers of duct tape. They could see one another, but the tape over their mouths prevented them from talking.

Jena found a sharp nail that protruded through the side of the bin. She scooted back to the nail and rubbed it against the duct tape on her wrists. After some considerable effort, Jena tore through a few layers of tape, cutting her hands and wrists in the process. She worried less about tetanus than what the blue-eyed man would do to them.

Jena's mind was a tumble of scattered images and voices. What had happened to get her to this place? She remembered going to a club with Holly to have some fun on their last night—what was supposed to be their last night on the island. They danced and enjoyed the nightclub scene. At some point, the man with the blue eyes started hovering around, offering to buy them drinks. He was the creep who gave them a hard time earlier out on the beach. He said he was sorry and wanted to make it up to them.

At the club, Holly and Jena moved every time he sat next to them, but he kept following them. Finally, to ditch him, they went to another club across the street. But he followed them to the second club and persisted. They finally retreated to the bathroom at the back of the club.

"Is that guy creepy, or what?" Jena said.

"He actually followed us here!" Holly said.

"I'm getting creeped out. I think we should go back to the hotel," Jena said.

"I can't believe that he followed us after he grabbed you on the beach when we didn't want to go on a tour."

They walked out of the bathroom, both in agreement to take a taxi back to the hotel, when they saw the blue-eyed man pour a powder into each of the drinks they had left at the bar. Holly looked at Jena with wide eyes. "Did you see that? He did something to our drinks!"

"What a sicko! Let's get out of here and get back to the hotel. Do you think we should call the police?" Jena said.

They ran, arm in arm, to the front door, where a hulking doorman stopped them. "Hey, what's going on? You two just got here. The party starting now; it's not even midnight."

"Yeah, well, I don't want to get date raped by some sick, disgusting old man," Holly responded and pointed across the club at the blue-eyed man.

"No Problem. Let me signal a cab for you. What hotel?" he asked as he stepped to the curb.

As the girls followed him to the curb Jena volunteered, "We are at the Grand Lido."

A taxi pulled up and the doorman opened the rear door for them. "Paulo, take these nice young ladies to the Grand Lido."

During the ride back to the hotel, Holly and Jena debated calling the police. They agreed that they would call the local authorities in the morning. The guy was probably gone from the club, and other than his icy cold blues they had no other particulars of the man to offer.

Safe back in their room, they finished packing and sat on their beds, too wired to sleep. The encounter with the man had spooked them. They both jumped at a knock on the door.

"Room Service," a voice said from the other side.

"It's one in the morning. Who in their right mind is drunk enough to order room service at this hour?" Holly whispered.

Jena looked at the door. "I know we didn't."

Jena tiptoed to the door, and with all the gruffness she could muster, said, "No room service here!"

The electric door lock clicked. She froze in place as the handle wiggled and the door opened. The blue-eyed man rushed in.

"There's always room service," he said as his hand whipped out and stuck a syringe in Jena's neck.

Jena felt herself fade and melt away. As she collapsed, she saw a Jamaican man, with long dreadlocks, go after Holly. Then everything simply faded into darkness.

The recollection of that night snapped away when Jena heard their keeper's footsteps on the wood floor. She stopped rubbing the tape against the nail and remained motionless. The blue-eyed creep pulled a large black gun from his waist and pointed it at them. He'd done it a dozen times to terrorize them. And, it worked—every time. He took pleasure from their whimpers. Though they tried with all their might not to react and give him what he wanted, fear came through.

When their keeper walked away with a satisfied look on his face, Jena rolled over toward Holly and wiggled her hands to get her friend's attention. It took a few seconds before Holly figured out what Jena tried to communicate.

Holly noticed the blood that dripped from Jena's hands. Holly's eyes grew wide with fear that Jena had cut herself on something.

Jena sensed Holly's confusion and wiggled her hands enough to show her a few layers of the tape that had ripped away from scraping on the nail. Instantly, Holly understood and rolled over to her side of their wooden prison in search of something with a sharp edge.

Nobody was going to rush to rescue them from this isolated patch of forest. Survival was up to them, alone.

Chapter 16

Grant paced the length of the patio, Jon-Pierre's demands bouncing inside his skull and threatening to explode. Andrea caught his expression as he turned. His eyes hollowed, and deep worry lines creased his forehead; he looked unsure, lost, desperate. Since the moment this incident threw the two of them together, Andrea considered Grant a decisive, independent man who didn't depend on, or need, anyone. Although he didn't talk about it much, losing a wife to a twist of fate would turn a saint into a callous ball of hate. Instead, she found him warm, tender and caring, especially when it came to Jena. The last contact from Jon-Pierre had him on edge and unbalanced.

Andrea stood in front of him, blocking his pacing path. "What's next?".

"I don't know."

"He knows who we are—that we're not millionaires."

"I'm sure he knows. Why fifty-thousand? Why did he give us twenty-four hours? Something about this whole arrangement sticks in my throat."

"He's greedy and wants the money. He knows we need time to gather the funds and get the wire transfer done," Andrea said.

"Don't get me wrong. I love my daughter more than any amount of money on earth. It's why fifty-thousand per girl, and why the time limit? There has to be something more to it."

"I don't know what the going rate for ransom is, but I'm willing to pay it, if it means I'll get Holly back. You don't think he'll release them, do you? Even if we come up with what he wants?"

"He is up to something more--something that I can't quite wrap my head around," Grant said.

"We don't have any choice but to get the money. We have to do whatever it takes. I'll call my bank and liquidate IRA's, money market and trading accounts. I'm not sure what that will give us. I could borrow against my house, but I don't think I could get that done in time from Jamaica," she said.

"I have some retirement accounts and a life insurance policy I could try to cash in," Grant explained.

"I don't have much, but I can come up with enough, I think." She picked up a notepad, jotted down figures and tried to come up with the fifty-thousand dollar price for her daughter. Annuities, retirement savings, even Holly's college fund went into the pot. Andrea would have her small two-bedroom home and little else, but getting Holly back was worth that heavy price.

They both called their respective banks, but dealt with expected resistance from officials over large transactions placed from outside the country. After a series of phone calls and four hours later, the banks were begrudgingly satisfied with their identities, as well as the concocted story about an island real estate purchase. The arrangements for the wire transfer were complete, with one minor detail: Grant and Andrea asked the banks to ready the wire transfers to the First National Bank of Grand Cayman, but not execute the transfers until they called back to authorize the withdrawal.

Grant thought Jon-Pierre might go for a transfer while giving the girls back. A trade of sorts, he hoped.

Andrea sighed, "I guess we wait it out now."

"Jon-Pierre has done this before. I think that's what this guy expects. What if we went on the offensive?" Grant said.

"What do you mean? Won't that put the girls at risk?"

"If we are smart about it, we may be able to get to them before he knows it," Grant said.

Andrea looked concerned, tipped her head, and waited for Grant to continue.

"He is not expecting us to do anything but sit tight. I can't do that. I can't, and neither can you. So if we go after the girls, we may have the element of surprise."

"We don't know where he is, so how are we going to do that?" Andrea asked.

"Andrea, let me see your cell phone." Grant pulled up the log of incoming calls. "The last call you got was from Baptiste, right?"

"Yes, that's right."

"Here is the number: 876-957-6743. I'm surprised it wasn't a blocked number."

"So, we have a phone number. It's probably a cell also."

Grant went over to the counter and pulled out the phone book. After a moment of searching, he found two cell phone companies that served the island. Grant called the first company, with no success. He called the second company. "Hello, this is Jon-Pierre Baptiste. My number is 876-957-6743." The voice on the other end verified that the company serviced the phone.

"What may we do for you, Mr. Baptiste?"

"I need to change the billing address for my account," Grant said convincingly.

"That's fine. We can do that for you. What is your new address?" the phone company technician inquired.

"I have been experiencing some trouble getting my bills in the mail. What do you have for the current address?"

Grant heard computer keys tapping on the other end of the phone. "We have 500 B8, Lucea."

Grant hung up the phone. "We have an address."

Andrea smiled, "That was pretty impressive."

"What say we take a drive out to the country? Maybe drop by the lieutenant's guy, Joseph at the Negril River on the way."

Chapter 17

Grant found the bridge at the Negril River within a few minutes. A wide, trampled grass path served as a gathering area and parking lot. He pulled in near a cluster of other vehicles.

"Let's walk to the river and see if we can find the guy Washington told us about," Grant said.

"Why did he tell us about this guy? Does he work with Baptiste?" Andrea said.

"Washington didn't say. I didn't get the feeling that Joseph the fisherman is one of Jon-Pierre's boys. The lieutenant said he was worth talking to, so let's go talk. If this doesn't pan out, we'll head up to Baptiste's address in Lucea."

"Then let's be good little tourists and check out the river," Andrea said. She grabbed Grant's hand and walked down the slight embankment to the river's edge.

The fishermen arrived with their catch and tied their multi-colored boats to the riverbank. There were dozens of the wooden vessels, no two painted alike. Some of the boats bore signs that offered scenic boat trips, or fishing charters. Most had makeshift shades, shielding the boatmen from the intense sun overhead and its reflection off the water.

Pointing at the wooden boats, Andrea said, "They're quite incredible. They all look handmade."

They walked slowly along the water line, stepping over mooring lines tied to trees, stumps and thick mangrove branches. Grant noticed a smaller white craft, with the words "Bottom Boat" scrawled in bright letters. Closer examination showed that the owner had added the word "Glass" at the water line.

"Some of these boats look like they are decades old; there is some real pride and artisanship here. They look well maintained and most seem freshly painted," Grant said.

A market sprawled in the shade of some mangrove trees near the water. Fishermen offered stacks of freshly caught fish, piled on canvas tarps. The buyers, mostly local women, bartered with the men for the fish. The atmosphere seemed friendly as each of the fishermen tried to outsell one another and loudly boasted his fish were bigger, then another yelled back that they were yesterday's catch. They laughed and continued bartering for a sale.

Grant and Andrea stopped and watched the activity for a few minutes. The quick back and forth banter captivated them.

One of the fishmongers rose from his canvas and approached Grant and Andrea. "A fish for da lady? We gots fresh fishes."

Declining the offer, they continued down the riverbank, past the fish salesmen, where they came upon a number of booths that sold beer, cold water, and food. At the far end of the alleyway of plywood and thatched booths was a bait booth.

"Well look at that. Like the lieutenant said," Grant said, directing Andrea's attention to the far booth.

An older man sat in an equally old wooden chair that leaned up against the back of the booth, seeming to have not a care in the world. As Grant approached the booth, the man peeked out under his wide-brimmed hat. He made no other movement.

"Ya, Mon, what do ya need today? You don't be fishermens, do ya? Da fishermans all be done by dis time of day," Joseph said.

"No, we aren't here for the fish, Joseph. We were told that you are the one to see for information," Grant said in a low voice.

Joseph looked up at the two Americans. "Now who be telling dat tale?"

Grant leaned closer and spoke in a whisper: "Our daughters were kidnapped, and Lieutenant Washington said you were the man to see."

Joseph looked from Grant to Andrea but didn't move.

"Please help us. We have to get our girls back. A guy named Jon-Pierre Baptiste has them," Andrea pleaded.

"Baptiste, huh? He has your girls?" Joseph asked, stone-faced.

Andrea nodded, "He wants money or he'll sell them and we will never see them again."

"Baptiste will never return da girls to you. He will sell dem, or kill dem," Joseph said.

"Help us--please," Andrea begged.

Joseph ran his hand over his beard. "Baptiste most likely have dem at his house in Lucea, or in da sugar plantation behind his home way back in da Cockpit."

Grant nodded, "We know about his place in Lucea—"

Joseph cut Grant off. "Dat won't be enough to get da girls back, if dey still alive. You need some fish."

"What?" Grant said.

"Fish. You need some of my special fish," Joseph repeated.

Grant shook his head. "I don't understand. Why do I need fish?"

Joseph leaned over, "You not too bright are you? Why you tink da lieutenant send you to me?"

"What do you want?" Grant asked, becoming impatient.

"I need two hundred dollars for some very special fish," Joseph whispered.

Grant, deciding to play along, peeled off two hundred dollars and passed them over to Joseph. The Jamaican quickly put the money in his pocket and lifted a large ice chest.

Joseph reached down to the bottom of the chest, moving ice along the way, pulled out two plastic-wrapped parcels and laid them on the counter. "Here be da fish…very special nine-millimeter fish."

Grant took the two packages and shoved them in the black plastic bag Joseph provided.

Joseph nodded and said, "Be careful, Mon. This guy, he a monster. Go get your girls and take dem home."

Grant nodded, and Joseph returned to his spot in the back of the booth, leaning against a wooden brace.

Grant and Andrea walked back through the fish market, wary that the heavy gun would fall out the bottom of the thin plastic bag. Some of the fishermen stood from their shady spots and chatted up the Americans.

"Hey, Mon, how come you didn't buy da fish here? You got old fish…probably rotten," one said, which started a roll of laughter directed at the gullible Americans.

Unseen behind Joseph's booth, Jon-Pierre's dreadlocked gunman overheard the entire conversation between the Americans and the bait monger. He followed the Americans from their bungalow to the river and crept close. Joseph provided information and weapons to the Americans, and he would suffer for that transgression. Jon-Pierre did not tolerate anyone who worked against him.

The dreadlocked man retreated into the thick brush above the river and followed a narrow red-dirt trail to his Land Cruiser. He pulled a cell phone from beneath the seat and dialed.

Jon-Pierre responded, "Yes?"

"The Americans are heading to your home in the hills. Joseph provided them with weapons. You want me to take care of Joseph now? Or follow the Americans?"

"Let them go to Lucea. They won't find anything there," Jon-Pierre said coolly. "You keep an eye on them until we have the wire transfer confirmation. You may want to be there ahead of them."

"Very well," the dreadlocked man said to an already dead phone line. He would wait to settle things with the fishmonger another day.

He became the watcher and followed the red rental car. As he neared the outskirts of Lucea, he bounded up a narrow side road that bounced the off-road vehicle from pothole to pothole. This track cut ahead of the main highway and put the gunman ahead of the Americans.

He stroked the steel barrel of the gun in his lap and planned how he would greet them.

Chapter 18

Rotted shards of sugar cane splintered underneath Jena as she worked her taped hands against the sharp tip of a rusty nail. The darkness inside the old wooden storage bin, coupled with the forest humidity, closed in on them. Restrained on their sides, arms taped tightly behind them, made it impossible to take a full breath. It bordered on claustrophobia. Panic fed the helplessness, a cycle that fed and consumed its own energy.

Jena leaned against the sharp point of the exposed nail and felt the fibers of tape give and separate. The bonds began to loosen, but still held their place; blood oozed from several cuts and punctures, slickening the tape's surface, making it difficult to continue. She tried again, wiggling back against the nail protruding from the wooden enclosure. Once more, she worked the tape, but slipped, puncturing the palm of her hand. Pain and terror welled up inside, but Jena continued. Her only hope for escape rested in a quarter inch of rusted steel.

From somewhere in the blackness beyond the enclosure, the creak of footsteps on the worn floorboards grew close. A heavy wooden door opened and slivers of bright light shot inside like bolts of white lightning. The door closed and the light vanished. The wooden planks vibrated underneath the girls. Jena and Holly knew that their blue-eyed tormentor approached. He checked on them often and didn't seem to care if they knew he was there. Before he reached their wooden prison, the girls rolled away from the nails and rested on their backs in the center of the pen. Both feared he would move them again and discover the partially torn tape.

The footfalls stopped, and from the gloom above, Jon-Pierre's olive face materialized. He stood over the pen, his hands resting on the front edge of the wood directly above the jagged nail that Jena used.

"It's almost over for you. Your parents will not be able to join us, so we will be going on a little trip. You are going to meet the man who bought you two little whores," Jon-Pierre said.

Holly cried out through the gag, afraid that something happened to her mother. She violently struggled against the tape at her wrists and ankles. The bonds remained tight during her convulsion, and her kicks fell on empty air.

Jon-Pierre stepped away into the darkness for only a second. He returned with a long-handled, wooden rake and drove it hard against Holly's chest, pinning her to the floor of the pen. He said nothing, but stared down at Holly until she stopped flailing.

Exhausted and fearful, Holly looked up at Jon-Pierre. Now past tears, locked eyes on her keeper without flinching.

Slowly, Jon-Pierre released the rake. "Behave. You are of no value if you hurt yourself." He tossed the rake away and looked back at his captives. "I will be back shortly with some clothes so you will make the right impression on your new owner."

Jon-Pierre's laugh echoed in the barn, covering the sound of his footsteps as he walked away. The usual flash of light preceded a thump of the heavy entrance door standing between them and freedom.

Jena rolled over, putting her back to the wall, frantically wedging her taped wrists against the nail's sharp tip. Holly returned to the small flange of tin and went to work on the layers of tape that bound her wrists.

Both girls grunted from the effort and didn't care if the blue-eyed man overheard their struggle. They knew they had little time before he passed them on to some pudgy, middle-aged pervert. Their future was closer to being swept away with each second that ticked off the clock. Tick-tock.

Chapter 19

Grant piloted the red rental car south onto the B-8 highway, which immediately soared past sugar cane fields up into densely forested hillsides. As they went farther inland, the road surface morphed into something slightly better than gravel. A rough, pothole-littered surface made for slow progress.

"I can see why Baptiste would live out here. You could do anything up here and who would know?" Grant crept the car around a large chunk of broken and buckled asphalt.

Andrea watched the lush, dense scenery pass her window. "It's so thick you can't see ten feet from the edge of the road." Dark shadows filtered from the canopy above sinister outlines that seemed to swallow whole sections of the road ahead.

They circled the contour of the hill, up to a plateau that flattened out. Higher mountains beckoned in the distance. A small metal sign, "500," painted in small white letters, stood along a drainage ditch. A two-track trail led from the main road.

"I don't know about driving up to his place. He can probably see a car coming up the road. It's not like he sent us an invitation," Grant said.

"There," Andrea said, pointing at a wide patch of dirt off the main road. "We can park the car there and walk in."

"That will work. Unless you were looking for it, you'd miss it," Grant shifted the car into low gear and nosed into brush behind the clearing. He pushed as far into the bush as he dared and parked the car. The last thing he needed was the two of them stranded in Jon-Pierre's backyard.

They retrieved the packages provided by the fishmonger and placed them on the trunk of the car. Grant cut the plastic wrap from one of the packages with the pocketknife he had purchased and rolled open the oily cloth. A black 9mm Takarov semiautomatic pistol and three loaded magazines glinted in the light. The gun looked old, but serviceable.

Andrea looked at the gun. "Do you know how to use that?"

"Proud member of the San Fernando Rod and Gun Club," he said, pulling back the weapon's slide.

Andrea stepped forward and timidly asked, "Can you teach me how to use it?"

"Are you sure you want to do that? I can handle this."

She nodded her head and stood a little taller. "I have to do this. I'm not a bystander. He has my daughter too. Teach me—please."

Grant picked up the old 9mm and explained how to insert the magazines into the bottom of the weapon's grip. She practiced removing and inserting the magazines a few times. She wasn't comfortable with the gun, but she understood Grant's instruction. Fortunately for Andrea, the old gun had a used spring in the slide, which made it easier to pull back. Andrea watched him pull back the slide and chamber a round as the slide pushed forward. She picked up the gun, inserted a magazine and pulled the slide back, putting a round in the chamber. Andrea pulled the slide back again slightly, to see the brass of the shell in the chamber.

Grant asked, "Are you comfortable with it? You seemed to pick that up very fast."

"I'll never be comfortable with this thing. I don't like guns, and I hope we don't need to use them. I've never fired one, so don't count on me to hit anything. I guess I could make some noise, but that's about it."

Grant unwrapped the second gun and tucked it in his waistband. "I hope we don't need them either, but if we need to force our way in and take the girls, these may come in very handy."

They each shoved the two spare magazines in their pockets. Silently, they walked up the rutted dirt road in the direction of Jon-Pierre's retreat, keeping as much to the shadows as possible, to disguise their approach.

The mixture of hope and dread of what they might find ahead grew with each step.

Grant watched the route ahead, and something struck him as out of place. He stopped, got down on one knee and peered into the bushes along the edge of the road.

"Andrea, stop. Stop right there!"

About two feet ahead, Andrea stopped in mid-step and turned to Grant. She didn't understand why, but decided he had a reason and put her foot back down.

"What is it?" she said.

Grant motioned her still. He slowly got up from his crouch and carefully approached her. "Look down in front of you. The bastard has the road booby trapped." Grant pointed down to the section of road in front of her.

Andrea followed the angle of his hand to the road, and there, inches in front of her, a slender wire snaked across the road. The wire was the size of fishing line, nearly invisible in the shadows. Her eyes grew wide, but she showed no panic.

"Why the hell would he do this to his own road?" she said.

"It means he doesn't want any visitors. I guess that means cookie-toting Girl Scouts won't be stopping by." Grant paused. "It also means that there must be another road to get to his place."

Andrea took a few measured steps backward away from the trip wire. "Is it connected to a bomb?"

Grant guided her back, and made sure he hadn't missed any more surprises. He pulled aside a small branch, which revealed a green canister that emitted the smell of fuel oil.

"It's an explosive of some kind," he said, gently returning the branch to its resting place.

Andrea looked up the road. "You think he has more of these?"

"I'd be willing to bet he does," he replied. "We need to get off the road, where we are less likely to get blown apart."

Andrea nodded and followed Grant off the roadway into the thick brush. The brambles thinned and they navigated through the dense vegetation. They pushed away draping tree vines and stepped over dense, low plants. Branches whipped at their legs and arms, leaving a collection of welts.

After a laborious slog, the thick vegetation transitioned into a large, manicured clearing. At the center of the open space sat a large terra cotta-tiled structure. Its outdoor terraces and patios were larger than the home itself. Two swimming pools were evident and a large fountain cascaded down the upper pool's edge.

Andrea pointed to three cars parked in a gravel-paved lot that could easily hold ten times that many vehicles. A white Hummer, a silver BMW 725i, and an out-of-place battered, green Toyota Land Cruiser sat along a circular driveway close to the home.

Grant saw no movement outside that indicated anyone had seen their approach. The home was so large, that a number of people could be inside and remain hidden from his vantage point. The home's heavily tinted windows made any direct line to the estate dangerous.

"Our girls could be in there," Andrea said, motioning to the large residence.

"It's possible, but checking it out could be difficult. We already know Jon-Pierre doesn't want any visitors."

Andrea looked from their location hidden in the brush. "What if we move down there, by that white outbuilding near the front side of the house?" She identified the structure that looked like a tool shed, approximately one hundred yards away from their position.

Grant nodded, and they ran from the brush line to the shed as quickly as possible, concealing themselves behind the structure.

"I didn't see anyone," Grant panted.

Andrea looked pained. She held the bandage on her side while she took deep breaths.

Grant, peered out from the side of the shed and saw what looked like the front of the residence. He detected no movement inside, or on the expansive terraces. After a moment, he looked back at Andrea. "Come with me. I think it's safe."

They ran to the corner of the home, to the point that connected with the uppermost terrace. Grant crept ahead, dropped to his knees and peeked in a window. It was an open living room arranged with heavy masculine furniture. Large timbers created a place for electronic equipment; a sixty-inch flat screen television was mounted on the far wall, with a number of dark brown leather chairs and matching sofas filling the space. There was no sign of Baptiste or the girls.

From their perch on the terrace, Grant and Andrea saw no one. They moved to one of the three French doors that opened to the terrace and were surprised to find it unlocked.

Grant half-expected to trigger an alarm when he tugged on the doorknob. No evidence of contact points, sensors, or wires or alarms sounded to warn Jon-Pierre of their presence.

Their feet caused a slight creak in the mahogany floor. It was faint, but in the silence of the home's interior, the noise sounded symphonic. A quick search of the living room yielded no signs that Holly and Jena had been there. Grant took the hallway on the right. He crept down the hall, his gun held in front of him as he scanned side to side. Andrea followed him, her gun held awkwardly by her side.

They looked though three bedrooms and a library, but there was no sign of the girls. Grant motioned to the other end of the hall, and they quietly walked in that direction. The first door was closed, but Grant tried the knob and found it unlocked. He carefully pushed, and the door opened into a large bedroom. As he took a step forward he caught a swift motion out of the corner of his eye.

Before he could react, the dreadlocked man brought down a metal baton on the back of Grant's skull. The blow dropped him like a rock.

Andrea looked on in horror and screamed, "Grant!" She froze in place.

Grant lay motionless on the floor, blood seeping from the wound on his scalp.

The assailant quickly knelt over Grant's body, pulled an ice pick from a leather sheath in his pocket and placed it against the base of Grant's skull, lining up a fatal blow.

Chapter 20

Andrea raised her gun absently, both hands tightly wrapped around the grip. "Stop!"

The murderer let loose a throaty, evil laugh. "I kill both of you. Then I kill your daughters." He stayed behind Grant with the ice pick poised at the hollow at the base of his skull. "You won't use that gun. You're nothing but a pathetic American soccer mom, soon to be without a child."

Andrea's arms shook with fury. A glance at Grant's unconscious form and she refocused. The gun felt heavy in her hand. This thug stood between her and Holly. She took aim at the middle of the man's body, closed her eyes and quickly pulled the trigger. The gun bucked more than she expected.

The shot went wide of the man. Surprised at the gunshot, he jumped aside and dashed farther back into the room. Against all instinct, she ran at him, past where Grant slumped on the floor. Andrea saw the man pick up a black automatic rifle, pull back the stubby slide on the weapon, and turn to her. Two bullets from Andrea's gun struck him in the chest.

She pulled the trigger four more times; two rounds hit the man in the chest and throat. The gunman collapsed backwards over a table and slid to the floor. Andrea held her pistol at him and walked slowly toward the fallen man. She saw his eyes, wide and vacant. Then she noticed the crimson stain spread from the wound on his chest, and from a ragged hole in his throat.

Andrea kicked the dead man's rifle away and tugged it to her by the sling. She backed away from the dead man and went to Grant.

"Grant," she said softly as she shook his shoulder. "Grant, wake up."

Grant groaned, and as he rolled onto his back, his hands went to his throbbing head. "Oh—what happened?"

"That ass over there, is what happened."

Grant tried to sit up, the slightest movement to his head made bright blinking spots in his vision. He tilted his head and saw the gunman's body at the other end of the room.

"He was going to hurt you, I couldn't let him do that…" She trailed off, a pained expression on her face.

"Help me sit up," and Grant reached up for her hands.

She grabbed both of his hands and helped him sit with his back against the wall. As his head started to clear, he blinked his eyes, and the room came into focus. Grant pulled himself off the floor and stood unsteadily. Placed a hand on the wall, he walked over to the fallen gunman.

"I didn't have a choice, Grant. I'm sorry."

"If you hadn't done it, we would both be dead—and the girls too." He walked over to her, a bit more steady, and lifted her head, looking into her beautiful face. "Thank you. I know that was hard."

She looked at him and whispered back, "I almost didn't do it in time. I almost let you die." She put her gun on the nearby table and hugged Grant tightly.

They paused for a moment, lingering in each other's arms, and then something drew Andrea's attention. "Grant, look at the luggage over there. I think that belongs to the girls."

Grant walked over to the wall and bent down. He lifted the tag on the blue suitcase. It was his daughter's. The second suitcase belonged to Holly. "Yep, it's theirs."

"They look full, but everything had just been tossed in," Andrea observed as she unzipped one of the bags.

"The girls were here," he paused. "Now we have to figure out where Jon-Pierre took them."

"I want to check the office we saw down the hall," Andrea conjectured.

They walked down the hallway to the second door on the left. Grant peeked quickly around the corner; he didn't want another surprise from someone who might have heard the gunshots. The room opened into a large office suite, complete with a large, antique mahogany desk, conference table and computer station. Grant went to the desk, and Andrea headed for the computer.

Andrea found the computer on, but the device needed a password. She tried a few random words, to no avail. She was about to give up when she saw a small note taped to the computer table.

"Hey, I think I found something. Do you think it's possible that Jon-Pierre wrote his password down?"

Grant walked over to the computer, "People do that all the time. They say it's one of the most common ways secure systems are hacked."

Andrea looked for the obvious post-it notes and handwritten cheat-sheets. Her eyes went to a large painting of a tall-masted wooden ship on the wall opposite the desk. She ran her finger on the bass plaque mounted on the bottom of the frame.

"We can't be that lucky," Andrea said. She went to the computer, plopped in the chair and typed the word "Amistad." "Wasn't *Amistad* the name of an old slave ship?" she asked as she pressed the enter key.

Grant watched as the screen came alive. Andrea quickly navigated to the computer's directory, displaying hundreds of file names, and series of numbers and letters. "I can't find anything in this mess," she sighed. She opened a few files—accounting ledgers of transactions.

Grant returned to the desk and looked through a stack of neat, orderly files positioned carefully on the desktop. He picked up the document on top of the pile and studied it. With his head pounding, Grant found it difficult to focus on the small print.

"This looks like a shipping schedule. A Libyan freighter named *Desert Song* docked in Montego Bay yesterday and is scheduled to depart tomorrow morning."

Andrea dove into the files on the computer drive, searching for key words in the files. She typed "Holly" in a search program, and the computer ground away, querying each file for the girl's name.

Grant opened a side drawer on the desk and found a .380 ACP Sig Sauer handgun. He took it from the drawer and placed it on top of the desk. He dug through the remaining drawers and found a thick file folder labeled "Real Estate." Grant opened the file to find the deed and documents dating the estate back to the 1700's as a plantation. In the back of the file, a satellite map of the estate displayed buildings, fields and irrigation lines. He took the map out and spreading it out across the desk.

Andrea's search on the computer pulled up on file with the word "Holly." She quickly clicked on it, the file opened, and the girl's named highlighted. Andrea's heart skipped a beat as she read the document. It described her daughter, listing her by name, sold date, price, delivery date and the name of the buyer. Scrolling down a bit, she found Jena's information also.

She looked over at Grant. "The girls have been sold! He sold them yesterday!"

Chapter 21

Grant threw the map down and ran to Andrea's side. The computer screen confirmed their nightmare. Jon-Pierre sold the girls before demanding money from them. The criminal never intended to return Holly and Jena.

"Look! It says the delivery is tomorrow morning before nine. That means they are still here on the island," Grant said.

Andrea printed the document and realized there were dozens of girls listed in the file, dating back over two years. "Look at this. All these women, sold all over the world. Holly and Jena are going to end up like them!"

"The timing of their delivery lines up with the ship schedule I found on his desk. The freighter is due to depart at ten in the morning. We have until then to get them back. We still have a chance."

"Well, they're not here at the house, so where is Jon-Pierre holding them?" Andrea asked.

Grant walked back to the desk and picked up the satellite map, spreading it out again. "This is this estate. See this here?" He pointed to an outline of a large building. "This is where we are now, and if you look off to the Southeast, there is another building."

Andrea furrowed her brow. "There are a half dozen buildings spread all over this map." She pointed at the large structure Grant had identified. "What is it, another residence?"

"I don't think so. Look at all the surrounding area." His hand swept the area around the building. "The terracing looks like it's for some kind of agricultural use, maybe sugar cane, since that seems to be everywhere around here. Remember what Joseph said about a plantation?"

"How do we get there?" she asked.

"The map shows a road to the building and another entrance road from the back side of this house."

Grant found a messenger bag on the floor near the desk. He poured out its contents on the floor. He put the Sig in the bag, along with his Takarov 9 mm, returned to the dead gunman and searched his pockets. He grabbed the keys to the Land Cruiser parked outside. Grant picked up the automatic rifle, slung it over his shoulder and tossed the messenger bag on the opposite shoulder. He wobbled slightly as his head throbbed.

Andrea held the computer printout that documented the lives of dozens of girls who were kidnapped and sold into slavery. She picked up her handgun. Andrea didn't like the feel of the weapon in her hand; after what she had done with it, the pistol felt dirty and evil.

They both walked out to the battered Toyota Land Cruiser and jumped in. Grant pulled open the map and handed it to Andrea.

"Over there," she said. Andrea pointed to a grove of thick rubber trees on the perimeter of the estate.

"The map says there's a road, but I can't see it from here," she said.

Grant blinked and tried to focus on the map.

They switched seats and Andrea took the keys from her woozy companion. She started the engine and headed toward the tree line. Grant gritted his teeth with each bump, his head throbbing. His vision started to clear and he pointed to a worn path ahead.

Tucked between a pair of huge rubber trees, a concealed forest road led away from the estate and into dense brush and undergrowth.

"We're close. I can feel it," he said.

"What if we're too late? If Jon-Pierre turned them over to the buyer…"

"He's not supposed to give them up until nine tomorrow. It would be too risky for him to move that up. Besides, he doesn't know that we're on to him. He's a greedy son-of-a-bitch, and we can use that against him."

"How are we supposed to do that? We already have the money ready to wire. What more can we do?"

"Eliminate the competition," Grant said.

Chapter 22

Jena felt the fibers of the duct tape start to yield and the circulation in her hands return, leaving her fingers feeling less fuzzy. She pressed once more, as hard as she could, and the nail gouged her injured wrist. She cried out under the gag while she pushed hard against the rusty nail tip. Through the pain, she felt the sudden release of the heavy tape that bound her wrists.

She quickly peeled the tape gag away from her mouth. The air entered her lungs and tasted sweet, even though it came from the entrails of a rotten old barn. Jena pulled layer upon layer of the sticky tape from around her ankles, rolled to Holly and removed the tape from her friend's mouth. Holly's arms and legs held tight. Jena tugged on the tape but only loosened them slightly.

"I'm going to find something to cut the tape," Jena whispered in Holly's ear.

Jena stood, rubbed her tender wrists, careful to avoid the deep lacerations from her struggle for freedom. She opened the short pen door and ran out into the darkness of the barn. Her footfalls slapped on the wooden barn floorboards.

Holly looked up into the darkness of the barn. "Don't leave me, Jena!"

"Shhh. I'm not leaving, I'm trying to find something to cut your tape off."

Jena walked to the opposite wall in the gloom and saw an assortment of rusted tools hanging on a rack attached to the wall. She picked out a six-inch, curved blade mounted on a round handle, which she guessed harvested sugar cane. Then she noticed an old machete, covered with what looked like bloodstains. Looking further, she found several tools stained with blood. Looking down at the one in her hand, she saw dried blood on part of the blade. She dropped it to the floor.

"Oh, God," Jena exclaimed. Her stomach turned as she reached down and picked up the blade. It was honed to a sharp edge, but very old. The bile rose in her throat as she held the weapon in her hand. Uneasy, she walked to Holly, knelt in front of her, and cut though the tape at her ankles. Holly turned and held her taped wrist out for Jena.

"Hold very still," Jena advised, while she concentrated on cutting the tape and not Holly.

Holly trembled to the point where Jena had to stop and wait for her to calm down. Jena pulled a gap in the tape to make a spot between Holly's arms. Holly took a deep breath and continued to shake violently. Jena timed her slice between tremors and cleanly cut through the tape, freeing her friend's arms.

Both girls got up and located the door that always made the heavy sound. They peered between the old wooden slats and didn't see their keeper. They pushed on the door, but it would not give.

"Look, it has a chain locking the door," Holly said as she pointed out through the wooden slats. Thick links of silver chain glinted in the hot sun.

"There has to be another way out of here," Jena said.

The inside of the barn-prison was a maze of shadows. With the sliver of light from the front door, Jena could barely make out the bloody tool bench.

They walked through the building, bumping into posts and abandoned tools strewn on the floor. As they approached the back wall of the old structure, a dark, rusted metal skeleton loomed. Jena approached the towering metal structure and put a hand on it. Her light touch caused dust and debris to rain down. She choked and spit out some of the dirt.

"What was this thing? Whatever it was, it's a huge pile of rust now," Jena said.

From her vantage point to the side of the structure, Holly saw the metal angle up from above the floor to a point high on the wall to what looked like a small door.

"This had to have been a conveyor belt to move cut sugar cane out of the building. Trucks would park outside, under that opening," Holly said.

"I don't see any other way out of here, but I really don't want to climb up there," Jena said.

"Let's get going before he comes back," Holly said as she reached out to the ancient metal structure.

The conveyor belt material had decayed years ago. All that remained was the fragile frame of the machine. Holly climbed up, one foot and one hand on each side of the structure, like a ladder.

"Come on, Jena, you can do this."

Jena watched Holly as she scurried up the conveyor belt frame like a squirrel. Jena pushed aside her fear of heights and climbed, very slowly, up the incline, trying not to look down, but once she thought about it, it was all she could do. The dust and red flakes of rust kicked up, making the air thick and difficult to breathe.

Holly made it to the top of the machine, pushing aside thick spider webs. From the coarseness of the webbing, the spiders must be the size of small dogs. She braced herself against the metal frame and pushed against the door. She felt it bulge under her weight, but it did not open. She waited for Jena and hoped that the two of them together were strong enough. Holly saw Jena a few feet away, when the sound of metal folding in on itself filled the barn.

"Hurry, Jena," Holly encouraged.

With every step Jena took, the machine buckled. The framework's deteriorated condition was not going to hold both of them.

Holly turned back to the conveyer door and desperately kicked at the slats. Jena finished her climb and joined Holly at the door. The wooden slats splintered and provided a gateway to the outside. Holly poked her head out and saw it was a long drop down, maybe fifteen feet or more. There was little on the ground to break their fall, just some brush that grew against the building.

Jena also looked outside, and the height made her dizzy. She was just about to suggest going back down when the metal collapsed under her. The sounds of crashing metal grew louder and louder, threatening to trap them within the sharp spines of the machine.

"We have to jump!" Holly said.

"I can't do it," Jena said.

"This thing is collapsing, and we will get trapped under the wreckage. You have to jump—now!

As soon as the words were out of her mouth, the machine buckled and fell in on itself. Holly grabbed her friend and pulled her out the opening with her. They tumbled out ungracefully and landed heavily in the bushes. A plume of rust colored dust followed the pair.

Bruised and scratched from their rough landing in the bushes was a fair trade for an escape from the awful prison. The crash of metal from within was enough to wake the dead, and they wanted to get as far away from the blue-eyed man as possible. He would have heard the sound and come for them. They stood, dazed and disoriented from their incarceration. They had no idea where they were, or where to go. This place was not safe, but the thick forest held the unknown. Better an uncertain terror than a known monster.

Holly and Jena ran into the shadows of the forest away from one fear and into another.

Chapter 23

Jon-Pierre Baptiste admired the pristine and private beachside view from an open-air café in Montego Bay. He sipped his Blue Mountain Coffee from a white china cup, the steam lofting from the dark liquid. It did not matter that it was late afternoon; a good cup of coffee was welcome at any time. The strongly caffeinated blend didn't interfere with his sleep, nor did any of his business activities, for that matter. From his perch on the café's patio, Jon-Pierre looked out at the deep-blue water and felt the ocean breeze on his face. It carried independence and self-determination.

The last time he had that feeling, Jon-Pierre was on his boat, a fifty-two foot yacht he had pirated for his escape from Haiti. He had sailed the yacht and landed on the Northeast Jamaican shore while the Jamaican Defense Force patrols were occupied pulling Haitian earthquake refugees from their small fishing boats, canoes, and oil drums lashed together in makeshift rafts. It had been too long since Jon-Pierre had gone on the water for his own pleasure. The island had started to make him claustrophobic, and a long, open-water cruise would blow away the cobwebs of doubt and isolation.

A tall, bronzed-skinned man came up to Jon-Pierre's table. "How are you, my good friend? Allah smiles on you, I hope." He pulled out a chair and sat down across from Jon-Pierre, who did not say a word.

A waiter approached the men and asked the newcomer if he cared for something from the bar. The man never looked at the waiter. "I don't drink. Perhaps you could bring me cold bottled water." The waiter scurried off from the table.

Jon-Pierre finally released his gaze from the surf and looked across the table at the Syrian. "Have you brought something for me, Ahmed?"

"Ah, so much for pleasantries," said Ahmed, while his leg pushed a cheap black nylon bag under the table to Jon-Pierre. "I think you will find all is in order. We agreed on $60,000 now and another $60,000 upon delivery tomorrow morning. No later than nine o'clock."

Jon-Pierre pulled the bag up to his lap, waiting to open it until the waiter finished filling his coffee cup and serving Ahmed his bottled water. He pulled the zipper about halfway back and saw packets of U.S. currency. He zipped it back up and placed it at his feet, under the table.

"I think you will be very pleased with this shipment. These two are very pretty," Jon-Pierre reassured Ahmed.

"You have provided us with very suitable items in the past. It is truly a shame they don't last very long. Like all precious things, they soon lose their value and we must discard them. When they become more trouble than they are worth…"

Jon-Pierre took a long sip of his strong coffee and looked back to the ocean. "A word of warning. These two are very headstrong. It's up to you to discipline them. If I were to keep them, they would most certainly require—instruction."

Ahmed took a pull from the water bottle, ignoring the glass with ice left by the waiter. He reflected silently, and then said, "We have a long ocean voyage ahead, so there will be ample time to train them."

Jon-Pierre, his gaze on the horizon, said, "I will see you in the morning with the two packages. You will be most pleased."

"I hope I am pleased. You would best be served to make good on this delivery. The people I work for will not tolerate another failure," Ahmed warned.

Jon-Pierre understood Ahmed's threat. The last woman he had delivered to Ahmed ran from the boat harbor and ended up floating in Little River.

Ahmed stood and headed out of the café. The Haitian crime boss watched as Ahmed walk away. John Pierre's muscles twitched in resentment. The man dared threaten *him*. His hand closed around the coffee cup tighter and tighter until it shattered in his hand. Though the hot coffee burnt his hand, Jon-Pierre made no move to soothe the pain. Instead, he focused on the pain until he felt it as anger, pure and hot.

The waiter came by the table and saw the shards of the broken cup. "Sir, what happened? May I get you another cup? I'm so very sorry, Sir."

"I've had quite enough," Jon-Pierre said. He rose from the table, reached down, grabbed the black nylon bag, and stormed out of the café. It was time to get the girls presentable.

Chapter 24

The thick forest growth, coupled with a full green canopy, made it difficult for Holly and Jena to see more than a few yards ahead in the brush, even though it was late in the afternoon. They had traveled less than a quarter of a mile from the old sugar plantation in thirty minutes. They continued to push their way through the dense brush, the branches slapping back at them with every step.

Exhaustion and dehydration took a toll on the girls. They felt as if they moved in slow motion. Jon-Pierre had fed them a single banana, twice a day, washed down with rancid water. Their energy reserves were at rock bottom. Only fear pushed them onward.

They took turns leading, and Jena cut a swath with the sharp blade she took from the barn. It was strenuous work, and the thick growth left red welts and small cuts on their faces, arms and legs. Jena whacked away at a vine and stopped, putting her hands on her knees to catch her breath.

Holly tripped in the overgrowth and fell. She looked up at the thick forest canopy overhead and said, "Where are we going?"

"I have no idea. I want to get far away from that place," Jena said, between ragged breaths.

"I can't even tell if we are going uphill, or down. We want to go down, right? Back to the ocean?" Holly asked, as she hoisted herself off the ground.

Jena was still trying to catch her breath. "We have to get far away before he finds out we're gone. If he comes after us, we're dead."

Holly got to her feet and took the blade from Jena's sore hand. "My turn."

Holly swung the blade and continued their escape from the blue-eyed savage.

In the vast green expanse behind them, a mechanical sound grew from a whisper to a roar. He came back. He knew they were gone. He would follow their trail.

They dove forward into the thick growth to put as much distance between them and their captor as possible. They flailed and fought the green arms that slowed their progress. They had to move. They couldn't let the monster get to them again.

Chapter 25

Andrea gunned the Land Cruiser's engine, shot up the dirt incline and bounced off the ruts in the road caused by the regular rainfall in the interior of the island. Navigating the twisting trail, she looked determined, and then she tapped the brakes. "Do you think this road is booby trapped like the other one?"

"Looks too well traveled to be set up like that. It's inside his security perimeter. But, I bet the road out will have some surprises."

Andrea nodded and increased her speed on the bumpy roadway. They traveled to a clearing in the middle of an overgrown sugarcane field. It looked abandoned, nothing cultivated or tended to in the field for fifty years. On the far side of the clearing, a huge barn-like structure that once served the sugar cane field lay in disrepair. As they approached, they saw how old the building was. It had been decades since this ramshackle structure had processed sugar cane.

Andrea drove a bit further and parked the Land Cruiser a short distance away from the building, behind a brush-line to the South. She and Grant got out, surveyed the structure, and noted there were no windows from which Jon-Pierre could watch their approach. Grant kept the rifle, and Andrea held her pistol. They made their way to the front of the building as silently as possible.

They knelt, listening for sounds inside but heard nothing. Andrea pointed at the door. A new heavy, steel chain and padlock secured the entrance.

"Looks like someone was here recently," she said as she hefted the sturdy chain.

Grant pulled on the chain and it held, secured by metal plates on the door. He walked around the outside of the building, finding no other point of entry. Finding a timber on the ground nearby, he used it as a battering ram on a section of wall that appeared rotten. At first the wall held, but after a dozen or so blows, the wooden wall splintered, and a small, dark hole emerged.

"A few more should do it," he said. The pounding on the wall kept time with the pounding in his head.

The wood shattered and left an opening the size of a basketball. They both grabbed the splintered boards and pulled until they had a space large enough to crawl inside. No sooner than the boards were out of the way, Andrea went on her hands and knees, and raced through the opening into the dark space.

Following her lead, Grant entered the shadowy, must-scented sugar-cane plant. They dusted themselves off, pulling jagged splinters out of their hands, waiting for their eyes to adjust to the dark.

"I wish I hadn't left the flashlights in the car," Grant apologized.

"I can see enough," Andrea said.

They found a series of wooden sugar cane pens, a tool bench, and an large work table where workers once cut the cane in from the field. In the rear, more holding bins sat alongside a pile of twisted metal. The dark-colored rust gave way to sharp, glistening edges, evidence of recent bends and breaks.

Grant walked by the pens, peering into each of them. His hopefulness faded when the girls weren't there. "Where are they? Maybe it's the wrong place." He sagged against the wall and rubbed his throbbing temples.

Andrea walked through the building's dark interior. In one of the pens, she spied what looked like paper wadded on the floor. She climbed over the ragged gate, stepped into the pen, and reached to pick it up. "Grant, I think I've found something over here."

Grant joined her in the pen and looked over her shoulder at a length of duct tape. On the ground amid the debris on the floor, he located two other pieces of tape, one stained with blood. He ran his thumb across the blood, and it smeared.

"They were here. Jon-Pierre has them. It hasn't been long. We just missed them," Grant said.

Andrea paused, "What about that shipping information you found down at the house."

"It was a freighter leaving out of Montego Bay at ten tomorrow morning," Grant recalled. "There is nothing else here; we ought to get down to the harbor now."

Andrea clutched the fragment of tape.

"The ship leaves at ten, and he is supposed to deliver the girls an hour before. Why would he move them from this place before he had to?" Andrea said.

"I don't know. Someplace closer to the docks, maybe?"

"He isn't coming back here with them," Andrea answered. She tucked the scrap of tape in her pocket. That scrap held a connection to the girls and it might be the last part of her daughter she ever held.

They returned to the hole they had made in the side of the wooden slats. The little bit of light that slipped into the dark room reinforced the darkness and despair that Holly and Jena had both experienced. Andrea took one last look into the abyss, tucked her head and squeezed out through the hole. Grant followed her outside into the bright sun, like gophers emerging into the daylight.

Grant took the keys from Andrea and got behind the wheel of the Land Cruiser. He unfolded the map once more, orienting their location from the position of buildings and nearby hills.

"There are two roads out from this side of the estate. One goes farther into the forest, and this one looks like a road back to the highway," he said, pointing at a trail that led past the barn.

They took the Land Cruiser down the heavily rutted road, bouncing over the irregular surface. Grant stopped the vehicle and got out. He looked into the forest on both sides of the road that ended at a line of thick, tight and tangled bushes.

Andrea stepped down from the vehicle and watched Grant. "Did the Great Navigator get lost? Just like a man, not to ask directions," she said.

Grant smiled, but his gaze held firm to the road. He sat on his haunches for a few seconds and said, "This is the road on the map. But it leads to the trees over there." He walked toward the end of the trail and squatted down. "It's here. These tire tracks run right up to brush and disappear."

Andrea followed where he pointed but couldn't see anything but a solid thick line of brush. "That can't be right, there's nothing there."

Grant walked over to a section of brush, reached into the thicket and shook it roughly. The section gave way, swung open and exposed a metal gate camouflaged with sections of heavy brush.

Andrea sat back down in the Land Cruiser and begrudgingly admitted, "All right, you can lead the safari—for now."

"Actually, that is what I had in mind. Get behind the wheel and follow me. I'm going to make sure that there aren't any more surprises tucked away on this road."

He walked slowly, scanning both sides of the road for explosive charges similar to the one they had encountered on the way in to Jon-Pierre's compound. This road showed more wear, with tire tracks, and Grant figured Jon-Pierre wasn't likely to take a chance on forgetting where he had buried one of his devices. After a slow mile, the road suddenly ended. Grant found another metal gate intertwined with foliage. He grabbed the gate and was about to pull it open, but his hand froze. Something didn't feel right.

He released his grip and walked to the far end of the gate. He parted the twigs and branches and exposed three short cylinders aligned on top of one another. Each contained a 12-gauge shotgun shell capable of killing anyone who attempted to open the gate. If the gate opened, a spring-loaded device struck the primers on the shells, blowing off the arm of the unsuspecting trespasser. Jon-Pierre would have a quick way to render the device safe, but Grant couldn't see it from where he stood.

Grant exposed the back of the tubes so that he could remove the shotgun shells. That meant pulling the gate open slightly. He took a deep breath as he placed his left hand on the gate.

"You may want to take a step back. If this goes bad, it could get ugly," he said to Andrea.

He pulled the gate open with a feathered touch and watched the spring loaded trigger gain tension every millimeter it opened. When the spring was as tight as he dared, he fed his right hand through the gate and carefully slid out the bottom shell. The middle shell followed and went into his pocket with the first one, but the upper shell was out of his reach. He tucked his arm deeper into the fence, directly in the shell's path. Now, if the shell discharged his arm would go with it. He extended his fingertips and barely touched the bottom of the shell. With the edge of his finger he coaxed the shell backwards. Slowly, the shell moved away until it fell out on the ground. A second later, the spring released the homemade firing pins down on the empty cylinders.

He leaned against the gate, exhausted, his head throbbing from the effort. He pulled the two shells from his pocket and tossed them as far as he could into the forest. He leaned over, picked up the third shell, and chucked it deep into the undergrowth. Grant pulled the gate open to the unobstructed road ahead.

He fell into the passenger seat, and Andrea drove the few hundred feet to the main road. She turned right and headed back down the hill to the driveway where they had parked their rental car. They dumped the Land Cruiser and pointed the red sedan back down the hill toward Montego Bay to intercept the hand-off between Jon-Pierre and the buyer.

Chapter 26

Jena and Holly learned that mosquitoes of every size were plentiful in the dense forest. It seemed that each breath came with a mouthful of the wriggling little critters. The girls tripped and cut their way through the brush, deeper into the lush, green forest.

"We're heading west. See the sun going down ahead?" Jena pointed, out of breath from the effort.

"We need to get as far as we can before the sun goes down," Holly said.

Jena agreed and added, "We need to think about shelter, too, because it looks like rain again." It seemed that it rained every night in Jamaica.

"Well, that's fine by me. I need a shower anyway," Holly held her filthy shirt out from her body.

Jena sniffed the air. "You are getting a bit ripe."

"Oh, ha, ha. You probably smell yourself," Holly looked up and saw a large, cream-colored Moluccan Cockatoo, perched on a branch high up in the canopy, watching them struggle through the vegetation.

Jena found a path cut through the forest. They followed the trail, thankful for the slightest assistance. The confines of the path restricted them to single file, and in some locations, bending down to get under a thick branch. The sunlight faded, making it more difficult to see very far ahead along this narrow brush-lined pathway.

Jena kept moving forward on the path, meandering in odd turns and angles. She couldn't tell what direction they were headed.

"Have we gone in a circle? I swear that tree looks familiar." Jena asked.

Holly couldn't see the sun, and what light there was didn't filter below the forest canopy. It was nearly dark on the forest floor. "I don't know where we're headed anymore."

"I'm getting tired. Can we rest?" Jena said.

"As soon as we find a way off this path," Holly replied, afraid of what lurked in the darkness.

A low, guttural sound emanated from the path in front of them. They both snapped their heads in the direction of the sound.

"What was that?" Holly asked.

"I don't know, but maybe it will go away," Jena said. The grunting sound got closer and developed an eerie, hollow tenor.

Appearing out of the darkness in front of them was a pair of red beady eyes. The eyes came closer, and the head of a two hundred pound male wild boar materialized. He lifted his head, grunted loudly and showed off his long knifelike tusks. He was close enough for the girls to smell his dank, musky odor.

Jena froze in her tracks; her instincts told her no sudden movement. The pathway they stumbled upon was this beast's domain, and he didn't look happy about sharing it with the girls. There was no way around him and he pawed at the ground with his front hooves. The boar charged a few feet forward and abruptly stopped. He challenged Jena and Holly for the path.

Holly slowly bent over, picked up a five-foot-long, dead tree branch and told Jena to move aside. As the boar charged again, Holly pushed the branch forward and frightened the animal back a few paces.

"This isn't going to work forever. Find us a way out of here!" Holly said.

Jena quickly looked around and found no opening off the pathway. If they gave ground and ran back, the boar would chase after them. She looked up and pointed to a tree they could easily climb. She caught Holly's eye, and Holly nodded in agreement. Jena scrambled up the tree like, grabbing limb after limb. She held tight to the tree's trunk to avoid falling.

Holly backed up toward the tree when the boar charged again. She stuck out the branch as before, but this time the animal clamped down on the pole with his jaws and snapped it in half. He pawed at the ground, ready for another charge. Holly ran to the tree and sprang up the branches to a safe height. The boar ran after her and rammed the tree with his head. He paced around the tree trunk and grunted when he realized that his prey was out of reach. The boar lost interest and continued down his path in search of slower food.

Jena looked at Holly, "I swear I'll never eat bacon again."

"Hey, look. Doesn't that look like the trees stop right over there?" Holly said. She pointed above the brush thicket to a depression in the hillside.

At the same time, they saw a faint light move along the depression. "That's a car! We have to get to that roadway and get someone to help us," Jena said.

Holly hoped no other wild beasts lurked below as she slid down from her perch. Jena followed, and they ran down the pathway, which held a strong left-over odor of wild boar.

They pushed in the direction of the gap in the trees where they saw car lights. Holly pushed a tree limb aside and revealed a paved road. They stood high up on a bank, some thirty feet above the road surface. Before they knew what to do, a small, white truck sped up the hill and disappeared around the curve.

They heard another vehicle coming down the hill and saw a small red car speed toward them. Jena waved her arms and shouted, "Hey! Up here! Up here!"

Holly joined in, wildly waved her arms back and forth over her head, "Stop! Help us!"

The car's lights didn't illuminate high up on the bank where the girls stood, and it sped down the road. The girls continued to jump and wave, trying to get the attention of those in the car.

Holly screamed at the top of her lungs, but saw that the car's windows were up. She kept waiving as she watched the car pass directly below them. Holly saw the person in the passenger's seat. She screamed, "Mom! Stop! Jena, that's my mom."

Jena stopped jumping. Her dad must be here too. "Stop! Please help us! We're up here!"

The low light obscured them from view, and the car sped out of sight around the curve.

Jena stopped waving and dropped to her knees in despair. "They didn't see us. No one will find us out here."

Holly stared at the point in the road where the car had vanished. Her shoulders sagged, and she took a step toward Jena. The red clay on the edge of the embankment crumbled where she stepped. Her face swept with panic as her footing gave way. Holly lost her balance, and grabbed at the air, reaching out for Jena. Their fingertips touched, but Holly plummeted down the steep embankment before Jena could grab her.

A shrill scream came from Holly's frightened throat as she started to fall. She pitched backwards and struck her head on some rocky debris on the side of the hill. She went limp and continued down, a lifeless rag doll, bouncing and tumbling to the roadway below.

"Holly! I'll be right there, hang on!" Jena called.

Seeing a depression in the embankment about twenty yards up the hill, she ran toward the low spot, tripping and falling more than once on her way to the crevasse. She could see Holly's still body tucked along the darkened roadway.

Jena carefully slid down the red clay embankment, safely reaching the bottom, but covered in red clay mud from the trip down.

She ran towards Holly and yelled her name. When she reached Holly, she stopped short. Her friend's body landed awkwardly on the pavement, and she hadn't moved. Jena got down on her hands and knees.

"Holly, Holly, can you hear me?"

The crumpled body didn't respond. Jena had thought there was no fear worse than the blue-eyed man. She was wrong.

Chapter 27

Jon-Pierre felt unsettled after the meeting with Ahmed. This would be the last time he tolerated the man's threats and demands. There were more than enough willing buyers for his kind of merchandise. It was time he prepared the girls for their trip, so he could hand them over before the deadline and be done with the Syrian.

His two American captives, like those before them, suffered from the mindless and promiscuous lifestyles that plagued young people who traveled to the island. Such young American women gave themselves to nearly everyone they met, even though they undoubtedly carried sexually transmitted diseases. Jon-Pierre considered it an extra bonus, after Ahmed's display of disrespect.

Jon-Pierre did not particularly care if they spread diseases in Ahmed's corner of the world. It would be far away from anything that concerned Jon-Pierre Baptiste.

Jon-Pierre sped up the hillside roadway in the well-used white Toyota truck he had taken from its former owner, who lay a half mile off shore, weighted to the bottom with a crate of weapons he had tried to sell to Jon-Pierre. The American Drug Enforcement Agency had tagged the weapons to snare Jon-Pierre in a gun-smuggling sting. The D.E.A. would find their operative, along with the guns, resting and rusting among the coral.

When he pulled into the parking area of his home, Jon-Pierre scanned the surroundings. Everything appeared to be in order, except that the idiot had parked the Land Cruiser down by the road. *That fool ran out of gas. I'll make him siphon gas through a garden hose and crush a cigarette out on his tongue.*

As Jon-Pierre looked over the expanse of his estate, he recognized that he could not have accumulated all this wealth and property in Haiti. He had been a street-orphaned hustler in Port-Au-Prince, where he scratched up enough to get by, far from the big time. He had snatched purses, robbed pharmacies, and carried drugs in from the Dominican Republic. On one of his drug runs, the Tonton Macoutes stopped and searched his vehicle. They wore blue shirts and straw hats and wielded machetes with depraved cruelty. Even though the gang of thugs threatened him with death, Jon-Pierre Baptiste found them kindred spirits.

Jon-Pierre told the Macoutes everything he knew about the man who paid him to pack drugs over the border, and the Macoutes ordered Jon-Pierre to kill his former master. After Jon-Pierre proved himself, they took him into the fold, and he came to relish the power and status of the sharpened edge of his machete.

When the administration of "Baby-Doc" Duvalier collapsed, the Macoutes dissolved and left Jon Pierre back on the street. Over sixty-thousand Haitians died at the hands of the Tonton Macoutes, and Jon-Pierre found his calling. The earthquake made it impossible to extort a decent living from people who had nothing but the clothes on their back. For a while, he sold relief supplies back to the organizations he'd taken them from, but he needed a new lease on life, far away from the wretched slums of Port-Au-Prince. So he made the jump to neighboring Jamaica and new found opportunities.

Jon-Pierre looked around at *his* island from the terrace for a moment before he entered the home. He tossed the truck keys on a rough-hewn table near the door and walked down the hallway to his office. At the doorway, he saw his computer powered up and the documents on his desktop not as he had left them. Someone had dared touch his possessions.

He shook with anger. *Who had the nerve to come into my home and do this?*

Jon-Pierre checked other rooms for signs of the trespasser, and he found his dreadlocked employee splayed over a table, bearing two visible gunshot wounds. He walked to the body and looked at the dead man with contempt.

"You were weak and you will never fail me again," Jon-Pierre said. He spit on the body, turned and walked out of the room.

A heavy cloud of anger fell upon Jon-Pierre. When these moods struck, his intense paranoia ratcheted up, and betrayal lurked everywhere. He couldn't shake the feeling that he was a step away from returning to the slums in Port-Au-Prince.

He hurried out, grabbed the keys to his Hummer, and trotted out to the oversized vehicle. He hefted himself into the driver's seat and spun the Hummer's rear wheels, flipping a hard turn in the parking lot. He threw the transmission into drive and dashed up the road to the sugar plant.

The ungainly vehicle bounced on a high-speed run to the abandoned plant. As Jon-Pierre made the last curve, the building came into sight. His heart rate accelerated, along with the Hummer. Jon-Pierre felt relieved when he saw that the chain still secured the door.

This was to be a quick visit to gather the girls for delivery to Ahmed. He took the key from his pocket, inserted it in the lock, and easily disengaged it from the thick chain. Jon-Pierre pulled the chain from the eyebolts he had installed on the frame and opened the heavy wooden door. The door moved easily, considering how old and big it was. His eyes slowly grew accustomed to the dark as he walked the familiar path to the pen where he had deposited the girls.

John Pierre leaned over and saw the pen contained only broken scraps of rotted sugar cane where the girls should have been. He quickly scanned the interior of the dark, dank building. They had to be here. Where were they hiding?

He called out for them. "Where are you, my little flowers?"

Jon-Pierre pulled a compact black .40 caliber pistol from his waistband and searched the remaining wooden pens. Then he saw the pile of twisted metal from the collapsed conveyor belt. The image brought to his memory the debris and wreckage after the Haitian earthquake—hundreds trapped under rubble, mangled or crushed to death. If the rusty remnants of the conveyor machine had maimed the girls, their value was diminished, and his deal with the Syrian was over.

Jon-Pierre stepped over and around the scattered remains of the crumpled machine, pulling sections of metal off the pile. His captives were nowhere in sight. Rage welled within and exploded. He grabbed a piece of metal from the broken conveyor and beat it against a wooden post with a fury fed by failure. A light caught his attention from the wall opposite the pens. A hole in the wooden siding was large enough for the girls to escape. He knelt near the opening in the wall and found scuffs and marks in the dirt, evidence that they had gone through this hastily made exit.

"You little whores! I'll find you. When I do you will wish you were dead!" he screamed.

Jon-Pierre had to get them back to keep his arrangement with Ahmed. That delivery must transpire, or he would have greater problems. Not only with Ahmed, but also with the people the Syrian represented, namely the Hezbollah, a fundamentalist Islamic group you did not want to offend.

He picked up another chunk of rusted iron and threw it with all his strength against the pen that had failed to hold his captives. At the tool bin he picked up his trusted, blood stained machete and struck the tool table. Chunks of old wood flew from the table under Jon-Pierre's assault. He stood in front of the table, his chest heaving and sweat pouring from his body. John Pierre lifted the machete, examined it, and smiled.

"There is nowhere you can run. I will find you and punish you."

He pulled his cell phone from his pocket and dialed a number. After a moment he said, "We have a problem to solve. Come up to the house."

Chapter 28

When Jena reached the bottom of the cliff, Holly lay sprawled, silent and still. Jena thought her friend dead from the fall, until a slight rise of her chest signaled Holly as unconscious, but alive. Jena called out Holly's name, but received no response from the fallen girl. Holly had no visible broken bones, although she had suffered a few cuts and scratches from the harrowing tumble.

Jena stroked Holly's face, pleaded to her friend and encouraged her to wake up."Please, Holly, please get up. Come on, Holly. Wake up. We have to get out of here."

She sat on the side of the asphalt road surface, Holly's head in her lap. Dark blood flowed from laceration on the girl's forehead, a stark contrast to the paleness that crept over her complexion. Jena tore a piece of material from her shirt and held it on Holly's forehead, to stem the flow.

"Please, Holly. Please be okay," Jena pleaded. Jena's tears dripped down onto Holly's matted hair. She wiped the blood from Holly's face, fearing that her best friend may not come back.

Tangled among the sobs, a throaty sound vibrated from the hillside. Jena sat up and looked for the source of noise that echoed from off the trees and embankment above. As it grew louder, Jena identified the sound as the thrum of a car motor. The first thing that flashed in her mind was the blue-eyed man coming to collect them. Jena considered pulling Holly off into the ditch to hide, but in Holly's frail condition, Jena was afraid to move her.

The car sound grew closer and closer, and Jena wanted to run. She couldn't go back with the blue-eyed monster. Every fiber in her being screamed for her to run far and fast, but she couldn't bring herself to leave Holly's side. Exposed in the moonlight, they would present a clear view of the approaching car. The car sounds and gleaming lights crested the hill.

The car's headlights flashed on Jena, nearly blinding her. She shielded her eyes with a hand and waived with the other. The vehicle pulled off onto the shoulder behind the girls, now bathed in the glow of the headlights. The car door opened and a single man got out. He approached Jena and knelt down next to Holly.

"You okay, Miss?" the man inquired.

"I'm fine, but she's hurt really bad," Jena said.

She looked up and saw the man was dressed in a police uniform, and the car was a local police cruiser. Relief swept through Jena's body. They were going to be okay.

"Sir, my friend and I were held hostage by a man up the hill. Please take us to our parents."

"Please, I'm not a "sir"; call me Sergeant Collins. Where are your parents?"

Jena thought, but realized she didn't know. "I'm not sure, somewhere in Negril, I guess."

Holly moaned, which the sergeant said was a good sign. "Let's get her in the car. Then we can go about finding your parents and getting her to a doctor." He took hold of Holly's legs. "We can put her in the back seat, and you sit up front with me."

Jena held Holly's arms and head while they carefully placed her in the police cruiser. "Thank you so much for helping us," Jena told the Sergeant after getting Holly secure. She noticed that his uniform was snug over his large frame, but thought nothing of it, relieved by their rescue.

"It's my pleasure," the sergeant said.

Jena buckled into the front passenger seat, and the police sergeant started the car, turned it sharply, and accelerated back down the road.

"Sergeant Collins? The man who had us … who is he?" Jena asked.

"If it is who I believe him to be, he is a man that you do not want after you. Some of the locals believe he is the devil. They may be right," he said in a tone that indicated he believed it.

Jena shuddered. "He was going to sell us to someone."

"Ah, then you were the lucky ones. You see, the women who do not meet his satisfaction, they end up dead in one of the rivers." He paused and looked at Holly in the rearview mirror. "He drops the women in the river where the salt water and fresh water come together. That is where the crocodiles feed. The bodies attract the animals. They have pulled partially eaten bodies from the Salt River, the Milk River, Martha Brea Rivers, and most recently, the Little River."

"Lucky? … I don't feel lucky," Jena admitted, while she rubbed her abraded wrists.

The Sergeant noticed her wounds. "We'll get those taken care of at soon as we get to the station."

The sergeant pulled out his cell phone and quickly dialed a number. He held it to his ear, while speaking crisply into the receiver. "This is Sergeant Collins; I have the two missing American women. I'm headed to the Montego Bay station, and both require medical attention." He listened for a few seconds, then hung up the phone.

Jena shut her eyes and rested her head against the headrest. The hum of the vehicle lulled Jena into a quiet state. She glanced at her friend in the back seat. Holly had not moved since they put her in the car. The sergeant drove down the road quickly and surely, as only a local could manage. Jena leaned against the window and slipped into a light sleep.

When Jena awoke, she saw lights all around and bustling city traffic. "Where are we?"

"Ah, there you are. We are coming into Montego Bay and we should be at the station in a few minutes."

Jena looked in the back seat, where Holly was still unconscious. "Maybe we should go to a hospital first?"

"She'll be fine. We have medical services available at our station," the sergeant said.

"I don't know. She doesn't look good and she's unconscious. I'm worried about her," Jena argued.

Sergeant Collins turned into the whitewashed police station and parked inside the fenced enclosure. He jumped out, opened the back door, and softly brushed Holly's cheek. He whispered, "Wake up baby girl. It's time to get up." He pinched the back of her arm and earned a response from Holly.

"Ouch! Stop it," Holly said sleepily.

Jena, on hearing Holly, reached over the seat and jiggled her a little bit. "Come on, Holly. Get moving, girl."

Holly opened her eyes and shut them immediately. The overhead light hurt her eyes. "Where are we?" she slurred.

"Sergeant Collins found us and had taken us here to Montego Bay," Holly explained.

Holly blinked. "I want to see my mom."

"All in good time," the sergeant countered. "We need to get you in the station so we can tend to you. Then we'll contact your parents."

"But I want my mom. I can tell you her cell number," Holly said.

Holly came out of the back seat more easily than she went in. She was unsteady, but more aware and awake. The sergeant partially carried the girl into the front door of the police station.

An officer behind the counter looked up. "Sergeant, what that you got there? More drunk college girls?"

"No, now get off your ass and help me with her. She's hurt. These are the girls who were missing. Remember that poster?"

The officer jumped up, and they carried Holly down a hall and through a heavy door. Jena followed but felt an icy chill on the back of her neck when she saw the sergeant guide Holly into a jail cell and lay her down.

Sergeant Collins, seeing her nervousness, tried to calm her down. "We need someplace to lay her down, and unfortunately this is all we have."

Jena froze, afraid and unsure. Something within told her this wasn't right. "I think we should sit out in the waiting area." Deep inside she knew she couldn't leave her friend.

The sergeant sat in the cell with Holly, tending to her with a first aid kit he took from the wall opposite the line of cells. "Why don't you lay down yourself? I need to take care of your wrists too," he said, while he tended to Holly's gashed forehead. Holly slipped back into an unresponsive state, and her skin grew pale.

Jena reluctantly took slow steps to the cell where Sergeant Collins tended to her friend. He had rescued them from the roadside, so she had some degree of trust, but something didn't sit right. She took small tentative steps, readying herself to bolt out the door.

"Don't you have a doctor here? You said the jail had medical services, right?" she said.

Now at the cell door, she stood there stiff and afraid. The sergeant looked up and held out a gauze bandage and a tube of antibiotic ointment.

"We need to take care of your wrists. If you won't let me do it, then you need to take care of it yourself."

Feeling a bit foolish, she did not even see the sergeant get up and walk over to her. He took the tube from her and squeezed a blob of ointment on Jena's finger. Jena rubbed the ointment into her injured wrists.

"I'm sorry. I was getting buggy and didn't know what to do," she admitted.

When she looked up, the sergeant was outside the cell. He looked at Jena, and his face transformed and took on an ugly quality.

"Little one, you need to trust your intuition," he said.

The sergeant slammed the iron bar door shut. The resounding clang boomed through the cellblock, and Jena knew instantly that they were locked inside, prisoners again.

"What are you doing? Open this door!"

Fueled by frustration and rage, she shook the cell door. Jena looked into the dark recesses of a cell across from hers. Her scream transformed into a shriek when she saw a man stripped down to his underwear. He lay in a dark pool of blood that trailed out into the hallway. From the flies that attacked the man's face and open wounds, Jena figured that the real Sergeant Collins had died hours ago, beaten to death and stuffed in the cell after his uniform had been taken. Jena now realized why the uniform of the man who had picked them up was unusually snug fit. She continued to rattle the door, screaming at the top of her lungs.

Without a word, the phony sergeant walked to the front of the cell door, took a short boxy device from his belt, and very quietly said, "Stop."

Jena looked at him. "Let us out of here!" She didn't see what he had in his hand.

The sergeant extended the antenna from the Tazer and shoved the probes through the bars and into Jena's chest. He held the trigger while fifty-thousand volts of electricity coursed through her system. The loud clack-clack-clack sound of the device almost drowned out Jena's screams. Seconds later, her protests ceased.

The sergeant pulled his cell phone out once again. "We have them at the station. They are not in the greatest shape, so you may not get much for them."

Jon-Pierre said, "I will be right there. We can clean them up in the usual way. I'm not lowering my price. These two have caused me a great deal of trouble. I may need to exact some discipline on them for what they have done." In his anger, he had slipped into a Creole accent.

Jon-Pierre had all night to discipline and ready the girls for transfer. If one did not meet his expectations, he would dispose of her like the garbage she was, using the local rivers to cover the girl's disappearance. The resort beaches and bars would provide a suitable replacement, but that would cost him time and trouble.

Jon-Pierre punched the gas pedal of his Hummer, heading down the road toward the main highway. He traveled much faster than was safe, pushed by his white-hot anger. "How dare they do this to me? They will be punished for their insolence," he said aloud, while banging on the steering wheel.

He swerved and took corners wide. Around a steep right hand corner, he veered into the opposite lane, into the path of a fully loaded local bus.

The elderly bus driver looked out his window in disbelief at the big, white vehicle coming straight toward him. He stomped on the brakes, but the forward momentum of the old bus barely changed. He spun the wheel to the right, sliding the bus to the shoulder of the winding road. It teetered on the small mountain slope for a few seconds before rolling over, crushing the top of the ragged bus. The overturned bus rested on its roof, before it began sliding further down the hill in the slick mud. It came to stop a hundred yards down from the road. Locals climbed out from broken windows and jagged holes in the bus's metal skin. The bus driver climbed out from the wreckage, clutching a broken arm. A score of others had similar injuries.

Jon-Pierre didn't glance at the bus in the rearview mirror. It was in his way, and the fools deserved what they got for their stupidity. His focus was on what lay ahead at the Montego Bay Police Station.

Chapter 29

Andrea held the map, navigating while Grant drove to the waterfront district in Montego Bay. She guided him to a frontage road, which took them directly alongside several fishing trawlers and chartered day boats. Down the pier, huge cruise ships moored for the night, their passengers mingling out on the railings, taking in the night air.

"What is the name of the ship we're looking for?" Andrea asked as they passed the docked cruise vessels.

"It won't be one of these." He paused. "Cruise ships have too many people—too many witnesses. It would be hard to hide the girls onboard without someone noticing."

Grant slowed the pace of the car when he saw the guard shack on the road ahead. Slowly approaching, they saw a tall, gangly Jamaican listening to reggae music in the shack. The guard slid from his perch on a stool. He did not appear to appreciate Grant's interruption.

"Wat chew want, Mon?" the guard asked.

"We are looking for a ship—"

The guard interrupted, "You jus passed a whole mess a ships back der."

"I'm looking for a particular ship, the *Desert Song*," Grant added.

The guard stepped back into his shack and returned with a clipboard. Tracing his finger down the list, he stopped about three-quarters of the way down. "Ya, Mon. We got dat ship here."

Grant asked, "Can you tell us how to get there?"

The guard laughed. "Oh, I can tell you dat, but you ain't gonna go der."

"What? Why not? We have something to get on that ship," Grant tried.

The guard put the clipboard away and pointed to the shipping warehouse on the far side of the port, well past the cruise ship terminal. "Dat's where all cargo is logged in, cleared by customs, and don't forget the drug dogs." The guard added the last part because why else would two Americans be out here in the dark, other than trying to take their Ganja off the island. Too bad for them. He told Grant to back up and leave.

Andrea looked at Grant. "Well, that went well."

"We know that the ship is here. I have to figure out a way to get to it," he said.

Grant pulled the car off the roadway and turned off the lights. The docks hummed with activity; cranes and forklifts heaved their heavy burdens from the holds of the docked ships. Spotlights lit the docks in artificial sunlight, but the spot where Grant and Andrea parked remained sheathed in darkness.

"We are running out of time. The shipping manifest said the ship leaves at ten tomorrow morning," Andrea said.

"Jena and Holly weren't in that old barn, so that means the girls are on the ship, or soon will be."

"I need to get on that ship and find the girls!" Andrea said.

"We have to plan this out. We can't waltz on in there and expect a welcome with open arms," Grant replied.

Andrea's frustration rose; they were so close to where Jon-Pierre was supposed to deliver the girls. "I can't just sit here and hope the girls come to us."

Grant looked into her eyes, and a smile spread on his face. "You're brilliant. That's exactly what we are going to do."

Chapter 30

Holly had a splitting headache from the blow to her head. She felt thick-headed, as if she were slogging through a bog.

"Oh—I feel like my head was used in a soccer game," Holly said as she tried to sit upright.

Jena hadn't left her friend's side, and when Holly's eyes focused, they saw a tearful Jena next to her on the bed. The jolt from the sergeant's stun gun wore off faster than she imagined, yet Jena stayed far away from the cell door. The sergeant and his men left them alone in the dark, empty row of cells. All alone, except for the real sergeant's body, with its fly swarm across the hall from their cage.

"I was really worried about you. I didn't know if you were going to wake up," Jena said through tears that traced down her cheeks. Both sat caked in red mud from the embankment. Their trudge through the brush left them stained with cuts and purple bruises.

Holly looked around, clearly confused at what she saw. "Where are we?"

"We are in the Montego Bay Police Station."

Holly's strength faded fast and she grew tired. She cocked her head and asked, "Are the police calling my mom and your dad?"

"No, they are not real police. I think they work for the asshole," Jena said.

"What? That doesn't make sense. If they aren't the police, then where are the real police?" Holly asked, while touching her bruised and lacerated forehead.

Jena leaned against her friend's shoulder. "I don't know where they all are, but one is in the cell across from us, and I think he's dead."

"What is going to happen to us?" Holly asked.

Before Jena responded, the metal door into the cellblock flew open and banged as it bounced against the wall. They heard footsteps and recognized the pattern and cadence. It was him, the blue-eyed monster.

Jon-Pierre came into view. "You have no idea the trouble you have caused."

Holly and Jena sat transfixed on the bed, trembling, fearful of what he was liable to do to them. Holly dropped her head and began absently picking dried mud from her legs.

"You destroy a wall in my barn and then you dare enter *my* home. You trash my office, and if that wasn't enough you left bloodstains on my carpet when you killed my driver," Jon-Pierre said accusingly. His face grew red with anger.

Jena was confused. They hadn't gone through a wall in the barn. They did destroy the rusty conveyor belt. But, they hadn't gone back to his home, either. That must have been someone else. Someone else trashed the man's home—her dad, maybe.

"Holly needs medical attention. You need to get her to a hospital," Jena said.

Rather than distracting Jon-Pierre, it further inflamed him. "She better not require medical attention, because if she does, she is worthless to me." To make his point, he pulled the Glock pistol from his belt, pulled the slide to chamber a round, and pointed it through the bars at Holly. "Do you need to go to a hospital?" He spat angrily, his French accent showing once more.

Jena screamed, "No…stop!"

Jon-Pierre ignored Jena's plea. "Tell me you need to go to the hospital and I will kill you right now!"

Holly attempted to get up from the bed, but stumbled and fell back down.

"You cost me a great deal of money. Look at you. I can't sell you to anyone in the condition you're in." He took aim at Holly's head.

Jena yelled, "Wait…wait. Let me help her."

She put her arms under Holly's shoulders, and whispered, "Holly, I'm here. We have to do this. Please try."

She held up Holly's weight, forcing her to stand. Holly's head sagged, and she seemed disoriented. Jena struggled and held her friend upright.

"See, she'll be fine. She needs a little time, that's all," Jena said.

Jon-Pierre was not impressed. "She is of no value to me like this." He did not lower the handgun.

Holly raised her head and saw that Jon-Pierre had again taken aim, directly at her head. She stared back at the cold blue eyes, knowing that this was her final moment. Her last memories would be of pain, grief and sorrow in a dark, dank jail cell. Tears formed in her eyes.

Jon-Pierre aimed carefully, then said, "Goodbye, whore," and pulled the trigger.

Chapter 31

Grant slipped into the dark shadows near the last cruise ship. All activity was focused near the roadway on the waterside. He crept along the opposite bank, out of the glare of the ship's spotlights.

Andrea climbed a section of fence at the back of the compound, making her own path to the dark dock area through the freight containers. She didn't like Grant's plan—it was bold and risky, but they had little choice.

Grant reached the first freighter and looked high on the stern for the name: *Mermaid's Dream*, out of Miami. The aft end of the ship was tucked tight against the dock, where forklifts unloaded canvas bags of cargo. He continued his shadow-covered trek down the row of ships, checking the name of each one. Four ships later, he came to a smaller freighter with a rusty exterior. The chipped and fading paint at the stern confirmed that this was the *Desert Song*. He hung in the dark, concealing his approach. A row of bright cabin lights glowed through large porthole shaped windows in the hull.

Materials and cargo were arranged on the dock for the scheduled morning departure. Cranes lowered island fruit and containers of coffee into the hold area. In the center container, huge open bins of bauxite from the mines in the hills were lowered into the holds below deck. Spotlights lit the mid-section of the ship, where most of the activity occurred.

Grant crept behind a line of trucks, forklifts and empty cargo containers. The only access to the ship was an elevated metal gangway, blocked by a guard shack at the dockside. A forklift loaded with layers of boxes sped past Grant's location, heading toward the cargo loading area, uninterrupted by security personnel or the ship's crew.

Andrea reached his location and crouched behind a forklift.

"Did you see anything?" she asked.

"A lot of lights on in the cabins. Looks like several passengers are booked on the ship."

"You sure this is the best way?" Andrea said.

"I don't know if it's the best way, but we have to do something. You keep an eye out for the girls," he said as he climbed into the seat of a parked forklift.

Grant turned the key and the electric motor powered up. He had no idea what the rest of the controls and switches operated. He flicked a lever and the front tines lifted from the asphalt. The lift moved forward and increased speed as it closed on the stern of the *Desert Song*. Grant managed to extend the front tines all the way up, and the steel forks threatened to topple the small machine. He aimed the forks at the huge propeller and rudder at the stern, holding the accelerator pedal down to the floorboard. The moment the forklift flew from the dock, Grant bailed out and landed hard on the rocks placed to control erosion around the harbor.

The forklift arced from the dock, clanged off the rusty hull, and one of its tines caught above the propeller shaft. The boat rocked from the impact. From inside, an alarm klaxon sounded, followed by a command in a thick Arab accent over the ship's communication system: "All ship's personnel report to fire stations. All passengers must disembark immediately."

"Here we go," Grant said after he scrambled back to Andrea. "The passengers will come down the gangway any minute now."

"We're going to get them to come to us. Not bad," she said.

"We need to get closer. What about over by those containers?" Grant said, pointing to a nearby ship.

"We need to act like someone from this ship," she said, pulling Grant by the hand.

Grant checked out his handiwork as they strolled by the rear of the ship. The top half of the rudder had jammed against the forklift. Crew members and dockworkers ran about, unsure if the fork lift's driver had fallen into the water under the ship.

"They won't be going anywhere for a while," he said.

Andrea monitored the gangway as passengers filed out. "How many passengers would a ship like this hold?"

"Not sure, I'm guessing no more than fifty—probably less."

The passengers, some dressed in nightclothes, gathered on the dock, inquiring of one another what had caused the disturbance. Some guessed the old ship's boiler had blown up. None of the passengers on the Libyan-flagged ship thought it was a terrorist attack. In fact, members of terrorist organizations preferred travel on these freighters, where they attracted less attention from immigration and customs officers in the countries they needed to enter.

Grant and Andrea watched as passengers continued down the gangway. The girls were nowhere among them. People gathered in small clusters, or alone, suggesting they did not know one another.

"Wait here for a second," Grant said.

Andrea reached out and grabbed his arm. "Where are you going? You're not going anywhere without me."

"I can do this by myself. You stay put." Grant attempted to pull her arm away but found Andrea firmly attached.

"Grant, stop it. I have as much right to go look for the girls as you do. I'm going with you."

The determined look on her face told him she wasn't going to give on this one.

"Okay, we are going to walk up and mingle with the passengers. So let's go mingle."

They walked hand in hand down the road and across the dock. There was so much commotion among the fire crew and emergency response equipment that they strode unnoticed up to the area where the passengers milled. Medical personnel checked on a few older passengers and offered words of assurance. Grant grabbed two thin blankets handed out by the emergency crew, even though the evening was warm. Grant and Andrea looked the part of a couple put out and inconvenienced.

"When can we get back on?" Grant asked a ship's officer at the gangway.

The officer apologetically answered, "No one gets back on until the Captain says so."

Grant turned Andrea and walked back into the crowd, complaining loudly about their inconvenience. They took a spot at the back of the pack, while assessing the crowd. There were a few couples, but most of the passengers were men who traveled alone. Holly and Jena weren't going to be paraded out on the dock. If the girls sat tucked away in a cabin, Grant and Andrea needed a diversion to reach them. The pandemonium on the dock was more than expected, but the ship's officer was steady, never leaving his post at the gangway.

From a loudspeaker mounted on the *Desert Song*'s bridge, a voice announced, "All passengers may return to their cabins. There has been an accident on the dock, and there is no danger to the ship."

"Come on, let's get in line with the passengers," Grant said.

"Won't they check tickets, or identification?" Andrea said.

"Only one way to find out."

Chapter 32

Ahmed stood among the small knot of passengers and crew at the bottom of the gangway. He had felt the impact from his cabin in the stern of the ship. It wasn't an explosion, more like a large hammer struck against the steel hull. It had rattled the glass in his cabin but caused no damage.

As Ahmed walked down the gangway and saw the forklift tangled with the ship's steering gear, his first thought was that a careless dock-worker had run the forklift off the deck. His suspicion grew when he realized that the forklift hit in the exact spot needed to disable the ship. The cargo-loading work was in the center of the ship, not at the stern. The dock foreman claimed all his workers present and accounted for, and Ahmed scanned the faces in the crowd as the crew assessed the damage. Two people seemed out of place.

The strangers were dressed too shabbily. In spite of the *Desert Song*'s dog-eared exterior, a deliberate illusion, a berth on this particular ship was lavish and very pricey. Service aboard the *Desert Song* was excellent, and a two-thousand-bottle wine cellar would be the envy of most large cruise ships. The two people Ahmed focused on were dressed in cheap western fashion, tourist-like rather than proper casual attire. He had not seen them on the ship before, but then he hadn't seen many of the other passengers who mingled on the dockside.

The Syrian unbuttoned his linen jacket and placed his hand on his 9mm CZ-100 handgun. The cold polymer of the Czech-made weapon reassured him. Ahmed wondered if the two were Interpol officers. American immigration agents had no authority in this port. If they came within reach, he would have no choice but to dispose of them.

The ship's engineers hooked towlines to the wayward forklift and pulled it away from the *Desert Song*'s huge rudder. They hauled the mangled forklift back up to the dock and swore at each other in rapid-fire Arabic, more concerned about who to hold accountable, as the damage to the ship was superficial.

Ahmed wasn't a man who believed in coincidence, fate, or chance. Everything happened for a reason. He saw the forklift as an attempt to disable the ship. That thought, coupled with the two passengers who seemed out of place, made him uneasy.

He held back while the passengers lined up and started climbing the gangway, including the two he suspected. They carried themselves like Americans, entitled and cocksure. Ahmed waited until they disappeared below deck with the others. He darted to his cabin, one level above. He opened the door into a deeply lacquered teak wood cabin, which covered the entire thirty foot width of the deck; it consisted of four distinct rooms, an expansive living room, large bedroom, marble-finished bathroom, and his special room. This special space was a sound-insulated holding room with leg irons fitted into the floor and a floor drain in the center of the scuffed tile surface.

The restraints, and everything he needed to transport the cargo was in good working order. Several dozen voyages required the use of the special room, and Ahmed's reward was more than a handsome paycheck. He often sampled the merchandise during the long, lonely cruise. His superiors never knew they received second-hand products, and if Ahmed suspected a woman would threaten his enterprise, he tossed her into the vast expanse of ocean between Jamaica and the African coast.

Ahmed removed a long, cylindrical tube from a drawer in his huge mahogany desk. He took his CZ pistol by the left hand and screwed on the silencer, checking to be sure there was a round in the chamber by giving the gun a short tug on the slide. Satisfied, he left the cabin to hunt down the Americans.

Chapter 33

Grant and Andrea merged with the group of passengers when the boarding announcement sounded. The ship's loudspeaker repeated the message in another language that sounded like either Farsi or Arabic. The crowd started to move up the gangway toward the ship's main deck. As the couple approached, the same ship's officer Grant had spoken with earlier was overseeing the boarding process. He nodded to them from the railing.

The freighter was less than two hundred feet long and maybe thirty-five feet wide at the beam, a small ship, so boarding happened quickly. The flow of passengers carried Grant and Andrea to a companionway that led to the deck below. They moved with the pack down to the next level of staterooms.

Grant and Andrea peered into the staterooms as they opened, looking for any sign of the girls. They were almost to the end of the hallway, only a few rooms remaining. The passengers assigned to those berths approached and Grant signaled that they needed to separate and look into the rooms. He stepped quick and startled an older man, but managed a look inside the open stateroom door before the door slammed. Andrea was in a better position when her passenger opened his door. She peered in and saw a woman's leg flung off the side of a bed.

"Grant, over here!" Andrea said.

Grant ran to the doorway and awkwardly pushed it open against the passenger who had just entered the room. As the man fell to the stateroom floor, Grant jumped over him toward the woman on the bed. The woman lay covered with a blanket in spite of the humid evening air. She was about the same build as Holly or Jena.

Andrea ran to the bedside, pulled the woman's shoulder and rolled her over on her back. The woman's hair fell across her face, and Andrea brushed it aside. The unconscious woman was older than the either of the girls. Andrea noticed a syringe and burnt spoon. A length of rubber tubing was wound tightly on the woman's left arm, and a drip of blood oozed from an injection site.

The man on the floor sat with his hands raised, babbling as if this were a police raid and his girlfriend's drug addiction was going to be the end of him. He'd purchased the heroin in Montego Bay, and she had shot up when the alarm bells sounded. Now the police were going to put him in jail. Probably in a cell with big, hairy Jamaican man who would make him do unspeakable things.

Grant turned to the man on the floor and asked, "Have you seen two young white girls on this ship?"

The man's eyes grew large, and he stuttered, "N….n…n…no."

Grant pressed, "Have you seen them?"

The man felt Grant's anger and wet himself. The dark stain on the front of the man's pants was evidence that the man knew nothing about Holly and Jena.

"This is a waste of time," Grant told Andrea. "Let's go."

The sheepish, pee-stained man sat on the floor, grateful his girlfriend was too doped up to notice.

Seeing an older couple in their seventies shuffle toward their stateroom, Grant decided to strike up a conversation with them. They spoke in a lilting French accent that seemed very proper and civil. The older couple entered their well-appointed stateroom and continued chatting with Grant, who stood at the doorway in the corridor.

Ahmed found the Americans in the passageway and crept close enough to hear their conversation. His blood pooled when he overheard the American ask about two girls. It confirmed his suspicions. They snuck on board to steal his girls. The girls were rightfully his; he bought them.

Ahmed overheard the older gentleman respond, "We haven't seen any young women, have we dear?"

An old woman's voice sounded from within the stateroom. "Why no, there aren't that many women on the ship at all; no young ladies whatsoever."

Grant rubbed his weary forehead and asked, "Have you seen a man with short dreadlocks and blue eyes?"

"My, he sounds marvelous!" the older woman exclaimed. She stepped out to the hallway.

Andrea piped up. "I assure you he isn't. He's taken my daughter—both of our daughters, actually."

"Goodness me!" the old woman responded, holding her hand to her chest. Cosmetic surgery prevented the emotion from registering on her face.

Ahmed drew the silenced pistol from his jacket and slowly raised it until it was only a few inches from the back of Andrea's head. The Americans were so engrossed in their conversation with the old couple they hadn't noticed Ahmed's approach.

The silenced end of the weapon was now less than an inch from Andrea. Ahmed slowed his breathing and slowly squeezed back on the trigger until he felt pressure against his finger.

A stateroom door flew open behind Ahmed. A drunken man staggered out into the corridor. Ahmed tucked his weapon away and walked in the other direction. The American's weren't going to find what they were looking for.

Andrea turned and saw the drunken man lurch across the corridor before slamming into the wall opposite his stateroom. She also caught a glimpse of a man in a white linen jacket, walking away as silent as a ghost. "Where did he come from?"

Ahmed walked up the companionway and returned to his suite. He placed the gun on the counter and pulled his cell phone from his jacket pocket. He flipped it open, stabbed in the number and looked out on the dark gangway below his cabin.

The phone rang once, twice, and on the third ring, a voice answered. "Yes?"

"Jon-Pierre, I am most displeased at present."

"Your delivery is not due until the morning. That was our agreement, yes?" Jon-Pierre said.

"That was the agreement. Two Americans prowling aboard my ship asking questions are most certainly not part of the agreement," Ahmed stated calmly.

Jon-Pierre paused and tried to play coy. "Which two Americans would that be?"

"Do not toy with me, you Haitian mongrel. If the delivery does not occur as scheduled…"

"I have the two packages here with me, and the delivery is on schedule as planned," Jon-Pierre said.

From the stateroom windows, Ahmed watched the Americans walk down the gangway, crestfallen after not finding the two whores. A few hours later, they may have been more fortunate.

"Jon-Pierre, you are to ensure that the Americans do not get in the way of our transaction."

"They are not a concern. As for your delivery, I have personally inspected them, and I believe you will be most pleased," Jon-Pierre said.

"You have not soiled them, have you?"

"I do not mix my work with pleasure," Jon-Pierre lied.

"The delivery will occur at eight in the morning. If I see the Americans, there will be no deal and you will be dead. Then I will take the packages out to sea and sink them with weights tied to their legs," Ahmed said.

"I will deliver them. I have my eye on a couple of new items that would be an addition to your collection," Jon-Pierre added.

"Your life depends on *this* delivery," Ahmed closed the phone and looked out into the darkness, pondering if he should simply kill Jon-Pierre and the two girls because of the unwanted attention they had attracted. Probably so.

Chapter 34

Grant and Andrea backtracked to their rental car and fell inside, weary and spent from their unsuccessful venture. Silence enveloped them for a period, until Andrea shrugged her shoulders and sighed, "I really thought the ship was going to be the key to this mess."

"I know. I can't believe the ship was a complete bust. When I found the document in Jon-Pierre's office I thought this rust bucket was going to be where the girls were taken after we missed them at the sugar mill," Grant said.

"Wait a minute. It may have not been a bust after all. You said it— after the sugar mill."

"What do you mean?" Grant asked.

Andrea turned in her seat and faced him: "They are still going to come here. We got here before Jon-Pierre. He hasn't delivered the girls yet."

"So we wait it out here, and hope they appear?" Grant said.

"It's the only thing that makes sense, Grant. Jon-Pierre said he was going to sell them. You found the shipping information in his office. The Desert-what-ever-it-is wasn't scheduled to leave until tomorrow morning."

Grant paused. "Okay, we'll hang out here and see if anything happens."

Andrea nodded and settled in next to Grant, prepared for a long night's vigil.

Grant started the car and drove through a largely vacant parking lot to an isolated area against the fence, where the stern section of the ship and adjoining dock was in clear view, approximately one hundred yards in the distance.

They grew weary after the first hour, beyond the point of exhaustion. Grant suggested they sleep in shifts, and if one of them saw anything, they would wake the other. The plan was that when the girls or one of Jon-Pierre's vehicles headed toward the ship, Grant and Andrea would climb the fence, run through the shipping containers and be there waiting before the vehicle arrived. If they timed it right, they could do it, while the vehicle made a slow circuitous route to the dock area.

Grant took the first shift and observed nothing come into the ship-yard. The freighter took on a number of containers, lifted by huge cranes onto the rusty ship's deck. It appeared that the freighter had suffered little if any damage from his forklift attack. He'd hoped the tines would have pierced the steel plate near the waterline, but the ship was much sturdier than she seemed. It was well past midnight and he needed a few minutes of sleep. He gently reached over and shook Andrea's arm. She woke with a start.

"It's okay, Andrea, it's okay," he whispered. "Can you take over for a while? I'm about to fall asleep."

Andrea, a little foggy, needed a few seconds to grasp what Grant asked.

"Sure–sure, I'll watch now."

The ship was bathed in light on the dock and she waited. Any movement or activity could lead her to her daughter, so Andrea watched with a hyper-vigilant attention to detail. A few minutes before two, a gray sedan cleared the security gate and headed in the direction of the *Desert Song*.

"Grant, wake up! There's a car on its way to the ship. Was Jon-Pierre's Beemer grey?" Andrea said, shaking Grant out of his slumber.

He was up and out of the car in seconds. He raced to the trunk, grabbed the automatic rifle and slung it over his shoulder. Grant hit the fence and was up and over it quickly. He waited on the other side for Andrea, who cleared the fence nimbly in her adrenaline-fed state.

They raced through the maze of cargo containers and arrived at their observation post, the corner of a container near the ship. Andrea pointed at headlights approaching in their direction.

The grey BMW pulled and parked under the lighting on the dock, adjacent to the ship. Grant and Andrea waited less than fifty feet from the car, ready to run up and snatch the girls before anyone could react. The plan fell into shambles when a front seat passenger exited the BMW with an Uzi and stood guard over the car.

The armed man said something to the driver, and the rear passenger door opened slowly. Grant tensed, hoping for a glimpse of Jena. A short, round man exited the vehicle. The gunman stiffened, then walked backwards, protecting the man from unseen assassins. The dignitary made his way up the gangway. Only then did the gunman return to the car. The BMW backed out of the dock and sped away.

Both Grant and Andrea felt heartache and frustration. Neither said a word to convey their feelings to one another. Grant tossed the rifle on the ground and sat back, his head in his hands. Andrea quietly sobbed as she sat across from Grant.

"I don't know how much more of this I can take," Andrea cried.

Grant could see her eyes filled with tears. "We can't give up," he said in a whisper.

At that moment, another vehicle approached. Both Grant and Andrea turned back and looked at the dock area. A service truck drove to the dock and parked in between an oil tank truck and a forklift. Grant felt a hard object press against his head.

"Don't move, either of you!"

Andrea turned enough to see three policemen, their guns drawn. One held his pistol against Grant's head and the other two pointed their weapons at her. She slowly put her hands up.

The policeman jabbed Grant in the ribs. "You put ya hands up now."

Grant put his hands in the air. As he tried to speak, he received another blow to the ribs with the policeman's gun barrel.

Andrea tried to talk to the policeman closest to her. "Listen, we are looking for…"

"Shut up. I don care wat ya be looking for."

Another policeman picked up the rifle and quickly found the pistols the couple had bought from the fishmonger. "Ya, mon, I be looking for people with this too," the officer said.

Handcuffs went on, and the officers escorted the two Americans to police cars on the other side of the cargo containers. A black hood went over their heads.

Andrea panicked and started screaming and writhing. "Get this off me! I can't breathe!" They shoved her into one of the cars and slammed the door after her, muffling her screams and cries for help.

The hood disoriented Grant, and each time he struggled, he got a sharp crack alongside his head. His captors guided him to a police cruiser and tossed him into the back seat. He leveraged himself up into a sitting position before he heard the driver's door shut.

"Take dem to Lieutenant Washington. He be expecting dem," a voice from outside the vehicle said.

The driver responded, "No problem, mon," and started up the car.

Grant blamed himself for letting the smooth talking lieutenant know about Holly and Jena in the first place. *That vile cop is involved in the sex slave trade and covered up all the kidnappings. He's probably the kidnapper! Who would have better access to locations where young women hang out than a police lieutenant? That bastard, when I get my hands on him, I'll beat him to an inch of his life until he tells me where Jena is, and then I'll finish the job.*

Andrea hyperventilated under her hood and grew dizzy, sprawled out in the back seat. She begged, "Please take off the hood. I can't breathe…please help me."

"Jus be quiet and take a deep breath, lady," the driver threatened.

Andrea feared that she had failed and she would never see Holly again. She cried unseen tears under the hood and whispered, "I'm sorry… I'm so sorry, Holly."

Every curve threw Grant across the back seat. After a time, the vehicle stopped and the driver's door opened. Hands abruptly pulled Grant out of the car and dragged him away. He listened for any clues as to where he was, but heard nothing besides the sound of the ocean. Grant knew they were going to execute them and dump their bodies in Little River.

Instead of feeling a final gun barrel against his head, Grant felt his foot hit a concrete step. Three more steps announced that he had crested a set of stairs and entered a building. Footsteps echoed, and the hood made it difficult to hear much more than the sound of his own labored breathing. Hidden inside a building was no less terrorizing than being out on the river.

Andrea was nearly unconscious from hyperventilating under her hood when the car stopped. Two officers grabbed her arms and dragged her into the building. They placed her in an empty room with a bare bulb that hung down from the ceiling. When the police removed her hood, the dizziness nearly made Andrea fall off from the chair on which they had parked her.

Grant was isolated in another room, and when his hood came off, Lieutenant Washington sat calmly in front of him, his legs casually crossed. Grant rose from the chair, but two officers, one on each side, forcibly pushed him back down.

"Hello, Mr. Turner," the lieutenant said in a carefree manner, a cigarette in one hand.

Chapter 35

The Lieutenant casually puffed on his cigarette, blowing smoke rings into the air. "We have much to talk about. Let's start with why you and the lady were heavily armed at the shipyard at this time of night? And why would I get a phone call telling me where to find you?"

"You know full well that we're looking for our daughters. Remember, you refused to help us?"

"Yes, that's what you say. But explain to me why a housekeeper found Benjamin Cooper's body at your rented bungalow?" Washington said.

"What are you talking about? Who is Cooper?" Grant said.

Lieutenant Washington leaned forward on his chair. "Mr. Turner, we know what kind of man Benjamin Cooper was, but we cannot allow people like you to take the law into their own hands. Tell me the truth. Why did you kill him?"

"I am telling you the truth! I didn't kill anybody," Grant said.

"We have more than enough to send you to trial. In this country, you will find the courts have very little tolerance for this kind of violence. I expected better of you, Mr. Turner." Washington stood up and stretched.

Grant lunged at Washington, but the two officers grabbed Grant and forced him back in the chair.

"Mr. Turner, don't push your luck here. Should I ask you about that damage to the motor vessel in my harbor? That act alone would carry a term of life in prison." He turned and opened the door. He stopped and looked back at Grant. "Perhaps Miss Carson will be more forthcoming." Heading out, he calmly closed the door.

Andrea waited in an identical bare room down the hall. Lieutenant Washington opened the door and greeted her as if she were a long lost friend, "Hello, Miss Carson, it is wonderful to see you again. You look a little tired. Are you feeling well?"

Andrea had trusted this man to be true to his word. He had set them up with the guns from the fishmonger, and now she felt duped and betrayed. "No, I'm not well. I want Holly back!" Andrea, now visibly angry, shook indignantly; her eyes burned holes in the lieutenant.

"I'm sure you do. I'm sure you do," the Lieutenant said dismissively.

"How could you do this? How could you be involved in kidnapping young women?" Andrea said through gritted teeth.

"We need to talk about you, Miss Carson. Why did Benjamin Cooper come to your bungalow, and why did you kill him?" Washington asked while he sat on a chair against the wall.

Andrea's face registered with shock from the information she heard. "What did you say?"

"You, or your companion, Mr. Turner shot, and killed Mr. Cooper. Why? That is the question I need you to answer."

"Who is Benjamin Cooper? No one came to the bungalow."

Miss Carson, the firearm taken from you tonight appears to have quite a bit of residue on the ejection port of the gun. "Did you fire that gun?" Washington said.

Andrea was afraid to answer the question because she shot and killed the awful man at Jon-Pierre's house. *Was that Benjamin Cooper? How was she going to explain that?*

"Miss Carson. Let us back up a bit. Is this the weapon you picked up from Joseph? Did you use it to kill Mr. Cooper?"

Andrea, now visibly afraid, breathed heavily, "Yes… I mean no. I mean yes, we did get the gun from Joseph. But you have to believe that we didn't kill anyone at the bungalow."

"The only thing I know is that Mr. Cooper is dead. The fact that he was a bad man does not matter. Someone must be accountable for his killing. Everything we have here suggests that someone to be you."

Andrea pleaded, "I don't know what you're talking about!"

"Again, what about the gun? Did you fire the weapon or not?"

Andrea stayed silent. The Lieutenant simply nodded. He rose, walked over to the door, and whispered something to a man outside. Within seconds he handed the lieutenant a small tube. The lieutenant approached Andrea and directed two officers to hold her hands.

Andrea fought the two officers, but they were much too strong for her. They quickly pinned her arms to the rough wooden chair.

"What are you doing?" she shouted.

"This small swab that I'm rubbing on your hands will tell me if you have nitrates from gunpowder residue on your hands after firing that gun."

He quickly swabbed her hands, placed the swab into the tube and shook it in a vigorous fashion. The swab turned blue. He held it out to Andrea.

"I don't care about that damn gun. I want my daughter. Are you the one responsible for taking her? You bastard! How could you?"

Ignoring her outrage, he said, "Let me change my question. When did you fire the gun, Miss Carson?"

Andrea looked across the room at the arrogant Lieutenant, she felt absolutely certain that he already knew about the shooting. "I want my daughter."

"Nothing, huh?" Washington held his large hands up.

She felt pinned against an immovable wall that separated her from Holly. Andrea needed a way around that obstacle. She would sacrifice her life for her daughter, if that's what it took. Andrea decided to give this man what he wanted, if it would give any chance to help Holly.

"I saw a man try to stab Grant," she sighed.

"When was this?" Washington probed.

"It was earlier today. A man hit Grant with a pipe and tried to stab him.

The lieutenant leaned back on the chair lifting up the front legs. "You say this man attempted to stab Mr. Turner? So why didn't he?"

Andrea looked down at her feet, avoiding eye contact with the lieutenant. She hadn't wanted to say the words. She murmured, "Because— I shot him."

Taking three photographs from his jacket breast pocket, the lieutenant walked over to Andrea. "Tell me if any of these men look familiar to you."

Andrea hesitantly took the photos, slowly looking over the first one. She had never seen the man before. The second man looked similar to the first but didn't ring any bells. Then she flipped to the last photo. The face dripped with evil and contempt. It was Jon-Pierre's gunman, the man she had killed.

Washington noticed her delay on the last picture. "Something there, Miss Carson?"

"This one had my daughter in a fishing boat this morning," she said while holding up the photo to Washington.

"Interesting. That is Benjamin Cooper. Is this the man you shot?"

"Yes, but not at the bungalow. We left him in at Jon-Pierre's home." Andrea braced for the worst.

"So you know about Jon-Pierre? I wish you hadn't gone there," Washington said.

Washington said nothing more, but simply stared at Andrea for a full minute before he got up and left the interrogation room.

Chapter 36

Click. The gun was empty. Jon-Pierre replaced the magazine in his pistol after the simulated execution. Holly fell back against the cell wall, all resistance broken. Jon-Pierre grew more restless and agitated by the second. He paced the corridor in front of the jail cells, contemplating the fates of Jena and Holly with each pass. The two captives were not as pristine as Jon-Pierre had hoped.

After a cold spray shower with a fire hose, he tossed clean clothes into the cell and ordered the girls to change. Jon-Pierre watched intently as Holly and Jena shed their soiled clothing and changed. He cared little about their nakedness, but their humiliation aroused him.

He stopped in mid-stride when his cell phone rang. He pulled the phone open, "Yes?"

On the other end, Ahmed said, "It is time. That is, if you can assure me that the meddling Americans will not pose a problem for you."

"I made sure they will not bother us. They are in police custody following an anonoymous call linking them to a murder. They are no longer an issue," Jon-Pierre said.

"I hope you are correct. When will you be here for the delivery?"

"I can be there in twenty minutes. I know you will be pleased. I have done well with my selection this time," Jon-Pierre said to a dead phone line.

"It is nearly time to go. Then I will be done with you," Jon-Pierre announced through the cell bars.

Jena watched the evil man walk out the door, then turned to Holly. "How are you feeling? You look a little brighter."

Holly nodded, "My head is pounding … but I can stand up without falling down, so I guess that's an improvement."

Jena whispered, "We are only going to have one chance to get free, and that is when they move us from this cell to a car or something. Can you run?"

"If I have to, I will. I don't know how long or how straight, but I'll run," Holly said.

"Act like you need me to hold you up. We might be able to catch them off guard."

Holly nodded her head and looked at her friend. "If you have a chance to get free, just go. Don't wait for me, Jena. I mean it."

The main door to the corridor opened, and the phony Sergeant Collins came to the cell front with an armload of objects. He opened the cell door, put a box on the floor, and shoved it to the center with his boot. He stepped out, relocked the cell door and instructed them, "Get cleaned up. There is toothpaste, makeup, a brush for your nasty hair and perfume to hide your stink. You will use all of the items. You have five minutes."

"I would really like to brush my teeth," Jena said to Holly.

Jena looked in the box and pulled out a worn stub of a toothbrush, stained with brown-crusted fibers. "I don't need to brush them that much." She threw the disgusting toothbrush back into the box, put a daub of toothpaste from the tube onto her finger and did the best she could. It did make her feel a little cleaner.

Holly joined in, finger brushing her teeth with care on the right side of her mouth where the bruises had begun to show. As she slowly guided the brush through her hair, dried blood flaked out from the wounds on her scalp. From a distance, the girl's hair hid the damage beneath.

Jena lifted a collection of half-used jars and small dried pots of makeup out of the box, "Oh, this is just nasty. There is no way I'm using this gross crap." She tossed the makeup containers back in the box.

"How many women have used this before us?" Holly said.

Jena pushed the box away as she realized that the cosmetics, brush and personal items belonged to others kept by this man—spirits of the others before them, collected like carnival prizes by the blue-eyed lunatic.

"Time's up for you," Jon-Pierre said as he entered the corridor accompanied by the fake Sergeant Collins. The Haitian keyed the lock on the cell door and swung it open.

The Sergeant Collins imposter, who had changed out of the stolen police uniform into black pants and shirt, approached the cell and pointed at Jena. "You. Come here now."

Jena didn't move.

"Listen to me. Don't make me come in there and get you. Come over here now!"

Jena slowly walked to where Collins directed. When she reached the cell door, Collins told her to turn around. She turned, and two sets of hands grabbed her. One placed her in handcuffs and the second attached leg restraints around each ankle. The leg restraints made certain that she couldn't take a full stride, dashing any hope of running. Fully restrained, Jena was pushed back into the cell.

Collins repeated the process with Holly. Jon-Pierre grabbed Holly while Collins took Jena by the arm, and they pulled the two hobbled girls to a windowless van that waited outside. Both girls went into the back of the van and landed hard on the bare metal surface. The phony Sergeant Collins sat in the back with the girls and held the fifty-thousand volt stun gun in his hand.

The van took off with a lurch, and Jena slid against the van's side. "Where are we going?" she asked.

Collins looked back at her and said nothing, weaving with the motion of the van.

"You probably don't know where we are going, do you?" Holly said, hoping for a reaction from Collins.

He looked away from her and did not respond.

Jena then caught on to what Holly was up to. "Yeah--you're right, he doesn't know where we're going; he's too low on the food chain."

"Shut up! Both of you!" the man said.

"I think you struck a nerve there, Jena. That's why he is riding back here with us. The boss can't trust him."

Jon-Pierre turned around in the driver's seat. "Be quiet, you miserable whore. All you need concern yourself with is that you are going to a place where you will be used like a paper towel and thrown away when you are worn out."

The girls grew silent. An unpleasant future awaited them. The unknown monsters and perverts who lurked in the hours and days ahead nibbled at their souls. Holly and Jena knew that every passing minute brought them closer to their fate. Inevitable and irreversible—their lives had ended when this man took them. Fear, disgust and even hope left them, replaced by numbness. Their only escape from the hell that awaited them was death. They didn't know how or when they would die, but die they would.

Chapter 37

Ahmed answered his cell phone on the first ring. "You are here, yes?"

"Your two packages await," Jon-Pierre confirmed.

Ahmed pushed the curtain aside at his cabin window and saw the familiar white van under the hot-white glare of the dock spotlights. Beyond the circle of light, Ahmed wondered if the Americans watched and waited. He also wondered if Interpol had finally decided to make a move against him. Let the Haitian take the risk. "Bring them up to my cabin, and we shall finish our business."

"We always conclude our transaction out here in the van," Jon-Pierre insisted.

"That was before you allowed the Americans to find my ship. I find it very unusual that they knew where and when my ship is leaving. For all I know they are out there now."

"I told you where they are!" Jon-Pierre said.

"Bring the girls to my cabin, or go away," Ahmed replied, and ended the call.

Jon-Pierre threw the phone against the dash, breaking it into pieces. "Get them ready," the Haitian ordered Collins.

The fake Sergeant Collins applied a short length of duct tape on each girl's mouth and clipped a ten-foot length of chain to her leg restraints. He wrapped the ends of the chains around his hands as if they were leashes for unruly dogs.

As Jon-Pierre opened the rear van door, the bright light from the dock startled the two girls. Their faces held fear and despondence beyond imagination. One at a time, Jon-Pierre pulled them from the van. Jena was first, and when he turned to remove Holly, Jena hobbled away in choppy quick steps as fast as she could. Jon-Pierre watched her futile escape attempt for a few seconds, until Collins pulled sharply up on the chain wrapped around his hand.

"Back here--now please," he said, like an animal trainer.

The force of the chain pulled Jena's legs out from under her, and she landed hard. With the handcuffs behind her back, she was unable to break her fall. She rolled slightly and took the blow on her shoulder. She struggled to her feet and walked back to Jon-Pierre.

"Up the gangway, if you please," Jon-Pierre directed the girls.

Jena looked around for someone—anyone. A crewmember or a passenger she could call upon for help. There was no one. The girls and their leash-holding masters made their way to Ahmed's cabin door.

Ahmed stood at the door waiting. He wore a sapphire blue silk robe over white-silk pajamas. "Time to meet your new owner," Jon-Pierre said to the girls as he prodded them through the door.

Ahmed watched the girls with a keen eye on his investments as they walked to the center of the room. He did not take his gaze off them when he closed and bolted the cabin door. He swaggered over to the girls and stood in front of them, his hands behind his back. He stepped forward and sharply ripped the tape from their mouths. "We shouldn't need this anymore."

Both Jena and Holly stood with their heads hung down, abject failure etched on their faces. Ahmed grabbed Jena's chin and lifted it up as he surveyed her face. Jena pulled her head away, repulsed by the man's touch.

Ahmed quickly jerked her back by the hair. "You need to be broken, young one. I am the one to do just that." He slapped her away and turned to Holly.

Holly trembled when he lifted her chin. She wept loudly and her knees buckled when Ahmed inspected her. Jon-Pierre caught her and propped her up.

Ahmed walked around the girls in a large circle, as if he were assessing the purchase of a new car. As he began a second circle he said to Jon-Pierre, "Un-cuff them. I need to inspect the merchandise more closely."

Jon-Pierre did as his buyer requested and removed the handcuffs from both girls. Jena rubbed her wrists where the handcuffs had opened up the lacerations once more. Holly stood in place and made no effort to move.

Ahmed approached Jena, so close that his cigarette-tainted breath washed over her. He leered at her, and she felt nauseated by his presence. Without warning, he grabbed Jena and fondled her. Jena fought madly, but the man was quick and incredibly strong. He released her and laughed; she was a plaything. Jena spit at him. He swiftly backhanded her and knocked her off her feet.

Ahmed issued a disgusting laugh again. "I think we will develop an understanding, my dear."

Holly looked back at Jena, clearly frightened for the both of them, caught in a living nightmare.

Ahmed stood in front of Holly, who tensed at his approach. She knew he was going to touch her as he had Jena. She cringed, but the creep didn't touch her. She opened her eyes a fraction and saw a scowl on the man's face.

He stepped close and rubbed his hand across Holly's forehead—not I a gentle fashion, but more in the way a butcher would inspect livestock. The laceration from her tumble down the cliff side was tender to his touch. He grabbed a handful of hair and noticed flakes of dried blood. His rough handling found the lumps from her fall and a couple of tender spots she didn't even know she had.

Ahmed stepped back and looked at Jon-Pierre. "We have a problem here, my friend."

Jon-Pierre became excited. "What do you mean? We had a deal for two girls, and here they are. Don't try to change the terms of the deal."

Ahmed retreated to one of the overstuffed chairs that adorned his cabin and lay back. He looked down his nose at the two girls and the Haitian.

"Maybe we have been doing business too long. Your selections have been inconsistent as of late. I need to find a better source of merchandise," the Syrian said.

"Give me my fee and I'll be on my way. We can renegotiate next time around," Jon-Pierre responded, in hasty effort to complete the deal.

"I will take this one," Ahmed said, pointing at Jena, who sat on the floor where she had fallen.

"I've got two here as you requested!"

Ahmed rose from the chair and shoved Holly at Jon-Pierre. "This one is damaged. She is unfit and cannot be sold to my friends. I will take one only. I have already paid you sixty-thousand, so our business here is done."

"I have put in considerable work on keeping these two for you. I will be compensated," Jon-Pierre said.

Ahmed walked to the bar, poured a glass of ice water into a crystal glass, and said, "Apparently you didn't work hard enough. You brought me damaged goods." Before Jon-Pierre could protest further, Ahmed pulled a pistol from the bar and pointed it at the Haitian. "Leave! Now! Don't bother me again."

Jon-Pierre grabbed Holly and used her as a shield while he backed to the door. As he reached to unbolt the door, Holly tried to pull from his grip.

"Jena. No. Help me!" Holly cried.

Jena got up from the floor and ran as quickly as her hobbled legs allowed. She hugged Holly around her waist and tried to pull her away from Jon-Pierre.

"Please don't take her away!"

Holly held onto her friend as tightly as she could, yet she felt herself getting tugged away by Jon-Pierre's overwhelming strength. She shook violently as he lifted her up off her feet. She screamed, and Jon-Pierre slapped the tape back on her face. Jon-Pierre backed out the cabin door with Holly between him and Ahmed's gun barrel.

Holly stiffened as Jon-Pierre backed her away from the open doorway; his touch hinted at the untold horrors that awaited her for ruining his deal.

Jena, seeing the panic in Holly's face, lunged for the door. Ahmed grabbed the leash chain that connected to her legs and yanked it toward him. Jena spilled to the floor and watched her friend disappear into the shadowed passageway. She fought the strong premonition that they would never see one another again in this lifetime.

"No, you don't, young lady," Ahmed said, his weapon now pointed at her. "I think it is time we begin your training."

Chapter 38

Hours seemed like days, alone in a humid, dank police interrogation room. Grant knew that every second he sat here put him further behind and could mean the difference in his daughter's life or death. She had depended on him, and he had failed her. He couldn't save his wife from the drunk driver, and now another man held Jena's life in his grip. He felt powerless.

Lieutenant Washington pushed the door open and sat down again. He sighed and looked at Grant through tired, hooded eyes.

"You have had a busy day, Mr. Turner. Miss Carson told us a tale of chasing a fishing boat that held your daughters, breaking and entering a private estate, and the murder of Benjamin Cooper."

"I keep telling you I don't know any Benjamin Cooper," Grant said, exhaustion evident in his voice.

"Benjamin Cooper is a local thug who, for some reason that I hope you will tell me, tried to stab you," Washington said.

"He was trying to kill me, and Andrea saved my life."

"Mr. Turner, ridding the world of people like Benjamin Cooper is a noble undertaking. He won't be missed by anyone."

"So are we free to go?" Grant asked.

"In a manner of speaking, yes. When you were arrested, we impounded a few firearms, and you were in possession of an automatic rifle, an H&K, I believe."

"That belonged to Cooper," Grant said.

Washington stood up. "Does not matter, Mr. Turner. There are some things the politicians in our government take very seriously. This year is an election year, and you seem to be their cause of the day. As I said, no one will miss Cooper, but the media here has painted this as an American crime spree. Now let's go talk to Miss Carson, shall we?"

Grant followed the lieutenant to the interrogation room next door. When the door opened, a dejected and visibly worried Andrea lifted her head. Seeing Grant, she rushed to meet him. He embraced her and held her close. Grant felt her tremble.

"I'm so sorry. I didn't know what to do." Fearing she had betrayed Grant, she slumped against him.

"Don't worry. It's all right," he said, hugging her close.

Washington cleared his throat, and both Grant and Andrea turned toward him. "We need to talk about what happens next. Please sit down."

The lieutenant took a chair by the door and gestured toward chairs opposite him. "Let me start out by telling you that no charges will be filed in the death of Benjamin Cooper, or possession of firearms."

Instantly, Andrea exhaled and relief washed over her. She did not relish the thought of time in a Jamaican prison. She waited for the other shoe to drop.

Grant asked, "When can we go? We need to get back on track looking for our girls." He started to get up but stopped at the sound of Washington's powerful voice.

"Mr. Turner, neither of you will be charged for the violent crimes. However, as I mentioned to you, the politicians in our government want to portray this as, I must admit they have a point, as a crime spree by non-Jamaicans."

"What do you mean? How is the whim of some fat-cat political hack going to affect us?" Grant asked.

Washington took a deep breath, "Once again, this island thrives on tourist income. Cash-laden tourists are reluctant to come to the island if crime runs rampant. You, my friends, are American, Cooper was Haitian, as is Jon-Pierre Baptiste. Jamaican people were not involved in this incident of terror."

Andrea softly asked, "What does that mean for us, Lieutenant?"

"It means, Miss Carson, that you and Mr. Turner have been deemed as persona non grata here on the island. You will be escorted to the airport this morning and put on the first flight out of Jamaica. I'm sorry."

Grant stood up. "You can't be serious! We can't leave yet; we have to find our daughters!"

At the same instant, Andrea yelled, "I'm not leaving without Holly! You know she's here and you are covering for Baptiste. You are no better than him." She sank back in the chair and put her face in her hands.

Grant came within inches of the lieutenant's face. "We won't be pushed off the island so some politician gets a few more dollars in his pocket. They don't want bad press? Wait till we get to the media. This island will dry up when we're done!"

"I'm very sorry. I must take you to the airport first thing in the morning. You will be here until then. Do you need anything, perhaps some food or coffee?" Washington obliged.

"You don't have any children, do you Lieutenant?" Andrea asked, her head still hidden in her hands.

Washington paused and looked at Andrea. "I used to have a daughter. She was raped and murdered last year. She was twelve years old."

Andrea looked up sharply, "Then you understand what we have to do."

"I understand, but there are some things that I cannot do for you," he said softly. He walked out, closed the door behind him, and threw the latch to secure the room.

Chapter 39

Jon-Pierre tossed Holly into the rear of the van where the Sergeant Collins impersonator waited. The Haitian slammed the door closed and jumped back into the driver's seat. He pulled the van's transmission into reverse and backed off the dock. Looking over his shoulder, his eyes flared at Holly.

"You have cost me. I will get my money's worth out of you. You will beg me to kill you before I am done."

Holly closed her eyes tight against the evil that poured from Jon-Pierre. The shock and trauma began to shut her body down, and she knew she was going to die.

Jon-Pierre pounded hard on the steering wheel and began talking to himself.

"Cheat me? Who does he think he is? That arrogant bastard—I'll teach him a lesson." Jon-Pierre pulled a cloned cell phone from the console of the van and quickly dialed a number.

"Tell me, is the Arab's ship leaving on schedule?" he said.

He paused, "Are you sure? When did he make that arrangement? I have a job for you."

Jon-Pierre tossed the cell phone in the seat and made a sharp curve onto a deeply rutted road. The uneven surface shook the van's old frame and bounced the occupants hard against the steel walls.

Holly slid forward as the van came to a skidded to a stop. Jon-Pierre opened his door and was out before the vehicle had fully stopped. He ran to the back of the van, threw open the rear door and grabbed Holly by the legs. He pulled her out of the van feet first and smacked her head on the packed dirt road surface when she fell from the vehicle. Stunned by the blow, she lapsed into semi-consciousness. Jon-Pierre held the length of chain that connected the leg restraints and dragged her across the roadway and up a wooded path. Holly's head bounced off thick, gnarled roots that snaked through the jungle floor. Clumps of her hair ripped away, stuck in the overgrown vegetation. She opened her eyes and saw the dark green canopy passing above.

Collins left with the van, a wordless transition that seemed all too practiced. Jon-Pierre reached the steps of a dark, weathered cabin, dragging Holly behind him, her head banging off each step to the door. Her head wounds had re-opened from the rough treatment. Dazed and limp, she couldn't have resisted even if she weren't restrained.

Jon-Pierre unlocked the door and pulled Holly into the dark room. She heard the door close and the terminal sound of a lock hasp. That click and ratchet was an omen, the sound of hopelessness. He dropped her in the center of a rustic cabin with a few pieces of mismatched furniture.

"I regret that we have less time together than I had hoped. I must leave in a few hours to catch up with the Arab. I'm sorry to tell you that your friend will not survive."

"Leave her alone."

Jon-Pierre grabbed her by the throat.

"Don't touch me, you pervert!"

"You need a change of attitude. Before you die you will learn respect."

Jon-Pierre released his grip on her neck and took hold of Holly's legs. He pulled her across the rough timber floor to a wooden rail that looked like a horse hitching post. Lifting one leg at a time, he secured heavy leather straps around her ankles to the heavy wooden cross member. The post was high enough that Holly's body lifted off the ground, only her head and shoulders scraped against the cabin floor.

His captive secured, Jon-Pierre removed Holly's shoes and socks. Without so much as a sound, he selected a long thin section of dried sugar cane from a bin next to the post. He raised it and paused to make certain that Holly saw him before he whipped down on the bottoms of Holly's bare feet. The jungle swallowed Holly's desperate screams.

Chapter 40

Sleep was out of the question. If a locked jail interrogation room, with its hard, dirty concrete floors, wasn't bad enough, the paralyzing reality that they had let the girls down, short-circuited their brains and made certain that Grant and Andrea stayed restless. The official order removing them from the island closed the official book on their hope of ever seeing Holly and Jena again.

Andrea sat on the floor, her head on her knees. "I'm to blame for this. I shot that creep, and I told Washington that I did it. It's my fault we didn't find the girls."

Grant rose from his chair and made his way to the wall next to Andrea. He sat next to her and put his arm around the woman's quivering shoulder. "Stop. You are not at fault here. If you hadn't shot him, I wouldn't be here, remember? So thank you Andrea, thank you for saving my life."

She didn't say anything back; she rocked back and forth gently. Grant tightened his grip around her, and she continued to rock. After a few long, silent minutes, Andrea propped her head up on one arm. "They are going to let us out of here, aren't they? He said that I was not going to be charged for the death of the man I shot, right? So we will get out of here soon and figure out where the girls are, right?"

Grant took his arm away and thought how to frame his response. He trusted nothing that came out of Washington's mouth, and he was only sure of one thing—he was going to find the girls.

"Whenever they let us out, we are not giving up. If they kick us off the island, we'll come back and they can deport us a million times, but we won't stop until we get them back with us," he said.

"Thank you for not being mad at me for getting us in here," Andrea replied.

"Are you kidding? What you did took a lot of courage, and not many people could have done it. I'm glad it was you with me and not someone else."

"I keep seeing him, all sprawled out, bleeding, even when I close my eyes. It won't go away," she said.

Grant put his arm back around her shoulder. "It will take time. We can deal with it together. I won't leave."

She raised her red eyes to his eyes. "For how long?"

"For as long as it takes. You'll have trouble getting rid of me."

She leaned against him, both sitting on the floor as daybreak cast a yellow tint on the wall opposite from where they sat.

A square steel plate slid open on the door, and Lieutenant Washington's face appeared through the small rectangular window. The door unlocked, and the lieutenant entered the stale interrogation room.

"Good morning. I have some coffee and fresh hot muffins," Washington announced.

The lieutenant placed a white pastry bag on the interrogation table and balanced two cups of coffee in Styrofoam cups. Crouching down in front of Grant and Andrea, he extended the cups to them.

They both took the coffee from Washington, steam wafting through the vented lids. Andrea held the cup and lost herself in the steamy tendrils that formed and disappeared. Disappeared like hope and dreams.

Grant folded back the plastic flap and took a sip. He nodded at the Lieutenant, "This is good. Thanks."

"You are quite welcome. Here," Washington said, as he handed the pastry bag to Grant. The aroma of the banana-nut muffins in the bag wafted over to Andrea. She reached in the bag and pulled out a huge, warm muffin. She broke the muffin in half and placed a napkin on her lap.

She pulled off a chunk of muffin and popped it in her mouth. She chewed and swallowed. "When are you letting us out of here?"

"Ah, yes. I am here to personally escort you to the airport. Your plane leaves within the hour," Lieutenant Washington said, thrusting his hands into the pants of an expensive, freshly pressed tan suit.

Grant asked in between nibbles, "Can't we to go back to Negril and collect our things from the bungalow? We need to turn in our rental car. We can't possibly leave in an hour. Lieutenant, Holly and Jena are here. We're close. You have to let us find them."

Andrea looked at the Lieutenant and tried to make her case one last time. "Please—I beg you. Let us find them."

"As I told you last night, the Ministry of Justice ordered you out of the country. There is no debate in the matter. As for your belongings, my men have retrieved them from your bungalow and closed your account with the property manager. The rental car has also been turned in for you."

Washington walked toward the door. As he reached the threshold, he turned and looked over his shoulder at the two Americans on the floor. "I'm sorry that it ends this way. I will continue to look for your daughters. This I promise you." Then he walked out the door.

Approximately ten minutes later, a smallish uniformed policeman came to the door and knocked politely. "Excuse me. It is time to depart for the airport. If you would kindly follow me, please."

Grant and Andrea followed the small policeman out the front door of the police station into the bright warm morning sun.

Washington sat in the front seat of the SUV waiting for them. The rear side doors of the large white vehicle were open, awaiting Grant and Andrea. They followed the policeman to the door and climbed in the rear passenger seat. Andrea slid across the wide bench seat, followed by

Grant. Behind them, their luggage, collected from the bungalow, sat in a heap. The baggage reflected failure and finality.

The small policeman closed the door for Grant and Andrea, ran around to the driver's side and jumped behind the wheel. The SUV took off toward the Montego Bay airport, escorted by a police car.

Andrea looked at the deep-green hills and cinderblock homes scattered on the hillside. A number of unfinished block structures dotted the landscape. Each building haunted her as a potential location left unsearched.

Grant felt a shared grief in her silence. He gave her hand a slight squeeze.

The SUV pulled up along the curb in front of the Sangster International Airport terminal, where the driver removed the luggage and sat the bags out on the sidewalk. Washington opened the rear passenger door and allowed Grant out. Grant helped Andrea down from the SUV, and they both stood solemnly in front of the terminal building.

Washington stood in front of the couple, thrust one hand in his jacket, and with an official flair took their tickets from his breast pocket and handed them to Grant. He looked from one to the other, and then said, "As I have explained to you, the Ministry of Justice has cancelled your visitation permit. They have ordered you to leave the island immediately."

Andrea blurted out, "You don't care about our daughters; you only care about what this might do to the tourist trade. I couldn't give a crap about that. I want my Holly back!"

The lieutenant accepted the barrage, then looked directly at Andrea. "You need to listen to me very carefully. There is no one who can sympathize with your plight more than I."

Andrea, catching the sharpness in his voice, responded with a similar edge. "Sympathy? What do you know about it?"

Washington took a deep breath. "These doors are as far as I go. I was ordered to take you to the airport. I and have fulfilled by responsibility. You are ordered by the Ministry to take your bags and tickets to the security checkpoint and then off to the gate. I have done all that is required by the Ministry of Justice. If for *some reason you need to leave the terminal*, the doors to the far left will bring you out to the baggage claim and ground transportation. I regret that I cannot see that door from here. Goodbye, Miss Carson, Mr. Turner."

Grant looked at Andrea, unsure he believed what he heard from the Lieutenant. He grabbed her hand, and they walked through the shaded automatic doors. They turned in time to see the SUV pull away from the curb. Grant swore he caught a slight smile on Washington's face.

Andrea expected swarms of police to escort them to the gate. She looked around, her head on a swivel. She saw nothing out of place among the tourists and airport workers.

"What's going on, Grant? We went from public enemies number one and two, to this?"

Grant led them from in front of the automatic door and shook his head, "I wouldn't have believed it in a hundred years." He paused. "I pegged Washington as either one of the bad guys, or a bureaucrat at best. I don't know why, but he has given us another chance at finding the girls. We need to make the best of it."

Chapter 41

Arriving tourists crowded around the airport baggage carousels, spitting out over-sized luggage, golf clubs and roller bags for pickup. As soon as a passenger touched a bag, uniformed porters, armed with wheeled carts, swooped in and spirited the traveler and their possessions on toward the resort lounges.

In the midst of this organized chaos, Grant's cell phone rang. He opened it, and before he said a word, a familiar voice sounded in his ear.

"Mr. Turner? We have some unfinished business, I believe," Jon-Pierre said.

"We want our girls. Where are you?" Grant said loud enough that passersby looked in his direction.

"All in good time. All in good time. Your deadline for the wire transfer is quickly approaching. Notice I said *dead* line Mr. Turner."

"We have the funds arranged for the wire transfer as you instructed. When the girls are safe and with us, then we'll transfer the money to your account."

"No, Mr. Turner, you will wire the money, and only then I will deliver the girls," Jon-Pierre said.

Andrea placed an ear close to the cell phone and overheard Jon-Pierre's demand. She tugged on Grant's arm, shook her head, and mouthed, "No."

Grant nodded his agreement. "We will exchange the money and the girls at the same time."

"Agreed. The wire transaction will occur in my presence, and when verified, I will release the girls to you. I will call you with instructions on where we shall meet," Jon Pierre said, and then disconnected the call.

Grant looked at the phone and tensed. "This guy is playing it very, very close. He wants to control the time and place."

"Are we sure he even has the girls? I mean, he was supposed to sell them to someone on that ship," Andrea said.

"I don't think we can afford to ignore him. We know they were in his barn and we saw them in that fishing boat."

"We can cover both ends if we watch the ship while we wait for Jon-Pierre's call," Andrea said.

"Wait a minute, I have an idea," Grant said, and he trotted over to a rental car counter. He came back a minute later: "They'll keep our bags behind the counter. I gave them a few dollars, and they were cool with it."

"We can't get arrested hanging out on the docks again," Andrea said.

"Agreed, but first let's figure out how to get to the harbor. I'm sure the Ministry of Justice is watching the rental car transactions, and our names will pop up if we try to get a car."

Once out onto the curb, an answer rolled up in front of them. A large man, stiff and ancient, got out of his multi-color taxi and asked, "Taxi, Miss?"

Andrea said yes, and the driver held open the door of his worn but very clean vehicle for his passengers.

Grant leaned up to the driver and asked, "Would you take us to the cruise line terminal in the harbor?"

The old man looked suspiciously in the rear view at Grant. "You have no luggage?"

"No, it seems the airline lost our bags. They are supposed to deliver them to the ship. I hope they get there before the cruise leaves."

The driver, satisfied with Grant's answer, put the car in drive and flew away from the curb. If they had not been preoccupied with their girls, the taxi trip would have scared Grant and Andrea to death. Two close calls and three run stop lights later, they pulled into the cruise ship terminal. Grant paid the man and added him a generous tip for getting them there safely.

The cruise ships from last night buzzed with activity in the daylight. Passengers milled all about, and scores of the ships' staff tried to gather all the passengers and board them. A frantic energy level pulsed around the huge ships as they prepared for their next ports of call.

The fence and security gate they had encountered last night separated the cargo docks from the cruise liners, and the *Desert Song* was further down the dock, out of sight.

"We can't risk a run for the fence in the daylight," Grant said.

"This is the only access road to the ship, right?" she asked.

Grant nodded.

"Why don't we watch the traffic coming in? This close, we can see the girls when Jon-Pierre delivers them to the ship."

They found a spot on a grassy median strip, ten feet from the roadway, from which they could watch the traffic. Incoming vehicles passed, and the faces of delivery drivers, passengers and dockworkers came into view.

Andrea sat, hugged her knees and watched the passing traffic like a hawk searching for a rodent. Each car held potential and hope. Each one provided only despair as time ran down.

Chapter 42

Seated at a teak and ebony inlaid dining table, Ahmed picked at a breakfast of eggs Benedict and sipped decaffeinated cinnamon-anise tea. The morning edition of the *London Financial Times* sat unopened on his breakfast tray. The business with the Haitian and the Americans had ruined his appetite. He grew weary of these business trips, and a night's rest in his own bed in Damascus was a precious gift from Allah.

While he pondered the best way to settle his business with Jon-Pierre Baptiste, the breakfast grew cold. He rose from his ornate table, took the plate across the room and unlocked the holding room. Inside, Jena sat against the far wall, with her legs chained to a thick metal ring mounted in the floor. Ahmed took the plate of breakfast leftovers and dumped them on the bare floor near Jena's feet.

"Time for you to eat, my little one," he said.

With less emotion than most would have for an animal, Ahmed closed the door and locked it securely. He returned to his tea and newspaper. He took a long sip of the tea and within a few minutes had read all sections of the paper that required his attention.

He reached to the side of the desk, picked up a large black phone and rang the ship's bridge. "Is the jet ready?"

Ahmed waited while the ship's first officer checked. When he was told that a Russian couple had booked the plane for an excursion to Cuba, he ordered the sightseeing trip cancelled. "I require use of the plane and crew. Offer my apologies to the Russians. Have it fueled and ready in two hours," Ahmed ordered.

Ahmed preferred a slow ocean voyage back to the Middle East, but the arrest of the two Americans last night complicated matters. They caused too much unwanted attention to the ship and his cargo. Attention too often came in the form of an Interpol inspection. That would be an inconvenience.

Ahmed stuffed a few essential items into two small duffle bags. The crew would ensure that rest of his belongings went untouched until he retrieved them later.

He finished packing and placed the bags by the door. He unlocked the holding room and walked to the chain on Jena's legs, unhooking it from the ring on the floor.

"Do not test me, for if you do, I will kill you with not so much as a second thought. Do we have an understanding?"

Jena looked at him and knew this was no idle threat. She nodded.

"Good," he said, and he tossed a set of fresh clothes in to her. "We are going on a little trip. Get changed." He closed and locked the holding room.

Jena quickly changed into the designer jeans and tee shirt. She stood up to work the kinks out of her knotted muscles. The fresh clothes felt good against her skin, until she realized where they came from. She felt dirty and wanted to tear them off. She grabbed the shirt and started to pull it over her head when her eye caught a dark spot on the shirt Jon-Pierre had given her. Blood. Was this Holly's blood?

Ahmed unlocked the door and entered the holding room with Jena. He looked her up and down. "That looks much better, my dear. We need to leave now. We are leaving this island, and I'm taking you to a much more pleasant location. For me, that is. I miss the warm, dry Mediterranean winds."

He held a small digital camera and took aim at Jena. "Please don't frown, it will detract from the bids we receive." He took several shots and put the camera in his pocket.

Jena got nauseous while he took her picture, certain it would go in a trophy album somewhere. *Don't frown, he says? What? I'm supposed to be happy that I've been kidnapped and sold to some pervert?*

He placed plastic zip ties around her wrists, but allowed them to remain in front. "I will allow your feet to remain untied as long as you behave yourself," Ahmed warned, then guided her from the holding room.

Once out of the holding room, Jena jerked away and broke free from his strong grasp. Ahmed issued a sharp blow to her kidney. Jena gasped and dropped to one knee. She had never felt pain that intense before.

He pulled her up from the floor and whispered, "Do not attempt to escape from me. I know many ways to cause you great pain without diminishing your monetary value to me. Do I make myself clear?"

Jena got a shallow breath as the sharp spasm diminished. She nodded her head, acknowledging his not so subtle warning. She straightened up as best she could with the intense muscle spasms.

"The pain will subside in about thirty minutes. Don't be alarmed if you have blood in your urine."

He walked her out onto the railing of the ship, where she caught the first wisp of fresh air in many hours. Even though the air was heavy with diesel fuel, she relished the cool sensation on her face. Jena walked slowly, trying to postpone the future.

Sensing her slow pace, Ahmed pulled her arm and propelled her down the companionway to the main deck. A small knot of deckhands secured cargo and hatch covers. Ahmed noticed that Jena's attention had honed in on the group of men.

Less than a syllable had squeaked from her lips when Ahmed's strong hand closed around the back of her neck. He squeezed the muscles and nerve endings, and it stopped her cry immediately. Her eyes went wide as the pain almost made her pass out. It would not have mattered if the deckhands heard her plea for help. She knew they were in Ahmed's employ, and from their reaction, they had seen him rough up young women many times.

Ahmed pushed Jena to the dock below the gangway, where a silver BMW sedan waited. An armed man opened the rear door, and Ahmed pushed Jena in the car. Once she was inside, Ahmed slid into the seat next to her. Jena attempted to open the rear door with her zip-tied hands. She managed to grab the lever, but it would not budge. She pulled and pulled with all of her strength, and then heard Ahmed's voice in her ear. "You think this is the first time I have ever done this? The door cannot be opened from the inside."

Jena slumped in the leather seat of the sedan and watched the armed man get behind the wheel. A throaty sound emitted from the BMW as the high-powered engine turned over and left the dock area. She looked over her shoulder and saw the ship recede in the distance.

The car slowed at the security booth, where a tall, skinny man with headphones stepped out onto the road. The pricey sedan drove up, and the man pushed a button, lifting the gate. Whoever owned this car was rich and made more money in a day than the man with the headphones did all year.

Jena watched the whole exchange happen without the silver BMW even coming to a stop. The driver signaled thanks to the smiling, skinny man in the guard uniform. The guard never saw her in the back seat, her bound hands raised in a plea for help.

Chapter 43

A deep throaty sound caught Andrea's attention. A silver BMW came from the direction of the cargo ships to the security gate. Even though this was a car leaving the dock, something about the flashy BMW drew her attention. It looked like the car at the dock late last night, with the armed security guard; but the girls weren't in that car, just a puffed-up dignitary. She turned away to watch for traffic that entered the dock area, not cars that left.

Grant's elbows were on his knees, and his head rested on one of his hands. He looked into the distance at the trucks and busses that deposited cargo and passengers at the cruise ship dock. Nothing came into the freighter area. He heard the exhaust sounds of a fast approaching car. Like Andrea, he gave it a quick look, and then turned back to the incoming traffic.

The BMW cruised past, and at the last second, Andrea caught the outline of a figure through the tinted window. She jumped up and pointed, "Grant! I think Jena's in that car. Do you see her?"

Peering into the passing car, Grant saw the outline of a girl's head. "Did you get a good look? I couldn't tell. It could be—God, it is!"

Andrea excitedly grabbed Grant and pulled him off the ground. "We need to follow that car. Holly's probably with her!"

The car cleared the security gate, and Jena looked out the window, taking in the huge cruise ships. She wondered if she would survive to sail on one of the floating hotels someday. She wanted to cruise around the world, but that seemed impossible now. She stared absentmindedly out the window, when something familiar passed by on the curb. She sat up and turned to the window.

"Oh my God," she said under her breath. When it fully registered that she saw her dad and Holly's mom, she yelled, "Dad! I'm in here. Help me! Please help me, Daddy!"

Ahmed reached over, grabbed her by the scruff of her neck and forced her to look straight ahead. Ahmed looked out the back window to see the two Americans stand up on the grassy area, pointing to the car. He turned his attention back to Jena. "They didn't see you, and that's a shame," Ahmed said. He looked up to the driver and directed him, "Please get us to the airport, my hanger, quickly."

The driver nodded, and the BMW accelerated, leaving the harbor area behind. Jena feared she had missed the only opportunity for rescue. She had come within a few yards but couldn't get her dad's attention. The urge to give up crested, and she slumped back into the seat. The nerve bundles on her neck throbbed after Ahmed released his grip. A single thought replayed in Jena's mind: *How am I going to die?*

Chapter 44

Grant's cell phone rang as he watched the BMW speed away from the harbor. He answered on the third ring. "Yes, what do you want?" Grant responded after the silver BMW disappeared around a bend in the roadway.

"That's kind of rude, don't you agree?" Jon-Pierre said.

Grant remained silent and listened to the background on the other end of the call. He did not hear any engine or road noise. Either the car had pulled to the side of the road, or Jon-Pierre was not calling from the silver BMW.

"Mr. Turner, you and Miss. Carson will meet me at the lighthouse on West End Road at the western tip of Negril. Let's say noon, if you please."

"Let me talk to the girls," Grant proposed.

"That's not very trusting, Mr. Turner. Jon-Pierre remained silent for a moment, then said, "Listen closely."

Jon-Pierre poured a pitcher of cold water on Holly's head. She spat and choked from the dousing. "Talk to your mother!" He held the phone a few inches from her face.

Holly's mind was not clear at all. She could not tell her mother where she was or how to get here. She croaked, "Mom…help me, please."

Andrea, hearing her daughter's voice, wanted to jump through the phone lines to be with her. She yelled back into the phone that Grant held, "We'll get you Holly! I promise."

Jon-Pierre's voice came back with a cold dark laugh. "Mommy, you should not promise things you cannot deliver."

Andrea snatched the phone from Grant. "Listen, you psycho, don't you dare hurt the girls."

"Oh, I'm afraid it is much too late for that. Please listen." Jon-Pierre's footfalls on the wooden cabin floor echoed over the phone line. A slap of wood against flesh rang out, followed by Holly's wail. "You were saying something, Miss. Carson?"

Andrea's blood boiled. "I will kill you," she threatened between clenched teeth.

Jon-Pierre laughed once again. "Well, that makes us very similar. I want to kill something too. I'm looking at her now."

Grant pried the phone from Andrea's hand. "Put Jena on the phone," he said.

"She's not able to come to the phone right now. She seems to be unconscious. Let me check," Jon-Pierre said.

Grant heard the wooden floor creak in the background.

"It seems I can't wake her up. I do hope that her condition is not permanent. I can assure you that it will be permanent if you don't show up at noon, or have not transferred the funds. Do I make myself clear, Mr. Turner?"

"Yes, we're clear. We'll see you at noon, at the lighthouse. I'll transfer the funds at that time, and then you give us the girls."

"Transfer the funds, or you won't see the girls again."

Grant hung up the phone and placed it in his pocket. He turned to Andrea. "Something is not right about this."

"No kidding! Some maniac has our girls and is threatening to kill them," Andrea said.

"What did you hear on the phone?"

"What do you mean? I heard him threaten to kill my baby, I heard her cry out in pain, and I couldn't do anything about it."

Not that. What did you hear in the background? What other noises did you hear?" Grant asked.

"I don't know. I listened for Holly's voice, and when I heard it I was rattled."

"But in the background, what did you hear? Close your eyes and think about it," Grant pressed.

Andrea closed her eyes and replayed the conversation over in her head. "I heard his voice, some kind of an echo, and footsteps."

Grant grabbed both her arms. "Exactly. The footsteps. We just saw Jena go by in that silver BMW, and now this guy claims he has the girls. I don't see how you can have footsteps in a car."

Andrea slowly realized the implications of what Grant outlined. "So that means the girls are separated?"

Grant nodded, "I think that's exactly what it means. Holly is in a wooden building stashed on the island, and Jena was in that car going God knows where."

"It also means that Jon-Pierre wants the money for two girls, but has no intention of releasing them to us," Andrea said shakily.

"I think you're right. Jon-Pierre is running a scam. We'll play along for now. We need to find out where Jena's car went, and, I don't know how, but we need to find Holly before the noon meeting. If we haven't located them, I don't think we have a choice but to meet with Jon-Pierre.

"So we keep playing his game. Fine, where do we start?" Andrea said.

Grant walked to the harbor security booth and stood at the door. The skinny man in a baggy uniform shirt had his earphones back on, listening to Bob Marley and ignoring Grant. Grant knocked on the glass window, his impatience showing.

The security guard turned casually toward Grant, slid open the window, and said, "Ya mon, wat do ya want?"

"Where was that Silver BMW going?" Grant asked.

"Why you want to know, mon?"

"We need to find out where they went." Grant paused, wondering how much to tell this man. "My daughter was in the car."

"Wat your little girl be doing in dat car?" The security guard thought of the money he had received regularly from the Arab and did not want to jeopardize that arrangement. He looked at Grant and said, "Sorry, mon, I don't know where dey be." He put his earphones back on and looked away from Grant.

Grant stood in place at the window for a few seconds before walking back to Andrea. He shook his head and said, "That didn't go well."

"Couldn't get anywhere?" Andrea said.

"Nope, that guy's a steel trap." Grant sat on the small patch of grass, uncertain of what to do next.

Andrea looked at the security guard and back to Grant. "Let me give it a try."

"You're wasting your time," he said as she walked to the security guard.

Grant watched her work the guy. She actually flirted with him. There's a flip of her hair, a laugh, and now she's talking with him. She turned and walked back to where Grant was. The security guard watched her the entire way.

She stood over Grant, leaned down and extended her hands to help him up from his perch on the grass. "We need to get to the airport. That's where the BMW went," she reported with a bit of a smirk.

"How did you get him to tell you that?" Grant asked as he stood.

"A girl has her secrets," she said.

"The airport? You're sure we go back to the airport?" Grant asked again.

"I'm certain. Do you need me to get us a cab?"

Grant smirked. "No, I can do that much. Come with me."

They jogged down to the cruise ship terminal. Grant raised his arm, and a green taxi stopped in front of him. Grant opened the door for Andrea.

Andrea nestled next to him in the cab and whispered, "Not bad. I'll have to keep you around in case I need a taxi."

Grant told the driver to take them to the airport. The words were no sooner out of his mouth when the driver hit the accelerator and sped away from the cruise ship terminal.

Andrea took Grant's arm and softly, but firmly, said, "We are going to find Holly and Jena. We're getting close. I feel it."

Grant melted in his seat a bit and looked out the window. "I have to keep hope. I mean, I don't know what to do when we find the assholes holding them—the police took our guns, remember?"

The driver's eyes shifted to the rear view mirror at the mention of police and weapons. "I don't want any problems. Okay, Mister?"

Grant assured the man that there were no problems coming his way. In spite of Grant's assurance, the driver sped faster to get these trouble-makers out of his cab. The taxi skidded to a stop at the airport passenger terminal. The driver hopped out and hurried Grant and Andrea out of the car. Grant handed a couple of bills at the driver, who didn't even look at them as he drove away.

They walked inside the terminal building to find that most of the passengers were upstairs past security. Grant pulled the tickets that

Lieutenant Washington had provided and confirmed the flight left over an hour ago. They walked down the corridor and joined the security line, some ten people deep.

Andrea reached the metal detector first and waved her ticket in the jacket to the man operating the machine. He took her passport, checked that it matched the name on the ticket, and Andrea walked through the metal detector, retrieving her passport and ticket from the security man. She turned and waited for Grant to clear his metal detector, but he seemed to be having some difficulty.

A large Jamaican security woman grilled Grant about his ticket. She had caught that it had been issued for a flight earlier that day. "This ticket is no good. You need to go back and get a new one." She pointed back toward the ticket counters.

Grant had learned a lesson from Andrea when she worked the security guard at the harbor. So Grant tried to apply a little sex appeal. "Sweetheart, I really need to get in there, and I know you—"

She cut him off mid-sentence and started waving a finger in Grant's face. "Don't you sweetheart me! No, you get your no-ticket-havin' butt out of here."

Grant didn't even see it, but Andrea approached the woman from the other side of the metal detector and begun talking to her. After a few seconds of friendly conversation, the woman smiled and laughed at something Andrea said. When the security woman turned back to Grant, the smile evaporated, but she waved him through the metal detector.

He collected his passport and ticket and walked over to the far wall, where a smirking Andrea stood waiting. "What did you say? I had visions of going back to jail. I swear that woman thought I was the underwear bomber."

Andrea headed for the stairs, motioning for Grant. When he caught up to her, she told him, "I simply explained that my husband had gotten us lost on the way here, and would not ask for directions. She had sympathy for me traveling with such a weenie, I think she said."

Grant stopped at the top of the stairs and asked Andrea, "Am I really that bad?" Grant was self-conscious now.

Renewed hope that she was closer to finding one of the girls made her a little giddy. Andrea gave him a peck on the cheek. "No, Grant, you're not that bad." She turned, took a step and then turned back around, "But you do have a nice no-ticket-havin' butt." She moved toward the passenger gates, leaving Grant speechless and blushing.

They went to the far end of the terminal at gate one, walking slowly, scanning the faces of every passenger in the gate area. After finding no luck at the gate, they backtracked, searching the passenger lounges. No sign of Jena.

The next two gate areas were almost empty, with only a few passengers who had gathered early. Grant checked all passengers in the remaining gates. He looked to Andrea. "Are you sure the security guard said to come to the airport?"

Andrea parked in one of the chairs to the side of Grant and patted the chair next to her. "He told me the car was headed to the airport, that the big man had a flight to take."

They looked out the window to the tarmac where planes waited at several gates. Baggage handlers tossed luggage into the open bays. Service trucks brought prepackaged food for the flights, and fuel trucks hurried between planes.

"Andrea, we are in the wrong terminal."

"What do mean, 'the wrong terminal'?" There is only one passenger terminal, isn't there? Is there another airport?"

"This is the right airport, but the wrong terminal. Look over there," he said. Grant pointed out the window to the left where a fuel truck passed. A dozen small private planes and jets were parked on the tarmac.

"That makes sense. They could come and go with less scrutiny," Andrea said.

"Think about it, if someone is taking our girls off the island, they are going to have their own private means to get out of the country. We thought it was going to be the ship, but this makes more sense."

They pressed up to the glass and looked out to the charter terminal, hoping for a glimpse of something that would rekindle their hopes. Grant tugged on Andrea's arm and pointed towards the charter hangers.

"Over there, by the corner of that building near the end, near those small planes. It's the silver BMW. It is parked right there. That's it. I know it. Jena's there."

Chapter 45

Ahmed's car breezed through the charter air terminal near the busy main passenger terminal in Montego Bay. As the driver slowed at the gate, Ahmed put his hand around Jena's neck, squeezing slightly.

"If you make a sound, I will break your neck," he whispered in her ear.

Jena nodded slightly against the pressure on her neck. She felt lightheaded. His grip cut off the nerve impulse to her brain. She panicked and struggled against his hand. Ahmed knew exactly how much pressure to apply. He wanted to see how long it would take before she struggled. She lasted longer than most of the women he tested. Unfortunately, some of the women had died. It was a cost of doing business, and they were all replaceable.

At the security gate, the driver handed over a false Brazilian passport with Ahmed's picture and one hundred dollars tucked inside. Many people, from rock stars to drug dealers, frequently required special handling, and most of the guards could, with a little encouragement, be enticed to assist in this swift processing. In this instance, the guard, finding the enticement sufficient, returned the lighter passport and motioned the BMW through the gate.

Ahmed released his pressure from around Jena's neck and directed the driver to a smaller hanger on the far end of the tarmac. They navigated around planes and hangers where the rich and famous kept planes they rarely used. The driver stopped in front of a hanger and ran around to open his employer's door. Ahmed nodded to his driver and pulled Jena from the car by her hair.

The driver moved the car alongside the hanger. Ahmed walked to a private door on the side of the building and used a key from his key ring to unlock the hanger. Inside, a small crew prepared a Lear Jet 55C for flight. Two cylindrical fuel tanks were mounted to the wings of the sleek aircraft, providing over 500 additional gallons of jet fuel, extending its long-range capability.

He shoved Jena to a room constructed of concrete block marked with heavy steel doors. One door sat ajar, exposing a jail cell with solid walls. Ahmed pushed Jena into the room, locked the door, and left her in darkness.

Ahmed went to the office next door and flipped on a switch activating a night vision camera in the adjacent cell. He would watch all of her movements while taking care of his business. He powered up a small desktop computer and waited for it to boot. Ahmed looked at the night vision image of the girl as she felt for walls around her. Ahmed thought there was something special about this girl.

Ahmed entered a password into a restricted dark-web internet site. Only those with sufficient money, or those with certain commodities to sell, had the password. He made a few key strokes and then entered Jena's description into an internet page. He removed the XD media card from his camera and slid it into an open slot on the computer. He selected the best pictures he had taken of Jena and copied them to the internet page. He posted a message on the bulletin board section that announced a new item up for bid.

Almost immediately, the bids came in from his exclusive client list. The first bid was sixty-thousand from a Lebanese gentleman, followed by seventy thousand by a Moroccan man. The two bidders, bid and counter bid for fifteen minutes straight, until the Moroccan lost interest at one hundred and fifty-thousand dollars. Ahmed smiled and shut down the computer. He would find out who the successful bidder was when he landed in the Middle East in a few hours.

He walked out to the hanger floor and watched the painstaking preparation for the trans-Atlantic flight. Blue uniformed men peered into the engines, turning the fan blades, while others checked the movement of the elevator, rudder and trim tabs. The crew supervisor directed all movement on the floor and checked off items on his clipboard. The supervisor, on seeing Ahmed, approached him.

"Everything is going well, Sir," the supervisor reported.

Ahmed did not look at him, but continued to assess the sleek aircraft. "When will my plane be ready?"

"We are finishing up the preflight checks. Then we have to fuel the plane, including the wing tanks. Then—"

"How long?" Ahmed cut off the reply.

"Thirty to forty-five minutes," the supervisor said.

Ahmed walked back to the office, closed the door against the noise, and seated himself in front of the night vision monitor. Jena sat huddled in a corner of the cell.

"You're going to make me a great deal of money, little one. It is a shame that the high bidder seems to be a man with unusual tastes. He will use you once and then kill you. It means he will require a replacement very soon."

Time passed, and a knock on Ahmed's door broke his trance. "Yes? What is it?"

An unsteady voice replied, "Sir, your plane is being fueled. You may board when you wish."

Ahmed took a deep breath, raised himself out of the chair and turned to open the office door. The crew had opened the hangar doors and towed the plane out to the tarmac in front of the steel building. Ahmed should have heard the hangar doors open, and his lapse of awareness disturbed him. That was the kind of carelessness that got you killed. He noticed that the air stairs were down and the door to the fuselage open.

A local man unhooked the thick, black fuel line from the jet and wrestled it back to his fuel truck. He waived to someone in the distance, apparently signaling that refueling on the Lear Jet was complete.

Ahmed quickly unlocked the cell. Jena shielded her eyes from the blast of light coming through the open door with her . zip tied hands. He pulled her to her feet and Jena was disoriented from the time in the dark isolation cell. She fell to her knees, and Ahmed pulled her up and shoved her out the door into the wide-open hangar. Jena froze when she realized her destination was a blue and white jet.

Jena tried to pull back from him with her restrained hands, but Ahmed pulled her along toward the Lear Jet without as much as a break in stride.

"No. I don't want to go anywhere with you! Help me! Somebody help me!"

Ahmed jerked the restraints and pressed his thumb into a pressure point on her neck. Jena fell silent and nearly limp.

"We are going to have a nice, civilized flight. If you have a problem with that, we have the cargo compartment in the belly of the plane. It is pressurized, but unfortunately is not heated."

No one responded to Jena's cry for help. The men who attended to the plane were her captor's people and paid no attention to her. Ahmed reached the bottom of the air stairs and shoved Jena ahead of him into the passenger cabin of the plane. The interior was opulent, appointed with crystal, deep-wood toned accents and large leather seats. Toward the back she noted a bathroom, bar, small kitchen and sofa.

Ahmed tossed her in one of the leather chairs and sat in one across the aisle.

"Once we are airborne, you will have the freedom to sit anywhere you like and walk about the plane," he said to Jena.

A man came from the cockpit and stood with a sense of reverence at Ahmed's side. "I have filed a flight plan to London. When we are over the Atlantic, I will file an amended plan to Milan. The deviation to our actual destination will go unnoticed."

Ahmed nodded his head in agreement, and the pilot retreated to the cockpit. One of the ground crew pushed away the air stairs after closing and securing the cabin door. Almost immediately, the jet's engines turned with a high-pitched whine that dissolved into a powerful rumble.

Jena heard the pilot say they were going out over the Atlantic, so wherever she went, it would be thousands of miles from home. Waves of panic swept over her. Her head felt like it was going to explode.

The engines revved up and the plane moved forward. Ahmed closed his eyes and relaxed. He had won this round.

Jena became more and more agitated. She felt her heartbeat in her throat. "I need to use the bathroom," she said.

She broke Ahmed's bliss. "You can wait!"

"I can't wait. I'm going to get sick right here," she explained. Her chest tightened with terror, and she could barely breathe.

Ahmed looked dismissively at the restrained girl and motioned to the rear of the plane, "Go—but be quick about it."

Jena stood slowly, unsteady as she made her way to the rear of the taxiing plane. She opened the bathroom and stepped inside. The marble counter and sink were cool to the touch. Jena ran cold water over her hands and threw some of the water on her face. She sat on the toilet seat, her head in her hands.

If I'm going to die, it will be on my terms, when I choose.

Chapter 46

Jon-Pierre retightened Holly's bindings, though it was not necessary. The swollen, purple lumps on the soles of her broken feet ensured that she would never run from him again. She shivered, cold and feverish from an inevitable infection that threatened gangrene and the loss of one or both of her feet.

Holly saw the Haitian stand over her. She braced for another beating and winced in anticipation of the pain to come. Instead, he held a syringe.

"I must take care of some business. This will make sure you don't make a sound while I'm gone. We can continue our little game when I return," he said.

The restraints kept Holly still when the needle jammed into her neck. She was too weak to move away, and at this point, she welcomed the warm deadness that crept through her pain-ridden body. She swore the Haitian smiled before her vision went dark.

Jon-Pierre locked the cabin and got into a battered, rust-pocked, blue pickup hidden behind his place. He put the old truck in gear and drove out from the dense forest toward civilization. As he hit the main road, he donned a ratty, faded baseball hat and sunglasses and slouched in the seat. Jon-Pierre headed to Montego Bay, planning his revenge against the Arab.

The old blue truck rattled down the coast road, and Jon-Pierre day-dreamed about his next capture. Seeing a group of young people playing volleyball on the beach, he pulled off the road for a moment. At this distance, he could not tell if they were worthy. A quick look at his watch and Jon-Pierre pulled back onto the highway; he had a timetable to keep.

He came to a sign that pointed left for the Montego Bay airport and headed directly for the coast road. Jon-Pierre chose the path to the right and drove to a secluded beach spot, near the base of the runway, a hundred yards outside the security fence. His faded blue truck was hidden under a small cluster of coconut trees. From this location, Jon-Pierre could monitor all flights in or out of the small airport. He pulled a short beach chair from the back of the truck and placed it on the warm sand.

He spotted and waived at the local fuel-truck driver on the tarmac who had tipped him off about the Syrian's change in departure. A few hundred dollars lined the driver's pockets for a few minutes work with a pair of bolt cutters. All set. Jon-Pierre stretched out in the beach chair and checked his watch.

Chapter 47

Ahmed sat in his comfortable leather seat as the plane positioned it-self in the cue for takeoff. The Lear Jet was in line behind a cargo carrier and a fully loaded American Airlines 767 passenger jet. Anxious, with only a few moments left on this miserable island, he swiveled his seat toward the back of the plane, while noticing that the bathroom door was still closed. *A few minutes more won't hurt*, he thought.

Once his plane had taxied to the apron near the end of the runway, Ahmed called for Jena. "Take your seat. We are leaving now."

She opened the bathroom door, walked back to her seat, past an emergency exit door, and plopped in her spot across the aisle from her captor. Jena looked out at the runway, pushing the hair out of her eyes with restrained hands.

"Where are you taking me?" she demanded.

Ahmed put down the Arabic newspaper that he had been superficially scanning. "Why do you wish to know?"

"I think I have a right to know where I'm being taken."

He picked the paper back up. "Get used to having no rights, ever again."

"So are you gonna tell me where we're going?"

Ahmad gave a deep sigh. "That all depends who pays the most, but for now you are going to my home in Syria. Now sit still, we are about to take off." He hid his face again behind his newspaper.

The jet received clearance from the tower for takeoff and rolled down the runway. The nose of the plane skipped down the runway, and the sudden thrust pushed Jena back into her seat. In desperation, she jumped up and ran to the rear of the plane. Ahmed caught her movement out of the corner of his eye and figured the nervous girl needed the bathroom again.

"Wait until we level off. Get back here!" he said.

The plane picked up speed, and Jena felt the rear wheels bumping along the runway. She felt the sudden lifting of the jet up off the ground and climbing into air toward her next unknown horror. The Lear Jet cleared the end of the runway, but made a sudden dip toward the blue ocean. A black puff of smoke blew from the port engine, followed by the starboard seconds later. The nose of the jet pulled skywards, clawing for altitude, but the lost airspeed stalled the craft. The Lear Jet banked over and dragged a wingtip in the water before its lightweight metal skin ruptured, spraying thousands of gallons of jet fuel across the surface. The crippled jet cart wheeled into the ocean, leaving a trail of engine parts, metal debris and bits of fuselage in the surf.

The fire started slowly, engulfing the intact portion of the fuselage that floated near the reef. The ruptured fuel tanks fed flames that spread like wings of death for anyone on board. From the shore, the water glowed orange for a hundred feet around the remains. Anyone caught in the inferno had little chance of survival.

Jon-Pierre watched the wreckage burn, satisfied that the Syrian no longer posed a problem. His buyers in the Middle East would send another emissary to take up where Ahmed left off.

Casually, Jon-Pierre picked up his beach chair, stowed it in the back of the pickup and entered the cab. Emergency vehicles raced down the coast road, lights flashing. Jon-Pierre drove the opposite way, back to his cabin to tie up one more loose end.

Chapter 48

Grant hadn't noticed the private jet take off and head out over the ocean, but when the plane splashed down and burst into flames, he and everyone else in the gate area pressed to the windows to see what had happened.

Andrea looked just in time to see the front portion tumble toward the ocean and heave into the water near the reef. "Grant, what was that? An explosion?"

"I have no idea. That plane fell out of the sky."

Concern and speculation grew among passengers and employees in the terminal. The faces on an older couple in their seventies expressed fear, and with trembling voices, they asked, "Was it a terrorist attack?"

That comment triggered widespread panic in the crowd. Airline employees did their best to calm the swelling mass of people in the terminal, but hysteria took over. People burst out of several emergency exits, setting off shrill alarms throughout the terminal. The alarms amped up the crowd, feeding the fears of the stampeding mob.

A frail, older man locked eyes with Grant, grasping his carry-on bag tight to his chest seconds before a wave of panic-stricken people bowled him over and trampled him. Grant rushed against the human tide, fighting his way to the fallen man. He reached down to help the old man, but the oncoming crowd knocked Grant to the carpet. Grant shielded the man's body as best he could with his own. The old man's eyes clouded over with surprise and fear.

"Can you get up?" Grant asked, after a pause in the crowd surge.

"Not on my own. If you give me a hand, I think I can make it."

In between crowd surges, Grant stood and pulled the man up from the floor. He was still clutching his carryon bag and had difficulty walking on his own. Grant directed him to a nearby chair.

"Thank you very much, young man. Shouldn't we be leaving the terminal like everyone else?"

"I think we'll be fine right here. The problem is outside the terminal."

Andrea flagged down an EMT and motioned to the old man in the chair. The EMT bent down to check the man's vital signs.

Grant gave the EMT some space and stood nearby with Andrea. Elsewhere in the terminal, medical staff tended to a couple of other people who had been knocked down and trampled by the crowd. Door alarms sounded all over the terminal, as the rush of the crowd spread to the tarmac. Through the boarding area window, Grant and Andrea noticed scores of passengers on the runway, mingling about the waiting planes. A young man in his twenties looted valuables from a baggage cart staged to load aboard an outgoing flight.

Security staff chased passengers off the runway while onlookers cheered on the passengers who eluded the airport's security employees. Others remained convinced they were victims of an Al Qaeda attack.

Andrea whispered into Grant's ear, "This confusion should give us a chance to get to the hangar over there without getting noticed." She motioned to the silver BMW.

Grant asked the EMT, "Is he going to be okay?"

The EMT looked up and nodded, "Very lucky he didn't get crushed. He's going to be fine."

Andrea tried to leave, but the old man grabbed her arm, pulled off the oxygen mask and spoke to Andrea. "I owe your husband a great deal. He didn't have to jump into the middle of that crowd the way he did." He pulled an expensive looking, embossed business card from his pocket and handed it to Andrea. It read in gold lettering "Joseph R. Pierce" and displayed a phone number, with no title or business affiliation.

Andrea read the card and responded. "Grant seems to find himself in the middle of things wherever we go." She did not bother to tell him that Grant was not her husband. The man resisted her pull. She asked, "What kind of work are you in, Mr. Pierce?"

"Oh, I dabble a bit in different arenas. Whatever strikes my fancy, like mutual funds, commodities, banking, mergers and acquisitions, and so on."

"Well, it's very nice to make your acquaintance," Andrea offered. "I need to go."

"You two call me if you ever need anything, you understand?" His gaze was a bit unsettling for Andrea.

Grant shook the man's hand, surprised at his strength. "We have to go now," Grant said, pulling Andrea away.

They found an open emergency exit door and ducked outside into the intense heat, amplified by the sun's reflection off the tarmac surface. At the bottom of a stairwell, they mingled into a group of passengers standing in the little bit of shade offered by the building. The group clearly valued the shade more than a potential terrorist threat, as they had parked themselves a few feet away from one of the fully-fueled passenger jets at the gate.

Through the heat waves reflecting off the tarmac, Grant and Andrea saw at least one hundred and fifty people on the runway, wandering about or attempting to eluded the exhausted security staff. Andrea saw someone tied to a concrete column under the terminal structure. She recognized him as the baggage looter. Apparently, mob justice is swift; his eyes were swollen and his nose bloodied.

Grant weaved through the crowds in the direction of the silver BMW. At the fringe of the pack, a single security guard stood between them and the silver sedan. The very big security guard reluctantly worked to contain this end of the disturbance, to ensure that pricey possessions remained safe, tucked away in the hangers behind him.

Andrea read his face before they had come within ten feet. The burly guard looked put out and frazzled.

"Go back with the others. You're coming no farther," the guard said, one hand ready on an expandable baton.

Before Grant could respond, Andrea shouted, "There is a man tied to a column over there, and he is hurt!"

Grant, astonished at her quick wit, stood back while she worked.

The security guard picked up his radio and spoke. "Johnny, can you check out a report of a guy tied up by the terminal?"

A voice came through the radio: "Do it yourself. I'm busy chasing people off the runway. The tower told us we have two planes on approach, so we need to get it cleared off. You need to get out here and help us."

The burly, out-of-shape security guard determined the path of least exertion and chose Andrea's report about the injured man tied to a concrete column. He told Grant and Andrea to stay put and not go anywhere. He hitched up his utility belt and waddled toward the terminal building.

"How did you know he was going to choose going to the terminal, rather than chasing down passengers? It was because he was out of shape, right?" Grant concluded.

As they began walking toward the BMW, Andrea said, "I wish I could say I was that good, but no. I thought he would go check out the report of the kid tied up. I almost choked when he pulled out the radio."

"Well, it worked," Grant said as they slowly approached the silver sedan. He peered in the tinted windows, seeing nothing that linked to the girls.

Andrea pointed to the open hangar door. She and Grant walked slowly to the front of the huge steel building. When they arrived at the door, they overheard a stern voice shouting in what sounded like Arabic. Whatever language it was, the message it delivered was terse, angry and accusatory. At least two other voices shouted back in response. Grant carefully pushed Andrea back against the outside of the hangar wall and crouched on his knees. Peeking around the doorway, he saw three maintenance workers, clad in blue jumpsuits, arguing with another man in a pullover shirt and khakis.

There was no plane in the hangar. Grant felt sick in the pit of his stomach. The workers in the hangar yelled at each other with an occasional word of English that carried blame for the plane that had plunged into the sea. Jena was nowhere in sight. He had to know, and without thinking, he stood up, resisting Andrea's pull on his arm.

She whispered, "Grant, don't do it."

Grant walked through the open hangar door, his silhouette lit by the sun behind him. One of the workmen spotted him and sputtered something in Arabic to the others, and they fell silent. The man in a khaki pants walked over to him, and one of the workmen pulled an AK-47 assault rifle out from under a table.

"I would like to charter a jet for some island hopping. Can you give me an estimate for a three-day charter?" Grant asked as the man approached.

The Middle Eastern man, worked up from his argument with the other men in the hangar and his brow lined with sweat, said, "You leave now. We have nothing for you."

"I'm looking for a charter. I'm willing to pay top dollar," Grant pressed.

"Get out now! We are closed." The heavily accented man pushed Grant with a hand on his chest.

"Don't you want the business?"

The khaki clad man lost his composure and yelled at Grant. He pushed Grant away, demanding, "Do you see a plane in this hangar to charter? We lost our plane twenty minutes ago. Do you see that jet burning in the water? That was ours."

Grant tightened, "I'm very sorry. Who was on the plane?" Grant held his breath for the response.

"My boss, Ahmed al Fiari, the pilot and a young woman," the man responded. "Now we need to find out what happened and which one of these incompetent fools was responsible for the crash."

"What did the woman look like?" Grant asked.

The man took a sideways glance at Grant, "She was young—his usual type. She didn't matter. Why do you want to know?"

Grant exploded and swung a fist into the jaw of the man, knocking him to the floor. His hand ached immediately. Grant saw the workman raise the AK-47, the black barrel pointing at him. He didn't care if the man pulled the trigger; he lost everything.

From the floor, the man rubbed his jaw and got to his feet. He put a hand up and said something in Arabic to the gunman. The gunman lowered the rifle, but looked poised to bring it back to bear in an instant.

The man approached Grant. "Who is this woman to you? I allowed you one shot; please don't make that mistake again."

"The girl was my daughter, Jena Turner, twenty-years-old," Grant said while looking the man dead in the eye.

The man nodded, "Leave here now. We have no issues with you. The boss mentioned a couple of Americans were looking for two women. Mr. al Fiari boarded the plane with only one young lady. There is nothing you can do now." He turned his back to Grant and walked away.

Grant stood there in the vast open expanse of the hangar and felt it close in around him. His chest tightened, and he felt his heart banging in his head. He did not hear the men tell him to leave. Andrea turned the corner of the hangar door, walked to Grant and took him by the arm.

The gunman raised his rifle and looked ready to fire, when Andrea appeared. He lowered it quickly, once the man in khakis put out his arm to stop him.

She guided Grant out of the hangar and took him to a bench tucked under an awning attached to one of the airport's outbuildings. In another time, the scene on the runway would be quite humorous. It looked very much like a game of tag between the passengers and the security guards, and the passengers were winning.

From the bench, they looked out over the spot in the ocean where the jet had gone down. A small number of vessels combed the water for debris. Debris, which included his daughter. Debris—he shuddered at the thought.

Numb, Grant leaned over to Andrea and laid his head against hers. She felt the tears fall from his face. She held him tight and let him grieve. She felt the same pain, not only for Jena, but also for Holly.

Andrea searched though her mind for anything that would help find Holly. The meeting with Jon-Pierre was in a couple of hours in Negril, and having witnessed Jena's plane plummet into the ocean, she did not trust that monster to keep his end of the bargain. For the first time, Andrea considered that Holly, like Jena, was dead.

Chapter 49

Jon-Pierre returned to his isolated cabin. He walked to the front door, a little self-satisfied hop in his step. He was very pleased with himself for the way he got the local to tamper with the fuel system to take care of that miserable Arab. Ahmed was off to meet Allah in pieces. The fish would eat what was left of the Arab's carcass, and that thought very much pleased Jon-Pierre.

He thought aloud, "The Arab paid for one, and the Americans are going to pay for two. Not a bad return—three for one."

He walked inside and confirmed that Holly was still restrained by her ankles and suspended, only her head and shoulders against the floor. She was awake and foggy from the dose of Ketamine he left her with. Holly registered movement in the room, but her mind was too cloudy to focus. She struggled to turn her body to see him. He played a cruel game and ducked to the other side when she turned over, and then back again, toying with her. She used what was left of her strength to see what he was doing but lost him in the haze in her brain. Holly rolled to her back again, and now his face stood directly over her.

"A little longer and you will get to see your mother--maybe," he said.

"Please let me have some water," she croaked through her parched lips.

Jon-Pierre walked to a rusty pail that gathered rainwater from a leak in the roof. He knelt on one knee, close to her face, and told her, "Here you go." He tipped the pail, and the rancid water filled Holly's mouth. She spit it out, fearing she was going to choke on the thick, murky liquid. From her suspended position, the effect was akin to waterboarding.

She gagged, coughed, and vomited up a large pool of brown mucus on her shirt. She aspirated some of the vile liquid, and gasped for air.

Jon-Pierre rose, threw the pail away, and left Holly struggling to get a shallow breath.

Preparing for his meeting with the two Americans, he looked at his watch. He would make sure the money was in the account before he did anything. By the end of the day, he would be thousands of dollars richer. In addition, there would be three more dead Americans—this worthless girl and the parents who had proven to be a great distraction.

He pulled an old map from one of the cabinets and laid it on the table in the middle of the room. He studied it intently, reviewing all the access points to the Negril Lighthouse. He ran his finger along a particular route and tapped a spot on the map. It was a slight rise, maybe seventy-five yards from the lighthouse itself. That was the spot where he would wait for the Americans. From that distance, he could easily dispatch them both with well placed rifle shots.

A metal vault protected his valuables from the heat and humidity of the jungle. Jon-Pierre went to the vault and withdrew an M-40 .308 caliber rifle with a large matte green painted scope mounted on top of the rifle's housing. The bolt action rifle was simple, but deadly and it looked sinister, painted with a brown and green camouflage pattern. Among the four rifles in the cabinet, this one's consistent operation made it his favorite. He had used the rifle for his first long distance assassination, a judge in Port-Au-Prince. It was the same rifle he had used to warn the American woman back on the resort beach.

From a drawer within the vault, Jon-Pierre selected and removed a box of handmade bullets he thought would work well for the occasion. He closed the vault, placed the rifle with the ammunition on the table, and examined the rounds. Designed to tumble on their way to the target, they caused more extensive tissue damage upon impact. There was a tradeoff though; these were slightly less accurate than traditional jacketed rounds. He figured that at short range, these slower but more deadly rounds would be perfect.

He pulled back the bolt on the rifle and slowly fed the ammunition into the rifle's magazine, entering five rounds before returning the bolt to its forward position, chambering a lethal round.

He grabbed the rifle, spare ammunition and map, and headed for the door. He turned to Holly and said, "I'm off to kill your mother. I will say hello for you." Her weakened condition made another dose of Ketamine unnecessary. As the door banged closed behind him, Holly jerked.

Trapped in her restraints, the leather harness securing her feet, Holly couldn't move the lower half of her body. The savage beating she had endured meant any movement to her seriously injured feet caused blinding pain. She felt open wounds ooze and saw flies circling around her battered flesh. Even the slightest pressure of a fly landing against the wounds on her feet made her wince.

Her hands, still bound behind her, were now devoid of feeling. The circulation to her arms had been cut off. She pushed against the post to secure her position, but it did not move. She thought about what to do next, when a sudden and violent wave of nausea hit. She turned her head in time to avoid choking on the thick, brown discharge.

Holly, on hearing the Haitian's truck leave, wriggled against her restraints with all the strength she had left. Nothing moved except for the flies that fed from the open wounds on her feet. As she turned her head, an object caught her eye under a table in the corner of the cabin. It took a second to focus on the object. Then it moved, and red eyes reflected back at Holly. A rat with its long thin tail, protruding teeth and feet that clawed at the wooden floor circled around her. The creature probed closer and waited.

Holly waited too.

Chapter 50

Collapsed on a bench at the airport, Andrea sat with Grant. She felt his grief as he trembled. It served as a reminder that her daughter risked a similar fate. But, she couldn't give up the search for Holly, not when she was so close.

"Grant, honey, we are supposed to meet Jon-Pierre in Negril at noon. I have to take this chance to get my Holly. I understand if you can't come with me. I really do understand—but I would like to have you by my side." She rose from the bench and faced Grant.

Grant's face was red and puffy. "Of course I'm coming with you. I can't change anything sitting here, but maybe we can change something in Negril." He took her hand and pulled himself lightly from the bench.

With the chaos at the airport, all the taxis were gone with their fares to hotels and establishments far away from the terminal.

"How are we going to get back to Negril? It's about an hour drive from here," she said.

A slight sparkle came to Grant's eyes. "Wait here, I'll be right back." He took off in a trot toward the hangar, the place where they encountered the gun wielding men.

Andrea held her breath and waited for the men inside to come running out with their guns ablaze. In the commotion of the frenzied throng of passengers, the men never heard Grant start the BMW's engine and pull away from the hangar. When the car rounded the corner, Andrea jumped in the front seat and closed the door.

Grant turned the steering wheel of the smooth sedan, and sailed between two other buildings, heading away from the main airport road. He looked at Andrea's concerned face, "Would you believe it—the keys were in the car. I thought I was going to have to hot wire this thing."

She turned in her seat, "You know how to hot wire a car?"

"Actually, no, I have no clue how to hot wire anything. But, I figure they owe me the use of this car."

Andrea couldn't leave it unsaid, "Grant, I'm so sorry about Jena. I don't know what I can say."

Grant gripped the wheel tight and drove west on A-1 toward Negril. "There is nothing to say. I've lost everything in my life that was important to me." He increased his speed on the coast highway, passing the slower vehicles on every straight section of road.

They made good time until they hit Lucea. The road narrowed between buildings on the main street through town, and a bus left the transit yard as they approached. It pulled out in front of him, the people in the back gawking, wanting to see who drove such a nice car. In the rear bus window, Grant saw a cage that held a chicken destined for someone's dinner.

Grant shot the BMW out past the bus, and raced down the coastal highway, reaching the Negril area with almost thirty minutes to spare. Andrea guided Grant to the Negril Lighthouse from signs posted along the route. Gravel crunched under the BMW as it pulled into the half-full parking lot.

They got out of the car and immediately blended in with the dozen tourists wandering about the grounds. Most of the tourists snapped photos of the lighthouse or took their time reading wooden placards that described the area. In a place noted for calm breezes and relaxed tourists, anxiety ruled. Holly was supposed to be here for the exchange. Andrea peered into every car in the parking lot and looked at the tourists for a sign.

Grant and Andrea walked hand in hand to the base of the lighthouse, expecting one of the sightseers to be working for Jon-Pierre. They waited for someone to make an approach. Andrea expectantly looked at every person who passed, wanting to grab them and plead for Holly.

"I know we are early. I think he's already here, don't you?" Andrea said.

"And he's watching us, waiting," Grant said.

"What is he waiting for? Let's get this over with."

"He's probably waiting for some of these tourists to thin out. Or, he's playing games with us again. Do you see anyone who looks like Holly, maybe wearing a hat? Anyone held close to another person?"

She scanned the tourists once more, "No, I don't see anyone resembling her. I thought that girl, with the crop top, may have been her, but when she got close, I saw it wasn't." She pointed at a young woman on the other side of the lighthouse. The girl was similar to Holly's build, but that was the only similarity. The face, nose and eye color were all different.

Jon-Pierre observed the Americans for fifteen minutes. From his position on the hill above, he watched the show unfold. It was about control and power, and about who wielded it in this relationship. It was time to remind them that *he* was the source of all power. He held the power over life, and he was the bringer of death. Jon-Pierre lay prone at the base of a small bush, his rifle trained on target. He looked through the scope as Andrea examined every face that came by. Her companion also tensed at each passerby. They grew frustrated and that was good; they were apt to make a lapse in judgment.

Hidden in the foliage surrounding his nest, he called the Americans' cell phone. He watched as the man jumped and pulled his phone out from his pocket.

"Hello?" Grant said.

Jon-Pierre waited for a few seconds to let the tension build and then instructed Grant, "You are to execute the wire transfer now and then I will let you see the girls."

"We agreed to see the girls at the same." Grant said. He knew this man didn't have Jena because of the plane crash. He doubted the Haitian's intentions of turning Holly over to them, but he had to try, for Andrea.

"I have changed my mind. You give me the money and then I will tell you where you can collect the girls," Jon-Pierre said.

"The girls aren't even here, are they?" Grant called the Haitian's bluff.

Jon-Pierre bent down to the riflescope and peered at the American man caught in the cross hairs. The American seemed to look straight up at him. Jon-Pierre's finger looped around the trigger.

"No. I did not bring them here with me because they have been far too much bother. Nevertheless, it is time for us to conclude this financial transaction," Jon-Pierre said.

Andrea grabbed the phone from Grant and told the Haitian, in a dark tone, "You harm my daughter and I will kill you."

"Oh, I'm afraid it's much too late for that. The girls misbehaved and tried to run from me. I've punished them and they won't be walking for a while, *if ever.*"

When she heard the threat on the phone, Andrea spit back, "Then you won't be getting any money from us, will you? You don't even have Jena, do you, you lying bastard?"

Stunned by the woman's outburst, Jon-Pierre realized he misjudged this pair. How could she possibly know? He looked down the scope of the rifle and spoke into the phone, "I'm going to get paid one way or another. Yes, you are correct; I only have one of the girls. So, I only need one of you to finish our deal."

Jon-Pierre gently squeezed the rifle's trigger and a loud bang sent everyone scurrying for cover. He didn't use a silencer this time. He wanted the panic.

The impact of the bullet knocked Grant off his feet. The force threw him hard against the base of the lighthouse. A second bullet whizzed by inches from Andrea's head and hit the cement between her and Grant. She grabbed Grant by the feet, pulled with all her strength and dragged him inside the lighthouse.

The crowds ran in every direction, moving as fast as their legs could carry them. Jon-Pierre surveyed the crowd through his scope and did not see the Americans. He was certain that he had hit the man, the second shot had kept the woman from helping her fallen comrade, as he intended. The picture within his scope failed to show the man's body and that was very frustrating. He wanted confirmation of his kill. Jon-Pierre couldn't wait them out any longer, someone had called the police by now. Even though he had an understanding with most of the local cops, there would be too many questions to answer. He picked up his equipment and tracked down to his old pickup truck parked along the road. He tossed the rifle on the seat and covered it up with a blanket.

He threw the truck in drive and drove back toward Montego Bay. His mood grew darker. His financial connection to the Middle East trade was temporarily off line. Jon-Pierre reasoned that the Arab did that to himself and took no responsibility for the Syrian's death. He lost thousands of dollars because of the American woman's irrational behavior. With the man out of the way, this woman would be easy to manipulate and extract the money. After that, he'd kill her. Now it was time to get rid of the girl.

Chapter 51

Andrea pulled Grant inside the lighthouse doorway and held his head. He slipped in and out of consciousness, but she saw too much blood seeping from a ragged wound three inches from the top of his left shoulder. She placed her hand over the wound and pressed. Grant groaned and the blood flow didn't stop. She gently rolled him over and found a gaping exit wound about two inches in diameter. Grant bled from both wounds, and the pallor of his skin grew pale with each second that passed.

Grant looked up at Andrea's worried face and said, "I'm sorry I didn't find Holly. I let you down. Cold, I'm so cold."

"Stay with me, Grant. I'm here. You're going to be all right." She turned and yelled, "Someone help us!"

He reached and tried to grab something to pull himself off the floor. "Don't worry about me. We need to go find Holly. Help me sit up."

While Grant's heart wanted to get up, Andrea saw his body start to shut down, going into shock. He stopped moving.

Again, Andrea called for help and heard faint sirens in the distance. The EMTs needed to get here soon, and she pleaded again, "Help me!"

She saw his eyes lose focus and close.

"Grant, wake up. Talk to me, Grant. Don't leave me!"

He was unresponsive when the ambulance crew arrived. She yelled and waved for them to come to her. The first EMT assessed the situation, and yelled back to call in a life flight and bring the trauma kit.

The EMTs worked efficiently, communicating with each other in clipped phrases. They established an IV drip in Grant's right arm, dumped an anti-coagulant powder into the hole in his shoulder, then applied a pressure dressing to both sides of the wound. His blood pressure dropped from blood loss, and the EMT hung another bag connected to his IV.

Andrea stood back, helpless as she watched the two professionals work over Grant's crumpled form. Alerted by a sudden movement from one of the EMT's, her blood felt like quicksilver.

"I lost a heartbeat."

They moved quickly, stripping open Grant's shirt and holding two defibrillator paddles over his chest while the unit charged up. A loud whine increased in pitch, and one of the men yelled "Clear!" The paddles went down on Grant's chest and his body convulsed upwards with the electric charge. The EMT listened again for a heartbeat. "Let's hit him again." Once more, the paddles jolted Grant's lifeless form.

"Where is the life flight?" Andrea asked.

"OK, he's back. Heartbeat's not strong, but we have one," the EMT said to his partner. He looked to Andrea: "The life flight helicopter should be here very soon."

She saw Grant's face and his ashen color. She whispered in his ear, "Grant, stay with me. Holly needs you and I need you. Please don't give up."

Andrea heard a helicopter in the distance, the sound grew as a red helicopter drew close to the lighthouse point. Afraid to feel relief, she held Grant's hand tightly and closed her eyes. The next thing she knew, one of the EMT's tapped her arm gently and said, "We need to move him now."

The helicopter flared for landing, sending dust and material flying through the air. Andrea watched the craft gently touch down. A crew member jumped out, opened the side door of the helicopter and signaled the EMT's that it was clear to bring their patient under the copter's spinning blades. The medical personnel placed Grant on the short gurney that lay next to him. The pool of blood that remained told that that the pressure bandage hadn't stemmed the bleeding. The EMTs picked the gurney up, and its wheels fell, popping into place. They pushed the gurney through the parking lot where the helicopter waited, its rotor cutting through the air.

One of the helicopter crew members pulled a long metal ramp that resembled a ladder from the belly of the aircraft. The helicopter crew member grabbed one end of the gurney and aligned it over the metal ladder-platform. Two Velcro straps secured Grant, and the crew member pressed a button inside the helicopter. A mechanical whirring sound came from under the gurney, and the ladder retracted, pulling the gurney into the helicopter.

One of the EMTs yelled to the crewman, "You've got a male in his forties with a through and through GSW, BP is low and falling, erratic heart rate. We defibrillated twice. He still has uncontrolled bleeding from the exit wound on posterior left shoulder."

The crewman nodded and started to slide the door shut. Andrea grabbed the door. "Wait, I'm going with you!"

The crewman shook his head and yelled above the rotor wash, "You can't. We don't have room for a passenger," and he pointed inside. Andrea saw a cramped space filled with medical equipment, monitors and IV machines, as well as the man who treated Grant, straddled over him, applying a new pressure bandage. There was no room for a passenger.

"Where are you taking him?" she inquired as the rotors increased speed and noise.

"What?" the man yelled over the whine of the helicopter's engine.

The doors closed, and the craft lifted a mere ten feet before it swiftly banked out over the ocean. It shot out, growing smaller and smaller, until it became a black speck in the blue mid-day sky.

Andrea rushed back to the ambulance, where the EMTs were putting their equipment and supplies away. "Do you know where they are taking him?" she asked.

One of the EMTs sat on the bumper of the ambulance, pulled off blood stained rubber gloves, and carefully put them into a red Haz-Mat plastic bag. "They are taking him to the MoBay Hope Medical Centre. They have good emergency and trauma staff available. They also have an arrangement for long-term care with South Miami Hospital. I think they will keep him in Montego Bay. Unfortunately, we are getting quite a bit of practice with gunshot wounds."

"Thank you for coming so quickly and saving his life," she said, exhausted.

"No problem. If you hadn't applied pressure when you did, he would not have survived."

She nodded, stood, a bit unsteady, and walked to the car. She remembered that Grant had the keys to the BMW. How was she going to get to the hospital?

She returned to the EMTs getting into the ambulance. "Can I get a ride with you?"

One of the EMTs handed her a plastic bag with Grant's possessions. "I'm sorry, that's against policy." He nodded toward the plastic bag. "It looks like there's a set of keys in there. Besides, you need to wait here for the police. They are going to want to get a statement from you."

She took the bag and held it in her hands as if it were fragile. She watched the ambulance pull away and looked at Grant's few possessions. Though they did not represent what he was, she held on to it tight, afraid that this would be all she might have left of him. No one could lose that much blood and survive.

She couldn't wait for the police. She and Grant weren't even supposed to be on the island. If she let them detain her, she'd never get another chance to find Holly. She went to the BMW and dug in the bag for the key. A few feet from the silver car, she pressed the unlock button on the key, and a high-pitched "chirp" emitted from the car, unlocking the doors. She opened the driver's door and placed the plastic bag next to her on the passenger seat. A sudden chill down the back of her neck made her look around parking lot. The skin-prickling feeling made her believe that Jon-Pierre waited for her. She braced herself for a gunshot, but kept moving. Forward was the only path to Holly.

Andrea needed to be at the hospital with Grant. Self-doubt smoldered within her and taunted that she would never find Holly on her own. She couldn't give up hope that her daughter was still alive. Jon-Pierre was not a man to be trusted, but the mother in her had to believe that he would give Holly back to her, if she played his game. That slender thread of hope was all she had. Her hands tightened on the steering wheel, knuckles white with the dark fear that Holly was already as dead as Jena.

Chapter 52

Andrea couldn't find a place to park and her impatience ratcheted up with each passing second. A glance in the rear view mirror, one of a hundred since she left she lighthouse, told her the police hadn't followed her. She spotted an empty slot, marked for physicians only. The BMW looked the part, so she pulled in and parked. She grabbed the plastic bag containing Grant's possessions and ran for the front entrance.

She entered a waiting room, filled with locals and a smattering of tourists. Complaints about the long wait, uncomfortable seating, and stifling heat overwhelmed the triage nurse. All the obnoxious people were tourists. The locals took the wait in stride. Andrea took stock of the activity and realized that one nurse behind the counter controlled all the incoming traffic. The woman ruled the waiting room with an iron fist, quick to toss out troublemakers. Andrea approached the window gingerly and asked the officious matron, "Can I see Grant Turner, please?"

Not sure if the woman had heard her, Andrea was about to repeat her request when the woman looked at Andrea over her glasses and said, "There is no Grant Turner registered." She looked over Andrea's shoulder at the line that had formed behind her, "Next?"

"Wait—wait. Grant Turner came here by helicopter less than an hour ago. Could you please check?"

The woman clearly did not like someone questioning her knowledge of who had been admitted to her hospital. She sighed at the futility of this task and picked up the phone. "Do you have a patient by the name of Grant Turner, possibly off of a recent life flight?" She listened and showed no expression from which Andrea could draw any hope. She said nothing further and hung up the phone.

"As I told you, we have no Grant Turner registered at this hospital."

Andrea interrupted, "But he—"

The gatekeeper cut Andrea off. "If you let me finish, lady, there is no Grant Turner here. But, a John Doe was received off of a life flight helicopter."

"Where can I find him?"

The prideful nurse, enjoying the fact that she had been technically correct, paused to let that fact sink in. Then she continued, "Go through the double doors and follow the signs to 'surgery waiting.' Next?"

Andrea pushed the thin metal doors open and walked down the hospital corridor. Like any other hospital, this one smelled of disinfectant and chemicals. She passed an emergency room with medical staff hustling from one patient to the next. She took a right turn down another corridor and found a small waiting room with a woman at another window. The matron of this waiting room could have been a twin of the nurse she had encountered in the front reception.

Andrea approached and was prepared for the onslaught she had suffered out front. "I'm here to see Grant Turner. He was brought in as a John Doe on a life flight a little while ago."

The woman measured up Andrea and said, "Would you please fill this out with as much of your husband's personal information as possible? She handed Andrea a clipboard and then added, "Do you have a picture identification for Mr. Turner?"

She said, "No, I don't." Then she remembered the bag in her hand. "Wait a second." She reached into the plastic bag and drew out his wallet. She removed his California driver's license and handed it to the woman. Andrea sat and filled out the forms while the woman took a few steps out of sight. Andrea fidgeted in the stiff-backed chairs, designed to discourage long-term use. In the background, Andrea heard the whir of a copy machine and muffled voices behind the counter.

"Mrs. Turner? Excuse me, Mrs. Turner," the woman called from the counter.

Andrea popped up out of the chair and went to the window. "I'm sorry, I was lost in my own thoughts," she lied. It had taken a moment for her to realize the nurse was calling her.

"I understand. Mr. Turner is in surgery right now, and when he enters the recovery room the doctor will come and talk to you. I'm afraid all you can do right now is sit here in the waiting room and pass the time," the woman said in a kind voice, handing Grant's identification back to Andrea.

Andrea fell into a chair in the vacant waiting room, holding the plastic bag that represented all that was Grant. She stared at the floor and considered that if Grant didn't make it, she will have witnessed a whole family wiped from the face of the Earth. Andrea noticed small drops hit the plastic bag; she hadn't realized she was crying.

The clock moved slowly as she waited. Unable to contain her anxious tension, Andrea walked over to the counter and asked, "Is he still in surgery? It's been three hours."

The woman walked to the back, checked a board and returned to the counter. "Yes, he is still in there."

Andrea returned to her chair and sat back down. Feeling numb, she rested her head in her hands.

The nurse at the window yelled at Andrea, but the message didn't register.

"What is it? Is he out of surgery?" Andrea popped up from her chair.

"You can't use that here." the woman said with an edge in her voice.

"Use what? What are you talking about?" Andrea said through the fog.

"Your cell phone. You can't use that in here." The woman pointed to the sign restricting cell phone use in the hospital.

Andrea wasn't using a cell phone. What did the woman mean? Then she heard the cell phone ring and visually traced the sound to the plastic bag in her lap. Grant's cell phone was ringing.

She dug into the bag, grabbed the cell phone, opened it and held it to her ear. "Hello?"

"Ah, hello to you, Mrs. Carson. I can't tell you how happy I am to hear your voice," Jon-Pierre said in a phony sympathetic voice.

"What do you want?" Anger dripped from her words.

"Now is that any way to talk to the man who has your child? I was merely calling to extend my sympathies about Mr. Turner."

"What do you care about him? You were the one who put Grant in that condition," Andrea shouted.

"I must apologize to you and Mr. Turner. I failed to account for the wind. I should have hit him in the center of his chest. I'm so sorry, but maybe next time."

Andrea took a deep breath. "I doubt you even have my daughter. That's why you didn't bring her to the lighthouse."

"Oh, I still have little Holly. We have become quite close in the past few days," Jon-Pierre said.

The woman behind the counter came out front and walked toward Andrea. "I told you that you can't use a cell phone in here," and attempted to snatch the phone from her hand.

Andrea turned at the last second and walked down the corridor to continue the call. "Don't you hurt her!"

Jon-Pierre yawned. "We have been over this before. I have hurt her and I will continue to hurt her until I get what I want."

"What is it you want now?" Andrea asked.

"I want all the money wired to my account in the Caymans, as we had agreed. But now it is for one girl, because of all the trouble you have caused me."

"When do you want it? You need to give me time to get Grant's share of the money together."

"I really don't care if you ever pay me. I am enjoying my little house guest," he said. Andrea heard the wood creak from his footfalls.

Jon-Pierre slapped the lesions on the soles of Holly's feet with a thin reed and held the phone down to Holly's face. She screamed, crying out for her mother. "See, I told you we were having fun," he laughed in the phone.

"Please don't hurt her; I'll give you whatever you want!" Andrea cried into the phone.

"I know you will," the Haitian said. "I'll give you another twenty-four hours. But if you are so much as a minute late, I will think of something to do with little Holly."

Jon-Pierre snapped shut his cell phone and thought it was time to plan for a new girl to package up for the highest bidder. He glanced at Holly, convinced that she was secure and in no condition to walk, let alone escape again. She had learned that lesson.

Jon-Pierre packed a black nylon bag with a 35mm digital camera, a telephoto lens, duct tape, and a box of syringes filled with Ketamine. He grabbed the bag, tossed it on the front seat of the pickup truck, and headed back into the Montego Bay hunting grounds. The Arab connection was vacant for the moment. Jon-Pierre fancied an Asian buyer this time. Asia was a growing marketplace, and the Asians paid very well for his merchandise.

Chapter 53

Andrea closed the phone after her unsettling conversation. Her child was alive. Andrea didn't want to imagine the suffering the girl had experienced. The mere thought of Holly's pain was like an icy hand around a mother's heart. Andrea didn't trust the Haitian, but she was afraid not to believe him. She leaned back on the wall, her mind flooded with fear. In that web of darkness, she looked for a glimmer of hope for Holly's return.

The nurse from the surgery waiting room came down the hall and broke her concentration. "Mr. Turner is in the recovery room now. The doctor will be out to see you shortly."

Andrea followed the woman back to the surgery waiting room and stood. She didn't think her nerves would let her sit right now. A few minutes later, a small, light-skinned Jamaican man in blue surgical scrubs approached and asked if she was there for Mr. Turner. "The surgery went well, once we got the bleeding controlled. The bullet did a great deal of damage. Nicked a couple of major blood vessels, broke the clavicle on the way in and the shoulder blade, or scapula on the way out. As I said, a lot of tissue damage, and he will require a good deal of rehab. He's sedated now, but we should have him up and walking within a day or two. You can go and see him for a few minutes if you would like."

Andrea's mouth went dry, and she nodded at the doctor. She followed him down the hall, behind the counter, and into the second room on the right. Grant lay covered with wires and machines hooked up to him. She approached the bed and searched for a spot on his arm that didn't have a tube or wire connected to a machine. Andrea was afraid to touch him.

"He's so pale,"

"He lost a lot of blood. We had to give him a transfusion. He should start to brighten up in a few hours." The doctor paused, and then added, "The blood loss was substantial. We have to wait until he regains consciousness to find out if he suffered any brain damage."

Andrea looked at the respirator assisting Grant's breathing and realized how close he had come to not being here, and how close she had come to being alone. She gently bent down and whispered, "You are going to be okay, Grant. I'll be here for you." She gave him a soft kiss on his cheek.

The doctor touched her shoulder, whispering that it was time to go so that Grant could rest. She took another look at the rise and fall of his chest, matching time with the respirator. Andrea left, following the doctor back to the waiting room. She took a chair, curled up on it the best she could and tried to figure out why Jon-Pierre had shot Grant rather than her. What was the reason Holly hadn't perished in the plane crash, like Jena? Andrea kept asking, why? Survivor's guilt. Holly was alive and Andrea was grateful.

Andrea pondered these questions when someone lightly placed a hand on her shoulder. The touch shocked Andrea, and she turned around quickly. Lieutenant Washington looked down at her, his suit still crisp.

"How is our boy doing? I looked in on him. He looks like he was run over." Lieutenant Washington walked around and sat in the chair next to Andrea, letting out a big sigh. "So why don't we start with what happened, Miss Carson?"

Andrea shuddered. "Jon-Pierre lured us to the Negril lighthouse and told us he would exchange the girls for money. Once we got there, he called us. But, he wouldn't show us the girls. Then the shots came from a little hill just above the lighthouse. The first shot hit Grant."

"So where is the money that you were going to hand over?" Washington questioned.

"We were going to wire the money to the First National Bank of Grand Cayman."

The Lieutenant asked, "Why is it that people seem to get hurt around you, Miss Carson?"

"Perhaps if you would do a better job, we wouldn't even be here. It's not our fault that you can't control the crime in your own country. You know full well Jon-Pierre kidnaps young women, and you ignore it, so don't tell me it's my fault."

Andrea stared back at Washington, refusing to back down. The Lieutenant nodded his head and looked deeply in her eyes. "Baptiste has protection very high up in the ministry. He pays well for that insulation and has access to our communication and operational plans. With that he has managed to stay at least two steps ahead of us."

"He still has my daughter, and I have to get her back before he hurts her again. He still expects me to wire money to his account. I know it's risky, but I can't give up on my daughter."

Washington hung his head. "I know you won't give up, Miss Carson. Unfortunately, I cannot help you in that matter. I hope you understand."

"No, I don't understand, Lieutenant," she touched him on the arm. "You had a child murdered, didn't you?"

"He looked away from her, clearly uncomfortable, and in a low voice told her, "Yes, my oldest daughter was murdered after being sexually assaulted. Her assailant was never identified. Supposedly, he was from a prominent American family, and they couldn't bear the shame."

"Put yourself in my place, Lieutenant. What would you do if you were me?"

"I honestly don't know, Miss Carson. I can tell you Baptiste will not simply hand over your daughter. Don't trust him, or you could end up like Mr. Turner in there," the Lieutenant said, motioning to the recovery room.

Andrea had struck a chord with Washington, and for the first time he appeared uneasy. He rose and walked out of the waiting room. To her surprise, there were no other police officers with him to arrest her.

She snuck back to Grant's room, where she found a nurse checking his IV and charting the vital signs from his monitor. She looked over her shoulder at Andrea and nodded, which told her she could enter the room.

She took a chair next to Grant's bed and watched him breathe with mechanical precision. She hoped each new respirator-fed breath brought him closer to recovery. She listened for any irregularity and held her own breath waiting for his next. She wondered about the doctor's warning; Grant may have brain damage from the blood loss. He had risked his life for Holly after watching the plane that carried Jena careen into the ocean. Andrea felt responsible for what happened to him. When she needed his strength and compassion the most, she couldn't have it.

They had begun their search together. Now she had no one else to rely on for strength or support. Where this journey would end, along with Holly's fate, was up to her—alone.

Chapter 54

With one girl dead and another dying, Jon-Pierre needed new blood for potential income. The sugary–white-sand beach at Doctor's Cove always attracted crowds from the adjoining resorts. Time for the hunt. It was his favorite part of the business, when he selected, groomed and picked off a ripe, sellable target.

He rummaged in his backpack, pulled out a thin binder and leafed through a stack of counterfeit nightclub. He put his finger on a brochure for Pier 1, a popular nightspot with tourists. His doctored brochure promised free drinks all night at the Gloucester Avenue bar. He pulled a copy of the brochure from the binder and stowed his bag.

The resorts chased off anyone who solicited guests as a general rule. Jon-Pierre's unique, olive complexion helped him blend in with the tourists, who napped and drank in the hot Jamaican sun. Among them, he spotted a potential target—young, athletically built, and most importantly, no male companion hovering nearby. He navigated through the hot sand to the lounge chair that held his quarry.

"Excuse me, Miss, I have something for you," he said in a very deferential voice.

Jennifer Mercer shaded her face and looked up into Jon-Pierre's piercing blue eyes. "I'm really not interested, but thanks anyway." She turned away from him.

"I'm sorry, but you'll want to see this. No cover and free drinks at one of the island's best nightclubs," he said.

Jennifer's eyes flickered open, and she asked suspiciously, "What do I have to do?"

Jon-Pierre got down on one knee next to the bikini-clad woman. "You don't have to do anything. We are doing a promotional event at the club and will be filming commercial spots, so we want attractive people there, having fun. You are over eighteen, right?"

Jennifer hadn't had her ego stroked back home in Pittsburg, Pennsylvania, and the thought of getting on camera appealed to her. Part of the reason she had come on this vacation was to forget about the jerk she had broken up with back home.

"I'm twenty-one. Can my friend Karen come too?

Jon-Pierre asked, "Where is Karen now?" The prospect of another duo sparked a rush of euphoria in him.

Jennifer sat up, adjusted the skimpy suit that barely covered her, and pointed to a dark-haired woman in the surf, walking in their direction.

"Sure, she can come too," Jon-Pierre said.

Karen plopped into another lounge chair under an umbrella. "What's going on?" she asked, toweling her hair.

"I'll leave it to you to tell Karen about tonight. I hope you two are able to make it. You would both be great in the commercial spot. Come by around ten this evening."

Jennifer looked excited. "Thank you. What's your name?"

He paused, then figured there would be no harm in her knowing. She would not be able to tell anyone who mattered. "Jon-Pierre. Ask for me at the door when you get to the club."

He walked away, confident that he had set the hook on this one. Looking over his shoulder at a safe distance, Jon-Pierre watched the two girls show animated excitement. That was a very good sign, he thought. When he retrieved his bag, he quickly removed his camera and took a dozen pictures of the girls.

The evening's activities required his full attention. Holly Carson was of no further value. He had enjoyed the brief diversion she provided, but Holly was now defective surplus, something to discard.

Before he disposed of her, there was a last opportunity for a payday and a bit of fun at her mother's expense. He opened his cell phone and redialed the last number.

Andrea scrambled for the cell phone stuffed in the plastic bag with the rest of Grant's property. She pushed the connect button and answered, "Hello?"

"Time to finish our discussion, Mrs. Carson. I understand that Mr. Turner is a bit under the weather, so it's just you and me this time around," Jon-Pierre said.

"How can I trust you? You didn't bring her last time," she said.

"Can you, or should I say, can Holly, afford *not* to trust me?"

Andrea knew she was utterly alone, without Grant to lean on. She drew a deep breath and gathered strength from somewhere deep inside. "What do we do next?"

"That's what I like to hear, Mrs. Carson. Here is what you are going to do. You will wire transfer the money by midnight tonight. You still have the bank information, I presume."

"I know where you want the money sent in the Caymans. Why midnight? You told me we had more time?"

"Something has come up which will take more time and attention, causing me to conclude this matter earlier than planned," Jon-Pierre explained.

"If I do what you request, when will—"

"There will be no *if* on your part. Any lapse will guarantee that you will never see your daughter again." He paused to let his point sink in. "You will do what I direct you to do. Is that clear?"

Andrea felt her nerves fraying, and she tried to sound composed. "When?"

"Once I see the money hit my account, I will call you with directions. There is no negotiation on this point. The money must be transferred by midnight."

"What assurance do I have that you will live up to your part of the bargain?"

"Absolutely none," and with that Jon-Pierre hung up the phone.

Andrea shook and collapsed into the chair. How was she going to pull this off alone? She had to do exactly what this pervert demanded if she had any chance at getting Holly back. She trembled and wondered what a mother could do to get her child back from an insane killer? That's when it hit her, she couldn't be like any other mother. That is what he was counting on. Jon-Pierre had never come up against a mother like her.

Chapter 55

Andrea saw Grant stir in his hospital bed. "Grant, can you hear me?"

He made a slight moan, and Andrea saw a flicker in his eyes. Sensitive to the light, he squinted. Andrea read the panic in his face when he tried to speak when the ventilator tube gagged him.

She put her hand on his arm and softly told him, "You're on a ventilator, so don't try to talk. You're going to be all right." The last part she hoped was true.

Grant looked at her and moved his hands in a weak gesture that asked for a pencil and paper.

Andrea went from drawer to drawer, slamming one after another in frustration. She ran from the room and returned in seconds with a note pad, pencil, and a nurse in tow.

The nurse gave Grant the once over and said, "Mr. Turner, you had surgery and your blood oxygen is still low, so we don't want to take you off the ventilator. You need help breathing. Do you understand?"

Andrea put the notebook in Grant's hand and held the pencil for him. He took the pencil and scrawled an undecipherable message. Frustrated, Grant tried again. It looked like the writing of a five-year-old child who needed more practice on a newly learned letter. He handed the pad back to Andrea and melted back on the bed, exhausted from the effort.

She read Grant's labored message: "Did you get Holly?"

"He never intended to give her to us. He still has her and wants me to wire the money. I don't know what to do," Andrea said.

Grant held his hand out for the note pad again. He carefully scribbled a message and handed it back to Andrea.

Andrea looked at his message. It read, "Jena would want you to get Holly back, and so do I. Take the money and get her back." Distress etched his forehead. She gently took his hand and told him to close his eyes and get some sleep. Andrea went to the window and pulled the blinds shut, blocking out the bright sun.

She had returned to her chair in the corner near the bed when she saw Grant try to turn his head. Andrea gently said, "I'm right here, Grant. You can't get rid of me that easily."

The monitors over the bed chirped a steady rhythm, which Andrea took as a good sign. She was grateful that Grant seemed to be able to communicate, and didn't seem to have the brain damage the doctor had mentioned, even though he had a long way to go for full recovery. She listened to the monitors for over an hour, and the mesmerizing sound lulled her to sleep.

A nurse entered the room and startled Andrea. She told Andrea that the next time Grant roused she would remove his ventilator tube.

"If Mr. Grant does exactly as instructed, then he will do well," the nurse added,

Andrea nodded her head wearily, glad to hear some positive words.

The nurse's words resonated within her: *Do exactly as instructed.*

She went out in the hallway and placed a call to an old family friend. Luckily, Andrea had reached him before he retired for the night. Andrea told him what she needed, though the seventy-five-year-old banker was concerned about why she needed that amount of money. He asked her if she was in trouble. Andrea did not want to worry the man who had suffered two heart attacks in the past ten years.

"Most banks in the Caymans operate under a veil of secrecy, so you may not be able to track the funds after they are deposited. A host of shady enterprises use the banks for that very reason," the banker said.

"Uncle Nigel" (that's what she called him, though he was not her real uncle, rather a longtime friend of her father), "I have to make this transfer happen for reasons I don't want to bother you with right now." She described the very specific way she wanted the funds handled.

Nigel begrudgingly agreed to help her, knowing that Andrea would never ask for this kind of help if it weren't urgent.

"Can we get this transfer done by midnight, Jamaican time?"

"If I had a staff of five on hand to certify the funds and develop all the transfer documents, then certainly, but all you have right now is this tottering old man," he told Andrea, even though she knew he was sharp and could out-perform the twenty-somethings he hired in his bank. In reality, he thrived on beating the younger folks and grinding them into dust.

"Can you do it? It's important, Uncle Nigel."

He sighed, "Let me see what I can do. I will call you--at this number?"

"Thank you so much. Holly and I both appreciate this more than you can imagine."

"Let me get hopping on this, dear," and he hung up the phone.

Andrea knew that if it were possible, Nigel could do it. He had to come through. Holly's life depended on it.

Chapter 56

Jon-Pierre returned to his remote cabin and stepped out of his battered pickup truck. He gazed deep into the vegetation surrounding the cabin, looking for anything that did not belong. He had grown more paranoid since the Americans violated his hillside home. Thankfully, all the weapons and material he required for his evening plans were in the cabin.

Satisfied that no one lurked in the jungle that enveloped his hideaway, Jon-Pierre unlocked the door and stepped inside. The cabin was very dim, and a strong smell permeated the thick, moist air within. He lit a gas lantern, casting a ghostly pallor across the cabin. Holly hung limp from the railing, and she'd soiled herself in his absence. Jon-Pierre recognized the first signs of dysentery caused by the bacteria infested water he forced her to drink.

Jon-Pierre was too busy planning the night's events to deal with Holly's disgusting condition. He set about the cabin, gathering duct tape and black pillowcases, stuffing them into his bag, along with a silenced Glock G-22. Finally, he bent down to a small wooden cabinet and spun a combination lock. He reached in and pulled out a small black box. He withdrew a small glass container containing more Ketamine and two syringes.

He slung the bag over his shoulder and picked up a container of water, collected from the rain over the past week, and poured it on Holly. The shock of the water caused the girl to convulse. Her feet remained suspended, and Jon-Pierre noticed that the flesh on the outer edges of the wounds had turned black. A sprinkling of blow fly maggots wiggling about on one of her feet.

"We'll soon be rid of you. I talked to your mother again, and for some reason she wants you back. I really don't see it, but that's her problem, isn't it, Holly?" He paused for a response from the girl and took her silence as arrogance.

"I asked you a question. It's your mother's problem isn't it?" Without waiting for a response, he kicked her in the kidney.

Holly rolled away and whimpered, "Yes--yes, it's her problem."

"That's better. If you were mine I'd let you rot." He laughed, "I guess you are mine."

He turned out the lantern, leaving the cabin pitch dark, Holly's muffled cries to be swallowed up in the dense black jungle.

Excited about the night's possibilities, Jon-Pierre headed toward Montego Bay. He needed a replacement for the well-worn pickup truck, something more fitting to the jet-setting nightclub owner he was to portray this evening. More importantly, he needed something that could not be traced back to him.

The Tryall Golf, Tennis and Beach Club was along his route, and he decided that this was a likely spot to pick up his new vehicle. As he slowed down, he could see the main villa brightly illuminated for an event being held at the posh and exclusive club. That meant a selection of top-end cars awaited. Jon-Pierre parked his truck on the side of the road. Anyone who passed by would mistake it for a broken-down derelict. He hopped a hedge parallel to the manicured grounds and kept to the shadows. There were easily forty cars in the dimly lit square of asphalt, but what he did not count on was a score of valets who scurried and retrieved the eighty-thousand dollar cars for a buck or two in tips.

Jon-Pierre was at the rear of the lot, on the edge of the shadows, when he spotted a red-jacketed valet trotting in his direction. Jon-Pierre pulled a black butterfly knife from his back pocket. As he silently whipped the knife forward, the blade exposed its sharp serrated edge as it freed itself from the handle. Jon-Pierre moved undetected behind the car to the right and watched the valet's approach. He did not need to kill the unsuspecting young man in the gaudy jacket, but if the valet compromised Jon-Pierre's position, he would have no second thought.

The valet trotted to a green Jaguar XKS, and Jon-Pierre moved behind it, ready to take the valet. He didn't start the car. Sensing something wrong, he moved over to the next row of cars so he could look and see what delayed the valet.

The valet entertained a fifty-year-old woman with a formal, blue-beaded gown. The straps of the dress hung down, and the couple seemed very much occupied with one another. What bothered Jon-Pierre was how he missed the woman's approach.

Jon-Pierre considered taking them both at this moment, but his primary goal was to get a car and leave unnoticed. Two disemboweled bodies in a Jaguar were likely to get noticed. He crept back into the darkness, his eyes locked on the odd coupling in the vehicle.

There was too much activity in and out of the parking lot. Jon-Pierre looked into the surrounding darkness and saw lights from one of the eight privately owned villas in the resort compound. He trotted in the direction of the lights and found a new Mercedes S550 on a narrow cobblestone driveway.

He moved closer to the luxury car and noticed a blue light blinking on the center console. A car alarm. Jon-Pierre went to the villa's front door and listened closely. He heard the faint sound of a television and smiled. With his knife, he wiggled the lock free, happy the homeowners did not throw the deadbolt. The next hurdle was to find out if the home was alarmed like the car. He pushed the door inward very slowly, looking for contacts, magnets, or pins. An inch at a time, he analyzed the door casing, pushing the door forward. Finally, Jon-Pierre found a magnetic contact in the top of the doorframe. He looked through the glass panel near the door and located the alarm control box. Bright green letters proclaimed, "Unarmed."

Jon-Pierre moved more swiftly and stepped into the villa. The television sound came from the rear of the residence. He entered the hallway and quickly found a large gold tray, holding an assortment of keys. Jon-Pierre picked up a Mercedes key and silently backed out the front door.

The electronic key shut off the car's alarm system, and Jon-Pierre got behind the wheel, while adjusting the soft leather seat. The car started with a considerable roar from its high performance exhaust system, and Jon-Pierre quickly backed out of the driveway. He drove back toward the main complex, passing the crowd of valets.

Jon-Pierre approached the security gate, where the man waiving cars through figured that people leaving weren't a problem for the resort. The security guard stepped out in front of his car and forced Jon-Pierre to stop at the security booth. As the sixty-year-old security guard limped slowly to the driver's window, Jon-Pierre's anxiety notched up. When the man tapped on the window, Jon-Pierre had no choice but to roll it down. The Haitian's hand tightened on his pistol.

"Yes, what is it? I am in a terrible hurry," Jon-Pierre said in an arrogant tone. He figured the people who lived in these decadent locations were always in a hurry.

"Your headlights aren't on. I didn't want you to get in an accident out there," the old man cautioned, pointing to the main road ahead.

Jon-Pierre felt foolish for not noticing this mundane detail. First, the woman in the Jaguar had crept up on him, and now this. He was coming apart. His chest grew tight, and he felt light headed.

The security guard sensed something wrong. "Are you all right sir? Do you need me to call for a doctor?"

Jon-Pierre didn't hear the man at first, but then shook his head and said, "No, I'm fine, but thank you very much."

"Are you sure, because you look kinda pale?" The security man stepped closer. "Don't forget to turn on your lights."

Jon-Pierre looked at the dash but couldn't find the control for the lights. He fumbled with every dial and knob he could find, turned on the windshield washer, the GPS navigation, and the CD player. He finally tripped over the correct knob, and the luxury car's lights illuminated the road ahead.

"Mister, you look real confused. I'm calling you a doctor," the security man announced.

"No need," Jon-Pierre retorted, and roared out of the resort.

He ran through a mental checklist of the tasks ahead, and this detail work calmed his mind. He could afford no further lapses tonight. Speeding toward Montego Bay, Jon-Pierre looked over the interior of the car for items that would detract from his persona as a high-rolling club owner. There was nothing like the sight of a child's car seat to burst that bubble. Thankfully, the car's owner kept the car free of clutter.

He pulled up next to his old truck and retrieved the bag with the Ketamine, syringes and duct tape. He left the truck on the roadside, unworried that someone would trace it back to him. The registration was in the name of a dead construction worker.

Jon-Pierre pulled up to the nightclub, located on a busy strip on Gloucester, and had the car valet parked. He stepped to the door confidently and shook hands with the doorman.

"Good evening, Mr. Baptiste," said the massive doorman.

"And a good evening to you, Jonathan. Please do me a favor; two young ladies will be dropping by in a bit. I would very much appreciate it if you would let them in and have them escorted to my table." Jon-Pierre handed the doorman a wad of cash, totaling five hundred dollars.

The doorman's eyes grew large. He told Jon-Pierre that he would look for the women he described and would personally see to it that they went to his table.

The doorman then took his position at the front of the establishment and made certain only the right people were allowed entry. If you were not on the list, your chances were not good, unless you are a patron like Mr. Baptiste.

Jon-Pierre wandered through the club and took his usual booth at the rear. Just as he sat down, a bouncer, equal in size to Jonathan the doorman, came to his table.

Jon-Pierre knew this man well from Haiti, and he had paid him to handle delicate situations for him. Jon-Pierre sat with both arms across the back of the massive leather seat that enclosed the booth. He looked up and said, "We may have a bit of work this evening. Are you up to making a thousand dollars tonight?"

The man smiled, "Always. Are we talking about taking a package out the back door?"

Jon-Pierre shrugged his shoulders, "Maybe--we'll have to see how it goes. I would like to get them out the front door so people can say they left under their own power, but we'll have to see how the evening unfolds."

The large man got close. "You said *them*, so we are talking about more than one, then?"

"Yes, we are dealing with two this evening. So I will need you to hang close, because when it happens, it will be fast."

"I understand. Let me know when we are in play, and I'll be ready."

Chapter 57

Grant's eyes flickered and his first vision was a tired, worried Andrea. She bit her lower lip, while staring at the yellowed linoleum tiles. All the weight of the world seemed laden on her shoulders. He had let her down, as he had let Jena down. Even tied and wired to the hospital bed, Grant knew he had to help find Holly, because Holly was the only remaining link to Jena. He hoped, in time, that Holly could tell him about the last days of his daughter's life. He needed to know.

Andrea caught movement from Grant's bed. She turned and found his eyes looked somewhat stronger than before, but still incredibly sad. She scooted her chair close to his bedside. She took his hand, and it closed around hers.

"How are you feeling? You look a bit better," she said.

Grant started to speak, but the ventilator tube stopped him. He nodded his head.

She pushed the nurse's call button, and moments later the attending nurse came through the door.

"I bet you want that thing off, don't you, dear?" the nurse said.

Within a minute, she had removed the tube and placed an oxygen tube under Grant's nose. She checked his vital signs and gave an approving look.

Once the nurse cleared the door, Grant spoke in a graveled rough voice, "What's going on with getting Holly back?"

"Jon-Pierre demanded the money, or I won't see her again. I have to play his game, even though this guy would lie to the Pope." She paused,

"I don't know where we are supposed to meet, but I'm going to call and try to control that piece. I need to figure out where."

Grant moved, trying to sit up on the bed, disturbed by how weak he felt. "Don't put yourself in a position where he can hurt you too. I couldn't bear that, Andrea, and I'm useless here. I can't do a damn thing to help you."

"You can help by thinking about where the exchange with Jon-Pierre should happen. In a public location, I'm thinking." she said

"The more public and open the better. He's not going to like being vulnerable, especially if Holly is with him. She will be in some sort of restraints, tied up like she was in the boat, and she will be difficult to hide out in the open." Grant paused to get his breath. "I don't know, Andrea, and I really don't like the idea of you going at this alone."

"I don't like it either, Grant, but what choice do I have? I can't exactly roll you up in a wheelchair and threaten to run him down, now can I? I'm stronger than I look. I can do this, and I have to do this for Holly."

Andrea pulled the cell phone from her pocket and looked at the list of recent calls. She scrolled down to the Jon-Pierre's number. He picked up after three rings, and she heard loud, thumping music in the background. Finally, in the voice that set her teeth on edge, he said, "Yes? Who is this?"

Andrea swallowed and then said, "Where are we making the exchange?"

Jon-Pierre took the phone from his ear and looked at it, "Woman, you have some nerve calling me now; it is not a good time."

"If you want any money, make it a good time," she said sternly, with Grant looking on.

"You are a pain in the ass. What do you want? Make it quick before I lose interest."

"We make the exchange in the hotel lobby of the Ritz-Carlton in Montego Bay at midnight."

Jon-Pierre looked across the club's pulsating dance floor as Jennifer and her friend Karen made their way to his table. The approach of the new girls caused a sudden smile on his face, and he answered Andrea, "Midnight it is. Don't be late. This is your last chance, Mrs. Carson."

Andrea trembled as she closed the phone and sat down before her legs gave out. She looked at Grant, shrugged her shoulders, and said, "It's done. He's agreed to meet in the hotel lobby at midnight."

Grant was impressed. "You did really well. You didn't let that bastard get the best of you. You set the terms and stuck to them."

"I hope it all falls into place, and I pray that Uncle Nigel completes the wire transaction for me. If he doesn't, it will all blow up."

With great effort, Grant sat up in his hospital bed, and Andrea stepped to his bedside. He looked anxious: "Nigel? Andrea, go get the nurse. I'm coming with you."

"You can't be serious. Grant, look at you. You barely had the strength to sit up, and then you broke into a cold sweat," she scolded him.

"I can't let you go meet with this psycho. He's crazy, and if you don't get the nurse, I'm going to pull these IV's out myself."

"You pull those out and who's crazy then? What could you possibly do but sit in a wheelchair? That will strike terror in him, for sure."

"Don't do this by yourself. Help me out of here." Grant tried to swing a leg off the bed, and after tremendous effort, all he got was a cold sweat. He looked dejected and worn.

He continued to struggle, and Andrea put a gentle on the center of his chest. "Grant, stop. You are going to hurt yourself. I'm doing this, but I can't deal with you doing something stupid and hurting yourself too." She pushed him back onto the bed and held him down for a moment.

He looked up into Andrea's determined face and gave up struggling. "I don't like feeling helpless when you need me the most." He looked away from her.

Andrea put a hand on his cheek, turned his face toward hers and softly told him, "I appreciate that you want to help me, but I'm a big girl, and I can take care of myself. I don't want anything else to happen to you. I thought I had lost you at the lighthouse, and that scared me. I care about you." She caressed his forehead and saw the pain in his eyes. She tipped his chin upward and softly kissed him.

"I can't take the possibility of losing you now," she continued. She rose from the edge of his bed and touched his cheek with a light fingertip. "I'll be back as soon as I can. Don't worry about me; you worry about getting better." She spoke with a shaky self-confidence that welled from within. With a tentative first step, Andrea walked toward the door, looking back over her shoulder as she left.

She left a good man to confront an evil one.

Chapter 58

Jon-Pierre settled into his act as a high roller in the club. The garish neon lighting reflected off mirror-covered walls, and dark leather seating, complemented by expensive booze, helped complete the facade. Jennifer and Karen, escorted to the table by the doorman, sat with Jon-Pierre, one on each side of the Haitian. The girls gawked at the activity in the popular nightspot and looked impressed.

"Thank you for inviting us. This place looks fun," Jennifer shouted over the music.

"You really own this place? Wow, that's impressive. This club looks like some of the high-end clubs back home, the ones I can't hope to get into," Karen added.

Jon-Pierre nodded his head and raised his hand for a waitress. When she arrived, he ordered a local drink favorite called a Green Grass for the ladies and top-shelf vodka for himself.

"Can we go dance?" Jennifer asked.

"Of course, go have fun. Don't look for the cameras, they will find you. We use small digital recorders so people don't play to the cameras. It wastes our time. Go--," Jon-Pierre lied.

The two girls stood up, walked to the dance floor a few yards away, and enjoyed the music. Jon-Pierre thought the sound was offensive and decadent. He watched the two of them blend into the crowd, looking for the cameras that weren't there.

The waitress brought back the drink order, and Jon-Pierre sent her away. He pulled his vodka toward him and downed it quickly, experiencing a pleasurable warm feeling. He withdrew a glass container of Ketamine from his jacket pocket and pulled the icy light green drinks close to him. He pulled the foil seal from the vial and poured half into each glass. He stirred it with a straw and placed the cocktails back in front of each girl's seat.

After nearly fifteen minutes of dancing, Jennifer and Karen returned to the table and plopped down in their seats. "That was really fun," Jennifer said, while blotting sweat from her forehead. She picked up the frozen drink and took a big sip through the straw.

Karen followed suit, then grabbed her temples. "Brain freeze--ouch." She waited a few seconds, then took another long pull. "This is really good. What did you call this?"

Jon-Pierre looked at her and smiled, "It is a Green Grass, and I know you've never had a drink like this before."

Jennifer asked him about the cameras and where there were, because she couldn't see anything that looked like a lens. Jon-Pierre randomly pointed to three or four people on the floor and said they were the staff with the recording equipment. Jennifer said, "It must be really small, because you can't tell at all."

Jon-Pierre played along. "It's very expensive."

Jennifer jumped up and grabbed Karen's hand. "Let's go get on camera," and they trotted to the dance floor together.

Jon-Pierre sat back and checked his watch. The dancing would only speed the drug through their systems. He had twenty minutes at most, so it was time to get into position. He located the bouncer, who looked directly at him, waiting. Jon-Pierre nodded his head, and the bouncer came to his table.

"It is time to make ready. Please have my car delivered out back," Jon-Pierre said, while handing the parking slip to the valet. The man took it and walked away without saying a word.

In the middle of the crowd, Karen suddenly stopped dancing and reached out for anyone, as though she were going to fall. Everything went blurry, and she felt fuzzy all over.

Jennifer saw her friend was unsteady and grabbed her before she collapsed.

"What's wrong" Jennifer asked.

Karen didn't verbally respond; she only shook her head slowly. Jennifer helped her friend back to the table and sat her down. Jennifer knelt in front of Karen. "You probably got overheated; look at the sweat on your face. Here, take another sip of this. It will cool you off." She handed the drug-laced drink to Karen, who obediently took several long sips.

Jon-Pierre was amused when the girl poured the drug down her friend's throat. "I'll take care of her, but you need to sit down and cool off yourself."

He couldn't believe it was that easy. Jennifer went to her seat and sucked down her drink while her friend did the same. He wouldn't even need the syringe to finish the job tonight. Jon-Pierre, seeing the bouncer step through the rear exit, and nodded to him.

Jon-Pierre looked at his watch, and if as on cue, Jennifer suddenly fell back in her seat and said, "I must have drunk that too fast; I don't feel very good."

Karen was in her seat, unconscious. Jon-Pierre figured it was time, and he subtly signaled for the Henri, the bouncer. Jon-Pierre told Jennifer, "You must have a bit of an island bug. I'll take you two back to your hotel."

The bouncer lifted Karen up and quickly took her out the rear exit, while Jon-Pierre assisted Jennifer to the door of the waiting Mercedes. Jennifer saw that a big man carried her friend, but it never registered that something was wrong. *This nice guy was taking them home in his flashy car. How cool was that?*

The bouncer skillfully applied duct tape to Karen's arms and gently placed her in the back seat. He then came up from behind Jennifer, took her hands behind her and bound them with the tape. Jennifer looked confused but could not respond. Jon-Pierre sat her in the front passenger seat and secured the shoulder harness. No sooner than the seat belt clicked in place, Jennifer passed out, leaning forward against the pressure of the harness.

Jon-Pierre walked around to the driver's side and told the bouncer, "Make sure to clean the table." He handed the bouncer a huge wad of cash for his assistance tonight.

The bouncer nodded and headed back inside the establishment to attend to Jon-Pierre's instructions.

The Mercedes pulled from the dank, trash-ridden alleyway behind the club and out onto Gloucester Avenue. Jon-Pierre headed back toward his cabin to complete his arrangements with these two new acquisitions. He had something special in mind for one of them and thought it would be something he would enjoy very much. He raced the Mercedes up the narrow roadway to the dark cabin.

By the time he arrived at the cabin, it was nearly eleven o'clock. The darkness had enveloped the location, all light absorbing into the surrounding forest. He slid the Mercedes next to the cabin, pulled the back door of the car open and yanked Karen out by her feet. She smacked her head on the ground. He dragged her by the legs, up the stairs and all the way to the small covered porch by the door.

He removed the chain from the door and walked into the cabin, which was as dark as the night outside. He paused and lit the gas lantern, before pulling Karen to the back of the cabin next to Holly.

"I have some company for you." Jon-Pierre secured Karen to the post next to Holly, suspending her in an identical position.

Jon-Pierre quickly stepped back outside and removed Jennifer from the car. He carried her into the cabin, as he did not want to damage this item, because it would most certainly affect the purchase price. He laid her against a wall and duct taped her legs. In addition, he put handcuffs over the duct tape and locked a retention chain to a metal hook high on the wall above the girl's body.

Now tired from the hurried effort, Jon-Pierre was nevertheless pleased with the night's results. He could notify his buyer network and start the bids. He looked at his watch again, and saw that it was time to meet with the American woman to collect another paycheck. The girl was as good as dead, and after the money hit his Cayman account, the woman was dead too. He checked his silenced Glock and tucked it into the back of his pants, beneath his jacket.

Jon-Pierre looked at the spot where Holly and the new girl were suspended. He grabbed a black hood and said, "Time to go see mommy."

Chapter 59

Andrea took a taxi from the hospital to the Ritz-Carlton, a long, fifteen-minute ride. She strode into the lobby, nearly deserted at this hour, yet the clerks remained on station at both the front and concierge desks. A few guests came in after a night on the town, and the staff attended to their every whim. As soon as Andrea reached the main marble floor, a bellman offered to fetch her bags. She politely waived him off, telling him that a friend was meeting her.

She searched along the walls and plush sofas for Holly and her captor. Andrea nearly jumped out of her skin when the cell phone rang. She fumbled with it and answered, "Hello?"

"It's Nigel, dear. The task you assigned to me has been completed," the old man reported.

"I can't thank you enough, Uncle Nigel. When we get home, I will fill you in on all the details, and give you a big hug."

"That's more than payment enough. I have to advise you, once again, that dealing with these offshore banks is tricky business," he cautioned.

Andrea, knowing he always protected her, responded, "I will be careful, Uncle. The account is set up as I asked?"

"Yes, it is, and I have a password for you: 'pirate.' Something told me that's what you are dealing with, and you are in the Caribbean, after all."

How appropriate. She thanked Nigel again before she hung up. She was ready. The hair on the back of her neck pricked with anticipation, and she nearly hyperventilated from shallow, rapid breathing. She tried to calm herself; Andrea needed to be at the top of her game.

She walked to the edge of the lobby overlooking the pools, sitting flat and silent at this time of night. A few guests sat at one of the bars, enjoying a nightcap before they retired. The huge, sculpted-iron clock behind the registration deck proclaimed it was a quarter past midnight.

Her cell rang again, and she hurriedly answered after the first ring, "Yes?"

"Where are you? We are waiting for you, Mommy," Jon-Pierre said.

"I'm in the hotel lobby, like we agreed. Where are you? Her tension rose like a weather balloon.

"I've changed my mind. Come out to the beach. Follow the path to the left after you pass the pool. It's more private, so your daughter and I can have some intimate time together. Better hurry."

Andrea had no time to respond. Jon-Pierre had hung up. She walked to the edge of the pool and spied the walkway that veered left toward the beach. The trail was thick with lush tropical plants and dramatically lit. The lighting ensured that Jon-Pierre would see her approach, and the glare would prevent her view of the beach. Once she stepped off the path into the deep sand, Andrea saw little beyond the darkness around her. All she could discern was the outline of a few palm trees and the faint luminescence of waves cresting off shore.

She walked a few yards into the sand when she heard the shuffle of footsteps behind her. She quickly turned and saw Jon-Pierre behind a large palm.

"Where's Holly?"

Without moving from the tree, Jon-Pierre responded, "Do you have my money, Mrs. Carson?"

"Check with your bank. It was sent."

He looked surprised and called his connection at his bank. He spoke in rapid French and listened, then spoke again, more urgently. He looked at Andrea and said, "What kind of game is this?"

"It's called an escrow account. You get the money so long as you do what I tell you to do, namely hand over my daughter. Then I'll give you the password. Now where is Holly?"

Andrea saw his anger, and then he pulled a dark hooded figure from the shadows behind the tree.

"Oh God, Holly!" In the darkness, she made out a wisp of Holly's hair sticking out from under the hood. It took every ounce of strength she had not to run and hug Holly. She demanded, "Let her walk to me."

"She has great difficulty walking. I will turn her loose when you give me the password for the account."

Holly's return was worth any price this extortionist demanded. *Be strong.* Andrea stood firm and said, "The password—the password is *pirate.*"

Jon-Pierre laughed, dialed his bank once again and communicated with his bank representative. Even in French, Andrea heard him use the password—*pirate.* A few seconds passed, and then he nodded his head and smiled. He put the phone back in his pocket.

"You have done well and now I must depart," he said.

"My daughter!" Andrea shouted.

Jon-Pierre pushed the girl in Andrea's direction. Hooded, disoriented and hobbled, the girl collapsed in the sand.

"I'm here, baby." She ran toward Holly and gathered the girl up in her arms. Andrea pulled the hood from her daughter's precious face, and her reward was a wide-eyed girl, her mouth taped closed. It wasn't Holly.

Stunned, Andrea froze as she looked into an unfamiliar face. When she recovered, Andrea spun towards Jon-Pierre, who stood six feet away, a large dark handgun leveled at her. She pulled the girl out of the way and insisted, "I did everything you asked. Why—why are you doing this?"

"Because, Mrs. Carson, you have cost me a great deal of trouble and money," he said, and looked down the barrel of the pistol at her head.

Andrea refused to back down: "Where is my Holly, you sick bastard?"

"Your precious little Holly is fish food by now. Now I'm finished with you," Jon-Pierre said.

She watched as he firmed his finger on the pistol's trigger. Her impending death was a final failure, and she would die with unresolved questions about Holly's fate. Andrea didn't flinch when she heard the gunshot, or when she saw the fine red mist that exploded from the back of Jon-Pierre's head.

The Haitian dropped his pistol in the sand, and the only thing Andrea saw was a small black spot in Jon-Pierre's forehead as he collapsed into the sand.

Confused, Andrea ran to Jon-Pierre, knelt down beside him and picked up his head; blood, bone and brain matter fell into her hand. At the top of her lungs, she beseeched the spirit of the dead man, "Where is Holly? What have you done with my baby?"

She sat back on her heels and whipped around at a sound behind her. She turned and saw Lieutenant Washington, pistol in hand.

He slowly placed the weapon back in his holster. "It looked like you could use a hand, Miss Carson."

Andrea startled Washington when she charged and beat his chest with wild furious blows. Anger and confusion exploded with each strike.

"You idiot! He knew where Holly was, and you killed him."

She looked out at the dark water and knew what Grant felt—intense grief that shook her to her very core. Her daughter was gone. Andrea wouldn't even have a body to bury.

Washington pulled the tape from the girl's mouth and used a pocketknife to cut the tape that secured her hands. She rubbed her wrists and untied the short rope hobble Jon-Pierre had applied to ensure that she could not bolt from him.

Karen clung to Andrea, fear hidden just below the surface of her drug-fogged eyes. She slurred when she said, "He drugged my girlfriend and me."

Andrea put her arm around the girl and replied, "He has my daughter Holly and killed another girl named Jena this morning. Did you see her? Tell me what you saw."

Karen nodded silently and slumped against Andrea. Washington Washington knelt alongside and said, "We need to get the young lady to the hospital to get the drugs out of her system and make sure she's all right."

Andrea walked Karen to the lieutenant's car, and his officers secured the crime scene with yellow tape strung among the palm trees. The sight promised to startle the early morning tourists who opted for a sunrise dip in the warm Caribbean waters.

Karen sat between Andrea and Lieutenant Washington as he drove to the MoBay Hope Medical Centre. The girl was dizzy and fell against Andrea when the car navigated sharp corners.

"I think I saw your daughter tonight," Karen said during a fleeting moment of lucidity.

Andrea's nerves caught fire, "What? What did you say? You saw my Holly? She pulled Karen's limp body to face her and shook her in an attempt to rouse her from the drug-induced stupor.

Karen slowly nodded and slurred, "I think so."

"Where did you see her? Oh God, was she hurt? That asshole said he hurt her."

"She didn't look good. She was, like asleep, or something. She never said anything. Maybe she was already--dead?" Karen passed out and became unresponsive to Andrea's pleas.

No, it can't be. I won't accept it.

Chapter 60

Andrea shook Karen, trying to rouse the drugged girl.

"Take it easy. She's in shock. We'll get the answers when we get her stabilized," Washington said.

"I can't wait for answers; I need to know where he left my daughter. You killed the one person who knew."

Karen slumped against Andrea and murmured, "It was a big, dark room. A girl was next to me. I heard her moan, and then she went quiet."

Washington pulled into the emergency entrance to the Medical Centre, where hospital staff awaited their arrival. Andrea helped Karen out of the car, but the medical staff gently pushed her aside, placed the girl on a gurney and rushed her inside. Before Karen hit the emergency room, nurses inserted an IV and pushed a saline solution into her system.

Andrea leaned back on Washington's car and took a deep breath. "She's the only link to my daughter. I have to find out what he did to Holly and where he—he dumped her. I need to take my daughter home."

Washington put his cell phone away. "It seems the news of Jon-Pierre's death is spreading quickly. His loose network of thugs will unravel—some will ask for protective custody. People will begin to talk."

"Couldn't that take days, or maybe weeks?" Andrea asked solemnly.

"It will take time, his network was large; we hope something breaks very soon. We knew he controlled a few marginal police officers, but within minutes of his death, we found four patrol cars abandoned, their engines running. We expect even more officers to disappear."

Andrea and lieutenant returned to the same crowded hospital waiting room. In a section of vacant floor space away from the registration counter, they huddled close so they could talk in the noisy room.

"When will Karen be able to tell us something?" she said.

"She's young and we got her to the hospital in time. That's her best chance. Depending on what drug Jon-Pierre gave her, she could come around anytime, or—"

"She might not remember anything when she does," Andrea said.

Washington nodded.

Andrea wanted to collapse into a waiting room chair, but she was too anxious to sit. "I have to know what happened."

"Go check on Mr. Turner. I will find you when the young lady comes around," Lieutenant Washington said.

She made her way to Grant's room, and in spite of the early hour, she found him upright in bed, his color having improved from just a few hours earlier. Grant looked up from a day-old newspaper and read the expression on Andrea's face.

"You look like you should be in this bed. Tell me what happened?" he said.

She sat on the side of the bed next to Grant. "Jon-Pierre is dead, and I don't know what he did with Holly."

"What?" Grant stiffened. The muscle tension shot an ache through his wounded shoulder. "Did he tell you anything about Holly? What happened?"

"He had a scam going. He had a girl with him that resembled Holly. I wanted her back so bad that I fell for it completely. I wired the money into his account but I didn't know it wasn't Holly until I took off the hood. Jon-Pierre was going to kill us. Lieutenant Washington shot him before he killed me."

"Good God, Andrea. How did Washington happen to be there? I'm glad he was, don't get me wrong, but it seems a little too coincidental, doesn't it?"

"I tried to find out what the girl knew about Holly. She's drugged up, but she thinks she remembers seeing another girl. It didn't sound good. She made it sound like Holly was in bad shape."

"So we still have a chance to get her back," Grant added.

"Yes, we do," said Lieutenant Washington from the door of Grant's room.

Andrea brightened. "Did Karen remember anything that can help us?"

"The doctors identified the drug and are pushing a combination of chemicals into her, something I know nothing about, but she is responding and has asked to see you." He glanced over to Grant. "Mr. Turner, it's good to see you looking better. Miss Carson, if you please," he motioned for her to follow him.

She rose from the bed. Grant grabbed her hand and winced. "I know you'll do it. You'll get Holly back, and please be careful. I'm getting used to having you around to torment me."

A warm smile briefly softening her tense features. She tightened her hold of his hand. She stroked his forehead and said, "I'll be right back." Andrea stepped out and followed the lieutenant down the hospital corridor.

The emergency room bustled with activity. Staff ran to a burly man, rushing to stop the bleeding from a knife wound inflicted by his wife; and in another corner, a doctor attended to an older Rastafarian gentleman with chest pain. In the middle of this madness, Karen sat, propped up on pillows, on a gurney with three medications administered through her IV.

She brightened when she saw Andrea and motioned her to come over. She hugged Andrea the best she could, with all the tubes and lines attached to her. Her eyes were much clearer now. She looked up and said, "Thank you for getting me away from him. I don't remember if I said that before."

Andrea saw a bandage on the back of Karen's head. Karen noticed her looking and said, "I needed a few stitches on my head, and they had to shave a spot in the back of my hair…that's gonna look great."

"Karen, what can you tell me about my daughter Holly?"

"I don't remember getting there, but I woke up in darkness and heard someone breathing, kind of raspy, you know? Anyway, I don't know how long I was there in the dark, but I saw this girl next to me and tried to talk to her, but she wouldn't respond at all. She was really sick."

"Do you know where this dark place was?" Andrea said.

"No. When he took me out to the car, he had my head covered. I know that once we went inside, I could hear his footsteps on a wooden floor. Then she stiffened. "Jennifer--he has Jennifer there. We went to the club together, and that's the last I remember."

Lieutenant Washington asked, "Can you remember how long it took to get from the place you were being held to the beach?" Anything about that trip you remember at all?"

Karen closed her eyes and shook her head. "I'm really sorry, but I couldn't tell you if it was five minutes or five hours. It kind of ran all together." Oh, wait a minute. I do remember something."

"Go on," Washington said calmly.

"Tonight, after he put me in the car to come and meet you, we made a stop for a while, I don't know how long, but we stopped, and I know he opened the door, because I felt the heat. I think he took something from the car. I don't know what it was."

Karen, though exhausted, looked at Andrea and clearly wanted to help. Andrea told her to close her eyes and think about that brief stop.

"Try to remember any sounds, smells or anything you may have picked up on. Tell me what you remember," Andrea urged. Washington nodded, affirming Andrea's approach.

Karen concentrated intently, evidenced by the creases in her forehead. "I know the door was open and I think I smelled the ocean, but there was something else there—something kind of musty, maybe. I heard water sounds and crickets, a whole bunch of them, really loud. After he came back and closed the door, the ride was bumpy, and I think we slid a little. That's about all I can remember."

Washington's cell phone chirped, and the head nurse gave him a disapproving look. He looked back at her and answered the call, in spite of the nurse's glare.

He listened intently to the call but said very little, taking on a serious look. "How long had Jon-Pierre had that?" and he listened again. He snapped the cell phone shut again and looked at Andrea. "We may have found the place Karen's talking about. We need to go and find out. Karen, will you be all right here for a bit?"

Karen said she would be fine, and she was sleepy anyway. Washington found one of his officers outside the emergency waiting room and ordered him to go watch the girl. Nothing and no one was to get to her without his approval.

Once in his car, Washington told Andrea, "We have been trying to find all of Jon-Pierre's locations for a long time. We knew about the house and sugar mill, but warrants were always blocked. I just got off the phone with a lieutenant here in Montego Bay. He found his sergeant dead and what he thought were girl's clothes. Four of his officers went missing tonight. He found one of them and broke him. It seems that Jon-Pierre moved his operation to a cabin high in the hills above Lucea after you stumbled onto his sugar mill location."

"How is it that no one knew about this place?"

Washington turned the car away from the ocean, heading inland. "We tried to find all of his holdings through tax records and property grants. He has nothing on record, not even the house and sugar mill.

Everything is recorded under different names. This was one more thing that caused us difficulty obtaining a search warrant. Our dirty cop in Montego Bay told us that Jon-Pierre paid him five thousand dollars to put the property in his name."

They missed the unmarked dirt access road. Washington stood on the brake and skidded to a stop. He backed up and pulled into the drive.

"Stop. He booby-trapped the road to his house. He could have done that here too," Andrea said.

Washington stopped the car, sliding on the dirt trail. Andrea was out of the car with a flashlight she had rummaged out of the glove compartment. She walked in front of the car, remembering how Grant had searched the road. She waived the light from side to side. Washington crept forward in the car and followed Andrea's path.

She approached a slight bend in the road and felt pressure against her leg—a wire strung across the road. She had barely pushed against it, but felt the tension. She signaled Washington to stop where he was. Gently, and ever so slowly, she pulled her leg back from the wire. She expected a blinding shotgun blast any second.

Washington approached and saw the trip wire. "Well, I'll be."

They each went to find the end of the wire. Washington found his end secured around the base of a small tree, while Andrea found hers tied to an improvised explosive device. It didn't look like the shotgun shell trap that Grant had found. This one had a number of wires that went into a plastic brick.

"Lieutenant, do you know what this is and how we get rid of it?" She looked for a switch or something that would disconnect the device.

Washington knelt down and scratched his head. "I haven't the slimmest idea of how to defuse this thing. Come with me, step over the wire carefully, and let's get above this point on the road. I have an idea."

They walked up hill above the tripwire, cautiously looking for additional traps. Washington asked, "Have you ever played cricket, Miss Carson?"

She looked at him as if he'd lost his mind. "Cricket? I haven't watched a cricket match in my life."

Washington picked up an old coconut from the ground and held it in his large hand. "A pity. You won't appreciate this. Shine your light down there, if you please."

He wound up, slung the coconut, sending it tumbling downwards, striking the trip wire straight on, triggering the explosive. A deafening roar erupted from the device. Thankfully, the shaped charge directed the blast toward the section of roadway in front of the device.

"You could have warned me," Andrea yelled, holding her ringing ears. She looked at Washington, who wore a self-satisfied grin.

They walked back down to the car, noting the blast damage to the foliage as they passed. The car suffered a few small scratches from flying debris. They completed the drive to the top of the hill, Andrea on point searching for additional wires.

At first glance, the old shack looked so weak that it wouldn't hold up to the next strong tropical wind. Upon closer inspection, the door was a new steel-plated model and the few windows were blacked out, with welded bars installed over them. A thick metal chain and heavy lock secured the door. This was a fortress, not an old abandoned shack. They listened for any sounds within, but heard nothing but the jungle around them.

Washington went up to the door and said, "I don't know how we are going to get past this. I don't have bolt cutters." He pointed to the chain.

"Can't you just shoot the lock off?"

"That works in the movies, but with a 9mm, all I will do is spray bullet fragments all over the place."

"Well, throw another coconut at it. Do something. We need to get inside," she said.

They walked around the outside of the building and looked for an unsecured way inside. Jon-Pierre had been careful, leaving no tools or materials behind.

Washington walked to the porch, jumped up on a post that held up the awning and pulled himself up to the roof. He walked around the roof, probed and pounded his foot in various places. He bent down and touched the roof's surface.

"I think we may have something here. It looks like a stove had vented here at one point. Hang on."

Washington pulled off wooden shingles and tossed them away until he had carved out an opening large enough to crawl through. He crawled down into the darkened space and hung from the rafters, suspended above the darkness below. He dropped down and landed on the hard floor with a thud.

Andrea heard the landing and yelled, "Are you all right in there? What do you see? Can you see Holly?"

Washington turned on his flashlight and tried to get his bearings in the pitch black room. He saw a table, surplus kitchen cabinets, dented metal lockers, and in the rear of the room a wooden structure that looked like a hitching post.

A faint sound, almost inaudible, cried out, and Washington stopped. Again, the faint sound repeated, it was a plaintive cry. Washington stood still. "Is there someone here?"

The sound turned frantic and grew in volume. He walked toward the sound, scanning the area with his flashlight. He walked all the way to the back end of the building but found nothing. He turned around, accidentally kicking an enclosed plywood firewood bin. He lifted the lid and shined his flashlight inside. A terrified young woman looked out at him.

"It's all right now, we are going to get you out of here," he said in a soothing tone. Then he yelled out to Andrea, "We have her. She looks okay, but scared as hell."

Washington lifted the girl to a sitting position and slowly pulled the tape from her mouth. The lieutenant saw the handcuffs around the girl's wrists. He took his cuff key and unlocked the restraints. He pulled the weak girl up and found a chair for her.

"Who are you?" the nervous girl asked.

"I'm police Lieutenant Washington," he said, showing her his badge. "We are going to get you out of this mess.

He found a lantern, lighting it with some matches he found on the table. The soft light gave a creepy glow to the interior of the cabin. Next to the front door, he found a tray with a set of keys. He examined them and yelled to Andrea that he was going to throw the keys out to her. He aimed and threw them at the hole in the roof. The keys struck a rafter and fell back to him. Once more, he aimed for the center of the hole, and this time the keys flew from the hole, landing on the roof, where they slid down to the ground outside.

Andrea fumbled with the keys, almost dropping them in a gap between boards on the porch. She found the right key and opened the lock. Her excitement grew as she pulled the chain from the door. She threw the door open and ran into the dimly lit space.

She saw Washington as he tended to the girl. She ran straight to him, "Holly! Oh Holly! We've finally found you," Andrea yelled with tears of joy that streamed down her face.

Andrea got to her knees next to Washington and looked upwards.

"Who's Holly?" the girl said.

Chapter 61

Andrea fell to her knees, the frustration unbearable. Jon-Pierre had won the final battle. From the grave, he had reached out and snatched away her last thread of hope.

"I can't do this!" Andrea said. She grabbed the girl by the shoulders. "My daughter, Holly, was here. Did you see her? What did Jon-Pierre do to her?"

The girl was groggy and confused. Lieutenant Washington held her up to keep her from toppling backwards.

"The last thing I remember was dancing in some club. My head is killing me."

"Your name is Jennifer, and you were with Karen?" Andrea said.

Her eyes sharpened, "Yes,--oh my God, is Karen here? Where is Karen?" Jennifer said.

"Karen's all right; we took her to the hospital. She's going to be fine," Andrea said.

Jennifer suddenly remembered, "We met a guy named Jon-Pierre at the club. He must have drugged us. We only had one drink, and that's all I remember. The rest is really fuzzy."

Washington told the girl, "The doctors said your friend Karen was drugged. She had Ketamine in her system. It was probably in the drinks. We need to get you to the hospital too."

Lieutenant Washington held the girl up as they walked, Andrea following close behind. The girl looked up at the dark forest canopy and saw the first rays of the morning sun slice through a few gaps in the foliage.

"Did you get him? Jon-Pierre, I mean. I was so stupid to believe him and thought it would be cool. What was I thinking?"

"He won't be bothering young women anymore. We got him. I know it doesn't feel like it right now, but you were very lucky. Most of the girls he takes are never found again," Washington said as he helped her into the police car.

Andrea buckled herself into the front seat. Washington saw her grow still in response. "Miss Carson, after we get this young lady to the hospital, we will track down your Holly."

Andrea silently nodded, and then after a bit said, "I don't even know where to start. I had my hopes set on that cabin. Maybe she died in that plane crash with Jena." She shifted in her seat and watched the cane fields pass outside the window.

They drove in silence to the medical centre and walked Jennifer into the emergency room. The hospital staff swarmed the injured girl and started her treatment. Andrea left the emergency room. She felt unneeded there, and Jennifer was another reminder of what she had lost.

Numbed, she walked the corridors to Grant's room. She hadn't recognized, until now, that she missed him.

Andrea's life, by design, had been a lonely, solitary one. She had vowed to never allow another person to hurt her in the way her ex-husband had. She didn't rely on or need anyone, but that had become a lonely and dark place. Grant made it okay, even good to have someone to lean on. Someone who wouldn't abandon and betray her when things got difficult. It took a tragedy to let her defenses down and let him in. This good man had tried to help her in spite of his own daughter's death. Her pride had told her she didn't need anyone. That was before. She needed Grant now.

She walked into the hospital room, stopping short at the sight of an empty bed against the wall. The bed linens had been replaced, the floor freshly scrubbed, and Grant's few possessions gone. A shiver of panic swept through her body and her heart sank. If something had happened to him and she hadn't been here for him, she'd never forgive herself. Her heartbeat thrummed in her ears and she collapsed into a chair as if she were going to pass out.

A nurse saw her and came in the room. "Are you all right, Miss?"

Andrea lifted her head, and it seemed like it was full of lead. "I don't know. Do you know what happened to the man who was in this bed? His name was—I mean, his name is Grant Turner."

The nurse checked her clipboard, running a finger down the list of patients. "I don't see him on my list, but let me go check the roster at the nurse's station."

Andrea couldn't wait alone in the room and went out the door in pursuit of the nurse. She saw the nurse's station and made a beeline for the counter. Three nurses chatted about everything but Grant, and it drove Andrea to the breaking point.

"Excuse me, can one of you tell me where to find Grant Turner?"

One of the staff turned her head and scolded Andrea. "Just a minute!" Then she turned her back.

Andrea's blood boiled. "Hey, can you tell me where he is, or do you lose patients around here on a regular basis?" She was loud enough that patients and staff in the hallway stopped in their tracks.

Two of the three nurses scattered like mice, and the one who remained had a look of disgust on her face. She stepped over to the patient roster and scrolled through it quickly. Her finger stopped and she haughtily advised, "Mr. Turner has been moved from the post-surgery section to the acute care section."

"And where would that be?" Andrea responded.

The nurse pointed down the hall. "Follow the signs," she said, not even glancing in Andrea's direction.

Andrea sped down the corridor and after a few wrong turns found the correct section and entered the doors. *Oh, crap, another nurse's station.* She prepared herself for another hostile encounter and asked where she could find Grant.

The nurse at the station came around and told Andrea, "Please come with me. I'll show you where he is. He may be pretty tired. He worked hard in the rehab room this morning."

The nurse escorted Andrea to a room at the end of the hallway, where lay one snoring occupant. Grant was resting. Andrea sat in a chair at the side of his bed and closed her own eyes. Her mind replayed every action and decision she had made that had condemned her daughter. What more could she have done?

She looked up when Grant's snoring stopped. Grant was watching her.

"Morning," Grant said with hesitation. "You must be exhausted."

Andrea was dreaming about Holly, nightmares actually, about what that bastard had done to her. "Grant, I didn't find Holly. There was another girl, but she didn't know anything about my Holly. I don't know what to do next."

She came and sat on the edge of Grant's bed.

He reached up and hugged her. He held her tight, knowing what she felt. Jena and Holly were gone.

She lifted her face a few inches and asked, "Do you think we will ever find them, so we can bring them home?" She did not say the obvious—*when we find their bodies.*

Grant stroked her hair, at a loss as to what to say. He stared off into the distance, and then something came to him that made him bolt upright.

He stopped, pushed Andrea up, and asked, "Did Jon-Pierre say anything about Holly right before Washington shot him?"

She looked confused. "What are you getting at? I don't want to think about him anymore."

"Follow me with this. What did he say?" Grant insisted.

Andrea pictured the arrogant dead man in the sand. Then she remembered: "Holly was going to be fish food, or something like that."

Grant nodded. "Do you remember going to the river where he dropped the body that Washington had us view?"

Andrea stiffened. "Karen—she remembered Jon-Pierre stopping the car on the way to the meeting on the beach. Do you think he dropped Holly there—in the river?"

Grant nodded. "I'm sorry. I'm so sorry."

Chapter 62

"If there is the slightest hope she's alive..."

Andrea's mind flipped to the memory of the poor girl in the Montego Bay morgue. Holly couldn't end up like that.

She hugged Grant, and her face betrayed the wish that Grant was alongside her.

"Hurry," Grant said.

Andrea rushed out of the room and found Washington with Jennifer in the emergency room. She grabbed him by the arm and pulled.

"I think I know where Holly is, and we have to hurry."

"What are you talking about? Where is she?" the Lieutenant said.

"Remember right before you shot Jon-Pierre? He told me that Holly was going to be fish food."

"Yes, I recall him—"

"And remember when Karen told us when she was in the car, that they stopped and Jon-Pierre tossed something out of the car? That was Holly."

Washington nodded. "Jon-Pierre's stolen vehicle was splattered with red mud and mangrove leaves. They grow near water."

"I think he dumped Holly at Little River where you found that girl's body."

Washington considered it for a moment. "Let's go find your daughter."

They jumped into his car and sped eastward toward Little River. Washington called his station and asked for available officers to meet him where the highway crossed the river. He also asked for an ambulance to stand by at the location. He turned to Andrea, "I don't know what we will find out here, so let me go first."

They approached the location and parked in the wide clearing on the other side of the bridge where she and Grant had explored. As Washington exited the car, two uniformed officers came to him. He directed them, and they scurried off into the brush and trees along the riverbank.

Washington, with Andrea in tow, walked down the incline to the bank and pointed to fresh tire marks in the moist red soil. The tire tracks stopped short of the river's edge, but Andrea was first to observe the drag marks that led upstream.

They clambered over thick mangrove tree roots and rocks, losing the trail along the riverbank. In a crevice of one of the sharp rock formations, Washington found a strip of cloth ripped from a garment. He pointed ahead and Andrea charged forward.

She climbed over the rock shelf and came upon a large pool of water where the drag marks reappeared at the water's edge. She pointed them out to Washington, who scanned the surface of the brackish pool for anything that indicated Holly's presence.

At the river's edge, shaded from the sun, shadows cut by tree branches drew dark images on the water. The current moved slowly out to sea and wound through this section of small waterfalls and pools. This was the point in the river where the salt water mixed with the fresh. Washington pulled Andrea away from the edge of the water and pointed out a thick, four-foot crocodile that paddled slowly in her direction.

"I didn't even see that thing," Andrea said.

"Most of the crocodiles are in the South of the island in the Black River, but a few north coast rivers have significant populations. These animals have been seen miles out to sea, so they do travel. They are rare in this river, but as you can see, they find their way here, if they have a source of food. They are an endangered species, and there were only a few hundred of them at last count."

"That is really not comforting news," Andrea responded, while pushing her way through the vegetation along the river.

She parted a curtain of vegetation, revealing a large green pool fed from a small waterfall above. The trees rose thirty feet over this section of river and sheltered it from the searing tropical sun. On the far bank, Andrea noticed a wary crocodile as it slipped into the water.

Andrea found a torn piece of duct tape with dried blood at the water's edge.

"I have something," she called.

"If Jon-Pierre dropped her here, the current would have moved her downstream into one of the parts we covered," Washington said.

Andrea pressed on, walking to the base of the waterfall, searching the other side of the pool, where she spied a small piece of fabric caught in the current beneath the waterfall. She walked on small slick rocks, pelted by the cascading flow. In the debris, Andrea saw something in the water. She drew closer, and horror pinched at her soul. Pale flesh of a human leg poked out from slabs of broken wood in the water.

"No! Not this way," Andrea cried.

She jumped into the pool and swam to the spot where the remains were tangled in with the wooden debris. Washington went to the edge of the water. He couldn't see what she swam towards, but from her frantic push through the water, he knew what she found. He hoped the water, or the animals, hadn't mangled the girl's body.

Andrea churned though the cool water, pushing broken pieces of wood away as she made her way. A couple of crocodiles took interest in Andrea's thrashing. Washington threw rocks and tree branches in front of the animals to distract and slow the reptiles' progress toward Andrea.

Andrea crawled on her belly over logs and jagged debris that cut into her knees and hands. She pushed a heavy mangrove branch away and saw the lump of a human body in the water directly ahead. Her excitement went full throttle and she pushed her way through the water to the spot.

Andrea clung to a log next to a ghostly pale female form in the water. The body faced away from Andrea and was tangled in the wooden debris, which kept her from drifting downstream.

Andrea clung to a log and ripped the shirt fabric away from the downed tree branch, releasing the body. Andrea grabbed a cold arm and pulled the girl to her. She gently lifted the girl's head and looked into Holly's face.

She yelled back to Washington, "It's her! It's Holly."

"Baby, can you hear me? It's going to be okay now. We are going to take you home." She held Holly in one arm and clung to the log with the other. Desperate for a sign of life, she whispered, "Holly, can you hear me?"

Holly was pale and pasty white. Her puffy, water-soaked skin revealed bluish veins. Andrea rubbed her daughter's face, and saw the evidence of brutal bruising, and cuts. Her legs were one large bruise from the knees down. She didn't look good, and Andrea feared Jon-Pierre was true to his word.

Andrea put her face in her daughter's ear and shook Holly, "Holly! Wake up! Wake up now!"

Andrea felt a stirring and a slight moan from her daughter.

"I'm tired, Mom."

Paramedics arrived at the location, and one swam to Andrea, pulling a small rubber raft. She let go of the log and fell into the raft. Then the paramedic helped pull Holly from the debris flow and gently lifted her in beside Andrea. They paddled to the shore, where Washington and others helped pull the raft on dry ground.

Washington patted Andrea on her shoulder. "Holly is a very lucky girl."

Andrea nodded, "You're right. She has always been a strong-willed young woman."

"I meant, she is lucky to have you as mother, Miss Carson. It's not every day that a mother swims through crocodiles for her daughter."

Chapter 63

The wounds Holly suffered as Jon-Pierre's captive were life-changing, physically and psychologically. People in the emergency room called her lucky, but nothing felt remotely lucky about her experience. She had suffered a concussion from her tumble down the embankment, as well as the lacerations and abraded skin that went along with the fall. The slightest touch to the infected lesions on her feet fired jolts of pain up her legs.

Holly's attending emergency room doctor had served his internship in reconstructive surgery in Miami before returning to the island. He closed the lacerations on Holly's face and scalp with very fine sutures that would heal with only the slightest visible scars. Andrea was grateful that her daughter wouldn't have a reminder of Jon-Pierre Baptiste every time she looked in the mirror. Difficult times lay ahead, including agonizing skin grafts for her feet and the grueling rehabilitation of learning to walk again.

Holly drifted in and out of consciousness, her mind beginning to clear from the drugs and shock her body suffered. She focused, with some effort, and found her mother's face hovering above.

"Oh, Mom, I didn't think I was ever going to see you again."

"I have you now. Everything's going be all right."

Holly reached out and took her mother's hand. She winced at the pain, but didn't let go. "That man—he took us, and I don't know what happened. We got away and I saw you—I saw you in the car. I yelled, but you couldn't hear me. Then I fell."

"You saw us? We were that close and didn't even know. I'm so sorry, baby," Andrea said.

"After that, things got a little fuzzy. I remember Jena and I got on a boat and then—oh God, Mom, he still has Jena," Holly said through a painful veil of tears.

Andrea held her daughter's hand and remained silent.

Holly finally asked, "Where's Jena, Mom?"

Andrea considered not responding to her daughter's question, but it was better to be honest. She had experienced enough lies and manipulations for a lifetime. Andrea sat straight, looked at Holly and said, "Honey, Jena was put on a plane by the man who took you." She paused. "That plane—it crashed into the ocean after takeoff."

"Oh, Mom, no. I can't believe that. She kept me alive when we were together. It's my fault; I should have been there with her."

"Honey, if you had been with her you would have crashed too."

"Like this is so great. I can't even walk."

"When they are done with you in the emergency room, we'll go down the hall and see Jena's dad. He's here. Jon-Pierre tried to kill him too," Andrea said.

The doctors stabilized Holly and hooked an IV that dumped strong antibiotics and pain medication into her system. With bandages on the fresh sutures and gauze-wrapped feet, Holly went onto to a gurney for the trip down the hall to her room. The hospital arranged for Holly and Grant to be in the same room, at Grant's insistence. Holly wasn't a reminder of what he lost. The girl was a gift—a remembrance of Jena in better times. It wasn't always like this.

When Holly wheeled into the room, Grant jumped out of the bed, not caring about the pain in his shoulder, and joined Andrea at the side of the girl's gurney. He bent down and kissed the tip of her nose that peeked out among the bandages.

"I'm so happy to see you, Sweetie. You had your mom and I pretty scared," Grant said.

She was a little groggy. "We were scared too. I'm sorry about Jena. Mom told me what happened. It's my fault. I should have stayed with her."

"There is nothing you could have done," Grant assured her.

"I don't believe it, I just can't believe she's gone," Holly said.

"I know, Honey, I know. I can't believe it either," Grant said as his eyes welled.

A wave of exhaustion hit Andrea. She plopped down in a chair near Holly's bed. She looked like she hadn't slept well in more than a week, and she hadn't.

"You need some rest, both of you," Grant said.

"I'm absolutely beat. Oh yeah, and I'm wet too, from a leisurely swim." She put her feet up on the edge of Holly's bed, her pants stained from the murky water of Little River.

"Swim?" Holly said. She had no recollection of being dumped in the water.

"You're amazing. You did it—you really did it. You got Holly back. I'm so happy for both of you," Grant told her, and he meant every word of it. He walked up to Andrea, tilted her head back and kissed her gently and passionately. She returned his kiss.

Holly's eyes grew wide. "Mom?" An amused smile formed on Holly's lips.

Catching surprise in the girl's voice, he said, "I'll let you two rest. The doctors told me to walk out in the halls to build my strength. So…"

"When did you start walking, Grant?" Andrea asked.

"Earlier today I went for rehab, and a peeping tom nurse gave me a shower. That was enough motivation for me to get up and get walking," Grant admitted.

Andrea coyly said, "Lucky nurse—now go walk."

Andrea turned to Holly, overcome by an entire range of emotion. She was ecstatic that Holly was back with her, but at the same time she felt a dark anger that Holly had endured the inhumane treatment at the hands of the Haitian crime boss. Andrea had killed another human being, and that weighed on her soul. She felt a strange survivor's guilt that Holly had lived and Jena had not. She felt deeply sorry for Grant's loss, yet this experience had joined them in a bond few would ever experience. Andrea knew the months and years ahead were going to be very trying for the three of them.

Chapter 64

Grant walked up and down the corridors, and while he felt his strength build, the exercise was pointless. Everything in his life had changed. All the thoughts, doubts and feelings rushed at him. *Why did Jena have to get kidnapped? What could I have done to prevent it? Was she afraid in her last moments? Why did she have to die like that?* He walked, collecting no answers, only more self-doubt and recriminations that he had failed his daughter.

The yellowed cracks meandered on the old linoleum hallway, and Grant followed their lines. Grant kept his gaze downward, unwilling to have direct eye contact with anyone. He wasn't up to the questions or the knowing looks. They knew he could have done something to save his daughter, and didn't measure up.

He wanted to give Andrea some time alone with her daughter. He had grown fond of Holly, but when he looked at her, it reminded him that Jena was gone. He had not come to grips with the loss of his daughter and didn't know how he ever could.

Grant rested his head on a wall and stopped for a short while. He started the trek back to his room on the other end of the corridor, his head down, one mindless step after another. About one-third of the way to his room, something familiar made him stop in his tracks. A feeling wafted over him. He hadn't heard anything, and no one had caught his attention. He discarded it as his imagination, or a spike in his blood pressure, and took another step. The feeling came back again, and he took a step backwards.

He looked into a room that held three beds stuffed into the small space. In the bed farthest from the door, he saw the tufts of hair from a blonde head. Grant felt pulled into the room. Cautious not to disturb the patient, he walked to the foot of the bed. The partially exposed face showed black and yellow bruises. The name on the medical chart at the foot of the bed was "Jane Doe."

His heart pounded. He slowly approached the head of the bed and pulled back the linens. In the hospital bed before him was Jena. He bent over the sedated, broken girl who was breathing on her own without the assistance of a ventilator. Tears streamed down his face as he sat next to his daughter and held her hand.

Her eyes flickered, opened a bit, and she smiled. Jena closed her eyes, leaned her head against his arm and said, "I'm sorry I'm such a pain. I knew you'd find me, Daddy."

Jena slipped into a deep sleep, and Grant took stock of the pain and fear his daughter had endured. The physical evidence of her ordeal would heal, but he knew she would never be the same person.

"Excuse, me," a voice called from the doorway. A doctor clad in a white smock looked surprised to find Grant in the room. "Do you know this lady? We have her listed as Jane Doe."

"She's my daughter, Jena Turner. How did she get here? I thought she was in a plane crash."

"She was. Witnesses said she fell from the emergency door in the rear of the plane as the plane left the runway. Quite miraculous, really. The impact dislocated both shoulders, and she nearly drowned. The water actually cushioned the impact of the fall. A fisherman pulled her from the ocean before the tide swept her out to sea. She still has serious injuries."

Grant looked at his daughter's arms, bruised, welted and cut from the ties that had bound her wrists.

"She had bruised kidneys and a lacerated spleen from the fall. We had her in surgery a couple of hours ago and repaired the damaged tissue. She's a tough one, but she has a long road back," the doctor said.

Grant turned and saw Andrea at the door. When Grant didn't return from his walk, she went to find him. Her face held disbelief and joy. She walked to Grant, put her arm around his good shoulder and looked down at Jena. He looked from one woman to the other.

It felt right.

Chapter 65

In the six months that followed their return from Jamaica, Jena and Holly required extensive hospital stays and outpatient visits to repair damage they had suffered during their ordeal. Tens of thousands of dollars went into treatment and recovery. Grant and Andrea liquidated most of their assets to cover the costs. Both parents accepted the cost and financial burden as they realized they had come within an eyelash of losing their girls forever. Any cost was worth having the girls back.

Holly healed better than expected and required only a single skin graft on her right foot. The other scarred over, but caused sharp twinges of pain when she walked. The nerve damage to both feet was permanent and left her with a numbed tingle in her toes, a constant reminder of the *dark time*, as she called it.

Jena's bruised kidneys healed and she herself recovered from the surgery that removed her spleen. The most annoying part of her treatment involved an elastic and carbon fiber brace that kept her shoulders immobile. It reminded her of when Jon-Pierre had held her captive. A series of CT scans and MRIs found no tissue damage that required further surgery. Jena's longstanding fear of heights had tensed every muscle before she hit the water. She cut through the surface rather than tumbling into it. Her rigid body position saved her life in her courageous jump from the plane.

Physically, the girls progressed, as the outward signs of trauma faded away. However, the inhumane treatment they had suffered under Jon-Pierre's hand routinely came back to haunt them at night.

Life wasn't the same for the girls. Holly and Jena rarely separated, and both decided to take a semester off from school. They couldn't afford the tuition or books, and both harbored a fear of danger in large gatherings—social anxiety the professionals called it.

Adjustment after Jamaica wasn't easy, for Andrea or Grant, either. They tried returning to work full-time, but the hours needed for the girl's medical needs and counseling sessions demanded more time away from their jobs. They had to reduce their hours, as well as income, to balance their schedules so that one of them was with Holly and Jena at all times.

The dire circumstances that threw them together set a foundation for a deep relationship. They had survived events that would make most people crumble. The common bond of getting the girls healthy drew them even closer. Andrea found a man to trust and love without reservation or fear. Grant discovered a strong woman who made him feel alive again.

Andrea and Grant decided to take their relationship to the next level and moved into a two-bedroom home in the Los Angeles suburb of Glendale, a new start for everyone.

The rented home was small, but it was the most they could afford, and a single bathroom for three women made mornings difficult. Grant developed patience and learned to wait for a break in the morning action to shower and shave, though hot water was usually gone by the time he got around to his turn. Andrea and Grant liquidated their savings and assets to get the girls healthy, and while they hoped for a bigger place, they both knew that was only a dream. But they had dreams.

Jena prepared the table for dinner while Holly hobbled with a cane as she helped her mom make garlic bread to accompany the angel-hair pasta that boiled away on the stove.

Grant closed one cabinet door and opened another, looking for a colander to drain the pasta. He stood in front of the open cabinet, looking like a lost puppy searching for a dog treat. Andrea smiled at his confusion and opened another cabinet. She withdrew the colander, hugged Grant and handed him the strainer. She didn't want to let go.

"Mom, the pasta's ready," Jena said, calling Andrea mom, something she started saying a few weeks after they returned from the island.

Andrea looked up into Grant's face and found contentment there. And something more.

She pushed away, both hands resting on Grant's chest. "Go drain the pasta," a sparkle in her eye.

The girls plated the angel hair, poured a mushroom basil marinara sauce and tossed it, coating all of the fine strands of pasta with Andrea's family recipe. Grant carried the garlic bread to the table and gave Andrea a big hug. Andrea responded by standing on her tiptoes and kissing him warmly. The girls nudged one another and giggled. "Oh, how cute!" one of them commented.

Tonight, Grant had a little glint in his eye. Andrea didn't know about the engagement ring in his pocket. Jena knew about it and had given him the go-ahead. He looked at Jena, and noticed Holly with a strange grin on her face. "Did you tell her?" he silently mouthed.

Holly put her chin in her hand and grinned back at him. Jena gave him an angelic smile and said, "Who, me?"

Andrea came late to the conversation. "Who me what?"

"Nothing—nothing at all," Grant said while both girls just giggled at his nervousness.

The front door bell rang and Grant went across the small living area to answer. He opened the door to find the elderly man he had helped during the stampede at the Montego Bay Airport. The old man stood stiffly, both hands clasped behind his back. There was businesslike formality in the man's demeanor.

"Mr. Turner, allow me to reintroduce myself. C. E. Pierce, at your service. Do you recall our last meeting? And may I come in?"

"Oh, I'm sorry. Of course, please come in," Grant said.

As Mr. Pierce entered, Grant commented, "You look much better than the last time we saw you."

"Yes, that was quite a day, Mr. Turner. One I hope I never have to repeat. Is Mrs. Carson here also?"

"Why yes, do you need to see her?"

"Actually, what I have concerns you both. Sorry if I'm being mysterious, but I should talk to the both of you together."

Andrea heard the conversation and came into the living room, trailed by Holly and Jena, who stood at a distance, still leery of strangers, even old ones.

The old man perched himself on a couch, his back ramrod straight. "Mrs. Carson, as it turns out, your Uncle Nigel is an old friend of mine. In fact, we are on the boards of several institutions, one of which is the Western Caribbean Banking Trust. When Nigel gave you the password of *pirate*, for the account, that set all kinds of wheels in motion."

Andrea said, "I don't understand. The money was transferred from my account and deposited. Jon-Pierre verified it by phone."

"Oh, it was deposited, I assure you. However, that password triggered bank officials, who saw that transaction as some sort of extortion attempt in play," Mr. Pierce explained.

"Are you saying that the money never actually hit his account, it only looked like it?" Grant asked.

"Exactly so, Mr. Turner. As of this evening, all the funds have been replaced into Mrs. Carson's accounts."

Andrea rose, shook his hand and said, "Thank you so much. That will help us a great deal. We had to downsize and with medical bills. It's been very tough."

"Dear, please sit down. I have more I must tell you," the old man said.

Andrea knew it was going to be about taxes, and she would only get half of her money back, but that was okay. They had the girls.

Mr. Pierce continued, "The board of directors has reviewed the matter and has concurred with my recommendation. You two were so kind and helpful in Montego Bay that I need to personally thank you for saving my life."

Grant said, "There is no need to thank us. You would have done the same thing if the roles were reversed."

"I'm not so sure, Mr. Turner. Even in my prime, I may not have done what you did. Nevertheless, the bank has turned over the account formerly held by Jon-Pierre Baptiste to you and Mrs. Carson, jointly, as a reward for bringing that criminal down.

Andrea's mouth dropped. "What? What are you talking about?"

"Regardless of what you may hear, we are interested in a clean bank."

"I don't want his dirty money. It came from drugs and worse," Andrea said as she glanced back at the girls.

"We don't want criminals to use our bank as a method of laundering dirty money. Don't think of this as money gained from various illegal means. Please think of it as money you can use to get your girls all the medical care they will ever need, and get them through any college they desire. Think of it as restitution from the man who caused their pain. They, and you, deserve it."

"How much are you talking about?" Grant asked.

Pierce pulled a folder paper from his jacket pocket and handed it to Grant across from him. Grant slowly opened the thick parchment and scanned the account details, which listed Andrea and Grant as the account holders. He found the current account balance and handed it to Andrea, who clung next to him.

She reviewed the form and finally hit the account balance. In a quivering voice she said, "Are you telling me that this account is worth three and a half million dollars?"

"That's quite correct, Mrs. Carson. You two have that money at your disposal. We certainly hope you continue to use our banking facilities."

Pierce rose, thanked them again for their assistance, and left instructions on how to access their funds. Andrea escorted the old man to the door, wished him well and closed the door behind him.

"I can't believe it. I don't know what to say," Andrea said.

From behind, she heard Grant, "Just say yes."

She turned and saw that Grant held an engagement ring in his palm, with both girls beside him.

Chapter 66

A limo waited at the curb while Mr. Pierce conducted his business inside the modest home. When the old man appeared on the porch, the driver smartly exited the vehicle and opened the rear door for his passenger.

Mr. Pierce ducked his head and entered the spacious limo, sliding onto the plush leather bench seat that spread across the rear compartment.

"Where to, sir?" the driver asked.

"LAX, please. I have a flight back to Langley in an hour," Pierce said.

"As you wish." The driver closed the door and returned to his seat.

Pierce pushed a button that slid a partition in place between the driver and the rear compartment. He waited until the barrier was in place to dial a number on the phone console next to his seat.

"It's done," Pierce said.

"Do they suspect?" Lieutenant Washington said over the phone.

"No. Three-and-a-half million would make anyone overlook a few things," Pierce said.

"My name didn't come up?"

"No. We've monitored the girls' counseling sessions. You weren't mentioned.

"Miss Carson hasn't questioned why I followed her, or why I shot Jon-Pierre before he talked?"

"No. She's been far too busy patching her daughter back together. That was very generous of you to split the bounty on Jon-Pierre with them," Pierce said.

"They led me to him. Without their help Jon-Pierre would still be out there hunting."

"Don't you mean that you owe it to them because you used the girls as bait?"

"All for the greater good. Jon-Pierre is dead. I wasn't the one who made him into a monster," Washington said.

"Weren't you? You helped shelter Jon-Pierre when he fled from Haiti. Was that a little sympathy for the devil, since you both had roots in Haiti and the Tonton Macoutes?" Pierce said.

"Ah, so you have done your homework," Washington said. "Then you know about Jon-Pierre's attacks on the refugee camps outside of Port-Au-Prince. The murders—the rapes. Getting him out of the country and away from the NATO forces was supposed to put an end to that."

"But he couldn't stop," Pierce added.

"No. He went into hiding, and I needed to flush him out into the open. I made certain that his people knew when Mr. Turner and Miss Carson landed and made it seem like they were hot on his trail. I made Jon-Pierre nervous."

"They could have been killed. You even tugged at their heart with that phony claim that your daughter died. You've never even fathered a child," Pierce said.

"It was worth the risk."

"It wasn't your neck on the line."

"If Jon-Pierre found out that I brokered the seven million dollar bounty on his head with the Tonton Macoutes and his Syrian connections, then things might have ended very differently. Jon-Pierre crossed many lines and became an embarrassment," Washington said.

"Human trafficking and laundering money from terrorist groups became an embarrassment to your government and mine."

"So it seems."

"So our business in this matter is concluded?" Pierce said.

"Jon-Pierre's network is in shambles. It won't take long until another worm rises to fill the vacuum. As long as his replacements stay less visible and stay away from the tourist trade, the government will be slow to do anything about them."

"Where did the other half of the seven million dollar bounty go?"

"Some went for resources to the refugee camps on the North shore. Most will go into additional resources for shelters for victims of trafficking. The constabulary added additional officers to the Trafficking in Persons Unit, but it isn't enough. There is too much money to be made."

"What about Jon-Pierre's buyers?"

"His Middle Eastern connection agreed to deposit the three-and-one-half million into the Americans' account. But they still want what they paid for." Washington said.

"The girls?" Pierce said.

"Yes. They will settle for replacements, once their new network gets back into operation. They will leave the two American girls alone unless they have a sudden epiphany in their treatment sessions that threaten the new structure. If they recall Ahmed, or places that Jon-Pierre may have mentioned, the Syrians will head off any threat from them."

"Then we will continue to watch and listen," Pierce said.

"And hope for their sakes, they remember nothing."

The End

Story published in the BETRAYED anthology from
Authors on the Air Press (2017)

WHEN THE MUSIC STOPS

by James L'Etoile

"I was supposed to die tonight."

Beth Walker tried to make herself even smaller, pressing against the arm of a lumpy, broken-down sofa. She sat in the drab living room of something the landlord called a one-bedroom "charmer." It was a place that, until recently, she shared with her husband. Beth fumbled with a cheap disposable lighter and couldn't hold her hands quiet enough to light her cigarette. She tossed the lighter and the unlit smoke on the coffee table.

"Why did you think you were going to die, Mrs. Walker?" detective Tim Hall asked. Hall kept his jacket on in spite of the oppressive heat in the small home. He pulled a rough wooden chair from the dining room and sat facing Beth. He adjusted his tie, loosening the knot, signaling he was going to be here for a while. Hall leaned forward and retrieved the photos of Ronnie Walker's body that he'd placed on the coffee table between them.

Beth had barely glanced at the photos and shrank into the sofa while crime scene technicians swept through the house, pawing through her possessions, exposing her deepest secrets. Her attention drifted and Beth's gaze was drawn to the home's only bedroom.

"Mrs. Walker?"

"Yes?" Beth's focus came back to the detective, but she didn't make eye contact with the man.

"Why did you say you were supposed to die?"

"Because the music stopped," she said.

The detective glanced at his partner, a middle-aged cop with a paunch around his middle. The second detective leaned against a wall, rolled his eyes and said, "5150."

Hall knew his partner meant that they should write Beth Walker off as mentally ill and go dump her in a locked psychiatric unit for a seventy-two-hour evaluation.

"Tell me about the music," Hall asked.

The other detective interrupted, "Why are you even bothering to listen to this bullshit? Let's wrap her up, drop her off at the PHF, and be done with it." Detective Robinson pronounced the acronym for the psychiatric health facility as "puff."

"'Cause it might matter, Robby," Hall said.

"Whatever. I don't have to listen to this delusional bullshit." Robinson left the living room and headed toward the kitchen area.

Detective Hall turned back to Beth, his jaw a bit tighter than before.

"Thank you," Beth said.

Hall's brow furrowed. "For what?"

"Nobody's wanted to hear what I've had to say for a long time." She peered out from under her shoulder-length brown hair, which shielded most of her face.

"Tell me about this music. What do you hear?"

A small crease in her lip shown through, not a smile, but it was something less hollow than before. "I don't hear music, Detective. I'm not ready for a padded room."

"So tell me about it."

Beth stood and pointed to the bookshelf on one end of the living room. "May I?"

Hall nodded.

Beth raised up on her toes, stretching her five-foot-three-inch frame to reach to top shelf. A fading bruise showed on her lower back as she reached. She gathered a small wooden box in her hands, gently cradling the box, before placing it on the coffee table. Beth opened the lid and perched on the sofa again.

The wooden container was a vintage music box—the kind that featured a small figure of a ballerina, which popped upright when the lid was opened. The figurine was faded and chipped, the once elegant hands broken off at a sharp angle.

Detective Hall remained silent while Beth positioned the music box on the table. She wound the key and nothing happened.

"My mother gave me this music box when I was six or seven years old. She told me to play it when I was scared. Mostly, I played it when my father beat her—to drown out the sound of everything going on down the hall. It didn't block them out, especially when Dad would punch a hole in the wall with his fist—it just gave me someplace to go—into the music."

"It doesn't work?" Hall asked.

"It does—or it did, until two days ago."

"Is this what you meant by the music stopping? I don't understand what this has to do with—"

"My husband was more like my father than I thought. Maybe that was the attraction at first. Ronnie said all the right things, was kind, and told me about the future we'd have together. Something changed over time. I don't know when it happened, or why, but Ronnie turned."

"He abused you?"

Beth nodded.

"Why didn't you leave? You saw what your mother went through. Why didn't you take off?"

"Because I love him—loved him."

"I don't understand."

"Unless you've been through it—it's hard to explain." She leaned back on the sofa and drew a soft breath. "It began like it always did. Ronnie started coming home from work late. It was the anticipation that was the worst. Not knowing who it was that was going to come walking in the door—the man I married, or the worst version of him."

"Tell me what happened," Hall said.

Beth closed her eyes and Hall watched her body tense. Whatever she went through left an imprint deeper than her faded bruises.

As Beth recalled how her life with Ronnie came to its violent end, she felt numb. She heard the words fall from her own lips, but they seemed foreign, separate and distant from her. She rubbed the scar on her arm. It was three weeks ago when Beth rushed to wrap a dishtowel around a gash on her arm. She remembered a clatter ringing out as Ronnie dropped the butcher knife on the floor.

"I'm sorry. I didn't mean to..." Ronnie said.

Beth tightened the dishtowel to stem the blood flow from the wound. The towel soaked though and she grabbed another one.

"I'll never do that again," he said.

Beth heard that hollow, familiar phrase and she knew in her gut that he meant it, until the next time.

Ronnie took her to the urgent care clinic as opposed to the hospital emergency room. He always said it was because they would get her "fixed-up quicker." Beth knew it was his choice because there were no cops roaming the hallways in the clinic like they tended to do in the ER. No cops—no hard-to-answer questions.

This was the first time he'd hurt her with anything but his fists. Beth figured it was her fault. She shouldn't have antagonized him; she didn't back down when Ronnie grabbed the knife from the butcher block and swung it at her.

"Mrs. Walker, let's get you checked in," a nurse clad in light blue scrubs said.

Beth and Ronnie followed the nurse to a small patient exam room where the nurse took down all the basic information and noted her elevated heart rate, borderline blood pressure, and typed it all into a computer file.

"How did this happen?" the nurse asked.

"She slipped when she was slicing vegetables for a stew," Ronnie said.

The nurse's eyes shifted to Beth.

"Is that right? It must have been one nasty carrot to do that."

Ronnie squeezed Beth's hand as a warning and prompted her to respond with the words they had rehearsed in the truck on the way over.

"Yeah, I cut myself."

"I'll get this cleaned up and then get the doctor to come and take a look. I think this is going to need a few stitches."

"Can't you just slap on a few of those butterfly bandage things?" A whiff of bourbon from Ronnie's breath saturated the small exam room.

"I'll let the doctor make the medical decisions, how about that?" The nurse didn't glance at Ronnie while she cleaned the six-inch-long gash.

When the nurse left the room to get the doctor, Ronnie clamped down hard on her hand. "You gotta get your story straight."

"Stop. My hand. You're hurting me," Beth said.

"You saw that bitch. She didn't believe you."

"I told her it was my fault, Ronnie."

"Don't you get it? If you blame me for this, I'll make sure you regret it." Still squeezing her hand, he said, "Don't test me."

A doctor came in the room, a smallish man who tipped the scales at a hundred and ten on a rainy day. In a soft, but tired voice, he said, "Mrs. Walker, I'm Doctor Carson. Let's say we have a look at your arm."

Dr. Carson gently lifted the gauze the nurse had applied.

"This is a nasty cut you've got here. How did you say it happened?"

Beth locked eyes with her husband's glare.

"It was an accident. I did it."

"Um-hum," the doctor said.

"It was," she repeated.

"If you say so. I'm going to need to suture this back together."

Dr. Carson worked a dozen sutures into the wound, closing the gash on Beth's arm. "This will leave a scar, but there's not much I can do about that."

Beth noted the doctor's demeanor change after she claimed she accidentally cut herself. He was too busy or too lazy to question the circumstances of the injury. Instead, he tossed her a bottle of painkillers from the in-house pharmacy.

"See there, honey, you need to be more careful." Ronnie said.

Ronnie pocketed the bottle of pills before they got in the truck and once he started the engine, he realized he'd gotten away with it, again. Beth leaned against the passenger door, as far away as she could get from him.

"You'd better be a good girl, or you won't get any happy pills," he said.

Ronnie took the bottle from his pocket, shook one of the opiate-based pills out and popped it in his mouth.

The drive back home was excruciating. Every bump and pothole jarred her arm and sent a jolt of pain up her spine. As they pulled in front of the house, Ronnie got out of the truck and left Beth to find her own way inside.

When she finally got up the strength to go in, Ronnie grabbed her by her uninjured arm and pulled her to the kitchen.

The first blood-soaked dishtowel sat on the edge of the sink, the knife with it's stained blade still rested on the linoleum floor, and blood from Beth's wound dried nearby.

"Clean up your mess," Ronnie said, followed by a shove into the kitchen.

"I think I need to take one of those pain pills," she said.

"Clean first."

"I need one. I'm hurting."

"You don't know what it is to hurt, you worthless bitch. All you do is cause me grief and cost me money. Your mess today cost me two-hundred and fifty bucks."

He left her in the kitchen and Beth heard the television switch on. She'd have a few moments of peace, she figured. Beth muscled through the cleaning chores, relying on one good arm for the most part. She found that cleaning up her blood was easier this time.

When Beth finished, she put the cleaning supplies away and stood at the kitchen door.

"I'm done. Where did you put my prescription bottle?"

"You can have one." Ronnie took the bottle from his pants pocket and shook out a single Oxy. He tossed the pill on the floor in her direction.

Beth bent and found the pill among the shag carpet fibers. She tossed it in her mouth and swallowed it down dry. She was too tired and the pain made it hard to concentrate. Beth couldn't deal with a confrontation now. That's how she got the slice to her arm—challenging him over some trivial issue. One trip to the urgent care clinic today was enough.

Beth left Ronnie watching some mindless sports channel show and she retreated to the bedroom. The throbbing ache from the knife wound pulsed with each heartbeat. From a shelf in her closet, she took down her music box, sat on the edge of the bed, and placed the box on her lap. She opened the wooden lid and the ballerina spun in little circles while a chime sounded a waltz. Her mother never told her the name of the song, but said that as long as the music played, she'd be okay.

Tears stained the worn satin lining in the box. Once red, now a mottled pink, the tiny figurine had witnessed loss, incalculable heartache, and endless pain.

After an hour, Ronnie entered the room. The Oxy must have done its work and sanded off the rough edges, mellowing him. Beth silently predicted what would happen next, almost word for word. Ronnie would apologize and make promises and vow to be a better man. It would hold for a few weeks, usually.

"Baby, I'm sorry."

Beth closed her music box but left it in her lap. She flinched when Ronnie reached over to grab her hand.

"I'm sorry. I got carried away. What can I do to make it better?"

She tilted her head, looking through the dark brown hair that had fallen around her face like a curtain. "Promise me you'll never touch me like that again. Swear it."

He nodded, and a somber Ronnie said, "I promise—I promise."

Beth knew the pattern. Ronnie would actually appear to make an effort for a week or two. This time was no different. He brought her flowers, picked up after himself and he'd cook—well barbecue, technically. It was predicable. He'd play at being the dutiful husband. And that's all it was—a play—and every play had an end.

When it was time for Beth to get the stitches out, Ronnie took her to the urgent care clinic. The appointment was a quick one and when it was time to leave, Ronnie asked, "Hey, can she get a refill on those painkillers?"

A different doctor saw Beth that trip. She shrugged and said, "You shouldn't be in too much pain now. Is it still bothering you?"

"Yeah, it bothers her. Why do you think she's asking?" Ronnie said.

"Mrs. Walker? Do you want a refill?"

"No, I think I'm fine," Beth said.

Ronnie's jaw tightened.

Beth recognized the physical reaction for what it was—an announcement that this period of calm between them was over. Beth spied a women's shelter flier on the bulletin board on the way out, and she took one, stuffing it in her back pocket without Ronnie noticing.

Ronnie burst out of the clinic entrance and slammed the driver's door on his truck. He made Beth wait outside in the sun. Finally, he reached over and unlocked the door. Beth climbed in the cab and closed her door.

"They said they'd bill us. You left before I checked out. Did you split because I said I didn't need any pain pills?"

"They owe them to us," Ronnie said.

"Us?"

"We can save them for when we need them, or, you know, we could sell them for a buck or two."

"When we need them, Ronnie? You barely let me have any when I needed them last time."

Ronnie started the engine and gripped the wheel tight.

"Shut up, Beth." Ronnie shot a backhand to her cheek.

"Ow! Jesus, Ronnie. What's wrong with you?"

"I said shut up. What's wrong with *me*? You're what's wrong."

They made it back home without another outburst, but Beth knew there was more to come. Instead of following Ronnie in the house, Beth turned and walked up the block, away from the truck and him.

Ronnie turned when he noticed she wasn't behind him.

"Get back here."

"I'm done with you. Anything we had is gone," Beth said from the sidewalk.

"What are you gonna do? Where do you think you can go off to? Nobody'd want you. Don't come crawling back and expect me to welcome your ass back."

Beth turned and put her back to him until she heard the door slam. She walked without purpose; her only concern was putting distance between her and Ronnie. She paused at a park and took a spot on a bench and sobbed. She'd hit the end of the line with her marriage. She knew that one truth, Ronnie could not—or more accurately—would not change.

A different kind of cry made her lift her head. The sound of children playing in the park. Squeals of joy, of unremitting happiness, struck a sharp chord in her soul. All the things she'd wished for and never had, a real family, children, and someone who loved her, made the tears well up. The justifications that Ronnie told her over and over—"You don't deserve a family. What kind of mother would you be?" rang in her head.

A police car crept down the park access road and stopped near the bench where Beth sat, head cradled in her hands.

An officer got out of the car and approached the bench. "What's going on here?"

"Nothing." Beth sat back and wiped her eyes with the back of her sweatshirt sleeve.

The officer eyed Beth and then asked, "You have a child here?"

"No, no, I don't."

"Why are you here in the park, alone?"

"I like it here. It makes me happy. There's nothing illegal about it."

"Are you okay? You need to call someone?"

"I don't have a phone and I don't have anyone to call." The whole truth was Ronnie refused to allow her to have a cell phone of her own. He said it was a waste of money. His reasoning was clear to her now. Ronnie cut her off and isolated her from the outside world.

"Need me to call someone?" the cop asked.

"No."

The officer noticed the fresh red mark on Beth's face, and before he could ask, Beth said, "It's nothing."

"If someone's bothering you..."

It was the opening she needed. It all came pouring out. She told the officer the secrets she'd kept pent up for years. The abuse, the hospital visits, and the broken promises.

The officer sat her in the passenger seat of his patrol car and drove her home. When he told her he needed to confront her husband about the complaint, she nearly bolted from the car as it cruised down the street. She needed to trust in someone—in something.

The patrol car pulled up the driveway and Ronnie met the officer the door. Beth was told to wait in the car. She watched as the officer explained with his hands and pointed at Beth in the car. Ronnie nodded and acted civil, pretending to be the model citizen. The officer looked at Beth and waved her over.

She got out of the car and walked to the door, careful to stay behind the officer.

"Thank God she's okay," Ronnie said.

"Why would she say you've been abusing her?" the officer asked.

Ronnie leaned toward the officer. "My wife has a problem."

"I've what?" Beth blurted out.

"Just wait, now. Let me hear what he has to say." The officer held an arm out to hold back an imaginary charge from the woman.

"Beth has a drug problem. She's addicted to pain pills. I beg her to get help, but she won't listen. She wanders off like this and God only knows what she does to get her fix. It's awful, officer."

"What?" Beth said.

The officer told her to be quiet.

On cue, Ronnie handed the officer an empty prescription bottle in Beth's name.

"This was filled a week ago," the officer said.

"I know. She's got a problem."

"That a lie! I didn't get those pills."

"I wish she'd get help," Ronnie said.

The officer's attitude flipped and Beth could tell he'd been suckered into Ronnie's pill junkie tale. He put his notebook away and turned to

Beth. "If I see you hanging around the park looking to score dope again, I'm taking you in."

"Thank you for understanding, Officer," Ronnie said.

The officer returned to his patrol car and backed out of the drive. While Beth watched him leave, Ronnie had come up beside her and clamped an arm around her waist. From a distance, it looked like a casual embrace. What others couldn't see were Ronnie's fingers digging into the soft flesh under her ribs.

"What the hell were you trying to pull, bringing the cops to my house?" Ronnie said with a fake smile plastered on his face.

"I thought—"

Ronnie turned her and pushed her back inside.

"You can't have a thought. You're useless and you pull some shit like that again—I'm gonna end you. You're more trouble than you're worth."

Ronnie shoved her away from him.

Beth escaped to the bedroom and perched on the bed. She took up the music box again and the chipped ballerina reminded her that she was the broken one. Unlovable. She turned the key and the chimes froze. The music stopped. She wound it again and nothing. The precious reminder of her childhood was ruined—just like her. Then her mother's prophecy echoed in her mind. "As long as the music plays, everything will be okay."

From the other side of the bedroom door, Ronnie yelled, "I'm going out with the boys. Don't fuck nothin' up. And clean this mess while I'm gone."

Beth opened the bedroom door after she heard his truck start. She knew Ronnie was off drinking and whoring around. When he got home, she'd have to walk on eggshells and anything she said would trigger a violent response.

She went to the window and made sure his truck was gone. A sense of relief washed over her when there was no sign of him. In that moment, she knew she needed to leave—to break the cycle.

Beth hurried to the bedroom and packed what she could carry, her clothes, a few personal possessions, and her music box. The duffle bag was heavy and awkward to lug, but she hefted it to the front door. Beth paused, set the bag down, and went to the kitchen. She opened every single bottle of Ronnie's beer and poured them down the sink. The sight of a dozen glass bottles heaped in the sink made Beth feel giddy. She'd never stood up to him before and it felt good.

Beth carried the duffle across town to the address on the flier she'd taken from the urgent care clinic. It promised a shelter and a safe place for women like her. She walked in the front door and dropped her duffel in the waiting room. There wasn't anyone at the small desk, so Beth ventured down the hall.

"Hi, can I help you?" A woman in her sixties tugged an apron over her head and brushed strand of gray hair from her face. She greeted Beth with a smile, one that seemed genuine and warm.

"I'm not... I've got no place to… I can't go back," Beth stuttered.

The woman noticed the duffel bag at her feet and the crumpled shelter flier in Beth's hand.

"You need a place to stay, hon?"

Beth nodded.

The woman gestured to the hallway. "Let me get you something to eat and we can talk. My name's Cynthia."

Beth followed Cynthia into a kitchen where a pair of women were cleaning up after the last meal. Both eyed the new arrival with a spark of fear initially, then their expression softened when they recognized one of their own.

Over coffee and a homemade cookie, Beth asked, "How many women live here?"

"We have a license for ten women and ten children. And we're always full."

"Oh."

"I keep a waiting list all the time," Cynthia said.

"How long would I have to be on the list until I could get a chance at getting in?" Beth gripped the coffee cup hard to stop the tremor in her hands.

"There's no way to tell. This is a temporary place until something more permanent comes along—with friends or family or what have you."

"Is there another place I can go? I really can't go back."

"Check with me in the morning. I can see what happens with one of my residents. She might be leaving. But I have other women—women with children—on the list already. They get first crack at the open beds. As far as the other shelters, all three of them are full up. I'm sorry, Beth."

Beth put the coffee cup down. "I—I understand." She stood from the table, and with as much dignity as she had left, she thanked Cynthia for her time. She fought back the tears even though Beth swore she'd used them all up. These were bitter tears of desperation, not borne of sadness, or hurt. These tears came from fear of the unknown and they were all she had left.

On the sidewalk outside of the shelter, Beth hefted the duffle bag and started down the block when a voice called out from behind her.

One of the two women who had been cleaning up the dishes, jogged over to her.

"You're Beth, right?"

Beth nodded in response.

"Listen, we've all been where you're at right now. It's tough—but you're tough. You survived." The woman held out something in her hand. "Cynthia wanted you to have this."

Beth took it. "What it is?"

"It's a hotel voucher. Cynthia had one left over. It's for two night's stay up at the Budget Inn over on Mission."

Beth turned the voucher in her hand and saw another woman's name written on the front.

"This isn't from Cynthia, is it?" Beth tried to hand it back.

"What does it matter?" The woman pushed Beth's hand away. "Listen, I know the manager. I used to work there. Tell him Emily said it's okay."

Beth tucked the voucher in her pocket. "Thank you."

"Talk to Bobby the manager, you hear? He might be able to take you on doing some housekeeping and stuff if you want."

"I will. Thank you."

Beth knew where the motel was. She'd passed it a dozen times, so she had no trouble finding the place as the daylight started to dim. The desk attendant said Bobby would be working in the morning, and he didn't question the voucher for a second.

She unlocked the door and stepped into the low-budget room. Sparse and worn with carpeting that held a broken-down path from the door to the bathroom, the room would give most travelers a reason to leave, but to Beth, it represented a safe haven.

Beth planned to take a shower and nap for a while, but she rested on the bed and fell fast asleep. For the first time in months, Beth didn't have to worry about Ronnie coming home drunk, her next beating, or waking up dead.

For two days, Beth stayed in the room and called the shelter early each morning. Cynthia finally told her there was nothing for her and referred her to an outpatient program for a support group. Which meant she needed to find a place to live—back home with Ronnie, or a new start somewhere else. Back with Ronnie was a death sentence. She had to get away from him forever, but to do that, she needed money and Ronnie had been careful to not let Beth handle their finances.

Beth made the trip across town, blending in with the city's migrant homeless population. That's what she was, really—homeless, with no money, no food and nowhere she could call home. The brief motel stay gave her a glimpse of what a life without Ronnie could hold.

By the time she'd reached the street where she and Ronnie lived, she knew there were two choices: put up with his bullshit while she tried to squirrel away enough money to escape or take what she could

find and leave now. The first option was the easiest. She'd done it before and part of her wanted to just go and get it over with. But she was-
n't sure she'd survive another go with Ronnie. The second option posed
less physical risk and could give her a quick path to freedom. It was
two days after payday, which meant if Ronnie hadn't pissed it all away
already, she could find enough cash to get a fresh start.

From behind an overgrown patch of weeds three houses down, Beth
waited until it was time for Ronnie to go to work. It was a Monday, so
he was always a little hung over and late. True to form, Ronnie stumbled out of the front door a half hour late for his shift at the plant. She
waited until his truck pulled out of the drive and Beth hurried down the
street.

Beth dashed across the road and tried to get in, but the front door
was locked. Beth fished her key out of the duffle, but it didn't work.
She went around to the back door and looked in the planter for the fake
rock that hid an extra house key for those times when Ronnie left his
keys at the bar. The phony rock was empty—there was no key. It
dawned on her that Ronnie had changed the locks. The bright brass finish on the deadbolt confirmed it for her. He'd locked Beth out and
thrown her away.

She pulled one of the loose bricks from the back patio and smashed
the window glass in the rear door. She reached in and unlocked the
deadbolt. Her first instinct was to clean up the broken and shattered
glass because if Ronnie saw that mess, he'd be pissed—and that only
led to bad things.

Something formed in her gut, an urge to make Ronnie pay for everything he'd ever done to her. "Fuck you, Ronnie. You clean it up."

Beth searched the house for places where Ronnie usually stashed
the money he'd gotten when he cashed his paycheck. She pocketed
some loose bills on the nightstand where he dumped them the night before, but it was far from enough. Ronnie must have kept the cash on
him, so he'd look like the big man down at the bar. But he wouldn't
have taken it to work with him. Beth scoured the place for anything she
could take and sell for a quick buck. Ronnie wasn't into jewelry,
watches, or electronics. A survey of the house confirmed there was little there she could sell for an instant score.

In the garage, she found all of Ronnie's power tools. She could take them, but they were too bulky and heavy. She grabbed a pair of sharp wire cutters and snipped off the plugs on all the tool power cords. She would have loved to see his face when he saw this little present. But then again, she'd seen where that anger led.

Beth went back into the house and tore apart the closets, drawers, and shelves for the hidden cash. Thirty minutes of fruitless searching left her exhausted and frustrated. She parked on the sofa and contemplated giving up and what that would mean—living penniless on the street, but that was still safer than living with him.

She wanted to toss an ashtray through Ronnie's precious big screen television, but something stopped her. Beth had seen the VCR player a million times, but never really looked at it. Ronnie warned her to stay away from it, which, of itself wasn't so unusual. But, Beth couldn't recall a single time when he'd played a VCR tape—ever.

Beth knelt in front of the television and pushed the power button on the VCR. Nothing happened, not a light, not the whirring of components inside the box—nothing. She reached around the back of the VCR housing and discovered there wasn't a power cord coming from the box. The top cover came off in her hands when she ran them around the edges of the VCR. The guts—all the electronics and gizmos that should have been inside a VCR were gone. In their place, Ronnie had stashed cash, pills, and a half dozen credit cards in other people's names.

She grabbed the cash and a quick, rough count told her there was more than ten thousand dollars in rubber-banded rolls. Beth shoved the cash in her duffle, poured the pills in the toilet, and flushed them away. She took the credit cards to the sink. As she cut the first card with a pair of scissors, Beth heard a noise from the front of the house. Heavy footfalls sounded on the front porch.

Beth parted the blinds in the living room and spotted Ronnie's truck parked in the drive.

She started to run to the back door, but the front lock was already turning. She'd never make it. She was trapped. Beth ran for the bedroom and pulled the closet door closed as Ronnie opened the front door.

"Shit," she whispered to herself. Her duffel bag was in the living room.

"What the fuck?" Ronnie's voice carried through the entire house.

She heard his footsteps in the kitchen, crunching on broken glass.

"Where are you? I know you're still here."

Beth pushed back in the closet as far as she could. She spotted him entering the bedroom, holding the butcher knife ahead as he pressed into the room.

He looked under the bed. "You can't hide from me, you worthless whore. I want my shit back."

Beth's arm brushed against a cold, metallic object in the back of the closet. Immediately, she knew it was Ronnie's shotgun.

She watched Ronnie through a crack in the door as he soft-stepped to the bathroom. He raised the knife blade overhead and with his free hand, ripped the shower curtain aside. He started to plunge the knife downward, but realized Beth wasn't hiding there.

He intended to kill her. It was clear. It was final. She was going to die today.

While the shower curtain was still in Ronnie's hand, Beth rushed from the closet. It didn't even register that she held the shotgun in her hands until she raised the barrel.

Ronnie turned. "What do you think you're gonna do?" The knife twitched in Ronnie's hand while he spoke.

Beth froze, the barrel pointed at Ronnie.

"The broken glass, your prescription abuse, and threatening me with a gun—the cops won't question why I had to kill you."

"Leave, Ronnie."

"Bitch, who are you to tell me to leave my own house?"

"I mean it," Beth said.

"So do I," he said and lunged at her with the blade.

Beth pulled the trigger and the sound was deafening in the small bathroom. Ronnie flew backward from the blast. An orchid of blood covered the tile wall behind him.

She stepped to where he fell, pointed the gun at him again and pulled the trigger. The shotgun clicked on an empty chamber. He was dead, his soul already claimed in hell. She felt nothing.

Beth moved in a numb, practiced routine. She needed to clean up her mess. She'd taken care of her blood before. This was little different. Ronnie's body was wrapped up in the shower curtain. The blood-soaked towels she used to clean the bathroom went in with him before she duct taped the curtain tight around his warm body.

With some effort, she dragged Ronnie to the back door, through the broken glass, and onto the back porch. The glass shards tore the plastic curtain and left streaks of blood behind.

Beth pulled his truck as close as she could and muscled the body into the bed. She covered it with a tarp she found in the garage. She gathered all of her cleaning supplies and went about eliminating obvious signs of Ronnie's death. By dusk, she was done. All visible evidence of a shotgun sendoff was erased, along with any indication that she'd broken into the place and ransacked it looking for his cash.

After dark, Beth still felt numb—no remorse, no sadness, and no regret for what she'd done. She drove Ronnie's truck out past Pine Lake, a remote wooded area of National Forest land. She drove for about a mile on a dirt fire road until she found a wide turnout on the shoulder.

Beth walked to the back of the truck, lowered the tailgate, and pulled Ronnie's body to the ground. It landed with a loud *thump* that made Beth jump. She half feared Ronnie would still be alive under all that plastic curtain and tape. She kicked the body over the embankment and it rolled a few feet down the incline before it came to rest against a tree. She looked at his remains one last time before she drove back home.

Entering the house felt different. Beth knew Ronnie wasn't going to hurt her ever again; she was safe—safe in her own home.

Beth unpacked her duffle bag, put her things away, and placed the music box on the living room shelf. It wasn't going to be stuffed away in a tiny bedroom closet anymore. Even if it were broken, like her, it would never be hidden again.

Two days later, Beth was arrested. Ronnie's body was found by a Forest Service employee, blood in the back of the truck, and trace fibers on the body led investigators directly back to Beth. She never once denied what she'd done. She recounted the ordeal a dozen times for the detectives. And here she was.

Flash bulbs popped and shook Beth from her memory.

"Mrs. Wallace?" Detective Hall asked.

"I'm sorry, what?"

"If it was self defense, as you claim, why didn't call us right away? Why did you clean up all the evidence and hide his body?"

Beth shook her head. "I don't know—I was afraid. Ronnie always told me no one would believe anything I ever said. He said I didn't matter. I did the only thing I could think of. I got him out of the house so he couldn't hurt me anymore."

Detective Hall leaned forward. "You came back here and hid with the intention of killing him, didn't you?"

"No, I didn't have a choice."

"You could have run."

"I have nowhere to run to."

"So you shot him?"

"Yes—yes I did."

The detective sat back, looked at the recent scar on her arm, the fresh bruises on her face, and closed his notebook.

"Mrs. Walker, I believe you. But you're going to be asked, in front of a jury—why you felt you had to kill him?"

"I was tired of running, of hiding and lying for him. I was supposed to be the one who died. No one would be asking those questions if Ronnie was the one sitting here. I don't have to run anymore."

Without being touched, the music box started to play. The music never sounded so rich, so vibrant and clear.

Beth was escorted out of the home, in handcuffs, but she'd never felt as free. The music told her it would be okay.

Author's Note:

While Beth's ordeal is a fictional tale of surviving spousal abuse, it is, unfortunately, based on three real accounts of domestic violence. For over twenty years, I worked in the correctional system—probation, prison and parole in California. During that time, there were several women who ended up behind bars, partially due to the failure of the system to protect them. The women I most vividly recall were failed by health care professionals, who were too busy to notice or question obvious signs of abuse. They were again failed by law enforcement, who were quick to find an easier answer and shift the blame. Finally, the social service network and the lack of available services to assist women in crisis failed them. Like Beth, they felt they had no other avenue but to take matters into their own hands with a final, deadly response.

I hope Beth's story, along with the other stories in this anthology, will bring added attention to the helplessness of the victims and scarcity of resources available to those touched by personal violence. If one person in Beth's timeline stepped forward, the cycle of abuse and trauma could have been stopped. Beth could have avoided entanglement in the criminal justice system and stepped out of an abusive environment. Look for the signs, listen to what's being said—and maybe someone's music will continue to play.

<u>Acknowledgements:</u>

I have to express my gratitude to so many who made this book possible and continue to pick up the story since its original release in 2013. Thank you for all those hours spent reviewing drafts, talking over story lines and looking at revisions. Without your tireless support, Little River would remain another story in my cluttered mind. Since this was my first published long from fiction work, I ask that you please read gently.

Thanks to Amy C. Drew, SALT Media Publications, Dan Drew, Brenda Pandos, for guidance, gentle persuasion and for pushing me beyond my comfort zone. Your energy, focus and encouragement in getting Little River out were awesome.

This book was, and remains a vehicle for, bringing attention to the plight of the nearly 800,000 thousand people trafficked across international borders every year, and the estimated 20 million men, women, and children trapped in modern day slavery. A portion of the proceeds from book sales is donated to not-for-profit organizations to help those caught in the grip of human trafficking

The bonus short story, "When the Music Stops," was originally published in Betrayed: Powerful Stories of Kick-Ass Crime Survivors, from Authors on the Air Press in 2017. My friend Pam Stack, the galvanizing force behind the anthology, pulled together a great collection of authors and donated all of the proceeds to the Naples Women's Shelter in Naples, Florida to rebuild the facility after massive hurricane damage. Thank you Pam!

The first release of Little River featured an original artwork cover that conveyed the emotion of the dark recesses of Little River. I will always be grateful to my late daughter-in-law, Larina L'Etoile for her original cover design. Such an amazing and talented artist, gone way before her time. The original artwork is rendered in the front matter of this book.

Thanks to my kids, Jessica Windham and Mike L'Etoile for putting up with their father's nonsense and writing induced craziness. I'm so proud of you and of everything you have both accomplished.

Thanks to my wife, Ann-Marie, not only for reading countless drafts, but also for the support, encouragement and everything in life. Thanks for giving me the freedom to write without thinking I'm completely off my rocker. You are my partner in all things and I love you.

Finally, thanks to the Jamaican people for their inspiration and love of life. Respect.

About the author:

James L'Etoile is a Northern California crime writer. His novels and short stories are infused with characters and situations he encountered in his twenty-nine years working in the California prison system. He served as an associate warden in a maximum security prison, facility captain, hostage negotiator, investigator and director of the California state parole system.

His crime stories and screenplays have been recognized by the Acclaim Film Awards, Creative World Awards, and BURY THE PAST was shortlisted as a finalist for the Silver Falchion Award for Best Procedural Mystery of 2018.

He is an active member of Mystery Writers of America, International Thriller Writers, International Crime Writers, and the International Screenwriters Association.

When he's not writing, you have find James with his therapy dog providing services to assisted living and memory care residents, hospice patients and reading programs for children.

To learn more about James, please visit his website at :
http://jamesletoile.com